Keeping Gideon

A Novel

Keeping Gideon

A Novel

Richard Samuel Sheres

Vendemmia
Press

Keeping Gideon

a Novel

Copyright © Richard Samuel Sheres (2020)

First edition published 2006.
Second edition published 2020 by Vendemmia Press.

Requests to the author may be sent to:
RichardSamuelSheres@Gmail.com
or www.RichardSamuelSheres.com

Vendemmia
Press

Also by Richard Samuel Sheres

Ingersoll

An Imperfect Certainty

For Giovanna
Ancora e Sempre

We become just by doing just acts, temperate by doing temperate acts, brave by doing brave acts.

We must as second best . . . take the least of the evils.

Aristotle, *Nicomachean Ethics*

How dreadful knowledge of the truth can be
When there's no help in truth.

Sophocles, *Oedipus Rex*

Chapter 1

2005

THE FLIGHT HAD BEEN late taking off. The captain said that with tailwinds they could make up most of the lost hour by the time they reached Paris. Victoria wasn't concerned. She had more time than she wanted to catch her connection to Pisa. Besides, a longer time aloft made her feel better about the splurge on business class; it seemed like more for her money. She had enjoyed the pre-takeoff mimosa, removed her shoes and, after briefly massaging her swollen feet, put on the blue stretch socks from the Air France toiletry kit.

As usual she had brought along more books than she could read on a single flight, the product of a life in academe. Aside from an emergency change of clothes, her carry-on was laden with the second volume of Manchester's biography of Winston Churchill, Tuchman's *Guns of August* for her to reread, a Joyce Carol Oates novel, and the how-to titled *Creating and Preserving Wealth Through Cutting-Edge Stocks*. This last was a gift from her only son, Will, who had already demonstrated he knew how to create wealth and possibly even how to preserve it, having gotten in on the dot-com explosion and out before the implosion.

None of these suited her mood, though. Even the in-flight magazine, with its facing pages in English and French, was more than she felt like concentrating on. She flipped open the glossy duty-free catalogue, quickly went past the perfumes, watches, and bottles of cognac; stopped briefly at the page called elegant writing instruments; and lingered for a moment on the jewelry, not that she wore so much of it.

The plane ascended above the clouds, visible mostly in silhouette amid the growing darkness. She gave her dinner order to the flight attendant, dropped the catalogue in her lap, and reclined the seat half way.

By now she had overcome most of the misgivings about the journey. This was no small accomplishment, as it required her to confront the spikes and burrs that defined her relationship—or, more to the point, the lack of a relationship, as the loss of a limb might define the empty space—with Daniel, her father. By the time one reached her age—not old, she would be quick to say, but well into mature—such misgivings as she had were imbedded in the fabric, a tenacious image that had faded evenly over time. Like the image, Daniel after all these years was faint and yet never completely gone, one of the many things in life that fell into the category of accepted dissatisfaction. His absence had not kept her from having a good, full life. But of course there was always the question: how much better, fuller, or at any rate different, might it have been?

Now Victoria reflected upon the phone call that had roiled her and set in motion the events that led to her presence on this plane at this time. It had come as she was running out the door for lunch. She was about to let the machine get it but changed her mind when she heard the man, familiar but not immediately recognizable, begin to leave a message, his obvious self-consciousness made all the more poignant by his disarmingly inflected English. "My name is Francesco," he said, as if he had found a lost cat, "and you may not remember me but I'm your" (how did he put it?) "step brother." He had sounded so sweet, she had to race for the phone and put him out of his misery.

"Hello, hello of course I know who you are," she said breathlessly.

She heard him exhale a small puff of relief followed by his cheerful voice. "Oh, I'm so glad to reach you, Victoria."

She tried to remember when she had seen him last and to imagine what he would look like now. After chatting for a few minutes they decided it had been in 1972, the year before Daniel died. They asked each other in voices of honest amazement how so much time could have passed, and proceeded in fits and starts to catch up. Afterward, she wondered what critical information she hurried through or omitted in this Rorschach conversation. What things did she simply assume he must know? What things did she automatically veer away from telling him?

He lived in a little place in Tuscany, as he had almost all his life, called Ponte di Maddalena. He told her there was to be a belated ceremony—he didn't explain why it was belated—to mark the fiftieth anniversary of the end of the war. They were unveiling a monument to the partisans who fought against the Nazis and the Italian Fascists. He said one of those being honored—and in fact being singled out among the top two or three people—was none other than their father Daniel.

She wondered if she had heard correctly. Daniel, a top partisan? She might as well have been knocked over by an Italian plume! Francesco assured her that it was so and said again how much he would like her to come.

She said she couldn't promise, but she would try.

He pressed. "But you must!"

She laughed, said again, more fervently this time, she would try. With a promise that she would call him soon, she hung up and left for her luncheon.

It was late in the afternoon when she returned, the yellow cab dropping her at the curb and the forest green canopy that sheltered the sidewalk in front of her graceful west side apartment building. "In need of a nap," she responded with a smile when the doorman asked how she was.

She picked up the mail from the polished brass box, then entered the elevator and punched nine. The elevator, with its warm wood paneling, had the feel of a library. Victoria could remember when a man would sit on a stool beside a heavy control panel and bring the car up or down, stopping with remarkable precision at the right point on each floor. Even after the elevator was automated with buttons, an operator was kept on for years to run it. The wood paneling was still there, but for a long time now the passengers had been on their own.

She turned the upper and lower deadbolts and entered her apartment, resolved that she would, indeed, take a nap. She placed the mail on the small antique table in the entrance hallway reserved for the purpose and removed her shoes, briefly stretching the freed toes on each foot as she did so. From the hallway it was possible to see through the living room to wide windows that looked down on the park below. Victoria had inherited the apartment from her mother, lived in it with her husband, Patrick, until he died, and now had it to herself. She never tired of the view.

Outside, the light was fading. She turned on a series of lamps as she followed a path to the bedroom. She began to remove her skirt, then changed her mind and only opened its button to relieve the strain on the zipper. She took a magazine off the bedside table and fell crosswise on the bed with the expectation that a few minutes of reading would devolve into the exquisite sleep that a long, wine-inclusive lunch could be counted on to induce.

But she found that she could neither concentrate on the magazine nor fall asleep. Thoughts of Francesco's invitation intruded with an anticipation she wouldn't have thought possible. She hadn't taken a real vacation in ages. Some project always seemed to prevent it. On some level she understood that the reason for not getting away had less to do with professional commitments than with a lack of enthusiasm. She had traveled widely in her life, much of it for historical research—her specialty was early twentieth century American diplomacy—or to attend conferences; the notion of doing so as a tourist failed to excite.

She had been looking forward to a trip to Paris with her friend Richard, but a business opportunity in Tokyo came along for him, and Paris was scratched. Perhaps, also, other things with him. Aside from that, vacation plans in recent years were made tenuously, allowing them to be preempted by the requests for speaking engagements or her participation in this or that project that continued to flow in with surprising regularity even after her nominal retirement.

Francesco's invitation was different, she decided. For one thing, there was an actual date attached to it, revolving around the ceremony. She could, with a clear conscience, rearrange her schedule to conform to Francesco's specific requirement. It annoyed her that, at her age and with her record of professional accomplishment, she still needed the excuse of a project to make her comfortable with the idea of getting away, but there it was.

For no particular reason beyond this train of thought, when the phone rang again before she was able to get settled, she thought it might be Francesco. It turned out to be her friend, Sam Bemis—Bem—asking why she had not phoned. It was a part of her routine to check in with Bem, who, old enough to be the sole remaining link to her mother and Daniel, she took it upon herself to look after. Fortunately, this had been a pleasant task. Despite his considerable age, he was in good health and sharp. The kind of condescension that people often adopt as a matter of course when dealing with the elderly was nowhere in evidence in their relationship—he would have rebuffed it unceremoniously for what it was—and she constantly prayed it never would be.

"You didn't call today," he said. "I was concerned about you."

She assured him that she had simply been busy but wondered if her oversight didn't have a subconscious author. She wouldn't have wanted to discuss Francesco's invitation. It would only have sparked the latest round in a seemingly ageless conversation about her attitude toward Daniel. Bem believed she had never come to terms with Daniel's absence from her life and that she failed to appreciate his admirable qualities. She disagreed.

The very fact that she referred to her father as Daniel was enough to get Bem started. Though always courtly, he could be relentless in rendering his judgments; not a verbal sledgehammer, but something smaller tapping on sheet metal until it was covered in halfmoon indentations. Calling him Daniel was hostile, he said, a way of tweaking his honor, a way of deflating him. Victoria didn't believe this was true and regularly pointed out that she called Bemis Bemis, or Bem. It meant nothing. It just fit him, she said, as was the case with Daniel.

The mere anticipation of the lecture, even when it didn't come, could cause her to wonder, irritably, why a woman such as she, mature, educated, and some would even say wise, could be roiled so easily over a long-dead—and even longer dead to her—father. Bemis possessed an unerring instinct for raising the truth that was most uncomfortable to her. Occasionally he could do so with unsettling directness, which he would say was a privilege of age: He had to get the thought out before he forgot it. She was old enough herself to understand that. Yet Bemis was still sharper than most people she knew who were half his age, and besides, he had been taking her to task for one thing or another since she was a girl. And she had to admit, she didn't like the edge that crept into her voice when the subject was Daniel, or that it came so automatically.

"You know his involvement in my life was practically zero," she would complain. "Not to mention the heartache he caused my mother. I'll never forgive him for that." Bem always seemed to defend Daniel. It was misplaced loyalty as far as she was concerned. Still, she found his devotion to his old friend endearing.

These were the kinds of things—predictable, tedious—she was not in the mood for that evening and that made her reluctant to mention Francesco's invitation. But then, faced with a sudden lull in their conversation, she impulsively filled it with a recounting of Francesco's call. "He invited Patrick, too," she said. "Of course he had no way of knowing about Patrick. It was a sweet gesture."

"Ah, so Francesco didn't know that Patrick died."

"No. Or that we had divorced ten years earlier. I didn't mention the divorce. It didn't seem important at that moment. What do you think?" she concluded, hoping even as she knew the hope was in vain that he wouldn't have much to say.

"I have the impression you want to accept."

"I have mixed feelings."

Bemis laughed and she could imagine the loose skin around his neck quivering slightly. "I love you like a daughter, dear. If you want my blessing, you have it. By all means, go. Why not, after all?"

"Jesus, listen to you! I can do without your blessing."

"Well, what then?"

In fact, she wasn't sure what she wanted from him. "Maybe you'd like to come with me," she said on impulse.

"A nice thought, Victoria, but it's more than I can manage. These days, it's all I can do to make it around midtown."

She felt a twinge of guilt at the immediate refusal, as if he had suspected the insincerity of her offer. In truth, she never expected him to accept and was only slightly disappointed when he didn't. It would have required a fair amount of effort to look after him.

"Anyway, weren't you planning on a European vacation with Richard?"

"Yes, Paris. That's on hold," she replied, hoping Bemis would let it go at that.

"Did Francesco say anything else—tell you anything about himself, his family?" Bemis asked. "He's married, I presume."

"Remarried, actually. I'm not sure for how long. He was widowed. He said he has two grown children from his first marriage and one from his second.

6

"He did say something else that intrigued me. He said—and his voice had a strange quality about this, as if he wasn't sure he wanted to tell me—that Daniel left boxes of papers that I might find interesting. I asked what he had thought of the papers. He was quiet for a long minute. At first I thought we were experiencing a delay in our connection, but he was evidently searching for the right words."

"And?"

"That's what I found intriguing. He said, almost as a confession, that he hadn't had a chance to read much of the material. The boxes had been found only recently. He said they'd been walled up in a basement and discovered during some renovations."

"Perhaps Daniel recounted his experiences during the war after all. Even with his closest friends he was always tightlipped on the subject, you know. In general, he wasn't a very retiring person, so I always assumed there was something more to this hole in his life. It could only have been a traumatic time for him. After all, he did lose his wife—his second wife, of course— and a child during the war. But you knew that."

"Yes, of course," she said, though she hadn't known about the child. "I'm sure I detected something in Francesco's voice that sounded troubled, even though he said he hadn't read the material. Oh, who knows? It's probably nothing."

She hadn't meant much by this last comment. It was just something to say. But clearly it irritated Bemis. "Then why bother going?" he asked.

"I don't know. New-found sentimentality, perhaps. Maybe I should skip it."

"For what it's worth, I think it'd do you good."

"Go on."

"It's not very complicated, really. I believe discovery is good. You're a historian; you should appreciate that. You may be surprised to find noteworthy things about Daniel." In a more forceful rush he added, "You know, Victoria, this kind of puerile display really doesn't become you. Believe me, I'm fully aware that age doesn't remove the freight parents and children take on board. You have as much right as anyone to be angry with Daniel. But surely you know there were admirable things about him—surely you know this?"

She accepted his chastisement without demur, and he went on:

7

"Let me tell you one thing about my friend, your father: Daniel Gideon was a striver. He believed passionately that he could make a difference. The Great War was the defining event of his early life. It affected him profoundly. It caused him to focus his medical education on treating the poor souls who had been gassed and maimed. And he possessed a keen and lasting curiosity, a desire to explicate the things that caused the war, so he worked for causes that he hoped would prevent such catastrophes in the future. In light of subsequent events that may sound naive, as I'm sure even he would agree, but there's little doubt that given the same circumstances he'd do the same things all over again.

"And now it appears you can add war hero to his resume," Bemis went on before she could respond. "That must really gall you."

"That's a cheap shot, Bem. It does no such thing. Why should it?"

"Because everything admirable about him always has. Your whole life you've made it clear that his failings as a father could never be balanced out by other achievements or qualities."

"Oh, for crying out loud, what achievements? What qualities? For years my mother said he would play a part in our lives. But he didn't. That's what I care about."

"Those were difficult times."

"So I told myself. So my mother drilled into my head, defending him to the end for reasons I'll never comprehend."

"He did try to contact you after the war."

"For what it was worth by then."

"Still, he did try, didn't he?"

"Yes."

"And as I recall, you were the one who said you didn't want to see him. Well all right, that's water under the bridge"—she could imagine him waving away any of her objections—"but as far as going to Italy is concerned, well, if I were you, I would make the effort."

She had replayed this conversation several times since she told Francesco that she would come. Each time she came up with a different riposte to Bemis. Each time she imagined persuading him that he was making too much of the so-called repressed feelings she had about Daniel—her *issues*, as they would say on the frothy talk shows. The very fashionableness of the word put her off. What kind of issues? True, the part Daniel played in her life was,

8

literally, negative; it was a tale of his absence. And by the time he had tried to make up for this, after the war when she was grown, it was she who spurned him. Bemis was right about that. Even if he was also right that she'd never come to terms with her feelings about Daniel—about his absence, his shabby treatment of her mother, his *abandonment* (now there was another of those fashionable words) of both of them—what was she supposed to do about it? It seemed to her that either she accepted these facts of her life or she didn't. For the most part, she believed she did. Was there anything to be gained at this stage of her life by delving into The History of Daniel? If the discovery of Daniel's heroism in the war simply galled her further, as Bemis said, what would be gained by rooting around in the details of his life or his heroism?

And yet, why not? What did she have to lose? She had never considered herself a timid woman, or one easily rattled, so why not do this thing? Daniel had a passion for history. Surely he would understand his life being subjected to rigorous inspection, even if the person writing the history was his daughter. Anyway, she had as much right as anyone to this particular bit of delving. History is written by the survivors, and she would never think of herself as anything but. Victoria Gideon, Princeton history professor emeritus, survivor of countless pre-women's liberation department skirmishes, survivor of one failed marriage and one good one claimed by death, raiser of a good son.

* * *

DINNER FINISHED, SHE declined the proffered cognac, chose a white piece of Godiva, and glanced again at the duty-free. A lapis and enamel pin caught her eye, reminding her of another gift from Will. His gifts tended to be brightly ornamental, and he made no bones about wanting to perk up her stodgy wardrobe.

Stodgy was his word. She made no pretensions to glamour, but she didn't think of herself as stodgy. Conservative, perhaps. She didn't stint on quality, but she didn't buy things just because of a trendy label. She preferred shoes she could actually walk in. She rinsed her hair to accentuate the silver, kept it cut short and easy to care for. She wore little makeup, believing her complexion was still nice. And anyway, she would ask, for whom would she be wearing it? "I love it. It goes with everything," is what she told Will at the time.

The cabin lights were dimmed for the short night. Normally, Victoria slept well on planes, even in cargo class, which her friends regarded as a major talent. Now, in her wide reclining seat, she closed her eyes but could not stop her mind's autonomous, undisciplined meandering.

It occurred to her that she had never been very professional in her approach to the story of Daniel. To any other subject she would surely have devoted greater rigor. Most of what she knew, aside from her own scant, if sometimes intense memories, she knew from her mother, Nora. Her mother was, as everyone who knew her would attest, an admirable woman: she was proud, self-possessed and disinclined to speak ill of others. As poorly treated as her mother may have been, Victoria could not recall a time when she raged or spoke of Daniel with anything but respect. Sadness existed, certainly, yet probably love for him to the end.

Victoria resented nothing more than this last fact. She might not have been raised in an age when female strength, independence, and self-confidence were widely celebrated, but she possessed these attributes all the same and resented it when those she loved appeared to find them in short supply. Her mother had the strength to recover from Daniel, but not the spirit to banish him from her life.

Before she left New York Victoria had entered the wood-paneled, high-ceilinged, book-lined room that was her study and sanctuary. She stood before the shelves that contained the miscellaneous scrapbooks and photo albums of her family, the oldest ones nearest the ceiling having been pushed upward over the years by new additions. She climbed the proper library ladder and removed a scrapbook, its old tan leather stained dark brown along the spines from the sweat of palms.

Now, at thirty-seven thousand feet, she reached into her briefcase and removed the volume. Before she could open it, photographs, letters, and souvenir postcards, the glue long turned brittle, slid into her lap. One of the photographs, its edges scalloped and the finish still glossy, was of Daniel and Nora, startlingly young. One of them had written a caption on the back: "Us. June '25."

Victoria looked hard at the photo, as if by staring intently she could inhabit it, could get into the skins of these beautiful people. She smiled at her mother's short, clingy dress and bobbed hair. Even Nora's taste for flapper fashion couldn't obscure her classic beauty. She had sharp, even features, though her small nose verged on being cute rather than elegant. Her wondrous, luminous complexion, which she had until the day she died, was evident even in the black and white photo. She had a small birthmark above her lip, which Victoria thought alluring but Nora never liked—though she never disliked it enough to do anything about it. Nora accepted what she was given as hers, not something to be altered on a whim. The green eyes with a fleck of something in one of them, like a flaw in a marble, looked light brown in the photo. Victoria thought her figure was beautiful, though the bust that was fashionably small at the time, requiring little flattening, later became a source of self-consciousness for Nora.

Then Daniel. Even smiling, his gaze retained an intensity, some seriousness of purpose that suggested impatience with such frivolous things as posing for a photograph. His eyes were dark and piercing. There was no mystery why Nora would be attracted to him. He reminded Victoria of JFK, Junior, right down to the thick dark hair and purposeful eyebrows.

She turned over another of the objects in her lap and was curious to see a letter in Daniel's hand addressed to Bemis. There was no obvious explanation for the letter's presence in these papers, and she resolved to ask Bemis about it. She removed the letter carefully from the envelope and smoothed it open.

Paris, Feb. 12, '26

Dear Bem,

Well, we made it. We're here. And it wasn't easy!

There is probably nothing that has the ability to affect one's point of view as powerfully as a bad case of mal de mer. From the first day to the last, when we docked at Le Havre, the ship either was tossed unpredictably, or more often and far worse for one's equilibrium, rolled under the beam by huge swells. Tea, bouillon, and saltines all the way across. Nora had it worse than me.

During the crossing it felt as if nothing on the other side could be worth the misery. Since I'm the one who has pushed so hard for the venture, I felt obligated even when my heart wasn't in it to remind Nora of the reasons for undertaking it and of the advantages of living in Paris. She'd been to Paris before, so it was easy to remind her of the city's many charms, though in her wretched state this approach was not especially effective. She is a sensible

11

girl, however, and the more ocean we put under the keel the easier it became to argue that we might as well go forward as back, back not being much of a possibility anyway.

To her great credit, the points that held the biggest sway had to do with the importance of the trip to me. To what I hope to accomplish. The work I want to do can only be done in Europe. She gave me The Smile, which is what I was waiting for. This is the look, at the same time bemused and askance, that conveys her affection for me while making it clear that she knows the score. It's the look that says I will have to hear her objections—especially her missing family and friends—but that she will yield in the end, not only because she's my wife but because she loves me and has faith in me.

Aside from that, I must admit I'm relieved to be away from America. The place appalls me right now, with its shallowness and hypocrisy. I still don't understand how an artist like you can live in such an oppressive atmosphere. Not to beat the subject to death (but to pick up where we left off anyway!), this is where you belong, Bem, here in Paris. I don't consider my line of work to require particular creativity, but I'm as certain as I can be that the muse flourishes here as nowhere else. Some would attribute this to the food and the wine, but this conclusion is shallow. The essence of the place is tolerance for diversity of mind and spirit—an irony when one considers the much-vaunted but untolerated so-called American Individualism. That individualism doesn't exist in New York (which is to say, certainly not elsewhere in the USA either), where people are jailed on the slightest suspicion of Redness or excessive libido. But it does exist in Paris, where the cafés and salons are full of good ideas and good art.

Just consider the absurd business over Joyce's daring book Ulysses. *I admit that my view on this is rooted in an anticensorship bias. But the fight over* Ulysses *was not only contemptible, it was ludicrous! Its only merit may have been in its ability to entertain. I would love to have actually been there when that codger of a judge woke up long enough to suggest that the women—the very defendants who had the guts to serialize the book in America—should be, in the interest of decorum, removed from the courtroom while the offensive passages were read!*

How you can work in an environment like that is beyond me. And lest these remarks be taken for lack of patriotism, let me remind you that I did my part for Uncle Sam and have the scars to prove it.

12

Enough badgering for now. Nora sends love, and I will continue to hope that you come to your senses and join us over here. In the meantime, I remain your friend,
DG

To Victoria's knowledge, Bemis never did leave New York. She picked up a postcard, which bore an elegant painting of a transatlantic liner driving into the waves. She turned the card over, but it was blank.

~ ~ ~ ~ ~

~ ~ ~

Chapter 2

Paris, 1935

THE DOOR TO THE small clinic opened, then closed with the usual rattle of ill-fitting glass panes, the sound distinctive only in its familiarity, in its banal announcement of comings and goings, the door's very disrepair a comforting reminder of the importance of maintaining a sense of proportion—there were always more pressing things to attend to.

Over time Daniel's memory of the sound would take on more profound associations. He would remember it as the day they first met, and as a day when, even after all that had gone before, innocence existed like a caul, allowing only shadows and intimations of the time to come. Eventually he would associate it with a deeper reverberation, more tympanic than rattling.

"Are we in time?" a familiar voice called out.

"Of course not, Alessandro, you never are. Come in anyway. I'm back here. Who's we?"

"I'll tell you who we are if you tell me where back here is."

Daniel laughed, a genuinely enthusiastic sound. "Follow my voice. It's not such a big place."

Alessandro was about as tall as Daniel, almost six feet, but much lankier and with a pronounced olive complexion. His brown nubby wool suit was too warm for the early September day. His shirt was open at the neck, revealing chafe marks below his ears. His shoes were scuffed.

With him was a petite woman with dark bobbed hair and anthracite eyes that Daniel understood at once missed nothing. "We are yours truly myself and my friend, Paola Rosetti," Alessandro said.

She put out her hand, smiled broadly, and said in beguilingly Italian-inflected English that she was happy to meet him. Her hand was small in his, but her grip was certain. The men embraced.

Before them a few canapés remained on a tray—cheeses beginning to sweat, thin slices of smoked salmon beginning to dry and curl at the edges, as well as most of a bottle of Bordeaux rouge. Daniel had just poured himself a glass.

The occasion was the first anniversary of his clinic. Located in cramped spaces on the Left Bank, the clinic was highly specialized, devoted to treatment of those, mostly veterans of the Great War, who presented the most complicated recoveries from their wounds. These were the men who should have succumbed first to trauma, then to infection, then to the struggle against chronic pain. Most had no money to buy the services of the great clinics of Zurich or Lucerne.

The event symbolized an enormous personal achievement for Daniel. For the moment he would set aside that the achievement came at a high cost: there was a failed marriage, and an accompanying failed effort at fatherhood.

Alessandro looked around. "So, it appears we really are too late." Like Paola, Alessandro spoke English well but with an Italian accent. His was thicker though, more difficult to understand, friendly but less charming. "Or perhaps the party wasn't a success?"

"It was quite a success, as you would have seen for yourself had you been a more reliable, punctual sort of person." He handed each of them a glass.

"You see how he persecutes me?" Alessandro said, turning to Paola. "I'm very reliable."

She laughed, revealing well-proportioned white teeth and an unfettered spirit. "Unfortunately for you, Alessandro, I think your friend has already shown himself to be an excellent judge of character."

Alessandro shook his head. "How is it possible that I am so perpetually misunderstood?" He raised his glass. "To the clinic. May it prosper."

Daniel was about to second the toast when Paola offered her own. "To the clinic. May it not need to prosper."

Daniel gave her a surprised smile. "Amen to that." He tipped his glass in her direction. "May we put ourselves out of business."

She took a sip and asked where she could find the bathroom. "She's lovely," Daniel said when she was out of earshot.

"And very demanding. As you can see, she lets me get away with nothing," Alessandro responded jovially.

"To your benefit, I think. Is it serious between you?"

"Serious? You know me better than that. We're just having fun."

"Ah."

"We met at a demonstration outside the Italian embassy. She's from a little town in Tuscany. Came here about a year ago."

"On the run, like you?" For over a decade Alessandro had been persona non grata in Italy. A devout socialist, he had felt betrayed by Mussolini's abandonment of socialism in favor of fascism.

"Not really. She can still go back. In fact, she does go back from time to time to see her family. Her family doesn't have the problems with the *Fascisti* that mine does. They're fairly wealthy—part of the class that forms the backbone of Mussolini's support, despite his populist rhetoric. But they aren't party members, and according to her, privately they're critical of The Great Buffoon. Still, I'm sure her family rests easier with her here. Paola's charm," Alessandro smiled at his choice of the word, "is that she speaks her mind."

"Oh, I'm certain that's a trait highly valued in Italy these days," Daniel said with a laugh. "As it is in Germany," he added.

"Yes, very highly valued. So much so that here I am in Paris." Alessandro looked around automatically, and his smile was replaced by an expression of furtive earnestness as he said in a lower voice, "It's not necessarily so safe here, either, you know. Il Duce's men have taken care of opponents here."

"So I've heard. Let's hope he doesn't consider you a significant threat."

"Ah, but that's the dilemma, isn't it? If I'm not a threat to him, I'm a failure!" Alessandro's voice was again bright. "Anyway, enough about me. What are you working on?"

"You mean aside from the endless lines of maimed men? Not much. A hopeless cause here or there. I'm still spending what little time I have

16

advising the League on Geneva Conventions issues. Given the shortcomings of the medical arts—to which, unfortunately I can personally and expertly attest—I assure you we're much better off trying to prevent suffering than relieve it. As it happens, recently I've been involved in an issue that concerns your beloved Duce."

"Whose beloved Duce?" Paola asked as she returned. "Not mine."

"What did you call him that time?" Alessandro prodded Daniel. "The great something-or-other."

"Ah yes. The great windbag. Don't go around quoting me, though. I may have to work with these people."

"It's a lost cause," Alessandro said, shaking his head. "Take my word for it. They won't be worked with. They're convinced an empire is in their future—deluded themselves, I should say."

"What are you trying to do?" Paola asked Daniel.

"Keep Europe at peace." Even as the words came out he was conscious of their pious-sounding glibness. Nevertheless, Paola's giggle offended him.

"You think that's funny?"

"No, no, I'm sorry. Forgive me." The smile continued to leak out.

"I'm used to skepticism. People don't usually laugh, though."

"I should be more polite." She picked up a small piece of bread and spread a thin bit of pâté on it.

"Too late," Alessandro said.

"For your information," Daniel said and immediately regretted the petulance he heard in his voice, "we—that is, I and the many people I am in contact with, including Alessandro—have succeeded in many areas. Over the years we have put in place—helped put in place," he amended—"several rules and conventions that encourage peace. At the very least future wars will be less bestial than the last one."

"Very noble." Paola shook her head gravely and took a bite; the absence of inflection in her voice left the words open to interpretation.

Daniel interpreted them as mocking, and his tone conveyed the irritation he felt. "Yes, it is."

"You said you were working on something to do with the Duce," Alessandro interrupted in an ungainly effort to reset the conversation. "What is it?"

17

Daniel broke off his gaze at Paola, who began to look around the room as she sipped her wine. "The Ethiopians have asked the League's help in trying to make sure that Mussolini's imperialist rhetoric remains just rhetoric and that he won't engage in military action. I'm particularly concerned to ensure that if there is an invasion the gasses we've banned won't be used.

"You might like to know," he said turning again to Paola and still conscious of the resentment he felt, "that our activity may have been to good effect. Our recent soundings have been quite positive. The Italian ambassador himself has assured us that Italy will stop short of military action against Ethiopia. Of course, we are seeking similar assurances directly from Rome. For their part the Ethiopians have found our work encouraging."

"I'm glad to hear it," she said with a nod, a smile and a tone that struck Daniel as just condescending enough to set his teeth on edge. "We'll hope for the best," she added.

* * *

ON A SUNDAY a month later Daniel was strolling along the Right Bank, not far from Notre Dame. Early morning rain had washed the city and given way to a bracing fall day; the air had some bite to it, collars were up, it was easy to see for miles. He paused at an artist's stall where he had lingered frequently but had never purchased anything. The artist, a gaunt man named Jospin, was framing a painting. He nodded and returned to his task.

More out of idleness than real interest Daniel picked up a small, brightly colored oil, a Montparnasse street scene. He was studying it, turning it this way and that, holding it close then at arm's length, when he heard a familiar voice behind him.

"It's not very good, is it?"

He turned to see Paola smiling at him. He hadn't seen her since they met at the clinic, but he had found himself thinking about her often, his musings alternating between attraction—to her looks and to her sass and intelligence—and annoyance. The annoyance was directed as much at himself as at her when he reflected on his priggish performance in response to her remarks that evening.

The artist looked up from his work to see who was speaking; his expression gave no indication he understood what the woman had said, though Daniel knew he spoke some English.

She held out her hand. "Paola. We met at your clinic. Remember?"

18

"Yes, of course. Still hiding your opinions, I see," Daniel said brightly.

She was dressed mannishly in pleated trousers and an oversized shirt, both of obviously good quality and neither able to mask the figure he had admired at their first meeting. She would never be described as classically beautiful. Under close-cropped chestnut hair her face comprised features that were vaguely irregular in their spacing. Her nose was slightly outsized.

And yet, he thought she was beautiful nonetheless. Her eyes were large and intensely dark and lively in a way that suggested it was through them that her essence found release. As on the first occasion, it occurred to him now that he might be drawn equally to her insouciance. There was something about her that suggested *she* thought she was beautiful, and this fact—the presence of true, unquestioning self-confidence—had a power of its own. As he had been the first day, he was immediately, agitatedly, and resentfully captivated by her.

"What good are opinions if they're hidden?" she asked.

"I'll try to remember that." He pointed to the painting. "There are aspects, like the figures there"—he swirled his finger close to the canvas—"that are quite evocative."

She looked up at him with an exaggerated arch to her eyebrows.

He smiled, shifted his weight a little uncomfortably and stated the obvious. "You don't agree."

"No. I think it's terrible."

He looked at Jospin, trying to conceal his embarrassment. To her he said, "The artist speaks English."

But any expectation that this revelation might cause her discomfort was dashed with a shrug. She fingered her brightly colored silk scarf absently. "False flattery is the death of an artist," she said.

At this even Jospin laughed.

"Apparently, you need a severe critic for your own good," Daniel said to him.

Jospin straightened, his smile a little strained. "But," he raised a finger for emphasis, "does the mademoiselle know what she is talking about? Or does she merely express an opinion? For the artist, the most difficult thing is to tell one from the other."

"I express a true opinion," Paola said.

Later, Daniel would reflect on this moment when he knew without a doubt he was in love with her.

* * *

THEY WALKED TO a café he knew on Ile St. Louis. Daniel asked about Alessandro. She said he was away at a conference, that she hadn't seen him for some weeks.

"And when he comes home?" Daniel wondered why he couldn't seem to say anything to this woman that didn't come out sounding ridiculous.

They took seats under the dark green sidewalk awning of the café. She looked at him and smiled.

"What I meant . . ."

"What you meant," she interrupted, "is am I available?" He reddened at her high-spirited laugh.

"That's not what I meant," he insisted. Then, with a smile of surrender, "Yes, that's what I meant."

"You see? All you need to do is speak honestly."

"Some of us are less certain than you of exactly what is the truth."

"No, you misunderstand. I don't always know the truth. Far from it. But in such a case *not knowing* is my truth—I admit it willingly. *Pretending* to know is a lie. Anyway, you are confusing truth and honesty. If you ask how I feel about something, truth has nothing to do with it. My opinion on that painting, for example. I would not tell you I liked it or thought it good if I felt otherwise. You, on the other hand . . ."

"I, on the other hand, must be dishonest! Is that what you're saying?" Even in light of his brief, if intense, experience with her, he half expected her to respond with a denial that would spare his feelings.

Instead, she stepped sideways. "You didn't like that painting, admit it!"

"I did. I told you the things I liked about it."

She shook her head in disbelief as she signaled to a passing waiter.

They ordered coffee. For a moment they sat silently, looking at the passers-by. "I take it," he said, "you don't think much of the work I do."

"Now, you see, nothing could be further from the truth. Your medical work is of inestimable importance. I only wish I had a skill that was as valuable to people." She gave a small shrug. "But we must contribute in the ways we can."

20

"And what does that mean in your case?" It occurred to him to end the question there, but once again feeling a desire, petty he knew, to put her on the defensive, he added, "What are your skills? How do you contribute?"

For the first time since he had met her, the playfulness fell away from her expression. "Ah, now that is the question I ask myself every day. The most useful thing I do is work with groups here that oppose the Duce. I'm a good organizer. I can get people moving. That's a good skill to have, is it not?"

"It is, indeed."

"And I do odd jobs—help put out anti-Fascist pamphlets and little things like that." She paused for a moment. "I'm a coward, though."

Daniel looked at her in surprise, unsure how seriously he was meant to take this confession.

"No, really," she went on, obviously responding to his expression. "I'm not brave, like Alessandro for example. His life is at risk. I keep my head down. If I write something for one of the pamphlets I never sign my name the way others do. Not even a *nom de guerre.*"

The waiter brought their coffees. Daniel stirred in sugar. "Maybe you're just being prudent," he said after he took a sip. "What would adding your name accomplish?"

"I don't know, but it makes me feel not very brave not to do it. I tell myself I don't want to put my family in danger, but I don't think that's the whole truth."

"Well, it would seem you're not overly afraid. You do go out with Alessandro, after all. You're not exactly in hiding. And as I think we've established, you don't exactly hide your opinions, either."

She shrugged and put the coffee cup to her lips.

"So," Daniel continued. "We've established that you respect my medical work. And my other work? What about that? When we first met, you didn't give me much chance for success as far as Ethiopia is concerned."

She looked at him with raised eyebrows, the insouciance returned to her face, turned her palms upward to match, said in a voice that could not contain more incredulity, "How can you say such a thing when only days ago the Duce's glorious Roman legions marched into Ethiopia?"

"Even now it's not irreversible." His voice lacked conviction.

She gave a dismissive wave. "It doesn't matter anyway. Just because you haven't succeeded doesn't mean I don't respect you or think you shouldn't try. I respect people who work seriously for good causes, especially for peace and freedom. Even if their chances of success are nonexistent."

"Nonexistent? Why? And what's the alternative?"

"Why does there have to be an alternative? Just because you want there to be one? You will not bring an end to wars, no matter what you do."

"And yet, you say you respect me for trying."

"Yes."

"You do believe there are some things that can be done to improve the world?"

"Some, yes."

"But nothing to prevent wars in Europe?"

"So far, the proof is on my side. By the way, I don't think I've mentioned that I have two brothers in the army. At this moment one of them is probably somewhere in Ethiopia. The thought of losing him is more than I can bear, and the thought of losing him in such a stupid cause is, well . . . Anyway, as I recall, the last time we talked you were telling me about the Italian ambassador's assurances that this invasion would not happen. Tell me, are the Ethiopians still pleased with your work? Are you still trying to help them?"

He put down his cup, leaned in toward her. "Yes," he said crisply over a pointed index finger. The couple at the next table turned in their direction, then resumed their conversation. "Moreover, . . ." He stopped abruptly, shook his head and laughed. "Lady, you are something else."

She smiled mischievously. "Is that a good thing?"

"I have absolutely no idea."

"How about a truce on the political front?" she suggested.

"Do you think there's anything safe for us to talk about?"

"There's art."

They walked back toward the river, pausing occasionally to look at the windows of the closed shops. It had become colder. Paola's scarf luffed in the wind.

They crossed the bridge to the Left Bank. When they reached Boulevard St. Germain, Paola stopped. "I have to go that way," she said, nodding.

"Oh," Daniel said, surprised at the abrupt end to their excursion and suddenly concerned that the exclamation revealed the disappointment he felt.

This was not a woman to whom he believed he could give a petty advantage. "Well, I think I enjoyed myself," he said, extending his hand.

"Well I should hope so!" she responded, brightly.

"You never answered the question."

"What question was that?"

"The one about whether or not you're available."

"Oh, yes, I remember. The one you were afraid to ask."

"I'm asking."

"Yes."

~ ~ ~ ~ ~

~ ~ ~

Chapter 3

A T FIRST, DANIEL'S DESIRE to ask Paola out was thwarted by the need for him to attend an emergency meeting of the League in Geneva. Then, when he returned to Paris it occurred to him that he didn't know how to reach her. The telephone directory was unavailing. He was reluctant to call Alessandro and face the awkward moment of, essentially, asking his permission to date her. He had hoped he might run into her again. The few strolls he'd had time for tended to gravitate, fruitlessly, toward the place along the river where they had met. Finally, annoyed with his dithering, he resolved to telephone Alessandro.

He called at eight o'clock in the evening, just before leaving the clinic. As the phone rang, he scolded himself for the schoolboy nervousness he felt. He had not been celibate since Nora left, but the liaisons tended to be brief, and he was keenly aware that there had been no one who appealed to him as elementally as Paola.

There was no answer. With a mixture of disappointment and relief, he was about to give up when someone picked up at the other end. Her voice startled him.

"This is Daniel Gideon," he said, haltingly.

"I recognize your voice. This is Paola."

"Yes," he said at last, "well . . ."

"I was hoping to hear from you."

"I didn't know where to call."

"So it's not me you're calling?"

He took heart at the hint of disappointment he read in her voice. "I was calling Alessandro," he said, satisfied for the moment with the ambiguity of the response.

"He's away."

"Again?"

"No, still. He hasn't returned from America."

"Ah, I hadn't realized that's where he went. And you . . ."

"I'm staying here."

"I see. When I saw you last . . . I must have misunderstood."

"So, it *was* me you wanted to speak to."

"In a way, yes. But . . ."

"But Alessandro? Is he the issue?"

"Well . . . yes."

She laughed. "I told you to call, didn't I?"

"Actually, you told me you were available. To be frank, I didn't expect to hear your voice when I called Alessandro's number."

"I'm living here while some work is done on my flat. Now do you feel better?"

"That depends. You and Alessandro . . ."

"I said I was available."

"You haven't answered the question."

"Are you going to ask me to dinner or not?"

* * *

HOWEVER MUCH HE tried to make light of it with Paola, Daniel was deeply disappointed when the Italians invaded Ethiopia. He had been confident that international pressure would at least continue to forestall the invasion. Yet when it came to Paola, what came to mind was embarrassment, less for being wrong than for appearing to be gullible and naive.

When Daniel replayed his conversations with her—he was actually inclined to think of them more as matches—he was embarrassed to have succumbed so petulantly to her flippant remarks and challenges. He resented her attitude, telling himself it was easy to be a cynic, but nevertheless chided himself for taking the bait. True, he may have been more confident than was warranted, but he wasn't as naive as he must have sounded. He knew well the limited value of official assurances such as the ones he had received from the Italian ambassador. For that matter, the ambassador himself might have been misled. Mussolini would have felt no compunction about this if it suited his purpose. Yet Daniel's comments must have struck Paola as a boast, as if he were saying he had, single-handedly, averted the Italian threat.

In the wake of the invasion Daniel had, in fact, remonstrated with the ambassador, who hewed closely to the official line: Italy had been provoked. Italy was a great power, and great powers could not afford to allow provocations to go unanswered.

Did the ambassador not realize how strongly the international community of nations felt about this? Did he not realize that Italy might be subjected to international sanctions? To which the ambassador simply reiterated that Italy was a great power and would act in its interests regardless of the opinions of other nations.

Daniel thought of Paola often amid this swirl of events. Because she could not be more different than Nora, he thought about her, too. In the two years since Nora left he had seen other women occasionally, but never with a serious future in mind and always with the resolution that, if he were to become seriously involved in a romance, he would do everything he could to avoid the mistakes he had made with her.

He was not self-critical in a contrived, harsh, or mawkish way. He was not one to wear a hair shirt. He knew, and Nora would agree, that the marriage was flawed from the start. When the infatuation wore off they were left with the recognition that they wanted fundamentally different things from each other. Victoria's birth only briefly arrested the spiraling down, it didn't—it couldn't—stop it.

Yet whatever the flaws in the foundation, Daniel recognized that he more than she was the cause of their breakup. It was he who in his driven state put his work ahead of her no matter how many times he promised to do otherwise. It did not even occur to him then—as it would now, he believed—that she could be a partner in his work.

He looked back ruefully on the night Nora told him she was returning to America. When she had asked him to try and get home early from work—she had to make an appointment to see him, for God's sake!—he said he would and didn't even have the presence of mind to ask why.

It was after ten when he returned home. He was surprised to find Nora sitting in the living room, dressed as if she were ready to be taken out, reading

26

a book. "Oh, Jesus," he said, putting his palm to his forehead. "I was supposed to be home early for"—he paused, guessed—"dinner."

Nora looked up from her reading. He expected anger, but she was serene.

"I wish you'd called the clinic to remind me," he said, weakly.

"I did. Twice." Her voice was even.

"I'm sorry, Nora. Honestly I am. The time got away from me."

"I know."

He was surprised to see a small, sad smile cross her face. "How's the baby?" he asked, filling the momentary silence.

"She's fine. Madame Tourneau is looking after her for the night. I thought it would be better."

"I am sorry," Daniel repeated.

She stood and walked over to him, surprised him by kissing his cheek. "I know you are. Come." She took him by the hand and led him to the sofa. "I'll pour us some wine."

He took the glass she held out to him. "I don't need to have my food taster drink for me?" he asked, and immediately regretted the weak stab at humor.

"I would be angry with you," she began, taking a seat next to him. "But really, I couldn't have ordered up a better example of what the problem is— what the entire night was to be . . . is . . . about."

"Nora . . ."

She put up her hand. "Let me finish while I can." Now her composure broke slightly. She wiped a tear from her eye, pulling it back across her temple.

"Nora, please . . ."

The hand went up again. "Of course, you must know what I'm going to say. We've been headed to this point for some time now, maybe from the beginning."

He considered objecting, but he remained silent as she went on. "I'm going to take Victoria home. We sail tomorrow."

"Tomorrow!"

She put a hand on his. "I don't want a chance to change my mind. This is the right decision. You do see that, don't you?"

"I . . ."

"If you're surprised it only goes to prove my point. I can't live here. I don't *want* to live here as we have been. I don't blame you," she added hastily. "On the contrary, I admire you. I love you. And I believe you love me."

She began to cry freely. He sat there, miserable, in fact feeling tenderness and love for her. But—and he thought about this often now—he didn't contradict her. However much he may have failed to anticipate this exact moment, surely she was right about the two of them. She had been dignified throughout, as he knew she would be. The irony was not lost on him that, at such times as these, when her bearing managed somehow to encompass both true affection and real nobility, he loved her all the more. Yet he also knew she was right—knew that however much he might love her, he could not be what she needed him to be. He recognized that anything he might say would lack conviction. He owed her more than that. He owed her, at least, his silence.

She went on to the end. She explained to him all the things that really needed no explanation. It came down to there simply being no room for them—for either her or Victoria—at this point in his life. However much he may have wished otherwise. Better for them to call it quits now, to face up to the reality while there was time to find other happiness.

He hung his head. But he did not contradict her.

Since that night he had seen them only once, a year before, when he traveled to New York to finalize their separation. At the time they promised each other that, for Victoria's sake, they would attempt to see each other as often as possible, either in New York or Paris. But something always intervened, and it was not without anguished soul searching that he had to admit that he had become a father in name only. If he was honest with himself, despite his best intentions, he had never been more; within days of Victoria's birth he was working nonstop and leaving Nora to do the job for both of them.

They still corresponded occasionally. It pained him to receive photographs of Victoria. Nevertheless, as time passed, Daniel concluded that he could no longer attempt to be involved in the child's life. He could not see her often enough in any event, and any effort to do so would go further toward assuaging his own guilt than to benefiting her.

* * *

DANIEL AND PAOLA met at a bistro in Montmartre. It was raining heavily. Daniel dashed from the Metro. He had forgotten his umbrella and his raincoat was soaked through. He shook it and hung it on a brass coat rack near the entrance. He was wearing a now-damp tweed sport coat and a fashionably wide tie. His shoes were soaked, as were his trousers below the knee.

She was waiting for him, sitting at a small table at the rear near a stone fireplace. She looked up and smiled with her eyes. "You're a walking puddle," she said.

"And somehow you're not. Have you been waiting long?"

"A few minutes. I took a taxi here, so the rain wasn't so bad for me."

He pushed the thick, wet hair off his forehead. "You were lucky to find one." He flicked his napkin open and placed it in his lap. It wasn't lost on him that he felt something approximating giddiness in her presence—a nervous exhilaration that pleased him, made him feel alive, and made him feel foolish and self-conscious.

They ordered drinks, he a Scotch neat, she Campari and soda. Her appearance was more conservative than the last time: a simple navy wool dress that clung to her shape, set off as before by a silk scarf in reds, blues and golds.

"Do you know," she said, "I had almost given up on you calling me."

"It's been a busy month at work, as I'm sure you can imagine. Plus," he smiled sheepishly, "I didn't know where to find you."

"Ah, so you telephoned Alessandro."

He nodded. "And if I hadn't found you? Would you have looked for me? After all, you know where I work."

She sipped her drink, the candlelight jumping off the red liquid and her dark, lucent eyes. "We'll never know for certain, will we?" she asked, her expression full of mischief.

He smiled back at her. With growing confidence that he understood the game she liked to play, he asked, "But your intention would have been, what?"

Now she laughed, a joyful sound full of her spirit. "I might have found you," she allowed. "It's hard to tell for sure."

Amid a sudden silence, they studied the menus. Both of them chose the lobster bisque to start; he followed with a steak, she with the *plat du jour*, quail. After the waiter took their orders, Daniel asked how she had come to live in Paris.

She explained that she had visited often. When she was a young girl her father would take her with him on business trips. She lived for three years in London and took frequent trips to Paris.

"Three years in London?" Daniel interjected. "So that's why your English is so good."

"My father has always believed it important to learn many languages, especially English. He did a lot of business in England and Scotland. I was raised speaking Italian and English almost equally. Then I learned French. After three languages the next ones are easier."

Daniel smiled at the thought of how difficult it had been to learn only a second language, French.

Paola continued, saying that, when she turned eighteen—which Daniel guessed must have been about ten years earlier—she moved to Paris to study art. "I loved the beauty of the city. It is simply the most civilized place in the world. But I also hated the things that were happening in Italy. Mussolini's thugs—his so-called Blackshirts, we call them *squadristi* in Italian—were taking over everywhere, ensuring that he would be treated like a Roman god." She smiled and added, "I'm not very good at bowing down to such people."

Daniel raised his eyebrows obviously. "Oh, really? I can't imagine!"

She laughed joyfully again. "Yes, I know you must think me shy and deferential!"

"Exactly."

"My visits home became shorter and shorter. The atmosphere there is so oppressive. And to be honest, I love my family, but I think they're a little dense on the subject of Il Duce. I don't believe they recognize how bad he is."

"He has done some good things for Italy, hasn't he? Building roads and putting people to work in the countryside and such."

"Yes, some good things. But fewer than people think. Much of it is for show. Italians have a great weakness for show. Someday when we have many hours to spare and you have unlimited patience, I'll tell you the parable of Cola di Rienzo. In any event, as much as my family loves me, I believe they are more comfortable with me here."

"And here you spend your time rabble-rousing."

She laughed. "I wouldn't put it quite that way."

"And art? Do you still study art?"

"Now and then."

"So, your opinion of Monsieur Jospin's work really was knowledgeable?"
She gave a small smile and a shrug.

"Do I take it you're a socialist, like Alessandro?"

"Oh, no!" She seemed genuinely shocked that he would reach this
conclusion. "One doesn't have to be a socialist to oppose Mussolini, you
know."

"Of course not," Daniel replied with a certain defensiveness. "I just
assumed that you and Alessandro . . ."

"It seems to me you assume too many things about me and Alessandro.
Let's just say we make common cause against the Duce. Anyway, I don't
really do so much. A little of this, a little of that."

"Meaning?"

"Meaning things too unimportant to detail. Certainly nothing as important
as I'd hoped."

Over their main courses he asked if she had any news of her brother in
Ethiopia.

"My mother telephoned yesterday to say they received a letter from him.
But it was sent just before the fighting began. So . . ."

"He's probably fine. In my experience, it's bad news that travels fast."

She shrugged. "You were in the war?" she asked after a pause.

"Yes."

"Here in France?"

"Yes."

"So, your quest for peace is not merely theoretical."

"Why would you think it was?"

"Oh, I don't know. Perhaps because some people who call themselves
pacifists know the horrors of war only in their imaginations."

"That's not necessarily a bad thing, though imaginations often aren't up
to the task."

"You've killed men?"

The question startled him. "That's not something I talk about."

She nodded, said quietly, "I assume that means you have."

He shrugged. "Killing is not a prerequisite for my kind of work now, if that's what you're thinking. Just witnessing the carnage would have been enough, I assure you."

"And now you are a pacifist."

He dabbed his mouth with his napkin, then returned it to his lap. "I don't use that word. Too many people have too many ideas of what it is."

"What is it to you? Do you believe, for example, that no wars are justified, or perhaps that some are?"

"In theory, yes, some are. Certainly defensive wars."

"So, the Ethiopians are justified in resisting the Duce's legions."

"Justified? Yes. But that doesn't mean there isn't a better way."

She pushed her dinner plate aside and leaned in. "What about wars to punish aggression? What if, for instance, Britain and France attacked Italy to punish it?"

"I'm not sure. I'm inclined to think I'd feel better about it if the action were taken under an international sponsor, like the League."

"Would you, personally, fight under such a flag?"

"No. I, personally, won't fight under any flag. I'm done with soldiering."

"But it would be all right for some other man to sacrifice himself."

With a rueful smile he said, "I can't be responsible for all the contradictions in the world."

"Well, for what it's worth, I wouldn't trust other countries to do the punishing, even under some larger flag. I could never trust their motives. Look, you know I'm no friend of the Italian Fascists."

He nodded, said "of course."

"So perhaps you'll forgive me if I say I believe your viewpoint is naive."

In light of his earlier experiences with her, he bristled at the label. "How so?"

"Because I believe it is naive to assume that any country acts for anything but its own selfish motives. In my opinion, there is nothing noble about a country like Great Britain coming to the aid of the poor Ethiopians. It's not as if the British are a disinterested party, after all, or charitable. More likely they would be acting with a view to their own colonial ambitions—to obstruct a rival. I'll oppose my own country if I think it's wrong, but I won't simply be used by someone else's country."

Still bristling at being called naive, Daniel said, "You obviously take a great interest in these matters. But what is it, exactly, that you do about them?"

She shifted in her seat. "I'm not sure what you mean."

"I mean," he responded with the sharp tone of defense, "other than *this or that*. Do you do anything more than shake your fist at the heavens and criticize people like me?"

"I resent that. I work hard for the causes I believe in. And I wasn't criticizing you."

He rolled his eyes obviously.

"I wasn't."

"Oh, please, Paola! Be serious." He considered whether to articulate his complaint, decided to let it go, then decided that she had never given him a single reason to be circumspect or even polite. "Let me tell you something. I don't like being called naive."

"I didn't . . ."

"You did. And anyway, more than once you've implied it strongly enough. Don't get me wrong. Many people think anyone who works for peace must be naive. One gets used to it. But critics are, as they say, a dime a dozen."

He sat back in his chair. If she was angry, she didn't show it. Maybe this woman actually could get as good as she gave. He gave her a propitiatory smile. "Perhaps enough debate for one night."

She returned the smile. "Only time will tell."

Outside, the rain had stopped. Daniel called for the bill and suggested a walk to Sacre Coeur to view the city lights.

The wet streets had an oily sheen that reflected the street lamps in dull dappled patterns. The only people about were those, like themselves, coming to or from dinner. As they ascended a steep cobblestone street, Paola took his arm to keep from slipping. She was so much smaller than he—almost a foot shorter—he had an impulse to put his arm around her and draw her close, protectively, even as he believed she would resist such a gesture as gratuitous. Still, something about the willfulness and strength contained in her small package made him feel, paradoxically, an enormous tenderness toward her.

They were almost alone when they reached the church. Paris glittered below them. Each pointed to landmarks. Now, wordlessly as they looked off into the distance, Daniel did put his arm around her and draw her close, and she didn't resist. To the contrary, she leaned into him, fitting his side like a missing piece.

They stood this way for some time. Finally, she said, "We're being very quiet. Not much like ourselves, I think. Is it this place?"

"Yes. And the person I'm with."

She looked up at him with a smile. "I'm not used to inspiring silence."

He laughed as he said, "No, I should think not."

They looked into the distance again. After a moment she said, "And what are you thinking about now?"

"I'm wondering whether, if I kissed you, you would kiss me back."

She stepped away from him slightly and looked up. "And how long were you planning on wondering this?"

He leaned and kissed her, at first softly, and she did kiss him back. "Until about right now." And then they kissed long and deeply, her taste sweet and her breath scented with coffee.

Now he took a step down the stone steps in front of the church, so they were more nearly the same height. "You see," she said, "not everything needs to be thought to death."

They kissed again, longer and with more heat, Daniel feeling completely at one with her. And they did this for some time before they proceeded back down toward the center of town. He held her close all the way.

~ ~ ~ ~ ~

~ ~ ~

Chapter 4

FROM THE FIRST TIME they were together it was clear she would make love the way she did everything else, with directness and unbridled certainty. It was a revelation to him. Here was a woman capable of giving and taking pleasure in equal measure. He never felt more old fashioned than when she pressed her desires unabashedly. And yet, the thrill he felt at these moments could hardly be described.

On those early winter nights no amount of external warmth—no amount of coal or wood or steam—could come close to matching the radiating, fusion-fired heat that is the realm of new lovers. As his mouth sought her out, explored her, found one after another and captured the graduated light coffee areola moons that capped her breasts, the breasts she presented to him so unreservedly, as he drank more and more deeply of her, trying to take all of her in, he was certain he would stop breathing before he could get enough of her.

When at last he entered her, pressed into her leaving not a hair's breadth between them, she would wrap her legs around him to ensure the lock and keep them bone on bone until she had captured every essence and secretion. And then, when they would separate, after scant moments she would aid in his recovery by kissing and licking, starting with gentle pulls on his eyes and lips and working to his chest where the flicks of her tongue separated the dark tangle that barely hid his nipples, and still lower until she could have no doubt he was ready for her again.

Afterward, the fire banked, archly she would accuse him of using secret medical knowledge for carnal purposes. "Isn't there a code of some kind, an oath doctors must swear to keep their women from fatal over-boils?"

35

To which he would reply if there were such an oath he would refuse to swear it, and in any case what could account for her own carnal knowledge and the profligacy with which she spent it?

And yet, when it came to the overall relationship, while the arc of his passion was ever sharply higher, hers was more gradual. Where he wanted to demonstrate his love by demonstrating his capacity for abandon, she seemed, despite her ardor, determined to hold something back.

At a time when his work was more demanding than ever, he found himself unable to concentrate on it. There were times when he would look for ways to pass tasks to one of his assistants, and it was Paola, displaying discipline both admirable and disappointing, who would try to persuade him to do otherwise. As mercurial as she could be in every way, she had the wherewithal to limit her passion with reason, and this disturbed him greatly. If she was capable of restraint, she must love him less than he loved her. The deflation of these moments aside, the irony was not lost on him that he and Nora might still be together if he had been inclined to spend even half as much time with her as he wanted to spend with Paola.

His insecurity led to their first real fight. Over dinner at a restaurant one night about a month after they had started seeing each other, she seemed unusually subdued. But as it was something he couldn't put a finger on, he let it go.

After dinner, they went to her apartment. He was eager to make love, but she put him off, saying simply that she wasn't in the mood. The moment might have passed without incident if not for the fact that Alessandro had returned to Paris the previous day. Paola had met him for lunch. She made no secret of this. To the contrary, she told Daniel about it with pleasure.

Now, he interpreted her reserve as a signal that perhaps she had been less than completely honest with him about her feelings for Alessandro. She had readily admitted that they had once been lovers, though she maintained the affair had ended well before she began seeing Daniel. But he also knew that at one time Paola and Alessandro had lived together, and he was upset that she had rebuffed his hints that they should do so.

So it was that at this slight signal that things weren't right—that Paola wasn't in the mood to make love—Daniel chose not only to ask about Alessandro but to do so in a way that directly questioned her honesty.

He was pacing distractedly when he stopped and looked at her. She was tucked into the corner of an oversized Chesterfield leather sofa that she inherited with the apartment, her feet curled up under her. The leather was a peculiar mottled ochre, the result of an ill-advised attempt to restain what she called, in disgust, English club brown. "You wouldn't be leading me on, would you?" he demanded. "You wouldn't be telling me one thing about Alessandro when you feel something else?"

Within seconds she stood and glared at him, her arms at her side, her hands balled into fists. "The only thing—the *only* thing," she repeated—"I ever completely insist upon in a relationship is honesty. I have never, ever lied to you . . ."

"I didn't say you lied."

"No? What would you call it?"

"There is the possibility you don't know your own feelings."

"Yes, that is possible. But it's not the situation now. Just because I don't want to make love tonight . . ."

"You have to admit, I have reason to be troubled by the timing."

"That's just so much nonsense! And as long as we're on the subject of honesty, why don't you tell me about your wife?"

"What are you talking about? You know all about Nora."

"You never told me you're still married to her."

"Because it's just a technicality . . ."

She cocked her head in disbelief. "Maybe to you. I'm not a prude, but I don't go out with married men."

"Where did all of this come from, anyway?"

"What's the difference? It's true, isn't it?"

"So, this is what's bothering you?"

"You misunderstand. I don't want to make love because I'm not in the mood. That's all, nothing more or less. It has nothing to do with Alessandro or your wife or anything else. But at this moment, yes, I am bothered by it. I am bothered by your so-called technicality." She stressed the word and left it to drip.

"It is a technicality, Paola. We are legally separated and we're only waiting for the final divorce to come through."

They stood looking at each other in silence for some time. At last, she said, "I demand complete honesty in a relationship. I give it as well as expect to receive it."

"I love you, Paola. That's as honest as I know how to be."

"I think I love you, too."

"Then that will have to do for now."

~ ~ ~ ~ ~

~ ~ ~

Chapter 5

IT WAS MID-AFTERNOON when Victoria arrived in Pisa. Francesco had said he would meet her. She wondered whether they would recognize each other after thirty-some years. It seemed incredible that so much time had passed. Surely with a modicum of effort they could have arranged to see each other before, she during one of her numerous trips to Italy or he on one of the trips she presumed he would have made to the States.

When the automatic doors opened to the greeting area, he was waiting with a hand-lettered sign that said, "Gideon. Welcome to Italy." The sign was unnecessary as Francesco rushed up to Victoria and embraced her. He placed a kiss on one cheek and then the other.

For her part, Victoria was glad for the instant recognition; it would have taken her longer to recognize him. Francesco shared little of their father's looks. Where Daniel was tall and solidly built and, having kept his hair, always looked younger than his years, Francesco was of medium height, slight, and distinguished looking. His hair was thin, gray at the temples, and perfectly cut. He wore a cream-colored shirt open at the neck and a lightweight, very fine wool black blazer.

"It's simply wonderful to have you here," he said.

She found the inflection in his voice even more charming than when she spoke to him on the telephone. "Oh, yes. I couldn't agree more. It's wonderful to be here."

He took her suitcase, dismissing her protest, and led her to the car. The sun was bright overhead, just beginning to fall off toward the west. It had been a blustery late March day in New York when she left. Now she was overdressed. She stopped to remove her jacket.

"Yes, it feels wonderful to be here," Victoria said again, leaning forward slightly in her seat. She thanked him for meeting her. He gave a dismissive wave, as if to say no other choice was imaginable.

They merged swiftly onto the *autostrada* and moved into the fast lane. Off to the left the flatlands led to the sea; in the distance to the right the sun was illuminating the mountains. "We have a clear day for you," Francesco said. "Yesterday it was quite hazy."

Victoria took it all in, sighed audibly. "Every time I visit Italy I'm astounded by how much beauty—how many different kinds of beauty—can be contained in such a small space. It's truly one of the earth's magnificent places. Do you still see it?" she asked after a pause. "Or have you come to take it for granted?"

"Actually, I do see it, but there are some days when I have to consciously remind myself how fortunate I am to live here."

"Once," Victoria began with a laugh at the memory, "I was driving with my husband down the Amalfi coast. I was absolutely overwhelmed by the view, not to mention terrorized to be traveling over roads where the slightest mistake would send us plummeting to our deaths! We stopped at a village grocery to pick up something to eat, and I remarked to the man behind the counter about how glorious the place was, how it was the most beautiful drive in the world, and so on.

"Well, he looked up at me with a sort of distracted expression, as if he couldn't figure out what in heaven I was talking about, even though he spoke perfectly good English. Oh yes, oh yes, he said finally in a kind of offhand way. He asked if I was American. I told him I was, and he said he lived in America for a year—near Seattle. Now *that*, he said, is a beautiful place." Victoria laughed again. "So it was my turn to look dumbstruck that anyone would think Seattle—and I love Seattle, mind you—more beautiful than the Amalfi coast. But there you have it. We do tend to take our surroundings for granted, don't we?"

They took the exit for Lucca. "The historic center of Lucca is completely surrounded by Renaissance-period walls," Francesco said, pointing, as they stopped at a traffic light. "They're the only such walls in Italy that are still intact, encircling the entire city. We're very proud of them. The walls are wide enough to have a park on their top. You'll see people walking and riding bikes all around. Lucca is quite a lovely city. Our house is in the hills not far from here. We'll just pass the old city now on the way home, but we'll come back. I think you'll enjoy it."

"I'm sure I will. The pictures in the guidebook are beautiful."

They entered a two lane highway, which was shared with trucks that Victoria thought far too large for the road but which nonetheless moved with remarkable agility. Twice they had to stop abruptly as the road narrowed to slightly more than a single lane where it cut through solid rock.

"This is the old Brenner road," Francesco offered as they waited for a truck coming toward them to clear the tunnel so that one in front of them could proceed. Now most people take the autostrada to Germany and Austria, but they used to take this road through the mountains. It's still a lovely way to go if you have very much patience and a strong stomach." He made loops with his index finger to indicate the tortuous route.

A few minutes later they turned off the highway and began climbing on a narrow winding road. They came upon a tractor-trailer moving in the opposite direction, and Victoria tensed as Francesco pulled over to the right as far as she thought possible given the sheer dropoff on that side. But he moved over further, then folded in his side mirror, which, given the height difference between the two vehicles, would have hit the truck's wheels. Miraculously to Victoria, but apparently quite casually to Francesco and the truck driver, they passed each other with what could have been no more than an inch to spare. "Can I breathe again?" she asked.

"It does take some getting used to." His smile was tinged with pride.

"I'm amazed at what these truck drivers are capable of."

"Now there's a comment that can be taken more ways than one."

She gave a low, throaty laugh. "I'd be hard-pressed to tell which way I meant it."

"I always say Italian drivers are high on skill and low on judgment. They can put their cars through the eye of a needle. Unfortunately, they often don't have a good sense of when it might be a good time to do so."

Francesco pointed to a rectangular sign which read in clear black letters against a cream-colored background, Ponte di Maddalena. "This is our town." Within moments the narrow road opened up before a piazza.

Francesco stopped the car and pointed. "This is where the ceremony will take place. A monument will be placed in the center. Of bronze and marble."

The piazza was approximately a hundred yards square. At the far end sat an ornate building, which could have been a theater or small opera house and which appeared to have been recently renovated. The remaining two sides were enclosed by shops, offices, and banks. At that moment the center of the piazza, where the monument was to be placed, was being used as a makeshift parking lot, cars parked head-in like spokes on a wheel.

"Where is the monument now?" Victoria asked.

"The sculptor is finishing it. It will be ready, I'm sure," Francesco said with a wry smile that seemed to mean that such things always went down to the last minute and yet somehow always got done. "Why don't we go to the house? Later we can walk around here. It's quite close."

Within a few blocks and another narrow, winding street, this one badly in need of repaving as bits of asphalt and gravel hit the underside of the car, they pulled up to large ornate wrought iron gates. "This is it," Francesco said. The house was encircled by a low stone wall out of which grew a substantial, dignified wrought-iron fence that continued the motif of the gates. The distance between the fence and the house was about thirty yards. Francesco pressed a button and the gates swung inward. They drove through and followed a gravel driveway around to the side.

"Oh, it's lovely," Victoria said as she stood and closed the car door. She scanned the property. The house was not palatial, but it was impressive nonetheless. It consisted of two stories, each quite tall—she guessed the interior ceiling heights must be at least twelve or thirteen feet—and might have appeared as an unexceptional cube except that it was set obliquely on the property and the main entrance was carved out of what would have been one of the cube's corners. This gave the house the impression of having two wings, while the added angles gave it a beveled feel. The exterior was stucco, painted ochre, trimmed in white enamel and with a white columned portico over the entrance, and set off by forest green shutters and a traditional Mediterranean red tile roof. The tall double front door was a light natural color that glowed with the patina of many layers of wax. Cyprus and olive trees filled the property, and the house was surrounded at its base by large red pottery amphorae filled with newly bursting spring flowers.

"How old is the house?" Victoria asked as Francesco began to unload the trunk.

"Oh, not so old, at least by Italian standards. Perhaps a hundred and fifty years, maybe a little more."

"It seems to be in excellent condition."

"The result of constant work, I'm afraid. We painted it only recently."

Victoria noticed an ornate band of color near the roofline. "Are they frescoes?"

"Alas no, it's only painted on," Francesco responded with a quick smile, as if he had anticipated the question.

"It's lovely anyway."

"There's also some interesting trompe l'oeil work on the side of the house, which I'll show you later."

"Later would be better. In my present state it wouldn't take much to fool my eye."

As they began to make their way up the front steps, the door opened and a woman stepped out to greet them. She was small, trim and elegant, her silver hair cut short and perfectly cared for. She had a wide, sweet smile and the smallest touch of sadness around her eyes. She wore a brightly-colored print dress that Victoria recognized from one of the shop windows on Fifth Avenue.

"Ciao, Chiara," Francesco called as he reached the top step and put down Victoria's suitcase. "Chiara, I present to you my sister," he said without qualification or sign of self-consciousness. "My wife, Chiara," he added, turning to Victoria.

Chiara stepped forward and embraced her, kissed one cheek, then the other. "Francesco and I are so happy you could come for this occasion," she said. Her accent was more heavily inflected than Francesco's, but her English was still easily understood. "Francesco has spoken of you so often over the years."

"Ever since Francesco called, I've been wondering how we could have let so many years slip by. And now I have a chance to get to know you! We all have so much to catch up on."

"But first," Francesco said, raising a solicitous finger, "I'm certain you will want to freshen up."

"But of course," Chiara added. "Please come in and we'll show you to your room."

"Have you heard from Roberto?" Francesco asked Chiara as he stepped through the doorway.

She looked at her watch, then back at him. "No, but it's only four-thirty."

"Of course. I don't know what I was thinking."

"Roberto is your son, right?" Victoria asked.

"Yes," Francesco responded. "He's at the gallery."

"Oh, wonderful," Victoria said. "I'd almost forgotten. You said you had an art gallery. I can't wait to see it."

They were standing at the entrance of a large living room, the high ceiling of which was ribbed with massive old wood beams. The room was filled with antique furniture and an overabundance of paintings of varying styles.

"It's both the blessing and the curse of a gallery owner," Francesco said with a smile as he watched Victoria scan the room. "The things I have no space for at the gallery end up here. Everything gets moved around all the time." His face lit up with sweet mischief. "The challenge for you will be to identify which paintings are really mine—the ones that really mean something—and the ones that are just here until I can find a buyer."

"I'll have to discover your true tastes," Victoria said.

"Even more, you'll have to learn something of our real persons, something of, what?" He paused, searching for words, then smiled. "Something of what makes us tick, as our father used to say. A good project for your visit, don't you think so?"

"I think it will be a very pleasant task."

Victoria unpacked her things and stood for a moment at the window overlooking a terraced garden in the back of the house. The sun was falling off, hitting the garden at sharp angles, brightly illuminating some places while others were cast in shadow. She breathed in deeply, contentedly. The change in mood from that of a mere twenty-four hours ago couldn't be more pronounced. From New York's rocket-fueled pace to this, as if the solution to the problem of a sane existence were as simple as a plane ticket. And yet, hard as it was to imagine, one of her purposes in coming to this place was to learn about a father's heroism during a time when nothing could have existed in this tranquil way.

She took a long shower and lay down on the bed with her book, hoping to unwind but not wanting to sleep, which would impede the adjustment of her body clock. It was a lost cause, however, as within a few moments she began to nod off.

* * *

THAT EVENING, THEY drove a short distance to Il Poeta, an osteria set into a terraced hillside. Victoria's energy level, as well as her attention span, ebbed and flowed, and she had to force herself to concentrate. Including Roberto, who came directly from the gallery, there were now four of them. Victoria was surprised to see that, physically, Roberto had little in common with Francesco. He was a larger presence, more substantial, with thick brown wavy hair and well-proportioned features. It occurred to her that, in Roberto, she could see more of Daniel than Francesco.

"This is a charming place," Victoria said, looking around.

"We come here often," Chiara said. "It's one of our favorites."

"Especially in summer," Roberto added. "They put tables outside and it's really very wonderful."

Francesco suggested beginning with a selection of antipasti for the table. Victoria said she would be happy to put herself in his hands. Soon the plates appeared: paper thin slices of prosciutto, olives, sliced cheeses, tomatoes, bruschetta, and what Victoria could only identify as thin slices of fat.

"Lardo," Francesco said with a laugh as he looked at the dubious expression on her face. "An acquired taste but one worth acquiring. Just spread a little on the bread."

"Tell me about the ceremony," Victoria said to Chiara "What inspired you to undertake the project?"

"Chiara deserves a great amount of credit," Francesco said with a slight flourish of his hand in her direction.

"Oh, I think that is too generous." Chiara's expression of pleasure overshadowed the modesty of the remark.

"She may not say so herself," Francesco persisted, "but very much work was required, and I don't mean only the work you might expect of organizing people, getting the memorial constructed, and so forth. The real work was cultural," he added in a way that suggested they were to appreciate something profound.

Perhaps concluding that some elaboration was in order, he continued, "You must understand that this is not a period of our history we are comfortable with."

"Yes," Roberto added. "Most Italians would prefer not to think about it. Even though other towns have done it, when Chiara suggested to the *commune*, the local government, that it was overdue to recognize the people from our town who fought bravely—who risked their lives, who lost their lives—to defeat the Fascists—it was not exactly welcomed."

"How did they oppose it?" Victoria asked.

Chiara said, "They didn't oppose it exactly. They had—how shall I say it?—a kind of nervousness at the idea. First there was a long silence, and then this was followed by polite agreement. 'Of course, of course,' the *commune* officials said. 'We should always recognize bravery.'" Chiara waved her hand as if to sweep away a pile of litter. "I think the real issue is that there are families around here who did not act bravely, and they know who they are."

"As I'm sure you know," Roberto offered, "this time was not only painful for Italians to live through. For many it remains also a time of embarrassment and shame."

"Let us be honest," Chiara added quickly, turning to Victoria, whose time-lapsed mind was trying to keep up. "Italy suffered horribly during those years, and it was our own fault. We supported our own Fascists, then went together with the German Fascists, and in the end we were hit from all over. By the end of the war, we had to fight the Allies, the Nazis and each other. Those who had the courage to oppose the Fascists—including my family and yours—paid a terrible price. I lost my mother and grandparents. Francesco lost his mother and sister and barely escaped himself, along with his father—your father too, of course," Chiara added with a nod.

"I know about my father's wife and daughter," Victoria said, "but what happened to your mother and grandparents? And you must have been very young at the time. Do you have vivid memories? If you don't mind talking about it," she added.

Chiara gave a sad smile. "Some things never stop hurting, but in doing this work I've found that dealing with these things every day, as I've had to, can be very"—she searched for the word—"catharting."

"Can be a catharsis," Francesco volunteered.

"Yes, catharsis," Chiara nodded appreciatively. "So, yes, anyway, I can talk about it. I don't know how much of the history you know. It was a time of great confusion. In 1943, Italy tried to get rid of Mussolini and come to peace with the Allies. But in many ways, this led only to bigger problems. The new Italian government arrested Mussolini and then signed an armistice with the Allies. But the Nazis rescued him and helped set up a new Fascist government in the north, in a place on Lake Garda called Salo`. So now we had Nazi occupiers, the Allies invading from the south, and all kinds of partisans fighting a guerrilla war. The economy was in a terrible way, of course. People were hungry. When your father's wife and his daughter were taken away . . . "

"Why were they taken away?" Victoria interrupted. "That's still not clear to me."

"Unfortunately, it's not too clear to me, either. One thing I've heard is that your family, especially your father's wife—Paola was her name—became too loud against Mussolini—had got on the wrong list. Your father was lucky to escape. And Francesco too, of course. I'm sure Francesco has told you the story."

"Actually," Victoria said, smiling at Francesco, "we haven't had a chance to talk about that. I would be fascinated to hear about it."

Francesco seemed to strain for a smile. "Of course, I'll tell you everything I know, though I'm afraid to say much of it is second-hand. I was quite young, you know, a child really."

Victoria asked if Francesco knew anything more about the reasons for Paola's arrest.

"Not much. I think, as Chiara said, the family got on the wrong list. It was easy to do."

As the main course was being served, Victoria turned to Francesco and asked about the papers he had discovered.

"It's quite a collection of things. I haven't had a chance to go through them nearly as thoroughly as I would like. I'm sure there are things I've missed. That's one reason it will be reassuring to have you look them over with your historian's eye."

"I'll try not to disappoint you," she said with a smile. "Is there any organizational theme or system to them?"

"Most of the boxes don't appear to be immediately interesting. Many have to do with Father's professional work. There are documents about the first war—the kinds of things he would have accumulated for his medical research, but also things related to his interest in using international law to avoid a second war. Mixed in among these things are diary entries, some personal letters, and so on. I say mixed in because the diary entries have an unusual kind of coding so as not to be immediately obvious what they are." Francesco gave a mischievous smile. "Do you want to know what the code is, or shall you regard it as a challenge to figure it out?"

Victoria laughed brightly. "You're full of challenges for me today! If you put it that way, I hardly see how I can resist. I find it fascinating," she went on, "that these materials should have been left undiscovered for so long. As I recall, you told me they were found during some renovations to the house."

"Yes, that's right. We were breaking through a wall in the basement storage area—what we call the cantina—and there they were."

"And you had no suspicion they were there?"

"Not really. I always assumed that whatever papers he had were lost in the chaos of the war."

Victoria shook her head. "Astounding, truly astounding."

"Not as unusual as you might think," Roberto offered. "Italians have much practice in hiding things. One of the best cases was the discovery in the nineteenth century of the correspondence of a wealthy merchant in Prato, near Florence, who lived during the thirteen and fourteen hundreds. Under a sealed staircase they found a vast number of letters—thousands of them—as well as records from his business and other things. It's one of the best pictures we have of that time."

"Anyway," Francesco said, "whoever did the original work on the cantina did a really fine job of finishing, as there was no evidence that anything lay behind the wall. We had quite a surprise when our workmen broke through."

"There was one other thing that was interesting," Roberto added, and Victoria thought she saw a momentary crease pass across Francesco's face. "As we broke through," Roberto went on, "there was a place where, if you looked closely, the patching was different from the surrounding area, as if it had been partially opened and then sealed again."

"Maybe the simple explanation is the best one," Chiara offered. "Maybe your grandfather wanted to remove some of what he put in there."

48

"Or," said Victoria the historian, with a smile, "to add something."

"Yes, or to add something," Chiara echoed.

Over coffee Victoria said to Chiara, "You never did tell what happened to your mother and grandparents."

"Yes, of course." She put down her cup and prepared to begin, but she stopped abruptly. "Actually, I have a better idea. Tomorrow we'll pay a visit to my family home. There I think the story will come more alive."

~ ~ ~ ~ ~

~ ~ ~

Chapter 6

THE ROOM WAS DARK when Victoria awoke at nine. She felt her way to the window and opened the shutters. Sunlight streamed in. She raised her hand to shade her eyes. Gradually, her surroundings came into focus. Outside, the gardens and the hills beyond shone with a bursting spring lushness. Victoria stared as she tried to orient herself. In the distance, she could hear the gas-powered whine of a weed trimmer. Reproving herself for sleeping later than she'd intended, she dressed quickly and made her way downstairs.

Chiara was on the terrace sipping coffee when Victoria came through the large double doors that were swung wide open. The long trestle table contained the remains of a simple breakfast: drained coffee cups, bits of toast and the small horn ends of croissants. A bowl of apples and clementines rested in the center of the table. There was a fresh place setting, which Victoria assumed was for her.

Chiara smiled, "Buongiorno."

"Buongiorno," Victoria responded. "My apologies. I'm a little slow getting started this morning."

"Not at all." Chiara waved off the thought. "Traveling is hard on the body. We didn't want to wake you. Roberto had to go to work, and Francesco went to run some errands."

"Of course," Victoria said, taking a seat. "You can't be expected to change everything to suit a lazy visitor," she added lightly.

"Would you like coffee? You can have it the Italian way or American."

"Whichever is the least trouble."

"Neither is trouble," Chiara said, moving toward the house. "We drink both."

"American, then. I do like to linger over it."

"Francesco will be home soon," Chiara called from the kitchen.

"Wonderful. He doesn't have to work today, then?"

"No. He wants to spend time with you. Roberto is watching the gallery."

Chiara returned with a tray. In addition to a pot of coffee there was a bowl of fresh fruit salad and a basket of rolls and croissants.

"Oh, my," Victoria said, bringing her hand to her breast. "Coffee would have been more than enough."

"Not at all," Chiara responded as she collected used plates and flatware. "Take whatever you like."

"Only if you stop clearing up and join me," Victoria said with gracious severity. "Please."

Chiara took a seat and poured half a cup of coffee for herself.

"Tell me more about the ceremony," Victoria said. "What made you choose this time to organize it?"

"Oh, well . . ." Chiara took a sip and put the cup down. She dabbed her mouth with a napkin. "It was one of those things I've thought about many times over the years. I would visit small towns where memorials had been placed to the partisans—often simple plaques saying that so and so was killed by the Nazis on this spot. As you may know, when the partisans killed one or two Nazis, the Nazis would respond by rounding up many ordinary citizens and shooting or hanging them. In some places, like St. Anna di Stazzema, which is not far from here, the entire town was wiped out—five hundred sixty people, some as young as three months, were rounded up, shot and their bodies burned. If you want to know what the Nazis were capable of, you don't need to visit the famous concentration camps. All you have to do is come to a place like this. The people of St. Anna di Stazzema built lovely, touching memorials to the victims. You should see them."

"I would very much like to."

"Anyway, I would see such memorials and wonder why we didn't have such a thing in our little town. Some famous partisans came from here, you know. Also, I began thinking, why should memorials only honor the dead? Many people, such as your father, made great sacrifices and yet survived."

"Yes," Victoria nodded.

"So, why should they not also be honored? I had these thoughts for many years. It also grieved me that nothing public has been done to honor my parents and grandparents."

"Were they actually partisans?"

"Well, not in the sense of battle. My grandparents were too old for such things, of course, and my mother was too busy looking after her children. Including me!" Chiara added with a smile. "I was my parents' baby. But I know that in every other way possible they fought against the *Nazifascisti*. There is an expression in English, I think—giving aid and comfort?"

"Well, yes," Victoria said, not bothering to supply the rest of the usual phrase, "to the enemy."

"My family," Chiara continued, gave great aid and comfort to the partisans. And to the Allied soldiers, too. In this area we had many Negro soldiers . . ."

"The Buffalo Soldiers."

"Yes, that's what they were called. And we helped them as much as we would have helped any other soldiers."

"Yes, I see." Victoria spread honey on a croissant. "Do you have memories from that time?"

"Not really. As I said, I was very young. Much of what I know is from my older brother—he's dead now, but he survived the war. At one time not long before he died—this must have been about ten years ago—my brother did approach the *commune* about some kind of memorial. The *commune* wasn't very interested. I'm not sure why. Politics probably." She shrugged as if to say, politics or any number of possibilities, or what else could be expected from politicians and bureaucrats?

"Anyway," Chiara continued, "in 1995 there were many ceremonies to commemorate the fiftieth anniversary of the end of the war. I thought more and more about my family. After all, what better proof could there be of their bravery and sacrifice than the fact of their being killed by the Nazifascisti? And I became determined that their sacrifice should not go unnoticed. Why should our little town not mark their sacrifice as so many other towns have done? One thing led to another, and the original idea of a memorial to the dead gradually grew to include others, like your father, who had served and survived."

"What a fascinating story, Chiara. Are we still planning to visit your family home today?"

"Yes, of course, if you would like to."

"Oh, indeed, I would like to very much."

"*Buongiorno, tutte*," Francesco said brightly as he stepped out onto the terrace. "How nice it is to find my lost family right at my table!" He gave Victoria's shoulder an affectionate squeeze as he passed behind her.

Victoria smiled broadly and dabbed her mouth with her napkin.

"Would you like something to eat?" Chiara asked.

"No, no, thank you. I'm still full from before." Francesco patted his flat stomach as if to suggest something needed to be shed.

"Victoria and I were just talking about visiting my family home," Chiara said.

"An excellent idea. First, though, Victoria, I thought perhaps you would like to see our father's things."

"Yes, certainly." She dabbed her mouth again, stood, and began to clear the table.

"Please," Chiara said, putting her hand on Victoria's. "I'll take care of this. You go with Francesco."

Victoria began to protest, but Chiara was insistent.

Francesco led her to a wide stone staircase just off the kitchen. At the bottom of the stairs he switched on the lights to reveal a large space, with several rooms leading off a corridor that ran the length of the house. The smell of fresh paint bespoke the recent renovation.

"What a surprise this is," Victoria said as she looked around. "I would never have guessed such a big, attractive area existed here."

Francesco walked along and showed Victoria the rooms. "Much of the area down here is actually used for storage and such. On the left, here, though, we renovated two rooms, which we use as guest bedrooms, and put in a bath."

They passed the first bedroom and entered the second, the door to which was off center to the right. As Victoria stepped in she saw that the room had been set up as a study. The center was occupied by a large country-style desk in pickled wood with an olive leather inset top. One wall contained book shelves, mostly empty.

Francesco smiled. "You should not interpret the way I've arranged the room as an expectation that you will spend all your time poring over records. I just thought that if you wanted to bring your professional historian's touch to them, the least I could do was make you comfortable."

Victoria laughed and squeezed his arm. "That's very thoughtful. I promise, I won't do any more work than I feel like doing."

Two framed black-and-white photographs stood on the desk, and Victoria walked toward them to get a closer look. The one on the left was posed as a traditional family portrait. In the center she recognized Daniel, dressed in a light summer suit, thick hair carefully combed, and smiling for the camera. Next to him stood a petite woman turned slightly oblique to the camera to present a baby. She, too, was smiling, and the smile made her face alive. A shy-looking young boy in short pants and suspenders was wedged between them. "This must be you," Victoria said, pointing.

"Yes. And that's my mother."

"Paola," Victoria said, as if to catalogue her correctly.

"Yes."

"She was very pretty."

"I think she was. People who knew her have told me her beauty was more a spiritual thing—from the inside out. And this is my sister," he added, indicating the baby in Paola's arms.

"So the photo must have been taken not long before they were taken away by the Germans."

"There's no date on it. From the way they're dressed in summer clothing, I would say it was taken perhaps six months earlier."

"And the photo on the right?" Victoria brought her face closer. Daniel, obviously younger than in the first picture but in similar attire, was holding a baby and smiling broadly.

"That," Francesco said with the satisfied voice and smug look of one who has given a successful surprise party, "is you."

"Wherever did you find this?" Victoria smiled with a delight she would not have anticipated. Here was an unexpected attack on the armor of determined indifference she had built, layer upon layer, year upon year.

"In the boxes. There's an inscription on the back, dated to 1930. I had it framed. I thought it might give you inspiration."

"Oh, indeed! What a sweet thing!" She touched his arm.

54

Looking around, her gaze stopped at several large cardboard boxes in the far corner of the room.

"There they are," Francesco said. "Enough to keep a dedicated historian busy for some time, I should think."

She walked over and touched the top box. From the gum residue she could see that the boxes had been sealed with tape but now were closed only by the carton flaps overlapping like lattice. "They're in remarkably good condition. No evidence of water damage or anything."

"No, they were completely dry. I opened them, of course."

She pulled back the flaps of the top box and removed a small notebook. A heading in Daniel's handwriting said, "Notes on Geneva Text on Blister Agents."

"Light reading, I see," Victoria said with a smile. "Where was all this stuff?"

"Come, I'll show you."

Francesco led her to the opposite end of the corridor and into a room containing tools and a workbench. Like the rest of the cellar space, the walls had been recently smoothed and painted a pale yellow. She followed him to the far end of the room where a door led to a smaller room, all of the walls of which were taken up by wine bottles in neat, new racks. "If you get tired of reading musty papers, there is an alternative here," he said, sweeping his hand at the hundreds of bottles.

"This could be a dangerous place," Victoria laughed.

He then led her back into the utility room from which they had come and pointed at the wall in which the door to the wine room had been cut. "One of the things I wanted to do when we decided to finish the cantina—this space down here—was to create a proper wine cellar. We knew there would be enough dead space on the other side of this wall. Like everything down here before we renovated, the wall was gray stone, patched in various places over the years—nothing remarkable really. The floor was packed earth. But when we broke through we were surprised to find not merely the open area we expected, but what amounts to a chamber, with interior walls that we didn't expect.

"Now, from the narrow perspective of the plan to build a wine cellar, this was actually a very nice discovery, as we were assuming we would have to build such a chamber ourselves. But of course the real surprise was that the chamber was filled with Father's boxes. It was really very well done."

"Well, I'm not sure whether it was you or Roberto who said last night that Italians are good at hiding things. I guess that extends to our quasi-Italian father."

"Indeed," Francesco said with a laugh.

"Did you find anything besides the papers?"

"A few things. Some jewelry, which we assume belonged to my mother. Some cash, too, but it was in Italian lire, which is practically worthless. The banknotes are quite pretty, though. You might like to have some of them as keepsakes."

From upstairs, Chiara called.

"Yes, we're here," Francesco responded.

"If we're going to my family's home, we should go soon."

"Is it far?" Victoria asked as they returned to the terrace.

"Less than a kilometer," Francesco said. "As a matter of fact, it's a nice walk, if you're interested."

"Oh, yes, the walk will do me good."

They set out on a path behind the house. Francesco explained that, though the surface was uneven and slightly difficult to walk on, the path was preferable to the road as it wasn't necessary to dodge cars. They walked through small vineyards and olive groves and passed a few small, abandoned houses, their terra cotta roofs in disrepair; some of the loose tiles were held in place by heavy stones.

Before long they came to a rise on the other side of which came into view the rear of a large villa, in good repair but with no signs of life. The villa sat on a hill; the area between it and the rise on which they stood formed a valley containing a patio, gardens and stands of olive and lemon trees. A terrace ran the length of the house and looked over the patio and gardens below.

"That's my family home," Chiara said, pointing, pride in her voice.

"It is absolutely beautiful," Victoria said to Chiara's obvious pleasure. "But does anyone live here?"

"Not for some time," Francesco responded. "Occasionally we talk about selling it, but it's hard to part with a home that's been in one's family for so many years. Chiara has so many memories. We do our best to keep it up, but it's not easy. Anyway, one of our children may want to move in someday."

"Come," Chiara said, encouraging them on.

They made their way along the path, which seemed to end at a garden wall in the rear of the house. There Chiara asked the others to follow her along a smaller path around the house, saying she preferred to show them the gardens last. When they reached the front they stopped before an old brick and stone wall broken by an ornate double iron gate large enough for cars to pass through. A heavy chain and padlock secured the gate. Francesco fished in his pocket for a key and opened the lock.

The house was considerably larger than Francesco's. The stucco exterior was painted a uniform ochre, but the overall structure had a slightly haphazard aspect, the result of additions and modifications over hundreds of years.

Chiara led them through the house, pointing out places that held particular memories for her. In the living room she stopped and breathed deeply as if to inhale one of those memories, then explained that the room was special. It was here that her parents loved to entertain. As young as she was—not much more than a baby, really—she could recall with amazing vividness awakening during the evening and being taken downstairs by her mother and shown off at the parties that were in progress. "Oh, it was so lovely and warm. Mother would hold me and Father would dance me around the room in the candlelight. I remember the men in their dark suits, so handsome, would make such a fuss over me."

Finally they stepped onto the long terrace at the rear of the house. Below the terrace was the patio.

"There's the path we came on," Victoria said, pointing beyond the wall that surrounded the villa.

"Exactly," Francesco said.

"How do you maintain the gardens in such lovely condition? It must be quite difficult."

"Not very difficult if others do the work," Chiara said with a smile. "We have a gardener twice a week, but that's mostly to take care of the flowers and plants. The olives are tended by local farmers who do the work in exchange for the fruit. Now, come and I'll show you the most important place here."

They descended a staircase from the terrace to the patio, then walked through the garden toward a stand of olive trees, their leaves glistening in the sun like silver chaff. Chiara led them to a small clearing in which stood a simple black granite obelisk, about five feet tall. Inscribed on the obelisk, one above the other, were the names: Bruno Buca 1880-1945, Hilde Buca 1884-1945, Renata Buca 1906-1945. And beneath the names: *Non Mai Dimenticare*. Never forget.

Chiara went to the obelisk and softly traced the letters with her finger. "On this spot," she said, looking at Victoria, "there was once a lovely patio. I remember it as a child. My grandfather would sit here, reading. I would hide from him in the trees. I never hid very well, of course. I always hoped he would see me. He would pretend for a few minutes that he didn't. Then he'd make a big fuss over discovering me."

Chiara's brief smile was replaced by a somber expression as she went on. "It was in this sweet place that my beloved mother Renata and my grandparents died. Shot dead by someone who never showed his face; who never even had the basic humanity to explain why.

"Who knows?" she said after a pause. "Maybe there was no explanation. Ours wouldn't have been the only senseless tragedy in those years. That was on 14 April 1945. My family came so close to making it through the war. A matter of weeks, that's all it would have taken."

Chiara looked at Victoria. She held out her thumb and index figure separated by less than an inch. "This close."

~ ~ ~ ~ ~

~ ~ ~

Chapter 7

VICTORIA STOOD NEXT TO the boxes, which were arranged end on end along the wall. It was late morning and the house was quiet. Francesco was at the gallery. Chiara was meeting with someone involved in the ceremony.

Francesco had told her that, in his cursory review of the material, he had found no great organizational scheme. It was, he said, roughly in chronological order. Almost all of the boxes contained things of little more than passing significance—conference notes, patient case histories, various articles, including some authored by Daniel, on such subjects as treatments for chemical burns or research into biological hazards—things which Francesco had assumed, furthermore, were long outdated substantively and thus of interest only from a historical perspective. He had discovered a few notes and a journal of a personal nature, but these primarily covered the years before the war, whereas it was the war years themselves, and especially Daniel's experiences with the partisans, that most interested him. It was Daniel's journal entries on these subjects that were the real find and which Francesco had challenged Victoria to decipher on her own.

Francesco explained that it was always difficult for Daniel to talk about Paola and their daughter—his sister—Isabella, but that he did his best to answer Francesco's inevitable questions. At first, the questions were the predictable, innocent ones a child would ask and then ask again and again as if for the first time. Was my mother pretty? What did her voice sound like? Did she sing to me, tell me stories? Which story was my favorite? Tell it to me again. Daniel would answer, and then patiently answer again. Francesco added that before he could ask these questions he had gone through a lengthy

59

period of "strong neurosis," as he called it, during which he refused even to acknowledge that his mother and sister were dead.

Francesco told Victoria that when he was old enough to have some understanding he was grateful that Daniel had been so tender and patient in the face of what could only have been the most painful of memories. He speculated that it was a strong sense of duty that enabled him to hide the pain. Or perhaps it was the very repetitiveness of the questions that enabled the answers to take on, if not a rote quality, then one that had more of the essence of a family legend, told with affection and even occasional hints of passion but nevertheless at a level of remove.

However, the war experiences were a different matter. As a child Francesco asked often to be told about the time he was left to be cared for by others while Daniel joined the local partisan group. Daniel's answers to these questions were bland and general. He would seek the first opportunity to change the subject.

Victoria said she could understand. Such a reaction was not so unusual for people who went through the horrors of war. "A brother of my late husband was a tail gunner in the Pacific. He flatly refused ever to discuss his experiences."

Now, standing before the boxes, Victoria considered how to proceed. That she would do so methodically, bringing the historian's trained eye to bear, was given. Yet she wanted to be not excessively dispassionate. This was, after all, an opportunity to learn something about her own past, however remote the connection might seem. Perhaps she would find nothing especially illuminating about Daniel. The story she could piece together from her mother, Bemis, Francesco, Chiara, or the few things Daniel left to her at home might be all there was. Possibly a detail or two could be filled in. Or, possibly even many details, which would suit her taste for completeness even if it added little to the overall outline. She considered it virtually impossible that her fundamental judgments about Daniel would be altered, however open a mind she might keep. After all, the new evidence before her covered a period after the one that directly affected her. She and her mother were themselves history by the time Daniel arrived in Italy. And yet, all this said, what was the point of undertaking the project at all if she was closed to the possibility of being moved by discovery?

With the exception of a few notes Francesco had uncovered from the early thirties, the earliest papers dated to 1938. Victoria presumed that at one point there must have been papers from Daniel's Paris years—surely he didn't wake up one day in 1938 and start to keep careful records—but she had no idea if they still existed. The personal journal Francesco had discovered, a single bound volume which he had read and set aside for her, covered only about a year and a half, ending in summer of 1939. She would begin there, of course.

Victoria took the volume over to the desk and sat down, holding it before her. It was a sturdy construction, typical of the time. It had the feel of a ledger, with a stiff faded green canvas-like cloth over heavy cardboard. A coffee or tea stain bled across the top right-hand corner. It opened unwillingly as if frozen in embrace.

Daniel's hand was instantly recognizable, if not easily decipherable. Most of the entries were written with a broad nib fountain pen, the ink faded randomly from black to varying shades of sepia.

The initial entry was dated 3 May 1938. Daniel began by noting that it was a convenient starting point, coinciding as it did with his visit to Italy. It was a good time, he wrote, to review recent history. "Maybe seeing it on paper will make it more comprehensible to me." What he wrote next was the first surprise to Victoria, who for whatever reason had always assumed that Daniel's move to Italy was a willing one.

The past year has been momentous in every conceivable way. I'll leave my work aside for the moment—it's clear enough that Europe is on the wrong course, one which could well end with all of us smashed on the rocks. If war comes, I hope we will at least have learned enough to make it less barbarous than the last time. I take some comfort in the international agreements that have been put in place to this end. I have treated, and continue to treat, all the gas and chemical burn cases I ever wish to see.

But now I am in Italy, I don't know for how long. At least until the baby comes, I should think. The simple fact is, I couldn't hold out against Paola's campaign to bring us here. Not that she especially wanted to come, but for all the ways in which she can be contrary and rebellious, she is still the dutiful daughter and in some ways more tradition-bound than one would ever believe she could be.

Two years ago Paola and the rest of her family were stunned and inconsolable when her brother, Luca, was shot dead in Ethiopia. When her father telephoned with the news, she let out an unworldly shriek. Even listening to only her part of the conversation it was clear that her unrestrained reaction shook free any control her father might have been fighting to maintain over his emotions. The crying that started with the phone call went on for hours. Nothing I could say helped her. At last, only a sedative I convinced her to take did any good.

None of this is to suggest that there was a straight line between this event and my presence here. In fact, the reverse would have seemed more likely as I heard the shocking news that she didn't want me to accompany her to the funeral because it would be too awkward to explain me to her parents at such a time. It never occurred to me that I had been a secret all that time—Paola certainly never behaved as if that was the case. I asked her what, if anything, her parents knew about me. It was one of the few times she'd exhibited embarrassment. At first, she made it sound as if she talked to them about me all the time.

As I pressed, it became clear that mentions of me had been in the breezy, noncommittal context of her many friends in Paris. She would tell them she'd gone to the theater or a play with a group of friends, one of whom was a doctor named Daniel, etcetera, etcetera.

"So," I said in a way I hoped would retain a sense of humor despite the irritation I felt, "it would appear that the saucy, irrepressible Paola Rosetti, avant-garde woman of the world who speaks her mind without reservation is, in reality, a meek, compliant daughter who fears telling her family she has a boyfriend." I reminded her that we had been living together for over a year.

Her answer shocked the hell out of me. "You're married," she said. "I don't know how to explain that to them."

After I stopped sputtering I reminded her that I was not married, that my divorce had come through.

"Not as far as the Catholic Church is concerned."

I couldn't believe my ears. "Well, that's true, of course. But, then, I'm not a Catholic, am I?"

"Exactly."

"And when did you start taking such an interest in the views of this church that, as far as I can recall, you've only found time to ridicule?"

"It's not what I think that's important. It's what my parents think."

My confusion only grew at that remark. Not that it was a major topic of conversation between us, but I was sure Paola had told me that her parents weren't very religious.

I reminded her of this and she said it was true that her parents, and especially her father, could be best described as agnostic where God was concerned. But the Church was a different matter. The Church was the one thing people could always count on. Neither one of them could abide criticism of the Pope or the Church.

"So," I said, "do I now understand that we are never to be more to each other than a couple of convenience who are restricted to Paris?"

"Now who's being ridiculous, Daniel?"

By this point, I confess I was becoming childish. "Oh, excuse me. Perhaps we can go as far as the French border."

"I intended to tell my family about you. Now is not the time, while we are grieving."

Paola said this with the conviction that it would be the last word—her grief could not be superseded, could it?—but in my anger I felt compelled to remind her that she wasn't the only one who had other people to care about. "As long as you have a problem with my marital status, I might as well remind you that I have other obligations that won't end. I am, after all, a father, too."

"I know that," she replied—an instantaneous, automatic, irritated riposte, which was followed just as quickly by a second, more considerate— and certainly more welcome—reaction. Fortunately, I had long before come to appreciate that it is such second thoughts that truly define her. "I'm sorry," she said, touching my hand. "I'm just upset."

I nodded, thinking that was the end of it, but softly she volunteered to finish making my case. "We don't speak of it often," she said, "but I know how bad you feel about your daughter. I know how much what happened hurts you, and that you miss her and feel guilt that you have not done right by her. You let such thoughts show more than you are aware." She gave me a little smile and put a silencing finger to my lips. "I know these things because I know what kind of man you are, and this is why I love you and why I also know in my heart that distance is the only thing that keeps you now from being the father to Victoria that you would wish to be."

I admit I was caught completely off guard by what she said. I was less surprised that she would feel these things or even say them than I was at the suddenness with which she did so—and even more because they came on the heels of the ridiculous contretemps over my marital status. However it came about, I was overwhelmed by her expression of love and by her very comprehension of the depth of my sadness over my failings as a father, even though, as she said, it was not something I had spoken of often. I could feel my eyes becoming moist and could only find it in me to say, "Thank you." But this was sufficient. We held each other close for a long moment.

She went alone to the funeral, staying for three weeks, and made two other brief visits home by herself. All of a sudden—at least to me—our relationship took on a forbidden aspect, which seemed at one and the same time absurd (we're hardly adolescents, after all) and intriguing.

I suppose this situation could have gone on indefinitely if Paola had not become pregnant. We were surprised. We had taken precautions (obviously not diligently enough). But as much as I was surprised by the fact, I was even more surprised by my reaction to it. I was happy. However sad I could be about my failings as a husband to Nora and father to Victoria, I loved the thought of starting a family with Paola.

It was a defining moment for Paola. The shock gave way to delight. (She never had a thought about ending the pregnancy.) But, of course, this new situation put a wry twist on the nature of our relationship, trumping as it did Paola's earlier concerns vis-à-vis my religious status. Now, having to tell her parents about a live-in, previously married Presbyterian boyfriend paled beside telling them she had been made pregnant by this boyfriend.

In the end we settled on a civil ceremony in Paris, the news of which shocked and greatly upset her parents, no matter how much they might not have been truly surprised by yet another rash act by their impulsive, sometimes reckless—but in her way loving and dutiful—daughter.

In any event, whatever disappointment they felt at the manner of our marriage was washed away when, after as decently short a time as possible, we went to Italy, introduced me, and announced that she was pregnant. As I write this, we are on our second visit together and she is within days of giving birth. Her parents are as capable as anyone of counting months but either are reluctant to do so or, more likely, are too refined to bring the count to our attention. Anyway, Paola's concern about their reaction was probably overblown from the start. It doesn't take a genius to figure out that, however put out they might be with her—and I'm sure they are and have been often— they adore her.

The nice surprise for me is that I have enjoyed her family, and I think they have enjoyed me. I have gotten on especially well with Paola's father, who is intelligent, engaging and far more worldly than I expected based on Paola's worries.

Victoria heard a door open upstairs. A few moments later, Chiara's voice called down.

"Yes, I'm here," she responded. "Just going through some of Daniel's things."

"Good. Francesco will come home for lunch. I'll make something for us."

"I'll be up in a moment to help."

"No, that's not necessary. I just wanted to let you know about lunch. You keep working and I'll call you when it's ready."

Victoria decided to finish reading the entry she was on and then help Chiara. She reflected with satisfaction that she had already read something surprising: Daniel's acceptance of responsibility—and remorse—over the way things turned out with her mother as well as, of course, the surprising depth of feeling for Victoria herself. She turned the page, hoping to find more.

It is sad to witness the disintegration of an illusion. Yet that is what I see when I look at the Rosetti family's reckoning with Mussolini and his Fascists. As I understand it from Paola, they were never more than lukewarm supporters, going along to get along, appreciating some of the regime's social reforms (especially in the early years), secretly ridiculing the Duce's theatrics, and generally benefiting from the Italian resurgence.

All of this came crashing down on them with the death of their son. Any pride they might have taken, or as Paola would have it, might have convinced themselves to take, in the Fascists' pretensions to empire ran up against the hard reality of losing their eldest in such a folly. What's more, another son is still in the army; the way things are going in Europe, he, too, will be at risk.

In the meantime, Paola's parents are doing their best to keep up a brave front. We had a great demonstration of this when, shortly after our arrival, we joined them at a party at their neighbors, the Bucas. In the presence of the Blackshirted faithful and a smattering of likeminded Germans, and in the face of the Bucas' overweening Fascist patriotism, the Rosettis were polite and gracious. (It came as no surprise that it was Paola who almost made a scene.) But they left at the first opportunity.

Victoria closed the volume, then opened it again. With a look of perplexity she read again the phrase "overweening Fascist patriotism." Could Daniel be in error, attributing this to the Bucas? Certainly it was at odds with the things she had heard from Chiara. Perhaps he misspoke. Or, perhaps he meant that they were displaying such fervor for the benefit of their guests?

From upstairs Victoria could hear more activity. She assumed Francesco had returned. She marked her place in the volume, closed it, and set it on the desk.

* * *

THROUGH THE OPEN door to the terrace Victoria saw Chiara and Francesco seated at the table. Francesco waved to her to come out.

Victoria squinted into the sunshine as she stepped outside. "I feel as if I've been cast out of a dungeon," she said with a laugh. She was dressed casually in dark slacks and a red and white striped shirt. She threw a cardigan over her shoulders.

"I hope it's not too unpleasant working downstairs," Francesco said with an appearance of concern.

"Not at all. It's quite comfortable. You've set me up wonderfully. I was just surprised by the brightness."

"I hope you don't mind," Chiara said. "The day is so lovely, I thought we would take advantage of it and have our lunch out here." The table was set with an assortment of salads and cold meats. A crusty bread sat in a basket in the center.

"We must make the most of this early burst of spring," Francesco added. "It probably won't last."

"Of course! It's a splendid idea," Victoria said quickly, pulling up her chair.

"Look at those clouds!" Francesco said, pointing behind Victoria. They were massive and billowing, illuminated silver white by the sun.

Victoria turned, shielding her eyes. "Oh, they are fabulous! You know, when a painter captures a sky like that accurately, the painting looks amateurish, as if he did it with a paint-by-numbers kit."

"I agree," Francesco said. "I believe capturing a sky well is one of the most challenging things for a painter."

"It's hard to explain to people who haven't been here," Chiara said, "but the cloud formations that roll in and out of this area are really quite exceptional. I don't see them anywhere else."

Francesco picked up a plate of cheeses, chose a few pieces of pecorino, and passed the plate to Victoria. "How is the research project going?" he asked.

"Very interesting. I've only just begun, of course. So far I've spent most of my time organizing. Probably the most interesting things will be from Daniel's journals. Much of the rest seems to be medical records and such. Not much interest to me, but perhaps medical archives would like them. We'll see."

She paused for a moment, reflecting on the journal entry she had just read and their odd take on the Bucas. She considered mentioning it, decided it was premature to do so but worth nibbling around the edges. "Tell me, Francesco, I know you said you've only scanned Daniel's things, but what were your impressions? You must have formed some, however superficial."

"Yes, certainly," he agreed. He put down his fork, followed the quick declaration with a pensive moment during which his eyes focused on Victoria only in brief stops. When he resumed he chose his words deliberately. "I think what struck me most had to do with the partisans. You may not have gotten that far in your reading."

"No."

"Father was very reluctant to take up with the partisans. They wanted his help. But he was probably concerned about putting the rest of us in danger. As I've mentioned, even long after the war he refused to talk about his experiences. But he did tell me how torn he was. He was a pacifist in the best sense—not a naive idealist, but someone who, having had a full measure of war, wanted no part of violence. Yet, as a moral man he believed he had an obligation to oppose evil."

"Especially," Victoria said, "since he was presumably in a position to help the partisans by giving them medical help, rather than by carrying a gun."

"Yes, but don't forget, the activities of the partisans were not always easy to stomach. Not to take anything away from them, but the kinds of honors we want to bestow fifty years on tend to smooth over the rough spots. When you consider the partisans' own brutalities, the equation can seem to be one of calculating the lesser of various evils. This was even more true in places, especially in the north and east, where the communists were most powerful."

"I agree," Chiara said. "The partisans wouldn't merely ask for help from the local people. Sometimes they could be quite menacing in the way they asked. A lot of families were caught in the middle, between the partisans and the Fascist squadristi. That's one of the reasons I'm so proud of my family. They risked a lot to help the partisans the way they did."

Victoria nodded. "How did you learn about what they did, Chiara? Did they leave some sort of accounts?"

"No, nothing like that. Mostly from things my father and brother told me after the war, when I was old enough to understand. And then, the way in which my family died suggests some things about their actions. Why would the Fascists have taken the trouble to kill them the way they did if not for some kind of revenge? Gradually the puzzle comes together, you know what I mean?"

"That's what we all hope for," Victoria said with a smile. "What will you say about them at the ceremony?"

"I'm not planning for any of the tributes to be very specific. But I do want to give a few examples. According to my brother . . . "

"Your brother is . . . "

"Carlo. He died several years ago."

"Oh, yes, I remember. You mentioned him the other night."

"Anyway, according to Carlo, Mother and Father hid several partisans in their home."

"Can you remember any of this yourself? You would have been, what, five or six at the time?"

"That's right. I'm not sure. I remember many people coming and going, men especially. But you would expect that in such times, wouldn't you? Certainly I was too young to be aware of politics and such."

"Yes, of course."

They were silent for a moment. Although she was eager to hear more of Chiara's version, Victoria was reluctant to appear to be pressing her. To Victoria's mild surprise, Francesco asked, "But what about specific incidents? We were practically the same age, of course, and like you, I'm sure I didn't understand who was who. But I have some very vivid memories, for example of being taken to the convent, of being devastated when my father left me and went away. I remember hating one of the nuns, Sister Margherita, and loving two others."

Chiara nodded and thought for a moment. "My memories aren't so vivid . . . except of course for the killings at the end. Things are more muddled for me. I recall emotions more than the events that caused them."

"Emotions?" Victoria asked.

"Yes. To this day, when I think about that time my immediate reaction is a kind of sick fear."

Francesco nodded sympathetically and patted her hand.

"Of course," Victoria added.

"But unlike Francesco," Chiara went on, "I can't seem to match my fears to specific incidents."

"I would think it's quite possible you've repressed these memories," Victoria ventured.

"Yes," Francesco added. "We know that many terrible things occurred here, especially in forty-four and forty-five. Citizens were shot and hanged in the piazza, less than a kilometer from where we're sitting. If you witnessed anything first-hand, it wouldn't be a surprise if you repressed the memories."

"I suppose so," Chiara said, looking troubled.

~ ~ ~ ~ ~

~ ~ ~

Chapter 8

A LFREDO, PAOLA'S YOUNGER BROTHER, was waiting for them as they alighted from the train. Daniel stepped off first and helped Paola, who was struggling to move her inconvenient shape through the portal, her small frame having resisted but finally yielding to the latter stages of her pregnancy.

Like Paola, Alfredo was small. He had a compact, sinewy build and dark skin. He was trimly dressed in the uniform of an Acqui Division infantryman, a *Bersagliere*. "I can't believe my eyes!" he cried in Italian. "My sister the Madonna!" They laughed and embraced, Alfredo arcing his body forward at the waist to accommodate Paola's melon middle.

Alfredo turned to Daniel, hesitated for a second as he chose the proper greeting—an embrace or a handshake—while Daniel, also hesitant, stuck out his hand. As they shook Daniel reached around the smaller man and placed his left hand in the small of his back. Their laughter reflected the awkwardness of the compromise. They had met once before, when Daniel and Paola visited after their wedding. Paola wasn't showing then.

"Truly, if I were being the proper soldier, I should have greeted you with the Roman salute," Alfredo said, still speaking in Italian. "Handshakes have been declared old-fashioned, you know."

"English!" Paola demanded.

"Okay, I'll try to remember."

"Pathetic," she said, shaking her head but still smiling. "He takes after my mother," she added with a nod toward Alfredo. "They both hate to speak anything other than Italian, even though they both speak English well."

"All the effort shouldn't be his," Daniel offered. "I am in your country, after all."

To Alfredo Paola said, "Daniel has been learning Italian, but it's been difficult to find the time. Almost all of his work is in French, of course—yet another language you don't bother to speak," she added, cuffing Alfredo lightly and then kissing his cheek. "I do love you anyway."

A soft rain was beginning to fall as Daniel and Alfredo loaded the baggage into the Rosettis' black Fiat sedan. Daniel helped Paola into the rear seat, then got into the front next to Alfredo.

"For how long will you be home?" Paola asked Alfredo.

"I have a week's leave. Compassionate. To look after Father. I'm happy you could come. Having you here, and in your present condition, will brighten him up, I'm sure."

"I hope so."

"Ever since Luca, he's been so depressed," Alfredo added as he started the car. "Even Mama's come back faster, which I would never have thought possible. The doctor believes *Babbo*—Dad," he corrected to English—"has had a small stroke. Maybe more than one."

"From what Paola has told me, that would make sense," Daniel said.

The distance was short, and within a few minutes they pulled up in front of the Rosettis' home. The house was of the traditional stucco, cream colored with dark green shutters and terra cotta roof. What might have been an austere design was softened by thick trees, bushes and plants, all of which were greening up in the early April rain. The spring-washed air was redolent of the new growth. The ground was soggy under foot as the three descended from the car.

"Mama? Babbo?" Alfredo called as, a suitcase in each hand, he pushed open the front door. Paola and Daniel followed close behind.

Paola's mother rushed up to them. She was a petite woman with sharp features and deep-set moist brown eyes. She had coarse dark hair, which had grayed significantly in the past year. She hugged Paola as close as the latter's shape would allow, and smiled at her, reserving sadness only in the corners of her eyes. Then she turned to Daniel, kissed him on each cheek, thanked him in English for bringing Paola home.

"Where's Babbo?" Alfredo asked.

"Napping," his mother replied. "I'll wake him."

"No, don't," Paola said. "Let him sleep, he needs it."

"Oh, but he made me promise to wake him when you arrived."

At that moment, Paola's father appeared at the door. He was a large man, tall but even more than that substantial, in a way that made him appear larger than he was. The hereditary dividing line was clear. Paola and Alfredo took after their mother, while Luca had taken after Antonio, the father. Daniel noticed that since he had seen him last Antonio had lost muscle tone; his body seemed to droop like a jacket too large for its hanger. His facial features, too, had given up much of the fight against gravity. Circles like tree rings fell below his eyes. His complexion, dark, was nonetheless lifeless. His hair, close-cropped at the sides, was not as gray as might have been expected to complete the package, and the small mustache, thick but carefully trimmed like a lintel supporting the prominent nose, was more dark than not. "I asked to be awakened," he said over his daughter's head as he embraced her in a bear hug.

"We only just arrived, Babbo," she said into his chest.

"Still . . ." He turned slowly and embraced Daniel, thanked him for taking the time to bring Paola home, turned back to her and made a delicate swirling motion over her roundness. "You look beautiful," he said, as she smiled with delight.

"Go freshen up and we'll have lunch," Mama said.

* * *

THEY TOOK THEIR places at the long table in the dining room. Alfredo poured wine. Antonio offered a toast. "To an absent son and coming generations." They drank solemnly, the absence of the son momentarily taking precedence over the future.

"How long can you stay?" Mama asked Daniel as she filled bowls of soup from a lustrous cream-and-red ceramic tureen.

"It's a little hard to say. We'll have to see whether Paola is on schedule or not." He smiled. "We've planned on at least a few weeks. But I'll probably have to go back before she does. My colleagues are being too generous in covering for me."

"Things are well, though, at your clinic?" Antonio asked, dipping his spoon.

"As well as can be expected. It will never be easy work. By definition our patients are among the most difficult, long-suffering. On good days I'm happy—perhaps content would be a better word—to be providing some comfort. On bad days I get depressed over how little we can do for many of them. Here we are twenty years on, and the wounds are still so horrific." Daniel became conscious of the somber tone of his voice and of possible renewed suggestions of Luca. "Anyway, we do the best we can, and that is gratifying. In the meantime, it's good to be in this beautiful place."

"What's new around here?" Paola asked.

"Oh, the usual," Mama said, and began to run through her list. "The past few years have been bad for us all, of course. Everyone's business is bad. But we all continue on—what choice do we have? Your friend Anna Maria is pregnant with her second. But I think I wrote you about that."

"Yes," Paola nodded.

"She's doing well. They hope for a boy this time. The Peroni boy got a part in this year's Tosca. We went to see it. He was better than I thought he'd be."

"And the Bucas?" Paola asked. "What's the news with them?"

"They're all well, I think," Mama said.

"I'm sure the Bucas are as ever," Alfredo added. He blew on a spoonful of soup. "As ever they seek to improve their position at every turn and through any means."

"There's no need to be nasty," Mama rejoined, "like some sour old woman."

"Sounds a delightful family," Daniel volunteered. "Not one I'd be in a rush to meet," he added.

"And yet," Antonio said, "you almost certainly shall meet them. They're our nearest neighbors, and actually they can be quite charming."

"Yes, quite," Paola said, her tone sarcastic.

"Renata has been asking after you," Mama said to her.

"No doubt to boast about this or that. Renata Buca is an old friend, if I may use the term loosely," Paola added for Daniel's benefit.

"Very loosely, obviously," he replied.

Mama continued her update, pausing only to pass around new courses.

"Where are you posted?" Daniel asked Alfredo, when Mama returned to the kitchen.

"On the Adriatic coast."

"And do you have any idea of what your division will do in the near future?"

Alfredo laughed. "More training, I assume. Now that the situation is stable in Abyssinia, there's not much else to do."

Paola put down her fork and looked hard at Alfredo. "Abyssinia?"

Alfredo looked back at her, furrowed his brow in incomprehension.

"Abyssinia?" she repeated. "With the price this family has paid, you can talk in the phrases of empire? Luca . . . "

"What is the mood in Paris?" Antonio interrupted, turning to Daniel.

Daniel looked at Paola, confirmed she would cede the floor. "Worrisome," he said. "As they are just about everywhere now. The French fret continually over the Germans."

"Nothing new about that," Antonio said with a smile.

"No, I suppose not. On the scale of fretting, the French start high and only go up."

"You don't really believe there will be another war," Alfredo said.

"I don't know," Daniel replied.

"We would hardly be shocked," Paola added.

Alfredo gave a dismissive shake of the head. "It won't get so far. No one wants a repeat of the last one. What's happening is a normal shift of power, as one would expect after twenty years. Germany can't be kept down forever. It's only reasserting itself as a great power. As is Italy. Everyone will step back in time."

"I hope you're right," Daniel responded. "I'll remind you, though, that people thought that in 1914, too. And even those who predicted war thought it would be over in a matter of months."

Daniel turned toward Antonio. "I worry about the bond between the Duce and Hitler. I'm frankly a little surprised that Mussolini was so accepting of Hitler's union with Austria. It's not as if Italy has no interests of its own in Austria. If Germany continues to have its way, I fear Italy could be dragged into something for which it's not prepared."

Antonio nodded. In the flicker in his eye Daniel thought he saw the fleeting image of the dead son.

"Nothing will happen," Alfredo said, certainly. "And I'll tell you from my own experience, if anything were to happen, this time Italy would be ready. The Duce will be decisive, and our country is strong. If only you could see

74

the fine spirit, equipment, and training in our division. You would not be at a loss for confidence, I can tell you that!"

"Confidence in what?" Paola started. "Confidence that I'll lose another brother."

All eyes turned to her. Daniel placed a calming hand on her arm. "Paola . . ."

Antonio wiped his mouth with his napkin and stood with difficulty, using the table for support. "Excuse me. I'll be back in a few minutes."

"I'm sorry, Babbo," Paola said.

He gave a tired wave. "That's all right. If I had been more assertive years ago, perhaps I wouldn't bear so much guilt now."

"Guilt!" Mama exclaimed. "How can you say such a thing? What responsibility can you possibly have?"

"There was nothing within your power to help Luca," Alfredo said. "Nothing could have been done differently."

Antonio nodded in a way that suggested to Daniel he was unconvinced but not willing to debate the point, and shuffled toward the bedroom.

~ ~ ~ ~ ~

~ ~ ~

Chapter 9

O N ONE OF THE first spring evenings that actually felt like a spring evening the Bucas' villa was thrown open wide, was incandescent. From a distance it radiated a gauzy, beckoning light. Silhouettes and shadows drifted past open windows. A muffled surf of voices punctuated by spirited laughs floated down the long drive where Paola stopped to catch her breath. She was now within days of her due date, but the baby was still riding high, pressing on her diaphragm. She filled the shallows of her lungs and reached behind to massage the small of her back.

Daniel, standing beside her, took over, pressing the heel of his palm into the hollow, pushing her forward for a moment until she gave resistance. "You have no idea how good that feels," she said.

"We didn't have to walk here, you know. We could have come in the car with your parents."

"Even going the long way it's not that far from our house. I'm not so feeble that I need to be carried. Besides, I need to clear my head before I go in there."

"I didn't realize it was enemy territory."

"Not enemy, foreign. You know the feeling—when you've been away for so long that home is a strange place to visit, comforting and yet foreign at the same time. All right, I'm ready to move this carcass the last hundred steps."

Daniel laughed and kissed her cheek. "It's a fine carcass, I'd say. The best I've ever had."

They stopped once more before the steps to the house. "Okay, *andiamo*," she said as she began the ascent. They reached a deep loggia at the top of the steps and stood for a moment in front of the highly waxed wooden double doors that were open wide to the night.

"Ciao, Paola!" came an excited cry from inside as a woman hurried to them. "Look at you!" the woman said, standing back after the awkward embrace. "I couldn't believe it when I heard you were coming back! Finally! And look at what condition you're in, also finally!"

"Not everyone can turn them out like rabbits," Paola said with a laugh. "You've just had your fifth is it?"

"Don't exaggerate. Fourth. A girl, Chiara. That makes two boys and two girls. Maybe we should stop."

"Good idea. That will give me some time to catch up. This is my husband Daniel."

"Ah, the American I've heard so much about," she said, switching to a heavily accented English.

He took her hand. "I won't ask what you've heard."

"Daniel, allow me to introduce Renata, one of my oldest friends. Renata and I grew up together."

"Until Paola ran off to live fast in Paris," Renata said in a voice of mock admonishment. She had a pretty face, with full lips and clear, olive skin. Her brown eyes, wide set and vaguely almond shaped, lent her an Etruscan look. She was full-breasted and slightly thick-waisted. She wore a rose-colored silk dress. "How long has it been since I've seen you?" she asked. "Five years?"

"At least. It's not my fault, though. I've come home during that time. Only you haven't been here."

"Just bad luck, that's all. Have you seen Nicola yet?" Renata asked and added for Daniel, "my husband."

"No, we've just arrived."

"Well you must make sure to see him. He's been asking about you." From inside the house, a voice called for Renata. "Excuse me," she said, as she tried another hug. "We'll talk later. We have so much to catch up on. And you haven't seen the children."

"Fast life in Paris," Paola mimicked as Renata turned away. "She's driven me crazy my whole life."

Daniel cocked his head quizzically. "One wouldn't have guessed by watching the two of you. She seems very nice."

"Believe me, things aren't always what they seem."

"But you're friends anyway."

"That's such an American answer."

"Actually, it was more of a question."

Paola's reply was lost in the enthusiastic greetings of friends who came up to her. She introduced Daniel one by one. In the background, a Gramophone that had been playing classical music made an upbeat change to cabaret tunes. Voices, mostly Italian but punctuated with English and German, rose in matching volume. Paola's parents and Alfredo flitted in and out of view as they mingled and sipped champagne.

"I'm so happy Mama and Babbo decided to come," Paola said to Daniel. "It's good for them to get out. Look how pretty Mama is tonight. And Babbo looks like he's feeling better."

"Yes, he does," Daniel agreed.

Paola nodded toward the several black shirts worn by the men with their dark suits. "Great fashion, eh?"

"If it were only a question of fashion, I'd say it was quite natty."

"Come," Paola said, nodding toward an older couple on the other side of the room. "I'll introduce you to our hosts."

The couple, both of whom possessed an old world dignity, was engaged in conversation with a man in a German army officer's uniform. They excused themselves to him and smiled at Daniel and Paola's approach.

"Signor and Signora Buca," Paola said, "it's very good to see you." She introduced Daniel. "You just met the Bucas' daughter, Renata," she reminded.

Daniel apologized for his halting Italian and told the Bucas he was pleased to meet them. To himself he observed that they were picture-perfect for the roles of host and hostess. They stood, the wife's arm hooked delicately inside her husband's. He was of medium height, stocky in a prosperous but not gluttonous way, dressed in a perfectly pressed black suit, black shirt, and pearl gray tie. He was bald except for an attentively trimmed semicircle of hair above the ears. He had a mustache but was otherwise clean-shaven; a trace of styptic pencil smudged his left cheek. He had a ready smile. She had a smile to match, as well as nicely proportioned, very white teeth. Her full, Bavarian figure was borne with confidence, as was the rinsed brown hair.

78

"Daniel is much more fluent than he admits," Paola said. "I believe he's discovered that he has a talent for languages, in fact. He's fluent in French, is coming along very well in Italian, and even speaks a little German."

"My wife exaggerates my abilities in all of these languages."

The Bucas commented on Paola's "splendidly full" shape and turned to the officer to whom they had been talking. Signor Buca said, "Allow me to introduce Major Eberhard. The major is liaison to our forces in this region. I might add that he has established a very fine relationship."

"Signor Buca gives me too much credit," the major said as he shook Daniel's hand. Daniel judged him to be in his mid-thirties. He was trim, his features sharply defined. A hint of gray at the temples diluted his dark brown hair.

"When two countries are as fraternally united as ours," the major went on, "the job of a representative such as myself is hardly taxing. I must say, though, when I received an invitation to come to the Bucas' beautiful home tonight, I assumed the occasion was to celebrate the *Anschluss* with Austria. Alas, I was mistaken."

Major Eberhard allowed just enough time for a flustered look to appear on Signor Buca's face before he delivered a full-throated laugh. "I'm joking, of course! The German union is being well celebrated in Vienna and Berlin. You may have a party for your own reasons!" Eberhard laughed again, showing horse-like teeth.

"I'm glad there was no need for Italian troops in Austria," Paola said with a thin smile. "My family has already given enough to the cause."

Eberhard cocked his head in a manner that suggested he was unsure how to take her meaning.

"Yes, major, it's very sad," Signor Buca interjected quickly. "Paola's brother, Luca, was killed in Abyssinia. He was a very fine boy. I'm sure you'll understand when I say he died bravely. A soldier's death."

"Ah, I see," the major said solemnly.

Paola's jaw was set. "So people say. But I've been searching for the noble reason for his death, so far without success."

An unsettled silence ensued during which Daniel shot Paola a quick look of disapproval. "As you can see," he said, "we're all still quite upset."

"Yes, of course," Signora Buca responded, graciousness suppressing obvious discomfort at the turn in the conversation. "You will see it in time.

It is very difficult for one to have the necessary perspective when so little time has passed after the loss of a loved one."

"Very true," her husband said. "The Duce has led us on an extraordinary path to national revival. Luca will be remembered as an important part of that effort. I'm sure with time you will come to see that, dear."

"Indeed, it is so," the major added. "You must not allow your personal grief to obscure the larger good. Your country and mine are in the process of building a great modern world—a world in which the artificialities and distortions of the early decades of the century are put right, a world in which Bolshevism and Jewish conspiratorial mercantilism no longer hold sway."

Daniel put a hand on Paola's arm, hoping to forestall the reaction he was sure was coming. At the same time, his polite smile melted as his desire to avoid a scene clashed with his own disgust at the major's remarks.

"I might add," a still smiling Eberhard said, turning to Daniel and pressing the point, "it would be an even better world if our natural allies Britain and America would show some understanding of what we are trying to accomplish. As it is, they put obstacles in our way, obstacles which of course we cannot allow to stand."

Paola started, but Daniel interrupted, returning Eberhard's shallow smile. "And I would have to remind you, major, that your country several times now has violated its solemn treaties ending the last war."

"Illegitimate treaties, you mean." The smile was still in place, thinner now. "Treaties forced upon my country under false pretenses. No sovereign nation is obliged to be bound by such pieces of paper. To be bound so is totally illogical. Surely you can see that Mister . . . Gideon is it?"

"Doctor Gideon," Paula interjected.

"Forgive me."

Daniel waved the matter aside. "There is nothing illogical about . . . "

"Oh, Paola," Signora Buca interrupted in an ill-disguised effort to change the subject, "I almost forgot to tell you . . . I was so glad when your mother told me you would be here. We're going to have dancing tonight, if you're feeling up to it. I remember how much you used to like to dance."

Paola smiled awkwardly. "I don't see my mother or father," she said, scanning the room. "They were here a few minutes ago."

"Oh, they've already left, dear. I assumed they would have told you they were going."

"So soon?"

"Yes. Your father began to feel ill. Poor man. His strength is still low. Your mother and he drove home. Don't be alarmed," the Signora added, obviously in response to Paola's expression. "I'm sure he'll be fine."

"Yes, I'm sure he will," Paola said, anger returning to her face. "It's only that his strength is sapped by my brother's contribution to our glorious empire."

Another unwieldy silence enveloped them before Signora Buca excused herself, saying she needed to check on the kitchen, while the Signor and the major followed her wedge and turned to other guests.

A short time later, as they walked home, Daniel again placed his hand on the small of Paola's back, this time more to gauge the tension behind her smoldering silence than to relieve physical discomfort.

"Smug prigs," she muttered, ignoring the hand.

"That may be, my love, but this is not Paris. You can't run around bad-mouthing the Duce and not expect to hear about it."

She pulled up short to catch her breath. "Let them throw me in jail, then."

"Stop it, please, Paola. You're not nineteen anymore. They won't play games with you."

"And since when did you decide to bow to them? What happened to my husband the antifascist doctor?"

"Your husband the still antifascist doctor is here to remind you that pregnant women take on new responsibilities and . . . "

"They wouldn't do anything to a pregnant woman! I'm a weapon in the Duce's battle for more children, after all. My shape gives me protection."

"I'm not so sure. But even if that's true, let me also remind you that the reason we came here in the first place is to help your parents. I hardly see how this behavior of yours can do that. They'd be better off if we stayed in Paris."

Paola's face relaxed into a small smile. She squeezed his arm, a reminder that she was grateful he had agreed to accompany her home.

Chapter 10

ANIEL DEFLATED THE PRESSURE cuff and removed it from Antonio's arm. He nodded toward the full ashtray. "You should stop smoking. It's bad for your heart. I've told you that more than once." They were in a small study on the main level of the house. Antonio sat on the edge of the day bed he kept there for reading and napping. Daniel stood over him.

Antonio rolled down his shirtsleeve. "Just as my own doctor has." He shrugged, as if to convey the futility of such recommendations. What could one do in the face of an immutable force such as cigarette smoke? "These things," he waved toward the ashtray, "have been a part of me for almost fifty years. We are old friends."

"Your old friends will be the death of you. Your own doctor's advice is as sound as mine."

Antonio's laugh ended in a wheezy cough. "One would think that bringing a doctor into the family would result in more agreeable advice."

"The most agreeable advice is that which keeps the patient alive."

Antonio stood. "It would be interesting to know if you feel that way when you've lived as long as I have."

Daniel shook his head as he packed up his medical bag. "Your daughter comes by her stubbornness honestly."

"It would seem that my grandchild is continuing the tradition. How late is he in coming?"

"He, is it?"

"Of course."

"Almost two weeks."

Antonio looked into Daniel's eyes. "You're not worried, are you?"

"Not yet." He was about to say he was concerned that the baby might have turned breech, but he thought better of it. "It's not so unusual with a first child. Especially one determined to continue your stubborn line," he added, patting Antonio's shoulder. "The problem for me is, I need to get back to Paris."

Antonio withdrew a cigarette from the package, lit it, blew a rebuking cloud into the air. "This holiday doesn't agree with you, eh?"

"Well enough for the first week. Now I'm anxious to resume work. And to relieve my overworked colleagues."

Antonio laughed. "So, taking my blood pressure and giving impossible advice doesn't count as work."

Daniel returned the laugh. "Not quite the work I'm used to, anyway."

"Well, I should tell you I've taken a certain liberty."

Daniel gave a quizzical look but said nothing.

"A friend of mine is ill. I suggested he might come by this afternoon to see you. I reasoned that, as long as you're waiting on Paola . . . "

"I don't have much experience treating routine ailments, you know. Does your friend not have his own doctor?"

"In theory, yes. But as you may know, doctors are in short supply around here. Getting to see one can take quite a long time. So, I must confess, when my friend said he was having trouble, I thought of you. And about how you're having too much holiday," Antonio added with a mischievous smile. "In any case, you wouldn't want to leave Italy before the visit by the German *capo dei tutti capi*, would you?"

"Ah, yes, the great Führer's visit. I must admit, the preparations are quite astonishing. The newspapers and the radio are full of reports. The *Italy Illustrated* shows these remarkable photographs of Rome in its imperial glory. Not a bit of trash in sight. And a new train station to welcome the two-bit Kaiser."

"Yes, I know. Don't underestimate him, though. He's not two-bit, as you call him."

"You're right," Daniel nodded. "My expression reflects wishful thinking. He's more masterful than I'd like to admit. He's putting the rest of Europe in its place, and with hardly a whimper of protest. The British and the French don't have the stomach for another fight."

"True," Antonio agreed. "Unfortunately, it seems the Germans always have the stomach for fighting. It's in their bones. They do it so well. Hatched from a cannonball, as Napoleon put it."

"So now we have the New Roman Empire playing host to the Third Reich. The Duce will strut as never before."

"Yes, even Hitler will be impressed. He'll be taken in by the show, and I don't say that lightly. He's no fool. Italy's in for a rough time."

"A rough time? I would think this visit to be something of a high-water mark."

Antonio smiled and stroked his chin. He nodded toward Daniel's closed medical bag. "The examination is finished, yes?"

"Yes," Daniel replied cautiously.

"Good. Then come into the kitchen and we'll have a coffee. I'll tell you some true things about Mussolini and I'll disregard the orders of two doctors and smoke."

Antonio ushered Daniel ahead of him into the corridor. He closed the door to the study. "We'll have to reserve this room for you to see the patient I arranged," he said with a smile. "And for the others who I'm sure will come when word gets around that you're bored here."

Daniel laughed heartily as he followed Antonio into the kitchen. Antonio put the coffee on and sat opposite Daniel at the big table in the middle of the room. He crossed his legs. "I know you think you and your Parisian friends understand Mussolini."

Daniel began to reply but Antonio waved him off and continued. "It takes an Italian to understand him. That's why Hitler will be taken in by the show. Don't mistake me. It's a good show. Mussolini is such a good actor and he's been doing the act for so long, he probably doesn't know the truth himself."

"And that truth is?"

"The truth is there's little real strength in Italy. Once you get past the thugs who surround Mussolini and tell him what he wants to hear, what you see is an illusion, like the things they make in Hollywood—the . . . what do you call them?"

"Movie sets."

"Yes, sets. Or like the Potemkin villages in Russia in the last century. Nothing but a false front to impress the Czar."

Daniel leaned in on his elbows. "Antonio, I don't like to think of myself as naive or gullible, and I'm hardly a fan of the Duce, but even you have to admit he's brought some good things to Italy—bridges, roads, harbors, factories . . . "

"Some of these things he's done, yes. Among his best factories, though, is his propaganda factory."

"But he has energized Italy, wouldn't you agree?"

"Yes, but that's part of the trouble. There's a false confidence in the air. People see the latest issue of this or that magazine, with glossy photographs of a power plant here or a squadron of airplanes there, and they believe Italy is ready to take on the world."

"Alfredo seems to think so," Daniel said, reminded of the confidence he displayed when Daniel arrived. "And he is in the army, after all. He should know something."

"Alfredo is young and impressionable. He knows he sees many tanks and field artillery. What he doesn't see—and what Hitler will see but fail to comprehend—is the same tanks and artillery moved around the country to make it appear that Italy is a military giant, just as the public sees the same shiny new factory over and over from different angles. Hitler knows his Germany has actually built the tanks it needs. He will assume, incorrectly, that Italy has done the same." Antonio placed small, steaming cups in front of each of them.

"Do you know this to be true?"

"If you mean, do I have evidence, the answer is no. But I do know it to be true. I know it in my Italian bones."

Daniel cocked his head in a way he hoped would convey friendly skepticism.

"You'll see for yourself," Antonio said with a paternal smile. "We Italians love a good show."

"That's what Paola keeps telling me. I can see where it comes from." Daniel laughed. "Do you know," he continued, "Paola once said she wanted to tell me about some historical figure she compared Mussolini to. I don't remember his name. Cole something or other. She never did tell me the story."

Antonio whooped with delight and slapped the table, startling Daniel. "Cola di Rienzo!" he shouted. "Ha! She remembered her history! You see?

Not everything you tell your children is lost in the air." Antonio lit a new cigarette off the remains of the previous one. "Cola was a fourteenth century Mussolini," he went on. "The similarities are truly striking. He was of humble origins. At a time when Rome was in shambles and a den of thieves and even the pope had fled it for Avignon, Cola had a passionate dream of its resurrection. He was a powerful and eloquent orator who knew how to tap into people's discontents and appeal to their dreams. He had a gift for pageantry; he devised magnificent flags and uniforms. Sound familiar?"

Daniel smiled.

"Here are more things that may sound familiar. At first, Cola fulfilled many of his promises. He revived Rome and made it safe for commerce. He put the noble families in their place. He developed broad appeal for a united Italy.

"But he also became seduced by his own powers of pomp and persuasion. The symbols he devised for himself became ever more ridiculous. He spent ever more money on spectacle. He launched debilitating wars. Eventually, he over-reached and was driven from Rome. Some years later, he staged a comeback, using a mercenary army and many of the techniques of show that made him successful in the first place. But by then he was corrupt beyond redemption and the spectacle didn't play so well. When the people rose against him this time, they didn't merely drive him away. He was captured and killed, his body hung in a public square and eventually burned."

"Let us hope," Daniel said, "that this allegory is not fulfilled."

"Indeed. It is difficult to imagine quite such a bestial ending for the Duce. Still, it illustrates the point I was making about the power of pageantry and illusion. Also, though Hitler's visit seems to be a feather in the Duce's cap, I believe it actually represents a rather fundamental change in the order of things. The spectacle accorded Hitler will vault him over Mussolini as the leader of the Fascist world. Though he may not realize it, the Duce will be bound to follow him."

"Perhaps Mussolini is more aware of his situation than you give him credit for being," Daniel said. "After all, he has just succeeded in concluding a treaty with Great Britain that, among other things, all but ratifies Italy's position in Ethiopia and solidifies its relationship with the British. Certainly, this has not been lost on Hitler."

Antonio stroked his chin, crushed his cigarette. "A good point," he said after a moment. "Yet I still have a bad feeling about the direction of things for Italy and Germany."

"Don't tell me," Daniel smiled. "You know it in your Italian bones."

Antonio returned the smile. "Yes, I suppose that's what it comes down to."

* * *

THREE DAYS LATER, Daniel had just seen his third patient when Paola's water broke. Accompanied by Signora Spaga, a local midwife, Daniel presided over the breech birth of Francesco Rosetti Gideon. "A good omen," he announced to Paola. "Landed in the world feet-first."

He stayed for a week before returning to Paris. Antonio said he expected to see him soon and said he would reserve a place for Daniel to see patients, "just to ensure you can visit without being bored." Paola and Francesco followed him back to Paris two weeks later.

~ ~ ~ ~ ~

~ ~ ~

Chapter 11

IN APRIL 1917, THE United States entered the Great War, and in June, after rebuffing his parents' pleas to finish his education, Daniel enlisted in the army. His sense of adventure extended even to enjoying, or at least not minding, basic training. Every pushup or bayonet thrust into a straw-filled sack brought him closer to France.

He was disappointed when he was chosen for additional training as a scout sniper. The extra training meant he wouldn't arrive in September with his enlistment group. It also meant the first sobering exposure to what lay ahead. The instructors in basic had impressed on the recruits the demands of battle. For Daniel, their efforts lacked reality. He put their warnings in the same category as those he had received on the dangers of venereal disease.

Scout sniper training was different. In short order he learned that being a good shot was just a prerequisite, as steady hands might be for a surgeon or an affinity for numbers and order for an accountant. The real requirements went much deeper, demands of will and self-control such as he never imagined he possessed.

"The value of snipers is not so much in their ability to kill as in their ability to demoralize the enemy," the instructor said. He was not what Daniel expected. The drill sergeants in basic used raw intimidation to impress the recruits. One after another, in Alabama or Oklahoma drawls that were all of a piece to Daniel, the instructors bellowed, bawled or screeched to get the recruits into line.

The scout sniper instructor, a master sergeant named Combs, was different. Compact and wiry, he had a self-possessed, understated dignity. He didn't yell, nor did he need to. He spoke softly in the flat inflections of his native San Diego. The confidence in his voice was compelling, the truth of his words self-evident, inspiring.

"Soldiers may be killed by artillery fire, but at least they usually know when they have to duck. But," the master sergeant paused for emphasis, "when there's a lull in the fighting, when the soldier thinks it's safe enough for the moment, when he thinks the nearest enemy is miles away, when the soldier lights a cigarette, when the match illuminates his face so briefly, so slightly in the sniper's scope, when lighting that cigarette is the last thing he ever does, when the insides of his head are sprayed onto anyone close to him—*that* is terror. *That* is knowing you can never relax for even a moment. *That* is demoralizing."

The army could teach Daniel the techniques of stealth and concealment. It could teach him tricks of concentration to help him maintain the same position for hours in freezing cold or brutal heat. It could teach him how to evade capture. It could improve upon, but not really teach him intelligence, alertness, confidence, self-reliance, and resourcefulness. The army tested for, but could not really impart, these qualities. They were qualities the instructors saw in Daniel when he wasn't sure he saw them in himself, at least not to the degree they were required.

Some things, even more important, would remain unknown until the fact. Could he kill another man? Could he do so without the passions of battle to drive him on? Could he do so when he was in no immediate danger or without immediate provocation? Could he commit the ultimate act of aggression? When the master sergeant talked about the brief illumination of the target in the sniper's scope, it was understood that the sniper would pull the trigger. Why else would he be there?

Daniel did his best to push the question out of his mind. He and the other recruits were told repeatedly that they were elite, that they were handpicked to fulfill the most important, most demanding missions. They had it drummed into them that the Hun was brutal and cretinous and had earned what was coming to him. The chaplain told the boys it was only natural that there would be times when they questioned the morality of their acts. After all, they were moral people, whereas the Hun had proven by his actions to have abandoned morality. The point was that the boys were acting in defense; they were not the aggressors, therefore the things they had to do in war were done out of necessity and were moral.

89

Still, Daniel was unable always to repel the doubts, especially those that came by stealth in the night. Once, at about three in the morning, Daniel awoke to the tossing and turning of his bunkmate, a Pennsylvania boy named Ben. "Do you think," Daniel ventured into the darkness, "when the time comes you'll be able to do it?"

The tossing stopped. "That's the whole point, isn't it?"

"Kill someone like us . . . ."

"Like us?"

"You know, ordinary people with parents and families, who maybe don't even want to be there."

"Hell of a time to wonder about that." Ben rolled onto his side, punched his pillow and cradled it under his head. "They're krauts, for Christ sake. I'll pull the trigger and so will you."

* * *

THE EARLY MORNING light of Bastille Day 1918 found Daniel concealed under thick brush about three hundred yards from a farmhouse a few miles east of the Marne River town of Chateau Thierry. He had reached this spot a few hours earlier under the cover of darkness and fallen asleep in a cramped position, one he had mastered over the previous year and which would have kept a less experienced, less exhausted man awake. A strange sort of slumber engulfed him, deep and desperately reparative, yet at the same time he remained alert to the slightest change in his surroundings—branches abrading opposite the wind direction, movement of a gravity greater than that of a small animal, a barely discernable change in the atmospheric pressure. Biting insects made no difference. After a year slogging in and out of the trenches, his body was owned by lice. He no longer doubted what species would be the true inheritors of the earth. Shells, bullets and gas might kill him; the lice were eternal.

At first light Daniel was awake, his rifle balanced on a small tripod, the muzzle poking ever so slightly from the brush. Often accompanied by a spotter, today he was alone. He was comfortable working alone. What he lost in companionship and a second set of eyes and hands he gained in stealth and mobility. He discovered in himself a peculiar exhilaration of aloneness—a freedom that came from being responsible for only his own actions.

According to intelligence, the farmhouse he had under observation was being used as a command post. His assignment was simple and one that he

90

had carried out many times before: Observe the house long enough to determine who were the highest ranking officers in residence, then kill them. More than anything, the job required patience and self-control. The sentries posted outside the farmhouse had to become complacent and certain there was no threat. Daniel had to place himself in a trance-like state in which awareness was keen but the needs of body and mind suppressed. Survival and the mission were all. They were, in fact, indistinguishable from one another, as there was no such thing as a captured sniper. On both sides, the price snipers paid for the disproportionate terror they wrought was the vengeance of the enemy, which knew no international law or code of honor. The best a sniper could hope for was a quick death.

He didn't have long to wait for a suitable target. A major came outside, ignored the privy and urinated in bushes, then splashed water in his face from a stone sink on the side of the house. Shortly thereafter, a general came out and did the same things. For the next half hour, little more than the routine of such morning ablutions suggested that there was a target more important than the general.

Once the target was chosen, Daniel would move to the next stage. He would continue to observe the general until he determined the most advantageous shot. This shot would be the one most likely to succeed, but also would provide him with the best chance of escape. It might be the shot whose origins he could best disguise. Or it might be the one he could follow with quick kills of the soldiers most likely to respond. If the general were in a small cluster of people, for instance, Daniel might be able to hit him and, in the moments of confusion that followed, the others as well.

Escape often meant not full-out flight but relocation to a spot, usually selected in advance, where he could hide. A long, disciplined silence and concealment thus might lead to a few minutes of pandemonium followed by another lengthy period of silence and concealment.

That was how it worked, assuming one was good enough and lucky enough. No one who had stayed alive as long as Daniel had doubted that it took both skill and luck to keep going. And the longer he stayed alive, the more convinced he became of the role of luck. In a war of gross attrition such as this one, it was the odd shell fragment, the odd bullet that determined life or death. No one in the trenches was safe, least of all the snipers who had to move along the line practicing their craft.

He watched the house. The general stayed inside and out of sight for the next half hour. Then he passed by a window of an upstairs room and five minutes later stood there, the window framing him. Daniel was considering a quick shot and a slithering getaway, when his attention was drawn to three staff cars making their way in a cloud of dust over the unpaved drive leading to the house. Within a moment, the general turned out of the neat space that would have demarcated his end.

But Daniel saw quickly that the general—or at least the general alone—would not be his target. Out of each of the staff cars stepped an officer of even higher rank than the one he had been aiming at. The question of how to wreak the most havoc quickly gave way to the thought that this was an unusual conclave—certainly not one that had been predicted by intelligence—and that the most productive course of action might be to report on it.

The officers stepping out of their cars were greeted deferentially by the general whom Daniel had been targeting. Aides stood to one side and saluted, then remained at attention. Through his scope Daniel could see the grim expressions on their faces. No easy camaraderie, not even polite small talk. Shortly, two additional cars pulled up, containing officers of lower rank and several ordinary soldiers.

Daniel considered his choices. He could slip back to his lines and inform his own leaders. He could stay in place, hoping something of the conclave's purpose might be revealed. He could seize the moment and fire into the crowd in the hope of causing destruction more valuable than his own life, for certainly he would not escape alive.

For an instant the fact that he could weigh these choices with equanimity startled him. How was it possible that death, of others or his own, could be considered as one might consider which shirt to wear? Was this, then, the definition of insanity?

When yet another group, this time infantrymen, approached the house and fanned out to create a protective cordon, the decision was made for him. Whatever was going on was unusual and needed more to be reported than interrupted. In any case he had already missed the chance to hit the officers en masse. They were in the house and out of sight.

The first opportunity to pull back didn't come for hours. During that time, watching the comings and goings of additional cars and officers, Daniel was certain he needed to get back to his own lines.

Shortly after noon he eased out of his position. At first, he made good progress, covering almost a kilometer. In the distance, the sound of shelling kept up a normal rhythm; it was a sound that was only noticeable when it was absent. He repaired to a place of dense vegetation he had scouted on his way to the farmhouse, intending to rest briefly before moving on. With luck he would reach his division headquarters by late afternoon.

Yet each time he began to move from his refuge a group of enemy soldiers came near. He thought this strange. The level of activity—as it was at the farmhouse—was greater than predicted for this sector. In the distance, the shelling increased.

He became concerned that the area of brush in which he was hiding was inadequate for a long stay. He was concerned, too, that the information he wanted to report was being overtaken by events on the ground. He was willing to take a greater risk than usual, but leaving now would be simply suicidal.

He pressed himself deeper into the brush. From his vantage point he saw a road with increasingly heavy traffic in German troops and vehicles. The earliest opportunity to move might not occur until darkness fell, several hours away at this time of year. He had eaten the last of his rations in the morning and was hungry. He was nearly out of water. His uniform was soaked through with sweat. Flies were drawn to him. At one point, a group of soldiers broke off from their column and went to relieve themselves in the woods. They fanned out, and Daniel pressed himself still harder into the ground. One of them, talking over his shoulder to another, almost pissed on Daniel, who at this point was left with no recourse but well-practiced stillness and silent prayer.

Night brought no slowing of the movement of troops, and dawn brought with it a deafening barrage. It seemed clear now the information Daniel had hoped to report was related to a major offensive, and any warning he might have provided was now useless. His only objective was to stay alive, and that required him to remain hidden, without water or food.

The day was spent in a trancelike state, broken only at short, terrifying instants when soldiers—and on two occasions shells, possibly from his own side—came too close to him. Late afternoon found him weak and dehydrated. His thought processes slowed, became muddled. But his hopes rose as fewer Germans passed his position.

Then, at dusk, two stragglers approached. For a moment it appeared they would move off without incident. Suddenly, the back of Daniel's leg was seized by a violent cramp. It jerked involuntarily and rustled the foliage in his hideout.

The Germans stopped, called out and raised their rifles in Daniel's direction. Daniel willed the pain in his leg to subside. The soldiers continued to approach cautiously, calling out as they came. They were now only about twenty-five yards away, and Daniel had them clearly in his sights. Even in the dim light he could see through his scope that they were baby-faced, dirty sweat glistening off smooth cheeks.

One of them said something Daniel could not understand but which seemed to be suggesting they move along. He prayed that they would, prayed he would not have to shoot them, and that the shots would not bring others running.

The second soldier called out again for anyone hiding in the brush to stand and surrender. Daniel was reasonably certain his position remained concealed. But when the German fired a shot that came within feet of him, he flinched, moving the brush. The other German then fired in Daniel's direction, missing wide, as the one who had shot first prepared to fire again. Before the soldier was able to throw the bolt on his rifle, Daniel cut him down. Then, expertly, he shot the other.

Braced by adrenalin, Daniel fled deeper into the woods. To his surprise, no one followed, and as darkness fell he managed to find a new area of dense undergrowth in which to hide.

It was the counteroffensive that saved him. He observed the Germans in retreat; then his own soldiers came down the same road. Personal salvation, at least for that day.

Sergeant Combs had proclaimed the military advantages of sniping—the demoralizing terror it created among the enemy. But he had failed, either by ignorance or design, to touch on the effects of sniping on the sniper. Daniel thought often about the night he expressed his misgivings to Ben and about Ben's confident response. Ben never had a chance to test his suppositions. He was killed the day after he arrived at the front. He had accidentally raised his head slightly too far above the trench line and was shot by a sniper. Before the war was over Daniel would see many such deaths, including not a few in which a desperate soldier made himself vulnerable on purpose.

Daniel carried out his assignments; he performed his duty. But with each killing, however justified by war, however praiseworthy, however medal-worthy, he felt a shrinking inside, a premature aging and a drying out, a sense that, when it was all over, if he was one of the fortunate survivors, he would have to spend the rest of his life performing constructive works. Not atoning, exactly—not cleansing his sins—but a sense that he had an obligation to correct the balance.

In his redoubt, Daniel had thought: If I survive, I will meet that obligation.

* * *

THE MAN WHO returned to Princeton in the winter of 1918 was changed to the core. His first two years, before the war, had been spent in a state of chummy callowness. He had finished the mandatory, largely classical, portions of the curriculum without undue exertion. He attended smokers, rowed, dated. He joined the eating club later made famous by his classmate Scott Fitzgerald. His interest in current affairs extended to reading newspapers and sharing in the reflected glory prevalent on campus that, in Wilson, Princeton had one of its own in the White House. More out of loyalty to this connection than to any real belief, he campaigned for Wilson in '16. He convinced himself and became willing to persuade others that Wilson would, as he promised, be able to keep the country out of the European war.

He had not become, as some who went through the war, embittered, lethargic or humorless. He remained spirited and adventurous and eager. Yet he deeply wanted to comprehend what he had seen. The lunacy of the trenches. The suicidal charges. The gas. Men blistered beyond recognition. The rat-eaten eyes. Yards gained in a day at the cost of thousands of lives and lost the next day at similar cost. Nations ruined. People starving amid once abundant fields, orchards and groves.

He had written his friend Bemis from France. "I don't know if seeing such things makes me believe more or less in God. It certainly makes me believe in the existence of the devil. Whether he is a supernatural force or a natural force within humans strong enough to erupt and cause the things I witnessed, I also don't know. Whatever the cause, I am in awe of the power of madness. Even as I call it madness, I know the word is insufficient, because it is mad only in the presence of an alternative, and what I've witnessed in my first visit to France has been so horrible—and yet so compelling in its internal logic of killing and surviving—as to question the very existence of an alternative."

He was determined to spend his remaining time at Princeton preparing for medical school and already had in mind a specialty. He would treat the wounded. He would specialize in the traumatic wounds caused by bullets and shrapnel and gas. Equally important, he would exercise a newly awakened social conscience. He would strive to understand the forces, events, personalities, and decisions that had led to the catastrophe of the war. He wanted to comprehend those who could wind a mainspring as tightly as it could be wound and then let it loose with the expectation that it could be stopped before it had completely uncoiled. These were people who, in 1914, envisioned a war of a few months.

He wanted to explore mechanisms that might be used to prevent a recurrence of these events. He was intrigued by the idea of a peace that, perhaps, could be imposed by an international organization like the League of Nations. Perhaps war could be outlawed entirely. Or, at least, its worst forms.

* * *

WHEN DANIEL, A newly minted M.D., met Nora Black in the summer of 1924, the two of them were primed to accept or even to actively encourage the kinds of illusions about each other that usually result in rocky marriages. He was captivated by her refined looks and social graces. If she was a bit too refined, that was all right. It was easy for him to envision them together, a handsome couple and eventually a handsome family. She was educated and articulate and would build the kind of stable home life his parents enjoyed, and he assumed he wanted.

Perhaps most of all, she was fresh, her spirit untainted by the war. Here he made an important distinction: It wasn't that she didn't know about the war or lacked the sensitivity to appreciate the toll it had taken. Yet there was no way she could have internalized the experience the way he had, and in this he found her uplifting. In times when he might become overly absorbed in his work, when he might have a tendency toward periods of pessimism or gloom, she would provide the antidote.

It was precisely his seriousness, which she took for maturity, that appealed to Nora, especially as it was tempered by a good sense of humor and a romantic spirit. He wrote her poems and sent her flowers. They went to the theater, art gallery openings and Luna Park. Her parents addressed him as Doctor Gideon, and this pleased her.

They married early the following year. Shortly thereafter, they headed for Paris. With financial support from his and Nora's parents, Daniel accepted a low-paying internship at the American Hospital in Neuilly. Here he would study traumatic injury. He would devote himself to remedying the kinds of destruction he himself had wrought just years before. He would treat those with shattered bones and blistered skin. Eventually, he would open his own clinic.

Perhaps things with Nora might have been different had not Daniel utterly failed to recognize her tentative metamorphosis from traditional, which was to say largely ornamental, concepts of a married woman. He gave patronizingly short shrift to her expressions of interest in his work. Not only did he fail to recognize her interests and abilities—only much later did he realize that she could have been an enormous asset when it came to lobbying for social change and in many other ways—he also failed to recognize her profound need for such growth.

They were both happy when Nora became pregnant in late 1929. Each thought having a child would improve things between them. He assumed she would find purpose and fulfillment in motherhood; she assumed he would devote more time to them. But the birth of their child, named Victoria after Nora's favorite aunt, only served to accentuate Nora's sense of loneliness and displacement, while Daniel's single-minded dedication to his work altered not at all.

~ ~ ~ ~ ~

~ ~ ~

Chapter 12

DANIEL WAS SITTING ALONE in the small office that doubled as a conference room. It was eight o'clock in the morning and he was trying to gather his thoughts for a meeting with the clinic staff. His face wore the flaccidness of the worried sleep-deprived.

Within weeks of France's declaration of war on Germany on September 3, 1939, Daniel was advised by the civil defense office responsible for his *arrondissement* that, like all medical facilities in the city, his clinic was to prepare to accept casualties. Hospitals and clinics were instructed to evaluate existing patients according to medical urgency. Cases that could be deferred should be so in order to ensure maximum availability of space for the newly wounded.

Daniel was confident that the practical problems he faced in operating the clinic could be overcome. He was used to solving such problems; the specifics might vary, but they were almost always solvable.

Futility was another matter. Lying awake in the early hours, in the rubbery, kaleidoscopic minutes of endless night, Paola breathing softly beside him, Daniel questioned the worth of all he had done. Barely twenty years since the most grotesque war in human history, and here they were looking to do it all over again.

He was not playing a game of self-flagellation; he was not self-pitying. He had no doubts about his chosen vocation. He could always hold fast to the lifeline of honest purpose. When all was said and done, over the years he had helped people—had relieved suffering—period. How many professions allow one to say that?

And yet, his occupation was also a constant daily reminder of just how much suffering was needless. Was it not enough for people to cope with the demands of daily living, with unavoidable diseases and natural disasters? How was it possible that there was no learning from the experience of war? How was it possible that, over and over, war could be presented as a fresh distraction appealing enough to get otherwise rational, self-interested men to march off while equally rational, self-interested women cheered them on? Nothing depressed him more than the futility of human beings' inability to pass critical experience from one generation to the next.

Sometimes, when he found himself pacing the apartment late at night, he would steal into Francesco's nursery. A nightlight barely illuminated the fantasia Paola had painted on the walls. Billowing clouds, laughing barnyard animals, storybook characters, all rendered in boisterous spirit and color, made even more striking the dissonance between child and adult.

As he would look down at his son and wonder whether insights and experience might be passed on to him—wonder how the species might advance—at least he could be cheered by the thought, even if irrational, of new chances. Why not be hopeful, after all? What purpose would be served by gazing upon his son only with the gloomy burden of experience or with the certainty that nothing could be better for him?

But in the quiet of his conference room Daniel was hard pressed to imagine that even such determined hopefulness could meet the challenge of the present reality. He could only wonder how a new war could be under way when his own experience of the last one seemed so fresh in mind.

Alone in the room, he reminded himself that however mindless the world chose to be in coming months, he could be of use, his own part could be constructive. If avoidable suffering in fact was not, for whatever reason, avoided, at least he could play a part in ameliorating that suffering. That was something, anyway.

✳ ✳ ✳

AT EIGHT-THIRTY the staff began to file in. The two doctors, Charles and Henri, arrived first. Both joined the clinic at about the same time, three years earlier. Both were in their mid-thirties. Both were dedicated and tireless. There the similarities ended.

Charles, tall, lean, and patrician in bearing, with thinning, prematurely gray hair, approached his work with the greatest sense of noblesse oblige.

The fact that he was ill paid was of no consequence. Indeed, looking for something in a desk drawer, Daniel once stumbled upon several months' worth of uncashed pay checks. Daniel learned early that the secret to keeping Charles happy—though Charles would deny it vehemently—was to treat him with the deference due a noble. Charles would do even the lowliest of chores as long as they were acknowledged by others to be beneath him.

Henri was a good foot shorter than Charles and almost elfin in appearance. Where Charles bore his thin frame as a heraldic heritage, one had the sense that Henri bore his even slighter form as a result of habitual lack of interest in food. He had a shock of dark hair and an equally unruly beard that filled in his gaunt face. Like Charles, Henri was unconcerned by the low pay in the clinic, but in Henri's case this was due to his long standing as a communist. The two were bound together by respect for one another's dedication and professionalism. They might even have been friends if not for Henri's determined refusal to defer to Charles as the latter thought was his due.

Each nodded silently, grimly as they took their accustomed places at the table. One at a time, the clinic's three nurses filed in: Juliet, middle aged and stolidly Germanic, with a work ethic to match; Alice, a small firecracker who reminded Daniel of Paola; and Janine, the senior nurse who had learned her profession at the Second Marne and whose natural elegance might have presented a good match for Charles had her elegant appearance in fact reflected her lineage.

Daniel craned to peer out the open door. He was about to ask if anyone knew the whereabouts of Eloise, the receptionist, when she rushed in. "Sorry to keep you waiting," she said in clipped English tones, which had not diminished despite twenty years in Paris with her French husband. "Claire from the office next door just arrived to cover the phone whilst I'm in here."

"Thank you," Daniel said to her. He leaned forward and clasped his hands in front of him. "As you all know," he began, "we need to address the requirements we've received from the defense office."

"There might not be much to address," Charles interrupted quickly, authoritatively. "Everything will be cleaned up before we know it. The Germans will test the Maginot line, realize that France will not be gobbled up like Poland, and some sort of agreement will be struck. They don't want to be in the trenches any more than we do."

"You make a good point," Daniel said. "Let us hope we're planning for nothing. Nevertheless, I'm certain you'll agree that the wisest course is for us to plan for the worst and hope for the best."

The others said yes and nodded.

"I agree," Charles said. "However, I very much resent the distraction from our real work."

Daniel pushed his fingers through his hair, then leaned forward again and re-clasped his hands. This time he looked around the table more generally as he spoke. "In fact, there may not be very much we must do immediately. We are, after all, a small clinic, and only very rarely do patients remain here. It seems to me, for the time being we can continue on much as usual."

"I agree," Henri said, and the others also expressed assent.

"But there are some things I believe we can do now. First, I believe we should review our patients' histories with an eye toward identifying those who can be seen less frequently if things get worse and we must treat many new patients. Second, we should take advantage of the government's mood of largesse and stock up on as many supplies as we can store. In the admittedly unlikely event things turn bad, at least we won't have to scrounge for basic supplies. So, if the doctors will divide up the patient charts for review, and the nurses will inventory our needs, we will be on the right track."

"Do you think the government is prepared to release larger stocks of morphine?" Janine asked.

"This would be the time to find out," Daniel said. "A possible problem," he went on, "over which we will have less control, is that the doctors who have volunteered their time to the clinic may find it more difficult to do so, especially if they are conscripted."

"It is a damned nuisance, though," Charles said. "There is no reason to believe things will be so bad this time."

"Still," Henri said, "as we've agreed, it is prudent to plan for the worst."

"In truth," Daniel added, "if things were to get as bad as the last time—if Paris itself were threatened—my guess is the clinic would have to close."

"I don't follow," Alice said.

"Nor do I," said Eloise.

Daniel nodded. "The reason is that, because we are so small, I think it most likely the government will want to make use of our expertise in treating war wounds by drafting us to work either in the major hospitals here or in field hospitals. In such dire circumstances, I fear our existing patients from the last war may be left to fend for themselves."

"Well, you are safe, anyway," Henri interjected. "You're an American. They can't order you to do anything."

"That will be small comfort if Paris is threatened. I may be an American legally, but this has been my home for almost twenty years. I don't know what I'd do with myself back there."

"Be safe, I should think," Eloise chimed in. "That's more than the rest of us can say."

"You also have an Italian wife," Henri added in a teasing voice. "You never know when being part of the Rome-Berlin axis might be useful."

Daniel gave a rueful smile. "What I have is an Italian wife who hates the Italian government and who, when I once mentioned casually that we could live in America, said something along the lines of preferring to slash her wrists. So the American alternative doesn't appear likely."

"For Christ's sake!" Charles jumped in with a backhanded sweep. "What is this ridiculous, maudlin talk? This will not be a repeat of the last war. Paris will not be threatened, that is certain."

"Well," Daniel said, rapping the table lightly for emphasis, "if anything is certain it's that we're not accomplishing anything by sitting here with our crystal ball. Let's get on with our work." He stood and the others followed.

~ ~ ~ ~ ~

~ ~ ~

Chapter 13

O N A QUIET SUNDAY afternoon on the 12th of May 1940 Daniel was on the floor playing blocks with Francesco. Daniel would take each blond wooden block and delight Francesco by passing it behind his back and miraculously making it reappear, zooming it in toward the giggling child's face, pulling it back, and finally depositing it on the pile that was becoming a haphazard tower.

Paola was sitting on the mottled leather sofa, reading. She was four months' pregnant and beginning to show. From time to time she looked up and smiled as Francesco got the pleasure of knocking the tower down, while Daniel feigned wide-eyed exasperation. "Not again, you silly boy!" he would call to the heavens, and Francesco would shout, "Yes, I do it!"

"Is your papa making you wild again?" Paola teased.

After awhile, as the child's exuberance began to verge on the recklessness of the overtired, Paola went over to him. "Nap time," she proclaimed as Daniel handed up his taut, protestant body.

Daniel stood and stretched, then walked over to the window. He listened for Francesco's inevitable cry of resistance to resolve into the equally inevitable slumber. Below, the sun reflected off the streets, which glistened from the showers that had passed through. A black Renault sedan skidded and was barely able to stop before it hit the curb.

Paola returned to the room, gave Daniel a weary smile, and bent down to gather the blocks. She put them one at a time into a canvas drawstring sack, then placed the sack on the small pile of odds and ends to be put away later.

Daniel turned on the radio; the station turned up jazz. "I was hoping to hear the news," he said looking at his watch. "A few minutes early, I guess."

Paola stood and stretched, arching and massaging the small of her back with her knuckles. "It would be nice to hear something good for a change."

"Wouldn't it, though?" There was nothing hopeful in Daniel's voice. "Two days since the Germans began their offensive and they're already having their way with the Dutch and the Belgians," he said. "We should have known the skirmishing that's gone on since last September wouldn't be the whole show. Oh, but the power of wishful thinking . . ." He shook his head and let the thought finish itself.

"There's no need to be too pessimistic," Paola said, returning to the sofa. "France is not Holland, after all."

"In either case, darling, we need to talk."

Paola cocked her head with grave curiosity.

Daniel sat on a chair facing the sofa. He leaned forward and clasped his hands as he looked at her. "The immediate problem is the clinic. Yesterday, Charles was ordered to report to his regiment."

"I can't say I'm surprised."

"Actually, I'm surprised we've been left alone this long. We've been on tenterhooks since the beginning of the war. The thing is, though, with Henri already gone two months ago, that leaves me and two nurses, both of whom are nervous that they, too, might have to work for the army. At this point, I'm handling only some of my oldest and most difficult cases, and these will have to be further curtailed. The money is drying up, too. The people and organizations that have supported us in the past are distracted by present events and their implications."

"Who isn't?"

"True. Unfortunately, even if the explanation is reasonable, the fact of our financial straits remains." He paused to collect his thoughts. "Charles's conscription is actually just the topper. Even before yesterday, I'd wanted to talk to you because Eloise informed me that she has to cut back on her receptionist and clerical duties."

"Did she say why?"

"Family problems, mostly. She understands what a bind this puts me in. She was very apologetic. Still and all, there it is."

Paola stood and walked over to Daniel. She stroked his hair. "What can we do?" she asked, quietly.

He reached around her waist, pulled her to him, kissed the baby's place, lingered with his cheek pressed to her. She kissed the top of his head.

"I don't know what's going to happen," he said, looking up at her. "I was wondering if you could come in and help out until, maybe, I can find someone else. If you could find any time at all to handle some of the clerical things—records and such—it would be a big help. Francesco could come with you."

She looked at him, skeptically, then laughed. "Leaving aside my horrible clerical skills, it is hard to imagine our two-year-old sitting still long enough for me to do any work. I can only imagine him throwing surgical supplies all over the place."

"I know, I know," he laughed. "Still it's worth a try. The thing is, I have a feeling it won't be for very long anyway. Because this entire discussion ignores the real issue—the one we've been pretending for the past eight months isn't there: What in Christ are we going to do if the Nazis take Paris?"

"I still have trouble believing things will get that bad." She resumed her place on the sofa.

"It was easier to be hopeful while the so-called phony war the American papers have been talking about was going on. Clearly, we've entered a less phony stage. I know France is not Holland, but . . . "

"All right," she said, leaning forward. "Let's assume the worst. Let's assume the Nazi flag is flying from the rooftops of Paris. As disgusting as the Nazis are, could we not hold our noses and continue to live?"

"No."

When he didn't elaborate, she laughed. "Well, I guess it's all settled then!"

"Sorry, darling, I couldn't live under those barbarians. Frankly, I'm a little surprised that you could. You're the rebel in the family, after all. It might be different if we didn't have a choice, but we do."

"I was just playing devil's advocate, you know. Don't you know how to play this game?"

"Okay, so now that you've played devil's advocate, why don't you play Paola Rosetti Gideon and tell me what she would do. Before you answer, let me remind you that Paola and her husband have one young child to protect and another on the way."

"I don't need reminders about that," Paola said, suddenly stern.

"Ah, so now it's not such a game."

"I don't know what alternatives you have in mind, Daniel. To me, there's only one: return to Italy."

"You mean the Italy that you fled because you couldn't stand it there? You know, the one with the fat charlatan on the podium and the thugs that keep him there?"

"Now who's not facing reality? I don't like any of these things now any more than before. But Italy isn't in the war, after all, and as an ally of Germany it isn't going to be attacked. And we have family and friends there."

"And you have an American husband, who might not be so welcome."

"Daniel," she said in a tone that suggested she was talking to a child, "we're talking about Italy, not Germany. All such things can be finessed in Italy, as you know very well. And you are lucky enough to have a profession that is valuable anywhere."

"There is another alternative for an American . . . "

"No. Don't even suggest it. My roots are in Europe. I won't live there."

"Even temporarily? To be safe?"

"We can be safe in Italy, with my family. Anyway, we said we were imagining the worst, didn't we?"

~ ~ ~ ~ ~

~ ~ ~

Chapter 14

SSISTED BY JULIET, THE only nurse still available to him full time, Daniel was examining one of his oldest patients. Janine, the most experienced of the nurses, had some time before been drafted into service at a military hospital, while young, eager Alice worked sporadically. But now it appeared she would be leaving Paris with her family.

Alice had been tearful when she told Daniel this. Even though the bombs that had begun falling on the city were still distant, they were driving her mother mad; she insisted on going south. "But I can't abandon you," Alice said in almost a wail.

"You must help your family," Daniel said after he gave her a hug. "None of us knows how this mess will play out. Perhaps some sort of normalcy will return, and then you can come back here. Or perhaps I, too, will have to flee."

She looked shocked at the thought. "Oh, no! It would be terrible! You are needed at the clinic. You still have patients who will be seen only by you."

He responded with a short, ironic laugh. He wanted to tell her that calling this place a clinic had long been a ludicrous exaggeration, and that even if he could keep it going it would consist only of himself and, perhaps, Juliet if she managed to avoid being taken, and occasionally Paola to help out any way she could. Instead he said, "I certainly intend to try." He hugged her again and said the best thing she could do was to be safe so that she could return to help him in the future.

Now, on a deceptively beautiful day early in June, he and Juliet were helping the patient, Claude Moschos, to get settled on the examination table. Daniel considered Claude to be a medical miracle. In a single battle in 1918 he suffered a leg wound that required amputation, caught a large piece of

107

shrapnel in the abdomen, and was gassed. As the internal injuries from the gas were not as extensive as usually was the case, Daniel speculated that the other wounds may have saved his life by occurring first. As Claude explained, he was found with his face in the mud under the weight of a pile of his dead comrades. He must, therefore, have taken in a reduced dose of the gas.

Not yet forty but looking closer to sixty, Claude suffered from a host of complications from his wounds. The stump of his leg gave him constant pain. The amputation had been done crudely at a field hospital. With the help of a surgical specialist recruited by Daniel they had tried three times over the years to repair the botched job. Still, it ached constantly. Claude also had many bowel problems related to the abdominal wounds, and frequent respiratory illnesses.

Daniel had reached the conclusion years ago that he had done all he could for Claude. It was now a question of treating whatever condition was giving him trouble on a given day, and in this Daniel had no particular advantage over other physicians. Nevertheless, his ingrained sense of humility caused him to underestimate the value he provided to his patients like Claude by simply continuing to give their war experiences the importance he believed they deserved. In any event, he knew Claude well enough to know that any suggestion that he might do just as well to see another doctor would be met with the resistance of an old soldier's last stand.

"You've lost weight," Daniel commented as he palpated Claude's back. "Have you not been eating properly?"

"It becomes more difficult by the day for my wife to find food," Claude said, his words reverberating slightly with each tap on his back, "as I'm sure you know."

Daniel did know. For the past month, as things on the front grew ever more precarious, Paola was spending more and more of her days hunting for food. In the middle of May, when the Germans surprised everyone by charging out of the Ardennes and trapping the British and French along the northern coast, Parisians responded with the surreal hedonism of the condemned. They bought, they consumed, they played. Then the bombs began to fall, and the roads and train stations filled up, and the daily necessities became scarce.

"Still, you must do what you can to eat more," Daniel said.

Claude shrugged. "If I had wings, I would fly."

Daniel and Juliet eased Claude off the table and supported him while Juliet began to help him dress. Daniel handed Claude his crutch. "I'll be back in a moment," Daniel said as he opened the door.

When he returned, he handed Claude a small paper bag.

"What's this?" Claude asked, peering in. The bag contained two oranges, four potatoes, and a yellowing stalk of broccoli, half of what Daniel had had the good fortune to find on his way to work that morning.

"Consider it medicine from your doctor."

"I couldn't," Claude said, handing over the bag.

But Daniel was insistent. "We have to do what we can for our veterans." As he said this he was aware that he had long ago given up any pretense of neutrality concerning his political sympathies. As a physician he would treat all who needed help, and he was no less committed to finding peaceful ways to resolve disputes. But, after all, he did fight against a German enemy whom he held mostly responsible for that war, and the new National Socialist Germans had given him no reason to think any better of Germany. "Who knows? You may be needed again," he added with a smile and without regard for the absurdity of the idea.

Claude grasped Daniel's upper arm. "Thank you."

"Think nothing of it."

A tear appeared at the corner of Claude's eye and began to make its way toward his cheek. "You know, doctor, since the war ended I've been able to cope with my wounds by telling myself that I suffered them for France. We kept the barbarians away. Now what can I tell myself? What was it all for?"

Daniel looked at him, decided not to try to cheer him with bluff optimism. Indeed, Claude was only voicing Daniel's own doubts. "My friend, in life one can only do what one can do. Maybe things will work out better than we think, or maybe not. But you can still take pride in the fact that the last twenty years have been good for France."

When Claude had gone Daniel looked around in surprise to find there were no other patients waiting for him. "I thought we had two people scheduled immediately following Monsieur Moschos," he said to Juliet.

"Yes, that's right."

"Perhaps they've only been delayed. It's getting more and more difficult to move around the city. Even the Metro has been disrupted."

He sat behind his desk and picked up a sheaf of papers from the in-box, then changed his mind and put them back. He leaned forward and placed his elbows on the desk and brought the tips of his fingers together in front of his lips in a prayer-like tent. He maintained this position for a few minutes, then picked up the telephone and dialed a direct number he had had the foresight to save.

The phone rang several times before a woman answered, her voice an impatient rush. "Political Section. Mr. Stewart's office."

"This is Doctor Daniel Gideon. I wonder if I could speak to Mr. Stewart."

"Mr. Stewart is not available at the moment, Doctor Gideon. He's quite busy, as I'm sure you can imagine. Is he expecting your call?"

"No. He's an old friend. I understand how busy he must be. If he can find a moment, I'd appreciate it if he could phone me."

"If I may ask, is it an official, or perhaps medical issue?"

"It's a personal matter."

"I'll see what I can do, sir. Does he have your number?"

"I think so, but I'll give it to you just in case."

A half hour later Daniel was reading when the phone rang. "Daniel!" the man's voice said with the kind of surprised alacrity that suggested he had received rather than made the call.

Daniel and Keith Stewart first met and became friends in the late twenties, during Keith's first posting to Paris as a junior consular officer. He had returned for a second tour several months ago as a newly appointed political first secretary. Shortly after he arrived, Daniel and Paola attended a dinner at his home. Talk that night was about whether the war would remain stalled. Few people in Paris were planning to leave, and when the subject came up, Paola made it clear—politely for a change, to Daniel's relief—that she was happy to be married to an American but had not the slightest interest in living in her husband's native country. There the subject ended.

"Thanks for getting back to me so quickly, Keith."

"No trouble. Just a bit of a zoo around here, as it must be for you."

"Funny enough, my schedule may have benefited from the chaos. No-shows have left me feeling like I'm in some bizarre kind of oasis. Anyway, I won't keep you. I was hoping I might stop by the embassy and see you for a few minutes. I'd like to talk to you about getting a visa for Paola to go to the States with me."

"You've decided to leave, then? Actually, I'm a little surprised. I took you to be more masochistic than that."

"Well . . ."

"Even more shocking, I suppose this means Paola has changed her mind."

"Actually, she'd probably kill me if she knew I was asking."

There was a pause at Keith's end of the line. Finally he said, "Listen, Daniel, you're welcome to come by and see me, of course. But I have to be blunt with you. This isn't the time for dithering. It may already be too late."

"I understand. Perhaps if I could see you briefly this afternoon. Say about three?"

"Let's say three-thirty. I'll have my secretary scribble you in, but I have to warn you, appointments aren't worth the pencil point right now. You might have to wait."

"Yes, of course. I appreciate it, Keith. I'll show up at three-thirty and take my chances."

No mid-afternoon repose was evident in the city as Daniel walked across the bridge to the embassy. The outbound streets were clogged and cacophonous. Parisians were flowing south as if a drain plug had been pulled from their city. Anything on wheels was crammed with people and sacred possessions. As elsewhere, shops Daniel passed on Rue Royale were being boarded up.

As he neared the embassy, he was caught in a crowd that, when it moved at all, moved as one with shuffling feet. It was close to four-thirty when he was finally shown into Keith's office.

Papers were strewn everywhere in the large, high-ceilinged space, all pretense of diplomatic refinement having been abandoned. Keith stood, came around from behind his desk, and extended his hand. Both men were tall, though Keith's lanky build and thinning sandy hair contrasted with Daniel's more muscular frame and still-thick, only slightly graying hair.

Keith ushered Daniel to a government-issue brown leather sofa, then took a place opposite on a matching overstuffed chair. "What a mess we're in, eh?" he said.

"Well, I suppose the papers can't complain about a phony war anymore, can they?"

"No, indeed."

"Do you think Paris can be saved? Can the French fight them off?"

"The official line remains that a settlement can be reached that would leave the French in control of Paris. I don't think anyone believes it, as you can see for yourself by the direction of the traffic." He waved his arm toward the streets outside.

Daniel shook his head. "So much for the Maginot line."

"Yes. Well, that's what happens when French hubris and stodgy thinking come up against Prussian military genius. The Germans simply go around rather than over the wall and the French find themselves with brilliant fortifications that face the wrong way." Keith gave a short laugh. "Napoleon most certainly would not be proud of this turn of events."

"Let's hope," Daniel said, "that in the best Napoleonic tradition, the Germans overreach."

"Right. In the meantime, we're encouraging Americans to leave."

"As I mentioned over the phone, I want to find out what's involved in getting a visa for Paola. We are married, of course."

"But she still doesn't want to go?"

"I have to confess, I decided to call you on the spur of the moment. As I said, she doesn't know I'm looking into it. The trouble is, I think she's got this strange idea that we can just waltz out of here and into Italy and everything will be fine."

Keith leaned forward. "Listen to me, Daniel. As I told you over the phone, this is no time to be accommodating of your wife's sensibilities. And by the way, I'm not a consular officer anymore . . . "

"I know that." Daniel leaned forward, mirroring Keith's posture. "But I was hoping you could advise me and perhaps intercede to move the paperwork along—to get Paola and Francesco visas just in case they're needed."

"It doesn't work that way, Daniel—especially not now. This is not something we can do without Paola's cooperation, and frankly, we haven't got much time even with it."

Daniel cocked his head and was about to speak when Keith went on. "I shouldn't be telling you this, and I'd appreciate it if you wouldn't pass it on . . . "

"Of course I won't."

"The first thing is, forget the French official line about resistance and all that. We have it on good authority that they're going to surrender the city rather than have it destroyed."

"Just like that?"

"In truth, it's probably for the best. Militarily, they're in an impossible position, especially after the debacle at Dunkirk. In case you haven't noticed, the British allies are headed in the wrong direction, and there's no way the French can turn the tide on their own. There's just no point to reducing the city to rubble."

"When?"

"I'm not sure, but we're talking about days not weeks or months."

Daniel leaned back and puffed out his cheeks. "So . . . "

"So, the first thing you have to figure out is whether you can live here under the Germans. Otherwise, you might want to consider getting yourself and your family out as fast as you can—possibly join the crowds streaming south and, if necessary, see about moving on again from there—maybe catch a ship from Marseille. In a rare moment of foresight, the embassy purchased blocks of train tickets for our dependents. Worth a pretty penny on the street right now, I should think, though with the frenzy at the stations I wouldn't be surprised if they're not worth the paper they're printed on. Anyway, I might be able to swing a couple for you."

"I suppose," Daniel said, "that if we decide to stick it out here, it will help that Paola is the bearer of an axis country passport."

"Maybe so—assuming that the fact Paola isn't exactly on the right side of the cause in Italy doesn't come to the Germans' attention for a while. What's more, old friend, the lord giveth and the lord taketh away. Here's the other bit of inside information you have to keep to yourself. I'm only telling you because it affects you directly."

"I appreciate it. Go on."

"Without going into detail as to why we believe it, we have reason to believe that the Duce is officially going to enter the war."

"What? Why? What's in it for Italy?"

"We could talk about that for hours. What it comes down to is the Duce smells a winner, and he wants to be standing on the victory podium next to his good friend Adolf. There's no telling how long the United States will be able to stay on the sidelines, but the one thing you can be damned sure of is that if we come into the war it won't be on the side of Germany and Italy. In any case, our relations with Italy aren't exactly at a high point."

"So," Daniel said, pulling on the thread, "holding an Italian passport might not be such a hot thing even if Paola does decide then that she wants to go to the States with me."

"Exactly."

The door to the office opened half way and Keith's secretary stuck her head in to remind him that he was running late for his next appointment. She backed out and closed the door as the two men stood.

"I probably haven't been much help," Keith said.

"Not true. You've been very helpful."

"If I can leave you with one thought, Daniel, it's not to play cute with Paola about all of this. You need to decide quickly if you want to go home, in which case we'll try and get the paperwork moving. If you decide you want to stick it out here, make sure you stay in touch. At the very least, check for embassy announcements and notices to American citizens. You can try calling me, too, of course, but frankly, I'm not sure I'll be able to help much in any case. Once the Nazis enter the city all bets are off. We've been giving American citizens red seals to put on the doors to their homes or offices, to identify them to the Germans as neutral noncombatants."

"For crying out loud! Shades of Pharaoh! Maybe the Nazi plague will pass over our house."

Keith laughed. "Just so long as you don't get confused and put a Star of David on your door instead."

"You've got a great sense of humor, old friend. I'm really glad I came." Daniel crossed the threshold into the reception area.

"What's humor for if not situations like these?" Keith called after him. "Anyway, for what it's worth, you might want to pick up one or two of the seals. My secretary can help you."

Daniel thanked Keith again and headed for home with renewed urgency.

* * *

THAT NIGHT, PAOLA prepared an early dinner for the three of them. Between bites and dribbled forkfuls for Francesco they talked about the situation in the streets. Paola described her efforts to find fresh vegetables, Daniel related his sad conversation with Claude Moschos. "I can only assume that he is not alone among my patients in questioning the point of his sacrifice and suffering."

It was not until after Francesco was put to bed that Daniel brought up his meeting with Keith. They remained in the dining room so that Paola could sit in the straight-backed chair she preferred. He reviewed the choices facing them, according to Keith's assessment.

"I'm glad you went to see him," she said to Daniel's surprise as she shifted to find a comfortable position. "It's the responsible thing to do in these miserable times. I still don't believe Italy will enter the war, though."

Daniel shrugged. "If Keith is right, we should know before long."

She reached out and touched his arm. "I know you think I've been a shrew on the subject of going to America."

He smiled. "Only slightly. Call it shrewish."

"It's strange. For as long as you've lived in Paris, I still think of you as being completely American. And yet, I can't actually picture you living there, either now or before."

"It seems strange to me sometimes, too. It might not be a bad place to live right now, though. Safer anyway. And you might actually like it there."

"I have visited there, you know. I have a good idea what it's like." She looked at him, then studied her hands.

"Go on," he said after a long pause.

"I wouldn't be happy there, that's all. I just wouldn't."

"Obviously, it's not my first choice either. But my decision to live in Paris in the first place was based on my work and the freedom and sophistication I always felt existed in Paris compared to America. Neither of these things applies anymore. My practice is in shambles, and even if it turns out we're safe here, it's hard to envision life in a German Paris. You talk about Italy as an alternative. But you fled Italy. Given what's happened in Europe, America is looking a damned sight more appealing."

"I don't know what to say, Daniel."

"Well that's something, anyway," he said with a strained smile.

She put her hand on his. They looked into each other's faces for a long moment before she continued. "I never thought I'd say this to any man: You're my husband and I love you, and I'll go anywhere you want. Even to America. All I can tell you is that I'm as certain as I can be about anything that I would hate living there—or maybe the way to put it is that I'd hate not living here. Also, my family may need me to be close by, and I'd hate myself if something bad happened to them and I wasn't here. So I suppose what I'm saying is that if you insist we have to go, then we will, but I'd like to try everything else first, including moving to Italy."

On his way home from the embassy that afternoon, Daniel had found himself slightly embarrassed to recall Keith's gentle chastisement about the need to confront Paola and to stop "dithering," as he put it. Daniel had been prepared for a truculent response from Paola and resolved to stare her down. Now he was taken aback and touched by her willingness to defer to him. He touched her cheek. "I love you very much," he said quietly.

She took his hand to her lips. "We're all living through a bad time," she said after a pause. "Maybe the worst is over."

"Maybe," he said with no conviction. "In any case, if Keith is right, it's probably too late to do anything more than keep our heads down and see what happens. The fact is, I don't know how I could have told my patients, dwindling in number though they may be, that I was leaving."

~ ~ ~ ~ ~

~ ~ ~

Chapter 15

T HE ITALIAN DECLARATION OF war on the 10th of June caused Paola to fall into an unremittingly foul mood. She slammed doors, drawers and windows, scrubbed things twice as hard as necessary, and slapped dishes on the table almost hard enough to crack them. Expletives flew at times predictable and unpredictable. An irritated Daniel accused her of having developed Tourette's syndrome.

"That big fat strutting fucking idiot!" she responded. "Fucking idiot," she blurted again just after it seemed she'd cooled down.

Only Francesco was spared; with him she was as gentle as she always was. In fact, it seemed to Daniel that she had a need to be even more gentle than usual, as if only she could compensate him for the insanity that was engulfing them all.

The next day, a Tuesday, Daniel and Paola watched in grim silence as the last waves of panicked Parisians fled in a jumble of cars, trucks, oxcarts and wheelbarrows. As the city emptied it took on a funereal quiet, which, in place of the joyous energy that should have been extant amid the magnificent last days of spring, had a surreal aspect.

They stood on the curb as the endless columns of German soldiers arrived to occupy the city. The soldiers were proud, polished, orderly, as if to rebuke the ragged flight of their inferiors.

Daniel suggested to Paola that they should return to the apartment and not give the conquerors the satisfaction of playing to an audience. Instead, following the lead of several of the Parisians who, like them, found the spectacle irresistible, Daniel and Paola remained in place but expressed their sentiments by turning their backs as troops went by. An officer in a passing staff car pointed at the gesture and laughed.

Despite the difficulty of holding a squirming Francesco in her arms, Paola wouldn't hand him to Daniel when he offered, but rather held him closer. "I hope we haven't made a mistake by staying on," she said, not looking Daniel in the eye.

Over the next few weeks a surprising normalcy settled over the city, a deplorable certainty having replaced the chaos in which some hope existed. Now there was no hope, but Parisians at least knew where they stood. The worst had come to pass and they had lived through it. The sight of German uniforms became less jarring. People returned to their jobs. Shops reopened. Routines were reestablished. Paola found fresh food more readily available. Some of those who had fled the city returned.

Contrary to Daniel's expectation that his practice would dry up, he had a new crop of patients. These were primarily wounded French soldiers who, having been treated in the hospitals, were referred to Daniel for further treatment. Charles was released from the army and returned to the clinic, as did Alice, who had returned to Paris with her family. With Francesco in tow, Paola received patients and resumed her clerical work.

"Well, it's not as bad as we thought," Daniel said one night over dinner. "At least we can do some good."

Paola nodded glumly. "Maybe we can hold our noses and stay here until the Nazi stench somehow disappears."

Three days later even this runt optimism was taken from them.

Early in the morning Daniel arrived at the clinic to find about fifteen men waiting outside. All were bandaged or, as with two who clung to a parked car for support, otherwise obviously infirm. Several wore the remnants of French uniforms stripped of insignia and medallions. Others had reverted to civilian clothing. "What the hell is going on here?" he exclaimed as he unlocked the door and motioned for the men to come in.

Within a few moments they had overflowed the small reception area. Some sat on the floor, their backs propped against the wall. Daniel quickly assessed those who appeared to be struggling the most and led them to examination rooms, telling them he would return as soon as he could.

"What happened? Why are you all here?" he asked one of the men as he helped him into a chair.

"We were at the hospital in Montparnasse," the man said, clutching a bandaged arm. Blood had seeped through the bandage. "I was waiting to be seen by a doctor. Some of the others were already in the wards. As I was waiting, a line of German ambulances pulled up with soldiers who, if I overheard right, had been wounded somewhere in Belgium. The place turned into chaos. I don't know that the Germans were in any worse shape than the people, mostly French, who were already there. But I think you can guess which patients were going to be cared for first." The man forced a grim smile. "A Nazi officer saw to that."

"But how did you end up here?" Daniel asked.

"When it became clear we wouldn't be treated anytime soon, one of us—that guy over there—stopped a doctor long enough to ask if there was something else we could do. The doctor said we might try another hospital or a private clinic. He ran off before he could suggest one, but a nurse knew about you. A few of us decided to come here, and then a few more came along, and then we found some of the guys who were hurt even worse—they may have been thrown out of beds at the hospital, we're not sure—so we helped them."

"A damned outrage!" Daniel declared as he was distracted by another man who was moaning softly. "I'll help you as soon as I can," he told the first man. "Don't worry."

At that moment Charles arrived and stopped short, surveying the scene.

"Thank goodness you're here, Charles. I'll explain in a moment," Daniel said in response to his bewildered expression. "We need to triage these men, though I've already taken the ones who seemed the worst and put them in the exam rooms. Why don't you start there. Juliet should be here any minute to help."

"All right." Charles removed his coat. A look of silent fury contorted his face.

As Daniel moved toward an exam room he called over his shoulder, "Telephone Alice and Paola and get them here, too."

They worked beyond exhaustion and used up many of their supplies. But by the end of the day they had succeeded in treating all of the men as well as the others who had arrived. Several had wounds that, with bandages long overdue for changing, looked worse than they were. Their wounds were cleaned and new dressings applied. They were sent on their way with

119

instructions to return to be checked. A few had wounds that were showing signs of sepsis. Almost all could benefit from additional surgery, but that would have to wait. The four worst cases were kept overnight. There were beds for only three of them, but Alice padded out an old cot and she and Juliet arranged to stay the night and take turns caring for the men. Daniel and Charles left for home at around midnight.

They returned before seven the next morning. Daniel was relieved not to have a new batch of patients waiting, though two men with minor, albeit painful, wounds had come in the middle of the night. Juliet cared for them and sent them home.

Paola found a neighbor who was willing to look after Francesco. She went to the clinic in mid-morning and helped clean up from the previous day, though she sometimes became queasy when facing the odors of blood and vomit. She made frequent trips outside for fresh air.

Daniel spent the better part of the morning trying to find hospital beds for the four men he had kept overnight. All four needed more attention than could be provided at the clinic. A practical problem was that none of the men who came in the previous day were paying patients. Before, when hospitals would make referrals, he could count on receiving some payment from the government. It might take forever, but something would be forthcoming. Now, it wasn't clear who was in charge. For that matter, the previous day's patients weren't formally referred to him. He hated to worry about the money, but there was only so much he could do for free.

Just before noon, several new patients walked in. Like those the previous day, they were bedraggled and dirty. They all had received some kind of primary treatment but were well overdue for followup. Unlike the previous day's men, this group had no single impetus for coming. They were not driven out of the hospitals. Somehow word had already gotten around that the clinic might be a better bet.

In an exam room one of the new men showed Daniel a dirty bandaged fist. Ordinarily Daniel would have asked one of the nurses to assist him in removing the bandage, but they were busy with other patients, so he did it himself. From the ripe, sweet smell suffusing the man Daniel feared he would find that the wound had turned gangrenous. Both of them stared wordlessly, waiting for the revelation. At last they reached what was left of the man's hand. Only the thumb remained, opposing the knuckles and the crude stumps where the fingers had been, and where the skin had been stretched to cover the bones and quickly sutured.

"How long ago did this happen?" Daniel asked, as he turned the fist over to examine it."

"Few weeks ago. Near Abbeyville."

"Hit by a shell fragment?"

"Yes. How could you tell?"

"The fingers appear to have been taken off in one go, fairly cleanly but not surgically. Is that correct?"

"Yes."

"What do you remember after you were hit?"

"Not much. A comrade wrapped it tight and got me to the rear. I passed out after that. When I woke up, this club of a bandage was on it."

"This very one?" Daniel asked, raising his eyebrows.

"Yeah. I couldn't find anyone to check it until today. I thought about checking it myself, but then I figured I wouldn't know what to do with it anyway."

"In any case, you're lucky," he said, probing the hand gently.

"Oh sure, I could have told you that," the man said, rolling his eyes obviously.

"I'm serious. It could have been much worse. You appear to have some nerve function in what's left of your hand. Most important, it's not infected as I'd feared. I'll put a new dressing on it. If you keep it clean you shouldn't lose any more than you already have. The stumps were repaired crudely— the kind of thing you see often at field hospitals. The surgeons have to work very fast, after all. At this point, my advice is to keep an eye on things and see how the healing continues. Sometime in the future you may need to have a little more repair work done. But for now . . . "

Daniel took fresh bandages and surgical tape from a glass-front cabinet and returned to the patient. Both of them looked up at the sound of some kind of commotion coming from the direction of the reception area. They heard an unfamiliar voice, then a chair scraping across the floor. Daniel put down the bandages and listened for a moment. When he heard nothing further, he resumed work.

A moment later, however, Paola knocked on the door and opened it without waiting for a response. "Daniel, you're needed."

"Can't it wait a couple of minutes?"

She caught sight of the man's hand and quickly averted her eyes. "No, it can't."

"What's going on?" he asked as he closed the exam room door behind him.

"We have visitors," she began to say in English. Switching to Italian she added, "of the fascist unwelcome kind. They insist on speaking to the Herr Director."

In the reception area a German officer was idly thumbing through the clinic appointment book on the desk. Behind him stood three soldiers, armed but not especially alert. Four patients were waiting in chairs that were up against the wall. Three of them averted their eyes; the fourth looked insolently at the soldiers, one of whom glared menacingly until the patient lowered his gaze to the floor.

The officer looked up as Daniel walked in. He was of medium height, solidly built. He kept his cap on, but Daniel could see his hair was close-cropped around the ears, light brown with flecks of gray. His features were chiseled, his eyes dark, penetrating and purposeful.

In French, Daniel introduced himself.

To Daniel's surprise the officer responded in English. "You are in charge here?"

"Yes."

"I don't speak French. Do you speak German?"

"A word or two. My colleague in the other room speaks it better. Shall I call him?"

"It's not necessary at the moment. English will do. I assume you are the American," he added.

Daniel gave the officer a quizzical look.

"Your red seal on the front door," the officer said, pointing.

"Ah, yes. I'd forgotten."

"I am captain Wagner." He did not offer his hand but again began to thumb through the appointment book.

"What can I do for you?" Daniel asked.

"We were passing by and saw your clinic. Some of my men are in need of medical attention."

"I see. Are any of them badly injured? These men with you appear fit enough."

Wagner stared at Daniel. "You will make your diagnoses when I tell you to." His sudden harsh tone startled Daniel. "The men I have in mind for you to see are waiting outside."

"All right," Daniel said, coolly. "Bring them in and we'll see what we can do."

Wagner motioned to one of the soldiers behind him, who left the clinic. "You don't seem to have many appointments in your book," he said to Paola. He turned back to Daniel and smiled slightly. "I hope that doesn't mean you're a poor doctor."

Daniel looked at Wagner without responding. Wagner made as if to say something else, but the door opened. The soldier who had been sent to fetch the others stood aside as his comrades crowded into the room. Daniel counted eight of them. None had what appeared to be serious wounds. "There are only two doctors here, myself and my colleague in the other room, and two nurses. We'll see your men as soon as possible."

Wagner looked at Daniel sharply and gave a short rumble of a laugh. "No, doctor, you don't seem to understand." He poked his index finger into Daniel's chest. "You will look after my men right now," he said poking anew with each word.

But Daniel continued to look directly into Wagner's eyes. Through pursed lips he said, "Captain, you may be in charge of this city. But I make the medical decisions in this clinic. I have patients here who are seriously wounded and ill, and I will decide who is treated and when."

Wagner turned to the armed soldiers behind him, then back to Daniel. "I think not," he stressed, again poking Daniel to stress each word. He picked up the appointment book, held it in front of Daniel's face, and tore out the pages. He ripped the pages in half, then in half again and dumped them back onto the desk. He turned again to the man who seemed to be his second. "New patients have arrived. The doctor's calendar has been cleared for them. Make sure none of the old patients are in the way."

As if he needed to set an example, Wagner nodded toward the Frenchmen in the waiting room. "Get them out of here!"

"Wait a minute!" Daniel exclaimed. "These men are seriously ill. This is not right."

"Now!" Wagner commanded. His soldiers grabbed up the men. Wagner turned again to Daniel. Suddenly, without warning, he struck Daniel hard across the face with the back of his hand. Daniel took a step back, astonished as much by the turn of events as by the blow itself.

The last of the Frenchmen in the reception area began to vomit on the floor. A disgusted soldier dragged him through it and pushed him out the door. Wagner looked at Paola, who had begun to retch. "You can clean that up, plus any mess you make yourself."

Daniel began to protest again, but Wagner ignored him. "Get the French trash out of the rest of the place," he ordered his men.

The soldiers pushed past and fanned out into the clinic. The four bedridden patients were rousted. "Out!" one of the soldiers barked. When Alice moved to object the soldier shoved her and told her to keep quiet. Two of the patients were barely able to keep their feet. Alice put the arm of one of them around her shoulder while the second leaned on her in a daze and followed her out. When it was clear that the other two bedridden men couldn't stand at all, the German called to another soldier and, one after the other like so many sacks of flour, the patients were thrown into the street.

In the treatment room next door another soldier grabbed Daniel's fingerless patient and pushed him out. The man had the presence of mind to use his good hand to snatch the new bandages Daniel had been about to apply.

Throughout the commotion Charles, with Juliet's help in his treatment room, had been suturing a dicey wound. "Pay attention to what you're doing!" he commanded as with trembling fingers she let a stitch slip. She apologized and forced herself to concentrate, but before they could finish soldiers threw open the door and grabbed up the patient, shoving Charles aside. "This is a violation of international law!" he called after them as they pushed the dazed and bleeding man toward the exit.

Meanwhile, Daniel and Paola remained in the reception area with Wagner. When Wagner stepped into the treatment area for a moment, Daniel took advantage of the opportunity. "Get out of here!" he said to her.

It appeared Paola was about to retch again, but she regained control. "I'm not leaving you."

"You can't help here. Go outside, see what you can do to get help for our patients, then get home to Francesco. I'll meet you there."

Keeping Gideon

~ ~ ~ ~ ~
~ ~ ~

Chapter 16

VICTORIA PULLED SOME OF the files from one of the boxes and laid them out. All of them seemed to be from 1940. "More patient records," she said out loud to herself, a clear note of disappointment in her voice. She had read all of Daniel's notes and journals through the thirties, none of which he had tried to disguise. That seemed to be the end of them, though she knew from Francesco that there were more. After all, she had taken up his coy challenge to figure out Daniel's filing system. Now she was becoming annoyed, both because she hadn't succeeded and because, especially since she hadn't, the game seemed ever more childish. Well, at least she could place his whereabouts: all of the patients by this time were Italian.

Daniel had been methodical in his recordkeeping. Each file was blocked into sections: biographic information and history, vitals, complaint, diagnosis, treatment (cross-referenced to a separate list of medications prescribed), comments.

Most of the cases were routine: Bruno Scarpatti, 38, lacerated finger, cleaned/disinfected/sutured, patient to return in one week for followup. Rosa Lazzi, 52, history of digestive disorders, probable colitis, referred to Lucca Hospital for x-ray. Fabio Strozzi, 29, boils, lanced/dressed, instructions given re hygiene. Massimo Prete, 46, chronic constipation, probably related to diet/allergy, prescribed laxative and discussed sequential removal from diet of several possible irritants. Daniel also saw some patients with more serious ailments—cancers, heart conditions, and so on—as well as some with war wounds. Only a few files required extensive notes.

Victoria was on the verge of giving up for the day when, perusing the file of a patient who presented several nuisance ailments, she noticed that the diagnosis was particularly lengthy. The first paragraph recorded the predictable dry details—cough, cold, stomach disorders, rheumatism, and more. Then, without signaling anything in the transition, the next paragraph caused her to do a double-take:

What is it about Italy that seems to cause Paola to give birth here? Francesco's birth here was somewhat predictable; her due date was close when we came to visit her parents. With Isabella, on the other hand, we had fully expected the event to occur in Paris. That was before the Nazis messed things up. (We do tend to see things in personal terms, don't we? The hell with the fact that they chewed up Europe and took Paris for a trophy. The important thing is, they failed to account for Paola's due date!) Of course, just to show how quickly one's perspective can change, at the point at which we fled, having the baby in Italy became the most desirable goal, since the alternative would have been giving birth on some way station on that godawful trip.

Paola's water broke at about two this morning. The labor was fast and uneventful. (Easy for me to say, as she was quick to point out.) Anyway, Isabella came down the chute (head-first this time, as opposed to Francesco's feet-first approach), and we now have a beautiful daughter. Her head was only slightly misshapen by the ordeal. She has lots of dark hair. There were no complications. Need to finish this later. My services are required.

Victoria looked at the top of the file to see the patient's name. *Osservatore, Amerigo*" She laughed out loud, then laughed again when she read the patient's date of birth, 22 November 1900. Daniel's birth date. She shook her head at the obviousness of his hiding in plain sight. Too clever by half, but then, Daniel probably didn't think he needed to protect his thoughts with much greater rigor. She started checking files again from the beginning of the box, noticed he had abbreviated the faux patient files OA in some places. Well, at least she could tell Francesco she'd cracked the code.

She spent the next hour culling OA files from the boxes and placing them together in chronological order. When she was finished, she had a stack that would have filled two of the boxes.

The earliest entry Victoria found was only a week before the one that first caught her eye. She began to read it with the excitement she'd experienced many times in her career when she hit pay dirt in a seemingly dry hole. In this entry Daniel's tone was far different. It was suffused with relief.

Never in my wildest dreams would I have imagined it possible that the Duce's Italy would be a beacon of freedom and a safe harbor. The very thought is ludicrous. Not that the officials have welcomed us, exactly. Americans are not in very good odor these days. Yet here we are, and grateful for it, a dispossessed doctor, his very pregnant wife, and their young son.

We fled Paris with what we could carry. Friends will look after some of our possessions—furniture, paintings, books and all the small things one never thinks about in daily life that now have assumed precious value in our minds—but it would be foolish to assume we will ever see any of our things again.

As for the clinic, there's nothing left of it anyway, and I can't shake the thought that this is probably my fault. I don't blame myself for being surprised when that remarkable specimen of a lower life form Captain Wagner arrived with his band of barbarians. His visit came from out of the blue, and after all, we had no experience living under an occupier's boot. Given the relatively civilized surrender of Paris, it wasn't unreasonable to expect correct—not barbarous, at any rate—behavior. So, I was truly shocked when Wagner struck me and started throwing the patients out.

The reason I blame myself for what happened to the clinic—the reason I can't stop second-guessing myself—is that I continued to insist on correct behavior long after it should have been clear that this was a ridiculous hope. I should have realized at once that to respond to the cretins by taking a principled stand and talking about international law and such was absurd. (Charles did this, too, but given his personality, I doubt much else could be expected. Anyway, I, not Charles, was the clinic's director.)

Who knows if it would have made any difference, but I can only wonder whether I might have saved the clinic if I'd acted in a compliant—even subservient—way. What if I'd set the example for Charles and the nurses by swallowing my rage and treating the soldiers deferentially? Our real patients wouldn't have been any better off that day, but they wouldn't have been any worse off, either. And, once the whirlwind passed, perhaps we'd still be able to treat them.

Instead, none of us hid our resentment at being forced to give preference to these Germans, none of whom was seriously wounded or ill. We made it clear we were working under protest. And they paid us for our services by taking with them everything that wasn't nailed down. Every piece of equipment, every roll of bandages, every bottle of pills. On his way out Wagner declared the clinic defunct, and to make the point clearer, he even stripped the embassy seal from the door (so much for sparing the "chosen ones"). By this time I was intimidated into silence, which is ironic. I might as well have continued my righteous protest! Then again, even as I now begin to write, "What else could they have done?" the truth is, what wouldn't they have done? What wouldn't they have stooped to?

Then I think about Wagner's parting words as he ripped off the seal. "If I were you, I'd go back to America while I still could." Would he really have checked to make sure I didn't reopen the clinic? Who knows? Probably not. In any case, I don't know how I could have replaced everything that was stolen. We were running out of supplies and money even before the Germans arrived. And yet, all this said, I can't help but feel that I have abandoned my patients. I rationalize it any way I can. I tell myself my first obligation was to protect my family. I tell myself I couldn't have helped my patients anyway. I tell myself that, in the end, I'll be able to do more as a doctor here—or wherever we land.

As far as leaving Paris was concerned, Paola said she would support me in whatever I decided. In the final analysis, once I decided to leave, it was the sooner the better. We were already playing maternity roulette.

The hellish journey itself might have caused us to wonder whether we did the right thing by leaving. Although we had heard the train stations weren't as clogged with refugees as before, when we arrived the station seemed as crowded as ever. Of course, by the time we wanted to leave we had to contend not only with our fellow refugees but with the Germans themselves, who take priority on the trains whenever they want. Soldiers and their munitions and supplies were everywhere in evidence. The Germans lost no time, after all, making the city their own.

We decided to head for Lyon, but we knew we might not have much choice. The real object was to get out of Paris, preferably in the general direction of Italy.

In the event, the journey became an object lesson in the absurdities of life in wartime. Keith Stewart was actually able to get tickets—for couchettes, *no less—on a direct train to Lyon. From there, we intended to connect to Italy. The train was supposed to leave at four in the afternoon, and of course we got to the station well ahead of time. It would have been difficult to move through the mob without baggage, let alone with it, as well as a severely pregnant woman and a two-year-old. With these things it was nearly impossible. Paola was game, as always, but there was only so much she could do. We agreed she should concentrate on looking after Francesco, who had to be carried most of the time, while I handled the baggage. When he wasn't crying and cranky, Francesco wanted to walk, but then the crowds pressed in and it was hard for Paola to hold his hand. Paola also had two small shoulder bags. We couldn't have been at the station for more than a few minutes before a pickpocket got into one of them and came away with some of Paola's jewelry. We were stupid to have carried the jewelry there, but we considered ourselves lucky: the other bag held our passports.*

That left me to carry the suitcases—two big grips crammed to the brim (it was hard even to lift them) plus one with a strap I could carry over my shoulder. At first it was almost impossible to move through the crowd. We were afraid to get separated. I learned the secret of using the suitcases as battering rams. It didn't take long to abandon the civilized impulse to apologize every time I jostled someone and instead use the bags to claim territory. Paola and Francesco were able to follow closely in the short wake I created.

But back to those precious tickets. When we finally made it to our track (by this time only ten minutes before the train was scheduled to depart), there was no train waiting. Given the circumstances, we took this in stride.

A few minutes later a barely audible announcement over the loudspeaker said our train—the one on which we had our couchette reservations and on which, even now with our journey hardly begun we were already looking forward to the refuge of a compartment—had been canceled. We looked at each other with eyes rolling.

Paola planted herself on the platform with Francesco and the baggage while I (joined by what seemed like about a million Frenchmen) tried to find someone to tell me what we were supposed to do. I went to the ticket kiosk, but gave up immediately when I saw the throng there.

I wandered around looking for anyone who could tell me anything useful. After about ten minutes of this I began to contemplate getting us all out of there and trying another day with new tickets, even if we had to sacrifice the ones we had in hand.

A railroad official of some kind—by then it didn't matter which kind . . . conductor, engineer, steward . . . any would have done—appeared close to me and was surrounded immediately. I decided to join the knot. The man—a conductor, as it turned out—in an evident effort to remain calm, had assumed an expression that must have been drug-induced! He was answering questions without the slightest emotion. His composure would have been strange at any time, but in the midst of this chaos it was positively surreal.

I pushed my way closer to him, but it was unnecessary to get up all the way, as he was already answering the same questions I had.

"My train to Lyon was just canceled! What am I supposed to do?" a distraught man yelled in a manner that presumed whatever answer he got would be unsatisfactory. As, indeed, it was.

"There is another train scheduled in an hour," the conductor said with otherworldly serenity.

"But I had a reservation on the canceled one! Are these good?" the man yelled, waving his tickets in front of the conductor's face.

"No. They will have to be changed."

"But are there places on the next train?"

Shrug.

"What the hell am I supposed to do?" the man yelled again, even more irate.

Another shrug, though more emphatic this time, followed by words that I concluded were as close to helpfulness as the conductor would get: "Whatever you can, Monsieur."

Dripping with sweat and wondering again whether we should try another day, I headed back to Paola and Francesco. As I approached the platform, I caught sight of Paola waving frantically with one arm while she held

Francesco in the other. She was red in the face. Francesco was crying hot tears, snot dribbling from his nose.

I charged through the crowd. "The suitcase!" Paola yelled as I got close. She pointed over her shoulder.

Finally, I got close enough to hear her say, "A man took one of the suitcases!" (the one with my things in it, as it turned out).

I looked at her in disbelief.

"I'm sorry, Daniel. This man just pushed through the crowd, grabbed the bag and went off. In that direction," she added, pointing. "I screamed every obscenity I could think of at him, but he was gone."

"Wait here," I said, heading off in the direction she had indicated. I reasoned that the one thing I had going for me was that the case was so heavy, the man who took it couldn't have gotten very far.

I was wrong. The man was probably more adept than I had become at using the case as a battering ram, because by the time I was able to get into a small clearing in the station, there was no trace of him or my things. I took a step toward a gendarme not far from me. But like the conductor, the gendarme was surrounded by petitioners, and I knew at once that my cause was futile.

I returned to the platform, this time not merely drenched but with no prospect of changing my clothes for the foreseeable future. We were discussing what to do, when the train scheduled next for Lyon pulled in.

Immediately we were caught between those exiting the cars (though I have no idea why, with all of us so frantic to leave Paris, so many others were apparently bent on arriving) and those, waving tickets in the conductor's face and yelling that this was their train, who were trying to get on before the first group could disembark. Among them was the man I had observed talking to the serene conductor and whom I presumed was waving a ticket that was actually for the previous train. Within a few moments this bluff was confirmed, as the conductor for the arriving train looked at the man's ticket and wagged his finger in the man's face, at which point the man, now apoplectic, made off down the platform to try again through another door.

When the train had emptied and before all the new passengers had boarded, I was able to ask the conductor what I could do to get aboard. Pulling out all the stops, I pointed to my pregnant wife and distraught child.

"This car is full, Monsieur," he replied in a voice that, while sympathetic, suggested he had witnessed more dire situations. "Perhaps try one of the others." I could see for myself that the car was not full, but by the time I began to protest he had turned his attention elsewhere.

Meanwhile, the crowd on the platform was growing, pressing us toward the train. Even if we had wanted to leave and try again another day, I can't see how we could have gotten out of there. The expression on Paola's face was grim, determined. She was still holding Francesco, who wouldn't stop crying.

As the crowd pressed in, we began to be swept down the platform. By this point we were more worried for our safety than reaching our destination. As we were pushed toward the next open door, the conductor guarding it suddenly turned his back to us in order to fend off a man who was, absurd as it was in the circumstances, proclaiming his importance and the right to have his ticket accepted. It was a valid ticket, the man said, and he would be allowed on the train or the conductor would hear from his superiors! The conductor looked again at the ticket and proclaimed it to be "insufficient." He handed the ticket back and said the man needed also to have a "special ticket." Within seconds, the man cursed and produced a wad of francs, which he pressed into the conductor's hand.

Immediately I reached into my pocket to produce the funds for our own "special tickets." In what turned out to be our good fortune, by this time the surging crowd had pressed us right up against the door. In the moment we had while the conductor's back was to us as he weighed the sufficiency of the man's special ticket, I nodded toward the train door and commanded to Paola, "Follow me!"

Before the conductor was aware of what was happening I gathered up all the strength I could and virtually threw the one remaining monster suitcase up into the vestibule and immediately followed it up myself. Just as the conductor turned I reached out and grabbed Francesco and practically threw him up after the suitcase. Next, I reached out to Paola and grabbed her by the arm to pull her up. When the conductor realized what was happening, he pushed my hand away, interposed himself between Paola and me, and demanded that I and Francesco get down.

With the crowd surging toward the door, I was damned if we were getting off. Of course, I write this now as if I was thinking rationally. In fact, it was *something else inside that took over. "We're going on this train!" I yelled, and shoved the conductor. Standing on the step when I did so, I had the advantage of leverage, and he fell back. He would have hit the ground had it not been for the pressing crowd propping him up. In the instant he was falling backward, I grabbed Paola and all but jerked her up into the car.*

I slammed the door behind us, but couldn't find a way to lock it. "That way! Into one of the compartments!" I yelled.

Paola gathered up Francesco and I pushed the two of them down the aisle toward the middle of the car, dragging the suitcase behind me. By then the conductor had succeeded in opening the door, but it hardly mattered as people on the platform began to climb in through open windows.

With Paola and Francesco ahead of me, and somehow still dragging the suitcase behind, we managed to get into one of the compartments and close the door. Perhaps because the windows of that compartment were closed, the compartment, which contained berths for six, three on each side, was still empty.

There's no telling what would have happened had the gendarmes not appeared in force to suppress what was clearly becoming a riot. They weren't gentle about it, either, as they swung batons with an energy I could only be sorry hadn't been applied to the Germans. It took probably half an hour to clear the platform, but by that time the train had become jammed with those of us who had managed to clamber aboard.

Paola suggested that we climb up into the topmost berth and the one below it and claim them. The compartment was sweltering, and she was feeling faint and nauseous, but we feared to open windows. With relief I noted that the shoulder bag, which contained my medical kit, was still strapped to me.

On the platform, the chief of the gendarmerie began a heated exchange with several of the conductors, who, incredibly, were arguing that the train should be cleared and properly reboarded. No doubt they were angry over having been deprived of their rightful bribes by those of us who forced the issue.

By this time four other people—a young couple and an elderly couple— had joined us in the compartment, bringing the total to seven, including Francesco, for the six berths. We ventured to open the window slightly to allow what little air was available and to better hear the argument on the platform. For an anxious moment as it appeared the conductors might carry the day I wondered what we would do if the gendarmes demanded we leave. Fight them off? Pay them off? Comply?

We were more than a little relieved when the chief ordered the train to depart. In a sop to the conductors, he pointed out that there was no reason they couldn't collect the "proper fares" once the train was underway. (This they later did, and with a vengeance.)

The moment we started to move I opened the windows wide. We had had the foresight to bring a canteen of water, but not the foresight to know it would be lost in the chaos at the station, and now I became worried that Paola was becoming dehydrated. She was drenched in sweat and the air coming in from the open windows was insufficient to cool her off. (Humor amid chaos: as the train began to move, the old woman, indulging in the atavistic but widely accepted European notion that drafts cause illness, pointed to the open window, the implication being that, no matter how stifling and sweltering our condition, I should close it! Fortunately she didn't press the matter when I pulled rank, explaining that I was a doctor and that at the moment the malevolent draft was the least of our problems.)

For the next few minutes none of us said a word. Paola was secure on the top berth. I got Francesco settled and placed him on the berth below hers, then went to the WC in hopes of finding cool water with which to make a compress for Paola.

The water that came out of the tap was lukewarm (and not potable of course). I realized too late that I hadn't brought in a cloth or towel with which to make a compress. A grimy towel hung next to the sink. I tore it in half, and rinsed it as best I could. At least it would give her some relief until I could find something drinkable.

I returned with the wet compress, and there ensued yet another example of how absurd things can get—though it is clearly more humorous in retrospect than it was at the time. As I entered the compartment I saw that we had been joined by a rough looking man who was standing near the window. Then I noticed he was talking to an equally rough companion who was lying in the berth in which I had left Francesco, who had been placed, presumably by one of the men, on the top berth with Paola. Paola had fallen asleep. In spite of the heat, Francesco curled as close to her as her shape would allow.

135

"What's this?" I asked, nodding toward the berth, my voice determinedly harsh.

The man by the window looked at me. Neither he nor his companion appeared terribly bright. "The boy doesn't need a place of his own," the man said.

"He didn't have a place of his own. He was in my berth."

"One of us has to stand," the man lying in the berth said matter of factly. "Might as well be you."

"No, I don't think that's how it's going to be," I said, not really knowing how I would follow up such a threat, the ambiguity or hollowness of which was demonstrated by the complete lack of response by either of the recipients. The two other couples looked on from their places silently, with frightened eyes.

I don't know how the idea came to me. Perhaps it was borne of the instant recognition that I wasn't likely to be able to force the interloping goons out of the compartment. They might not have been very bright, but they were certainly very large.

Thus I surprised myself—not to mention the others—when in a firm but controlled voice I asked the man by the window if he didn't know he was in a quarantine compartment.

He looked at me with a sort of dull suspicion and asked what that was.

It amazes me that I was able to keep a straight face when I explained that I was a doctor (I displayed my medical kit to bolster the point) and that everyone in this compartment had been exposed to typhus. This got the attention of the one lying in my berth as he shot up so quickly that his head hit the berth above. "My uncle's whole family died of typhus," he said.

I could see out of the corner of my eye that my announcement startled not only the intended recipients, but the old couple. The woman began to protest. Fortunately, the young man in the opposite berth must have caught on to what I was about as he had the presence of mind to say quickly, "Just listen to the doctor. He'll explain everything." Which must have done the trick, as the woman stopped in mid-sentence.

I continued to play my hand, telling the men in the most stern physicianly demeanor that a half hour of contact with an infected person was all that was required to contract the disease. Then, looking at my watch, I suggested that the men had only a few minutes before they became sick.

Needless to say, it didn't take long for them to leave. I followed up by writing the words "Disease Quarantine" on a piece of paper and posting it to the outside of the compartment. And that is how we managed to get to Lyon in the relative comfort of six berths for six adults and one child.

We spent two days in Lyon, where we regained our strength—I was relieved when Paola recovered from the ordeal faster than I expected—and I was able to purchase some clothing to replace the things in my stolen suitcase. (By that time the clothes I was wearing must have bolstered our disease quarantine ruse.) The city was crowded but we lucked into a room at a reasonably clean hotel with a bath two doors down.

Things were looking up when we resumed our journey. The train from Lyon was blessedly uncrowded.

Then we stopped at the Italian border.

Two policemen entered our car. I passed them our travel documents as they requested. We had made the trip from France to Italy before, of course, so we were unconcerned as they began to inspect our passports and my French residence permit.

But to say the least, things had changed since the last trip, and the policemen gave particular scrutiny to the documents, looking especially at my passport, holding it this way and that to the light—looking for forgeries, I presume. After what seemed an eternity one of the policeman returned Paola's passport and the laissez passer we had obtained for Francesco. These were in order, he said. However, my documents were "questionable," and he asked me to follow him off the train to meet with one of his superiors.

If my impulsive reaction to the situation on the train to Lyon was a creative one, my reaction this time was not. I immediately became huffy. "I've entered Italy several times on this passport," I said, indignantly.

"The situation has changed," the officer replied simply. "The status of Americans is of greater concern now that Italy is at war."

"You're not at war with America!" I protested.

"Still," the officer said, motioning to follow him.

Now it was Paola's turn to make things right. As Francesco began to cry (I found out later that she had pinched him) she looked up at the policemen in the most pathetically Madonna-like way. "Please," she said. "This is my husband, and a doctor, and we are trying to return to our home in Tuscany in time to bring our child into the world," and so on and so forth.

And then, taking a leaf from the Paris conductor's manual, she said the magic words: "Perhaps in the circumstances we need a 'special travel document' for my husband, and perhaps you might be kind enough to arrange this? Of course, we could provide the necessary official fee."

The officers excused themselves, stepped back and spoke gravely to each other. But there was little doubt that the only thing to be settled was the amount of the "fee."

It only remains for me to end this entry where I began it: Here we are in the Duce's Italy, and grateful for it, a dispossessed doctor, his very pregnant wife, and their young son.

Victoria put down the pages and smiled.

~ ~ ~ ~ ~

~ ~ ~

Chapter 17

ARLY ON A BRITTLE morning at the beginning of February 1941, Daniel was already seeing his third case of influenza of the day. Meanwhile, in the antechamber that served as a waiting room for what was now Daniel's office in the Rosetti home several people sat in a state of heightened anxiety, the usual small talk replaced by subdued stares at the floor and distracted fidgeting.

In the waiting room he said goodbye to the patient he had just examined and motioned for a woman in widow's weeds whom he knew well by now as Signora Marchetti to come in. She was in her late forties but appeared much older. She wrung her hands and looked up at Daniel with moist eyes.

"Have a seat in my office, Signora," Daniel said in a tender voice. "I'll get my wife to help."

Although he had become comfortable dealing with routine illnesses in Italian, he had more difficulty treating a patient like Signora Marchetti, whose symptoms were more psychological than physical and therefore required a considerable amount of conversation, much of it in local idiom. She emitted a slurry of words, and made it worse by doing so with stupefying rapidity. Daniel would ask her to slow down, and she would comply for the next few words, then revert to machine gun speed.

Daniel had several patients like Signora Marchetti, and he had come to rely on Paola, or sometimes Antonio, to help translate. Paola and Antonio were able to help in other ways, too. Older, traditional women were more comfortable seeing Daniel when his wife was present, and even some of the men preferred to see him in the presence of a real Italian like Antonio, though this could cut both ways when the patient was reluctant to share his problems with a neighbor.

Most of the local citizens, and especially the less prosperous among them, considered Daniel to be a godsend. In the past, they would have been seen by one of two doctors in the town, or they would have made the trip to Lucca. But the older of the two doctors had recently died, and the younger had been called to the army. Antonio loved to claim credit for Daniel's success, never missing an opportunity to remind him that he had arranged for the first patients when Daniel visited in 1938.

A few moments later, Daniel returned with Paola, who was greeted profusely by the people in the waiting room who asked after her health and the health of her children. All were very well, she was able to say with truthful cheerfulness. Francesco, at two and a half, was bright and energetic. Isabella, at a little over six months, had passed through a bout of colic and also was thriving. Paola herself had regained her form and energy. Daniel believed she was happier to be home than she cared to admit; perhaps her reticence was out of consideration for his feelings. She was concerned that he was still at loose ends, but maintained he was in the best place possible under the circumstances.

Daniel ushered Signora Marchetti and Paola into the examination room. He offered the signora a seat next to the examination table and sat behind his desk. The ritual of who sat where was not a minor consideration. Some patients preferred him to sit close to them in a show of empathy and compassion; others—to further complicate things, sometimes the same patients on different occasions—preferred him to maintain a clinical, officious distance, as if compassion and competence were at odds with one another. The decision was easier with Paola in the room. She pulled up a chair next to the patient and provided the soft counterpoint to his foreign clinical brilliance. To the people of Ponte di Maddalena—as would have been true in any Italian town—he was, and always would be, a *straniero*, a foreigner, while she, no matter how foreign her actual experiences or views, would always be one of them.

"Are the sedatives I gave you helping?" he asked the signora.

"A little," she responded, though her bearing seemed to suggest that the relief she was reporting was out of consideration for Daniel's professional pride.

"Perhaps you can tell me a little more about your symptoms." This was the point at which he would rely on Paola to translate while he nodded sympathetically. The sympathy was crucial, often the most effective therapy at his disposal, since as with several of his patients, many of Signora Marchetti's ills were the product of anxiety brought on by the war. In particular, she was sleepless over the presence of her two sons in the army, one in North Africa and the other in Greece. Their letters home had become ever less frequent, and for the past few months she had heard nothing at all.

In the absence of contact Signora Marchetti, and the growing number of people in her situation, were forced to rely on rumor and the debilitating power of their imaginations. Increasingly, the government's propaganda machinery was unable to hide the debacles of the country's military adventures. Setbacks in Libya were bad, but they were nothing compared to the disasters in the Balkans. In October the Duce's forces, confident of victory, had invaded Greece from Albania. By December those forces had suffered a humiliating rout, which was stemmed only when Germany rushed troops to bolster its ally.

The government's proclamations of victory notwithstanding, Daniel, Paola and Antonio provided the sympathetic ears for the panicked men and women in the community. Their tales were increasingly alike: the word of mouth reports of brutal winter warfare for which the Italian troops were unprepared. It was supposed to be an easy victory in Greece, after all, begun in October and ended before the cold set in.

And then there was the real evidence before their eyes. Some of the sons who had managed to come home were mutilated and embittered and—worse for the parents of unaccounted for sons—not reluctant to talk about the horrific conditions they faced, the insufficiency of their supplies and equipment, and the callous incompetence of their officers. They spoke of the rains and the mud and the lice, then of the cold and the snow, of vehicles abandoned in the mire and forced marches without food, of jammed guns and futile charges. Above all, they spoke—though usually with more self-consciousness and circumspection—of betrayal. The entire edifice of their cause—the righteous glory of the new Rome and the masterful military preparation in which they believed—had proved to be a hollow shell.

Those who were merely disillusioned had by far the better of it, compared to the wounded. Many of the latter became Daniel's patients as word spread of his specialty in this area. To his own amazement the practice he had started as a way to pass the time, with the expectation of treating the routine ills of a small community, suddenly had more in common with the specialized practice he had left behind in Paris. Once again he was treating the aftermath of ragged gunshot and shrapnel wounds and battlefield amputations, many of the latter the result not of traumatic injury but of frostbite and infection. He volunteered time at the hospital in Lucca, both seeing patients and instructing other physicians and nurses in the treatment of such conditions. For the first time since he left Paris, he felt useful.

None of this was merely academic to Paola and her family. It had been a month and a half since they had heard from Alfredo. With each passing day—with each day of seeing sleepless parents or mangled sons—their anxiety grew. Daniel reflected on the confidence Alfredo had displayed barely a few years ago. He wondered what Alfredo would say now.

Once again, Signora Marchetti explained her symptoms. She could not sleep, had little appetite. In a lower voice, more to Paola, she said her bowels were giving her trouble and that her periods had become erratic. When she said these things, Daniel lowered his gaze in a way he had perfected to let the patient know that, as a doctor, he understood the seriousness of the complaint without, as a man, displaying unseemly interest.

Daniel prescribed a stronger sedative, made some suggestions with regard to diet, and told her to see him in a week. Sometimes he imagined himself providing true relief for Signora Marchetti and others by the simple, impossible act of inventing encouraging news about their sons. The signora thanked Daniel and Paola and stood to leave. She inquired about Daniel's fee, and as he did routinely with his less fortunate patients, he replied that his fee would be covered by the *commune* and she was not to worry. It was a lie that satisfied them both.

They showed the signora out. Before Daniel called in the next patient, he beckoned Paola back into his office and closed the door.

"What is it?" she asked, surprise on her face.

"Just this," he smiled and drew her to him, and kissed her lips softly. "In case I haven't told you recently, I love you very much."

She looked up at him. Her eyes were suddenly moist. "And I love you," she replied, touching his cheek. "More than you'll ever know."

Keeping Gideon

~ ~ ~ ~ ~
~ ~ ~

Chapter 18

A S FEBRUARY CAME TO a close there was still no word about Alfredo. The mood in the family turned ever more somber. The places rent by Luca's death had barely closed over with the thinnest of membranes. Antonio's recovery from that shock was endangered anew as he paced the nights away.

Paola's mother was better at masking her concern, better at the dramatic arts. Still, the dull pain that never left her eyes was becoming more intense by the day as requests to the army for information went unanswered.

One night at the dinner table Paola turned to Antonio, whose head was bowed close to his soup bowl, and said, "Babbo, I think we've relied for too long on official channels."

Antonio looked up, a slightly startled expression on his face.

"What do you mean?" Mama asked before he could respond.

Paola put down her spoon. "Only that you keep inquiring through the established lines—the official chain. You know, letters to Alfredo, letters to his commanding officer . . . "

"But," Antonio responded, "we're only making use of the contacts we were given by Alfredo in the first place."

"That was before his division went to Greece!" Paola said, her voice rising.

Daniel, sitting to her right, put a hand on her arm. "I think what Paola is trying to say . . . "

"I don't need you to interpret for me," she snapped, pulling her hand back and picking up a fork to use as a pointer.

Daniel looked at her evenly. "Yes you do. Let's not make things worse." He looked back at his in-laws. "If I know your daughter as well as I think I do, what she's trying to say is that she's frustrated by waiting for some official—some incompetent official, I think she'd put it . . . "

Paola tried, failed to suppress a smile.

"She's tired of waiting for some incompetent official to tell us what's going on. God only knows how long that could take."

"How?" Mama began, her face brightening slightly at the prospect of taking initiative.

"By taking advantage of our own contacts," Paola joined.

Antonio wrung his hands. "You're right, I know," he said in a somber voice. "It's just that . . . well . . . sometimes you don't want to press too vigorously."

Paola flashed impatience, then visibly reined herself in. "I know," she said softly. She reached across the table and put her hand on top of his.

For a moment Daniel was confused, thinking Antonio meant he was concerned about ruffling official feathers. Then he realized that Paola understood his real concerns. "We're all afraid, Babbo," she said. "We're all afraid of what we might learn. It's better to know, though."

"Who should we talk to?" Mama asked.

Antonio smiled thinly. "Our friends among the cognoscenti aren't as numerous as they used to be."

It was true. Daniel and Paola had worried this problem between them. The Rosettis had never been—perhaps more importantly, had never pretended to be—party stalwarts. In the early years this was not much of a problem. Outwardly, the family kept up appearances. In the twenties and early thirties Antonio overcame the reluctance inspired by a liberal education to support the Duce and his squadristi. As his business thrived he was able to convince himself that the leader's bluster might be a necessary evil to get the country moving. There was a certain noblesse oblige in his reasoning; the educated classes might not need such coaxing and diversions, but the others, well . . . . If the prosperity of his business and the wellbeing of his family could be assured by the occasional Blackshirt dress-up, by the occasional tactical smile or Fascist salute, by the occasional forced bonhomie or the occasional payment to the right person, what was the harm in it? Granted there had been some excesses, as well as some waste and inefficiency. But the country was more prosperous than ever, and the outlook was bright. "Liberal thinkers like ourselves," Antonio would caution in the self-deprecating tones of enlightened self-criticism, "have a tendency toward self-righteousness and a kind of naive purity that ignores the tradeoffs of the real world."

In the privacy of their home the Rosettis retained at least some of the rhetoric of liberal purity. They sighed at the thuggery that accompanied the revolution. They laughed at the pretentious pageantry. They ridiculed the buffoonery of the leader.

Luca went into the army, then Alfredo. The parents basked in the community's admiration. The daughter was a problem. She seemed to be only capable of seeing negatives. She spoke her mind. She proposed going to Paris to study and live. The parents were privately relieved, both for her safety—at least there her politics probably wouldn't land her in jail—and their own.

Then came the North African conquest. And the growing influence of Hitler. And the contemptible racial laws. The Rosettis' private judgments grew harsh, their private conversations scathing. They tried to maintain the well cultivated public visage. Two sons in the army made the family unassailable. Still, inevitably the private views began to seep into the public demeanor. At dinner party discussions they were more willing to inject contrary opinions, though they did so gently, saying things like, "Granted the party's policy makes sense now, but perhaps in the long run . . ."

But then, above all, there was the defining moment of Luca's death, which bestowed public heroism on the collective family and private embitterment on each of the members. Grief was amplified by regret and guilt. "How could I have been so blind as to where all of this was headed?" Antonio would wail. He could not be talked out of the belief that he had contributed to his elder son's martyrdom in a cause that was as ludicrously hollow as any in history.

And now there was, perhaps, Alfredo.

"I hate to be the one to suggest it," Paola said, "but the Bucas almost certainly have the contacts to find out about Alfredo."

"You'd think they wouldn't have to be asked," Mama said without attempting to disguise her resentment. "They know of our predicament."

"Yes, but then, they are the Bucas, aren't they?" Paola responded.

Daniel smiled. "It's a complicated relationship you have with them, isn't it?"

146

"Of course it is," Paola said briskly, allowing the irritation to flow freely from one object to the next. "The relations between Italian neighbors are always complicated. There's always too much personal history involved. It's not like in America where one generation doesn't know the next."

"Sorry for observing," Daniel responded with determined sarcasm.

Which drew no apology from Paola but did draw one from Mama on whom, as usual, sarcasm was lost. "There's no reason for you to be sorry," she said. "You couldn't have known."

"And there's no reason for you to be so harsh," Antonio said, pointing to Paola. He turned to Daniel and continued. "It's not unlike marriage, you know, this dealing with people who have lived near you for generations. You come to expect that things will not always be smooth. But you accept the need to go on. The Bucas are a perfect example. Our families have been side by side for more generations than I can count. Bruno and I went to school together. That's not to say things don't change. People are added and subtracted to the equation. Mama married me and became a new part of our community. Bruno's wife Hilde came from an Italian-German family up north, and she joined the community as well. Sometimes the two families are close, sometimes they're not. When Paola was a child, one day she'd be as close as a sister to Renata Buca; other days they'd scratch each other's eyes out."

Antonio lit a cigarette, which drew silent rebuke from the others, and went on talking through the cloud. "But the history itself becomes the overriding thing. It becomes a force of its own, which demands that people maintain perspective if they are to get along. We may not see eye to eye with the Bucas now. So what?" he shrugged. "We've lived together on this mountain for generations and will live together in the future as well. If you keep the long view in mind, you take the ups and downs in stride. As I said, it's like marriage."

"Even married people do unforgivable things to one another," Paola said. The fork slipped from her hand and hit the plate, almost as if she had timed it for emphasis. "Even married people change in fundamental ways," she added, picking it up again.

"What is it about the Bucas that you think has changed so?" Antonio asked. "What have they done that's so unforgivable? Is it that they haven't lost a son, or a brother?" At this tears came to his eyes, as if he had been caught by surprise—as if he hadn't realized what he was saying about his own son.

Paola pressed on without pause. Daniel knew her well enough to understand that this was her way of ensuring that she would not be drawn into a new round of tears over Luca, and possibly Alfredo. "What I hate about them," she said, "is that they have turned into real and fervent believers in the party's cause."

"What's new about your feelings about that?" Mama asked. "You've always hated the party. It's a wonder you didn't hate your own family. We've had dealings with the party, after all. And we believe the party has done good things for the country."

"When I was younger I did hate you."

Had these words come from anyone but Paola, the shock might have been serious. Instead, her father merely said, in his quiet way, "But you've grown up. You know things aren't so simple, don't you?"

"I know that I've been proven right, that's what I know!" she said, her voice rising again. "Look at what these barbarians are doing to our country! Look at what they've done to our family! Even when you've said you supported the Fascists, you had some reservations about them, and especially about their methods.

"What I hate about the Bucas is that they never questioned anything, and they still don't. They make their cozy deals and to this day are happy to be the area's best hosts as far as the Germans are concerned. We sit here talking about asking them to use their contacts precisely because they have such contacts and are willing to pay any price for them as long as it suits their family. Do they have a dead son?"

"Paola!" Daniel interjected. "I think that's enough."

"No, it's not enough! Someone needs to say these things! The Bucas don't have a dead son because the only son they've given up to the army, cute little Stefano, has a comfortable job behind the lines in Arezzo. Now, I wonder how that was arranged." Paola threw her napkin onto her plate and surveyed the grim silence she had wrought. She added with a dismissive wave, "Oh, hell, maybe their family is just smarter than ours."

"Are you finished?" Daniel's voice was cold.

She folded her arms and glared.

After a moment, Antonio gave a thin, ironic smile. He reached across the table and patted Daniel's hand. "And to think," he said, "you married her willingly."

~ ~ ~ ~ ~

~ ~ ~

Chapter 19

A FEW DAYS LATER, the weather turned mild and Antonio took his constitutional in the direction of the Buca home. Bruno Buca was sitting on the loggia overlooking the gardens. He waved as he caught sight of Antonio, who gave a slight wave in return and made his way along the gravel path leading to the house, the stones crunching underfoot.

Antonio was breathing hard after he climbed the steps to the loggia. "You're out of shape," Bruno said, smiling.

"Easy for you to say, sitting there like a lump of clay."

Bruno laughed. "Well, all right, come and be a lump next to me then."

Antonio let himself down into the green wicker chair that matched Bruno's. The chairs were set obliquely to each other, facing the gardens with just enough angle to allow the occupants to engage in conversation without craning, if they wished.

After the usual pleasantries the men sat quietly, looking out. "What do you hear from Stefano?" Antonio asked after a few minutes. "He's still in Arezzo?"

"As of a couple of weeks ago. That was when we received his last letter."

"He's still working in the supply command?"

"Yes."

"Good. Good. He's safe then."

Bruno made no reply. "And Alfredo?" he asked after a moment. "What have you heard from him?"

"Not a word, I'm afraid."

"When was the last time you heard anything?"

"Indirectly—from a comrade of his on leave—a few of months ago. Actually, Bruno, that's something I wanted to talk to you about."

Bruno nodded, silently.

Antonio went on. "Frankly, I'm worried. This lack of contact isn't like Alfredo. He's very good about writing. After Luca . . ." he paused and continued, "After Luca, well, you know, my wife is very nervous."

Bruno leaned forward and patted Antonio's hand. "Of course. Our boys have been very busy, though. I have to believe that if anything really bad had happened you would have been informed."

"I hope you're right, but I'm not so sure. Things are a disaster there, as I'm sure you know."

Bruno sat back in his chair, adopted a mask of exaggerated skepticism. "Nonsense, Antonio! Surely you're not gullible enough to fall for the rumors."

"They're not just rumors. My son-in-law . . . "

"Ah, yes, how is your family doctor?"

Antonio continued, ignoring the attempt to shift the discussion. "My son-in-law has been seeing more and more patients who have returned from Greece. They tell horrible stories, Bruno, and I have no reason to believe they're exaggerating."

"Of course they are, Antonio! Of course they are! By definition, my friend, you are hearing a distorted version of events. After all, these are the ones who have returned because they were injured. What we do know for certain is that our forces are secure in their occupation of Greece. Was it more difficult than we predicted? Yes, I'm afraid so. But wars always are that way, after all. There is always the unexpected. For instance, there was no way of knowing in advance that the weather would be unusually harsh. Our German allies recognized quickly that the situation was more challenging than anyone predicted, so they came to our aid—what are allies for, after all?—and in no time the objective was achieved. Now that things are settling down I would be very surprised if you didn't hear from Alfredo very soon. Don't look so downcast," Bruno added after a pause. "I'm sure I'm right."

"I can only hope so," Antonio said, his voice laced, not with optimism or stoicism or even resignation, but with ill-concealed irritation and resentment. "We've been through enough with the loss of Luca . . . "

"I know you have," Bruno interrupted, again patting the hand of his friend.

"I don't know how my wife could stand another loss," Antonio continued. "And frankly, Bruno, I must say it, I believe your understanding of events is somewhat"—he sought a word—"distorted." He went on before Bruno could respond. "It is, perhaps, too susceptible to the official version. The word that has reached us is more disturbing. It tells not only of bad weather, but of bad equipment, inadequate supplies, incompetence and, yes, even cowardice by the leaders."

Bruno sat back again in his chair, this time his posture rigid. "Or, perhaps, Antonio, you are too willing to accept the word of the poor soldiers who couldn't cope." He smiled thinly. "And you should be careful not to be influenced unduly by the views of your daughter and her American husband. That would not be wise."

Antonio stood and faced Bruno. "How dare you say that to me!"

"It's sound advice for an old friend," Bruno replied evenly.

Antonio turned and began to descend the stairs. His knuckles turned white as he gripped the handrail.

"Anyway, I'll see what I can find out about Alfredo," Bruno volunteered to Antonio's back. "He's a good boy. I always liked him."

* * *

TWO WEEKS LATER, Bruno telephoned Antonio and informed him that he had made inquiries about Alfredo but, so far, without success. His friends promised they would look into the matter, and that's where things stood. He wanted Antonio to know that he hadn't forgotten. He added that, if it made him feel any better, he still hadn't heard from his own son even though he had no reason to believe him to be in any danger. "It's a busy time, after all."

Antonio thanked Bruno and, without bothering with the emollient of small talk, rang off.

"Nothing," he said to Mama, who had overheard the conversation. "As Bruno says," he added after a pause that ruined any chance of his being convincing, "it's a busy time for the soldiers. They have more to worry about than writing letters." Antonio touched her shoulder. "I think I'll go and see if Daniel needs any help with his patients."

A week later, it was Mama who answered the phone. In trembling voice she called to Antonio, who, when he took the receiver from her, was instantly infected by the terror in her eyes. "It's a Captain Greve. He says he wishes to speak to you," she said, hoarsely, her hand covering the mouthpiece.

Antonio took the phone from her as if it was to be the instrument of his own execution. "This is Antonio Rosetti." His voice was strong, didn't betray him. He was on for only a few minutes, and his responses were unrevealing. "Yes . . . Yes . . . I understand . . . Where last? . . . I understand . . . Thank you so much for taking the time."

Mama reached out to touch his arm, her eyes brimming. "Yes?" Her voice was a wind in the rushes.

Antonio took a deep breath, steadied himself. "There's no news."

She looked at him with a perplexed expression.

"There's no news," he repeated. "That was Captain Greve," he said, as if it were necessary to start from the beginning. "From Alfredo's division," he added. "Captain Greve said he doesn't know where Alfredo is, but he hastened to add that, in the circumstances of the fighting in Greece, this doesn't necessarily mean the worst. It could be a matter of confusion or bad lines of communication. He apologized for not contacting us sooner. He knew of our inquiries but delayed because he hoped he would have something more definite to tell us. He confirmed that Alfredo's unit had been at the head of the fighting and that the fighting had been difficult. But Alfredo wasn't the only one who was missing"—Antonio stopped at hearing himself speak the word out loud. It was a word that conveyed a special terror, as some of the returned soldiers Daniel had treated told of comrades blown to bits or lost under waves of ice or mud. Often these unfortunates were listed as missing, the soldiers reported, even when it was clear they would not be found.

Antonio went on quickly: "Many of the soldiers were still being accounted for, Greve said, and many were turning up all right. Still . . ." He hung his head.

Just then, Paola entered the room. Seeing the expressions on her parents' faces, she rushed to them. Before she could speak, Antonio held up his hand. He began in a brighter voice to relate Captain Greve's call. Yet as the retelling progressed his voice became increasingly morose. Finally he said, "The captain said, since soldiers were still turning up he was reluctant to add Alfredo officially to the list of the missing. He may have to do so in a week or two if we hear nothing."

Following Greve's call the Rosetti home became permeated with gloom, though it was occasionally relieved by spikes of optimism, usually the result of word that this or that soldier given up for dead had returned, but sometimes the result of nothing at all, it seemed, or perhaps of some dynamic of emotion that decrees that all states of mind must be punctuated by some other state if only to show that the basic emotion actually exists, can be contrasted with something, is a real thing.

Then, at the end of March, the family was jolted by a completely unexpected event. It was a cold, clear afternoon. Daniel was working at the hospital in Lucca. Paola had just set off to do some shopping before the sun went down. Antonio was nearing the end of his afternoon nap. Mama was looking after the children and was beginning to prepare supper when she heard a knock on the door.

At the sight of Father Claudio, the local parish priest, she almost fainted. "Oh, God, not Alfredo too!" she exclaimed as the priest reached to steady her.

"No!" he said, quickly. "I'm not here about Alfredo. Come, let's go inside and sit down. I'm worried for you," he added.

He held her arm as he led her to the kitchen. "What can I get for you?" he asked, as if she had just come to visit him. "A glass of water? A brandy?"

"I'm all right," she responded, shaking her head. "It's just that, you know, we haven't heard anything about Alfredo. I thought . . . "

"I understand, Signora."

She offered him coffee. He declined, saying he could not stay long. He had a somber task ahead of him. "Although I have nothing to tell you about Alfredo—or any of your family," he added hastily—"I do have sad news."

It was then that the priest told her that the Bucas' son, Stefano, was dead. He had been accompanying a supply convoy into Greece when the truck he was riding in hit a patch of ice and tumbled into a ravine. "Apparently, he didn't suffer. At least we can thank God for that," the priest added. He went on to explain that the body would be returned for a funeral later in the week. The Bucas had asked him to inform members of the parish personally. "Signor Buca sends apologies for not coming himself, but neither he nor the other family members are up to the task, as he hopes you will understand."

"Of course, of course," Mama said quickly, her voice a rush of relief that verged on unseemly elation. "As you know very well, we have had our share of experience bearing such losses," she added with a corrective solemnity.

There was a large turnout for the funeral, which took place under a winter sky. Relatives, neighbors, and friends of the Bucas crowded into the church. Several party representatives attended, as did a number of the Bucas' German acquaintances. One of the party men gave a eulogy, the dignity of which nevertheless failed to deter Paola from whispering to Daniel—too loudly as far as he was concerned—that for once the Fascists' clothing was right for the occasion.

At the graveside the Rosettis embraced their longtime neighbors, bringing them into the community of loss. Signora Buca, who had managed to maintain her composure in a trancelike state during the eulogies, wept fiercely at Mama's touch. Bruno and Antonio, each with a face the ashen color of the sky, embraced stiffly, wordlessly. Paola and Renata embraced as well, and conversed in a low voice until Daniel appeared at Paola's side to tell her it was time to leave. He offered condolences once again to Renata on the loss of her brother. Renata thanked him and said to them both that she prayed for Alfredo.

Later, Paola railed to Daniel that, even in grief, Renata had to be superior. When he asked what she meant, she said that before he had come upon them Renata had offered her prayers for Alfredo no fewer than three times. "She couldn't live with the idea that we might have roughly equal causes of grief, Luca for us and Stefano for them. You'd think it was some kind of grotesque competition. She had to keep reminding me with her prayers that there is always the chance that something dreadful has happened to Alfredo, which would put us back in the position of needing their pity more than they need ours."

"Don't you think that might be a bit strong?"

"Not even a little bit."

~ ~ ~ ~ ~

~ ~ ~

Chapter 20

NO MATTER WHAT TIME Mama went to bed, she woke regularly at two-fifteen. On cold nights she would bundle up in a thick robe and, not wanting to disturb Antonio, wander the house until, about an hour later, she became sufficiently tired to return to sleep.

Often during the wandering hour she would stop and look at family photographs. Some were propped in ornate frames atop chests and dressers, others hung on walls: A photograph of her wedding, she and Antonio surrounded by their families, all of them wearing an expression of solemnity that would have been equally suited to a funeral. A photograph of Luca, smiling proudly in his uniform, and one of Alfredo taken some time during his middle school years. Paola's first communion—it had taken five tries to get her to stop fidgeting. In the still of the night Mama would stop before each photograph and stare into it—become transfixed and attempt to be one with the time and place.

On this night, she was roused by more than her internal clock. First there was the indistinct rattling sound from downstairs. She lay on her back, trying to identify the sound over Antonio's snoring. She persuaded herself it was the shimmy against the wind of a poorly fitted windowpane. A few minutes later, she heard what she thought was a pot lid hit the hard floor and wobble on its axis until someone muffled it like a cymbal. She relaxed now, assuming that Daniel or Paola had gotten up to fix a snack. Or perhaps something was being fetched for one of the children.

She eased out of bed, put on her robe and the yellow raw silk slippers Paola sent from Paris a few years earlier, and made her way downstairs.

She padded around the corner to the kitchen and stopped short. The man had his back to her. From the pot on the counter he was using his fingers to scoop cold polenta into his mouth. Stringy, greasy hair hung down well below his collar, almost to his shoulders. He wore the rough brown clothing of a common laborer. His shirt and pants were stained with grease and caked with mud, his boots scarred and the heels worn to sharp angles.

She took a step backward at the sight, reflexively clutched her hand to the top of her robe to ensure it hadn't gapped. None of these actions, including the sharp intake of breath, made much noise, but they—or perhaps it was her very presence, the addition of mass to the surrounding space—were sufficient to cause the man to whirl and face her.

"It's me, Mama, don't be frightened!" the man said, and in an instant she ran to him, opening her arms wide. Tears flooded her eyes before she could cross the room. She hugged him and babbled his name and the words of God and gratitude.

"I'm fine, Mama," he said in a hoarse but reassuring voice as he held her. "Really, everything is all right."

She pushed him to arms length, to see him, to make her own assessment. Beneath the grime he appeared to be whole. He had grown a beard. The exposed skin of his face was raw and weathered. But it was her son. It was Alfredo, whom everyone had mentally placed in a grave alongside Luca.

She ran to call the others.

✻ ✻ ✻

ALFREDO INSISTED THAT there was to be no special celebration to mark his homecoming. He said it would be unseemly to celebrate when so many of his comrades had suffered and still suffered. He spoke only in generalities about the brutality of the fighting and the severity of the conditions in which it occurred. Clearly, there was more to be told, but the family didn't press him. As if they knew not to ask, they especially didn't press for an explanation of the circumstances of his return or the disheveled condition in which Mama found him. He looked reasonably well when he was cleaned up and had rested. He had lost a good deal of weigh. Because he was slightly built to begin with, this wasn't obvious until he put on his old clothes, which now hung off him.

The most noticeable physical change, however, was the limp with which he walked and the pain that so clearly accompanied it. Especially when he might have thought he was not being observed, the grimaces would appear, and although perhaps he thought he hid it, his face constantly wore the strained, fatigued appearance of chronic pain.

Daniel offered to examine him, of course, but Alfredo refused. He was fine, he said, merely in need of some rest and good food. The limp was the result of a broken foot, which hadn't had time to mend properly. Daniel said it should be looked at by someone, even if not himself, but Alfredo continued to put him off. The most Daniel was able to secure was Alfredo's a promise that he would not hesitate to call on him if the pain became worse.

Although Mama and Antonio were concerned about Alfredo—and especially about the moroseness that seemed to have replaced his formerly optimistic demeanor—their relief at having him home was elemental. This son, at least, had been spared.

In spite of his refusal of any kind of celebration in his honor, as word of Alfredo's return inevitably spread around the small town, there was no way he could keep his parents from inviting people to drop by. To those who asked, Alfredo responded that he was home on extended leave. He had been wounded in the fighting, he said—though he was vague about the nature of the wound, the limp was sufficient proof—and the terrible conditions had prevented him from healing properly at the front. Now that the victory over Greece was secured, he was permitted to get the necessary attention at home.

Antonio made a special point of calling Bruno Buca to thank him for whatever role he might have played in the happy ending. It had been a difficult call, requiring the right balance of happiness, gratitude and solicitude for the still-grieving Bucas. Antonio invited Bruno to stop by whenever he felt up to it.

Bruno said he would, and on a Saturday afternoon not long thereafter he came to the door. He appeared sleepless and drawn, but was dressed neatly as usual, in a handsome hound's-tooth check sports coat. He was accompanied by Renata, herself looking pinched and fatigued, and her daughter, Chiara, who held her hand.

Antonio embraced them in turn. He picked up Chiara and gave her a warm kiss that startled the child and made her reach for Renata.

"It's such a nice day," Renata said, "I insisted Father join us for a stroll. He simply had to get out of the house."

"Of course," Antonio responded, leading them into the sitting room. "This was an excellent choice of destination. Only Alfredo is home with me at the moment, but I suppose he's the one you'd especially like to see." He handed Chiara back to Renata and went to find him.

A few moments later, the two of them returned. Alfredo, dressed in shiny corduroy pants and an old, pilled sweater, limped obviously toward Bruno and Renata, who rose to embrace him. Almost in unison they said how wonderful it was that Alfredo made it home. "Your parents were very worried about you," Bruno said.

"I know. I was shocked to hear about Stefano. I was planning on coming to pay my condolences," he added, weakly.

"I'm sure you would have," Renata responded in a voice that might have contained a note of disbelief or reproach.

"These are difficult times," Antonio offered, filling a momentary silence.

"Indeed they are," Bruno agreed. "We have all sacrificed. Thankfully, we can take solace that our sacrifices haven't gone for naught," he added, turning to Alfredo, who seemed taken aback at being called upon to add his concurrence.

Alfredo nodded.

Renata looked at him curiously, but was distracted by Chiara, who had begun to fuss.

"At least we have secured victory," Bruno went on, looking again to Alfredo for agreement. "Albania and Greece are secure. The country continues on its path to greatness. Our families have contributed to that."

Alfredo again gave a slight nod and smiled thinly.

"We must be content with that as our reward, I'm afraid," Antonio said, filling another awkward silence. "Besides our losses of Stefano and Luca, Alfredo has had a hard time—as you can see," he added, as if to suggest that Alfredo should be excused for his reticence. But Bruno and Renata both wore an expression that suggested dissatisfaction, an expectation unmet.

At Antonio's prompting, the four went on to talk about recent events in the community. Births, deaths, so and so off to university or the army. There were the Christmas and New Year holiday celebrations that Alfredo had missed. But with seeming inevitability, the Bucas brought the conversation around to the affirmation they sought from Alfredo. "A delightful time, Christmas was," Bruno said, "even though this year some traditional foods were harder to come by. We didn't realize then how small a sacrifice that was compared to what lay ahead. But that is what sacrifice is about—securing the future—is it not, Alfredo?"

Once again, Alfredo smiled thinly. "Yes," he said. "That is what sacrifice is for."

As each round of the conversation thus came back to the point where Alfredo was expected to show, but withheld, enthusiastic agreement, greater irritation became evident in the Bucas' faces, while greater embarrassment became evident in Antonio's as he would look hopefully toward Alfredo for relief. Still, Alfredo only smiled politely.

"I think it's time to be on our way, Father," Renata said after a time.

"Yes, yes," Bruno responded a little absently, and then, as if he had marshaled his strength for a final assault, "I was hoping to hear more from Alfredo about his experiences . . . about his service."

Alfredo looked at Bruno evenly. "You'll forgive me, Signor Buca, I'd prefer not to discuss my experiences."

"But it's important that our young men returned from the war convey the right message to those yet to serve."

"You do agree that this is important, do you not?" Renata interjected to spare her father the need to press in the face of yet another silence. "You do agree?" she said again.

"Since you ask, I'm afraid I don't."

Bruno tapped his foot at an ever faster rate. "How can you not agree?" he blurted at last. "My son and your brother have given their lives to our cause."

Now it was Alfredo who could not, or would not, contain himself or his bitterness. "That may be. Unfortunately for all of us, to say one has paid a million lire for an empty bottle of olive oil doesn't put any more oil into the bottle."

Bruno stood, the veins in his neck pulsing. "That is outrageous!" he said between gritted teeth as his daughter, no less distraught, attempted to calm him.

"But true nonetheless," Alfredo said evenly. "I have no desire to talk about the hell I experienced, because those of us who went through it—as opposed to those who sat behind and cheered as if it were a football match—inevitably came to the realization that we were serving not a worthy national goal but a fantasy perpetrated by the Duce, the biggest fool of them all."

"Alfredo!" Antonio interjected.

"I'm sorry, Father. I had no intention of saying these things. But if Signor Buca and Renata insist on the truth, I won't stand here and lie to them. "The truth is, we have sacrificed for nothing. My brother died for an absurd conquest in Africa—you have no idea how much it grieves me to say that, Father—and your son, Signor Buca, my friend, Stefano, wasted his life in an equal farce in Greece. We have been lied to by our leaders, we have been tied to the fortunes of the absurd German and his Italian puppet, and our forces have been all but abandoned in their hour of need." And with that, Alfredo left the room, each limping step an emphatic syncopation.

"You're not fit to wear the uniform!" Bruno called after him, and he, Renata, and his granddaughter left the house.

* * *

IN THE FOLLOWING days, Alfredo reverted to the reticence that preceded his outburst with the Bucas. Nevertheless, there was also a pronounced change as his mood became more sullen and angry, as if whatever he had been holding inside, having boiled over, now continued to simmer past the point of containment. With long nights of rest he became, not rested, but increasingly irritable and snappish. He declined all offers to be entertained and refused to visit the clubs and bars he had once enjoyed. His physical actions became impulsive. A book in which he seemed to be absorbed would be suddenly shut and tossed onto a nearby table. Innocent, even kind questions, drew barbed responses.

When Daniel mentioned these things to Paola, she said she, too, had observed them but professed to be unconcerned. "If there's anything to tell, I'm sure Alfredo will tell it." And, for one of the only times Daniel could recall Paola denying, rather than confronting something, she added, "We shouldn't look for trouble where none exists."

It was the worsening pain in his leg and the onset of headaches—searing, blinding things—that finally convinced Alfredo to allow Daniel to examine him. Even then, the course of events was not simple. Before the appointed time, Alfredo began to feel better and told Daniel the examination was no longer necessary. They went through two more cycles of pain and broken appointments before Daniel, insinuating himself as family as much as medical practitioner, all but forced Alfredo into the examination room.

Once inside, Alfredo became more compliant. He began to disrobe as ordered, removing his shirt and placing it on a hook on the back of the door. On his chest and arms Alfredo still had the remnants of deep yellow-green bruises, as well as the marks of lice and bug bites everywhere. Daniel wasn't surprised. After all, he had seen much worse.

Daniel peered into Alfredo's eyes, mouth and ears, and held a stethoscope to his chest and his back. He asked Alfredo to remove his trousers and lie back on the examination table, which he did but without removing his shoes and socks. "Your feet are cold?" Daniel asked as he palpated and listened.

Alfredo turned his face to the wall.

"I think I should take a look at them," Daniel said softly. He expected Alfredo to resist, but he remained silent.

Daniel removed the left shoe and sock. Immediately he could see that at one time the foot had been frostbitten. The toenails were missing, and thick crusted patches remained where once there had been blisters. Still, there seemed to be no permanent damage, and he said so to Alfredo, who still said nothing. He tensed as Daniel began to remove the right shoe.

When the shoe came off Daniel could see crumpled newspaper stuffed into the toe. There was dead space in the sock. Gently, as Alfredo remained rigid, Daniel peeled it off. Only the big toe remained, and it was badly scarred.

"How did this happen?" Daniel asked. When there was no response he said, "The toes were obviously removed surgically. Where? How?"

Alfredo kept his head turned to the wall. "Some butcher who called himself a surgeon."

Daniel probed the wounds, was relieved to see Alfredo flinch. "You've got reasonably good nerve function. If it makes you feel any better, the surgeon wasn't such a butcher. I've seen much worse from battlefield operations. Frostbite, I presume."

Alfredo nodded slightly.

Daniel brought a lamp close. He turned the mangled foot, examining it from various angles, then asked Alfredo to roll onto his back. He held both feet by the heels, comparing them. His hands moved up from the ankles to the calves and back down. "Sit up," he instructed, and he helped Alfredo swing his legs off the examination table.

Daniel looked into Alfredo's eyes. "Listen to me," he said evenly, clinically, "I understand how terrible this must be for you. The good thing is that you're healing well. The surgeon didn't do a pretty job—they never do in a front line hospital—but that can be improved upon later. The important thing is that there's no sign of invasive infection and you're regaining nerve function. That in itself may be part of the problem you're experiencing. When there's so much trauma involved, the nerves behave in unpredictable ways. It can be very painful, but we should be able to do some things to alleviate that. Believe me, it could be worse. I've seen cases of frostbite that were so bad the toes didn't have to be removed, they came off with the boot."

Alfredo nodded.

"The rest of you looks pretty good, too. The bug bites and bruises are healing." Daniel tried for a smile. "You're malnourished, but I imagine Mama will take care of that before long."

Still Alfredo stared ahead, vacantly, with no acknowledgement that there was some good in the news he was hearing.

"I can't be certain about the headaches," Daniel said. "They could be a result of nerve damage or a reaction to the cold or changes in diet. It's hard to tell at this stage. They may very well go away on their own. In the meantime, we'll do our best to control the pain." Once again, Alfredo only nodded.

"And they could be caused by whatever you're bottling up inside," Daniel added in a soft voice. "I would have a much better chance of helping you if you would talk to me." When there was no response he told Alfredo he could get dressed and helped him down from the table. "At the very least I can fix up something for you that will work better than newspapers in the shoe."

Alfredo shrugged. He slipped into his clothes. "Thank you," he said, finally, and turned to go.

With Alfredo's hand on the doorknob, Daniel tried one more time. "You know, it's obvious to more people than me that the source of your suffering is not only physical."

To Daniel's surprise, Alfredo turned around slowly and faced him. "If I were to talk to you, could I talk to you as my doctor and not as my brother-in-law?"

"If you like."

"And you wouldn't tell even Paola?"

"Not if you didn't want me to."

"Or my parents or . . . anyone else."

"No."

Alfredo nodded, turned to go. Then, still facing the door, he stopped and hung his head.

~ ~ ~ ~ ~

~ ~ ~

Chapter 21

"MY DIVISION WAS ONE of the first into Greece," Alfredo began as he took a seat opposite Daniel. "We were very proud of that. In my unit in particular spirit was very high. We sang as we marched. The Greeks were going to get what was coming to them. There was no doubt about that. We were well prepared, too. Supply lorries would pass us as we marched, and we knew we would have all the food and equipment we would need.

"The first shock was our discovery that the Greeks can fight like hell. We had been told for weeks by our officers that, especially in the hinterland, resistance would be light—that the Greeks would concentrate on defending their cities. Even now it's hard to know whether the officers were lying bastards or just stupid.

"Let me tell you just how stupid they were," Alfredo said, picking up steam as he went. "In early November three units, mine included, were making their way through a ravine. We had been assured that it was safe to do so. The area was clear. Intelligence said the Greeks had pulled back to defend a new line. So I can tell you we were more than a little surprised when the damned Greeks seemed to open up on us from everywhere. Within an hour, half of the men were shot to hell.

"We took cover behind some rocks. The dead were left out in the open. We did our best to help our wounded. But the Greeks had the high ground— and don't ever let anyone try to convince you Greeks can't shoot straight— and they used the wounded guys as bait. So we lost more of our comrades that way. The only medic we had waved a white flag and pointed to the red cross on his uniform. The bastards shot him in the head.

"We managed to radio for help. We cheered when two of our planes appeared overhead. They dropped some bombs on God knows what, strafed some rocks, and took off. We radioed again, and the imbecile on the other end said we should hold on, two planes would be there shortly. The radioman screams, 'you mean two more planes?' And the idiot says, 'Oh, you mean they've already come? Then they'll have to refuel and rearm.' So that was the end of our air cover.

"The rocks gave us good protection, but we were still right in the middle of the ravine and we knew we had to get the hell out of there somehow. We managed to re-form into two units. Two lieutenants were left, so each took one of the units. But they couldn't agree on which way to go. One of them wanted to fall back, the other to press on. So rather than come to an agreement, the stupid asses decided we would split up; each would take his unit in an opposite direction. My lieutenant was the one who wanted to go ahead. To this day I don't know for sure who was right. I don't know if any of the ones who retreated survived."

Alfredo stopped to collect his thoughts. "It's hard to believe things could get worse than that day. I don't even know where to begin."

"What happened when you reached the other end of the ravine?" Daniel prompted.

"At first, we were jubilant just to have made it through. We ran into some units that had come through the long way around. They were in good shape. We re-formed units again. Things were looking up.

"The next day it was back to reality. It started to rain like hell. It was a cold rain, the kind that lets you know snow isn't far behind. We were still in our summer uniforms. We were soaked and cold, and the wind whipped our faces. But we pressed on.

"Now the Greeks began to harass us. They didn't oppose us in force, but it seemed like they had snipers everywhere. The rain wouldn't let up, and within a few days everything was mud. Sleeping was impossible. There was nowhere to take shelter. We had no tents. A supply convoy got through, but the stupid bastards didn't have anything we needed. Assholes! When the rain kept up, everything—including, we assumed, the supply lorries, since we never saw any more of them—started to become bogged down in the mud. We became filthy, of course, and the lice literally ate us alive, as you could still see."

166

Daniel nodded.

"But none of this," Alfredo continued, "absolutely none of this did us in like the cold. The temperatures dropped like an anvil. Our stupid guns, which first jammed because we couldn't keep the mud and water out, now froze up. Daniel, it was stupefying just how unprepared we were for the weather. It was impossible not to realize how badly our brilliant generals had fucked up in every way. They so obviously thought—if they thought at all—we would have the whole campaign wrapped up in a matter of weeks.

"And let's not forget the Greeks. It seems never to have occurred to anyone on our side that they might fight like the devil for their own territory—and that they might even have warm coats and boots to do it in! In the meantime, our hands were so swollen with cold, we could barely get our fingers into the trigger guards. But if you think our boys lacked bravery, think again! When we could barely walk, we charged! Our dumb shits of officers would give the order, and we'd charge! We were shot to hell but that didn't keep us from attacking. I learned an important lesson, Daniel. Do you know what it was?"

Before Daniel could respond, Alfredo went on. "Do you know the difference between the commands, 'Charge!' and 'Follow Me!'? Well I'll tell you. The first one is what Italian officers say from the rear. The second is what the Greek commanders yelled when they attacked us."

"I have a question for you, Alfredo, because something isn't adding up for me."

The momentum Alfredo had built in the telling of his story stopped, he looked at Daniel warily. "What?"

"I understand how difficult all this must have been for you. I've heard similar stories from some of my other patients. What I don't understand is why you've sworn me to secrecy. From everything I've heard so far, you should be proud just to have survived. So what haven't you told me?"

Alfredo was silent. He stared at the floor.

"How did you lose your toes?"

Alfredo looked up. "Oh, that's it! I see what you must be thinking! You think I shot them off on purpose! Is that it?"

"No. I could see from your feet that's not what happened."

Alfredo brooded for a minute, then looked at Daniel again. "All right. What happened was this: One day, I and two other guys accidentally got separated from the rest of the unit—not that there were so many left by now, maybe twenty-five of us in all. We knew the others weren't far away, but the visibility was shit. We saw a hollowed out place in the rocks that looked like it might give us some shelter from the wind. I can't tell you how cold we were, and night was falling fast. We couldn't build fires because the Greeks would pick us off.

"So the three of us spent the night in this hollow—that's all it was. It didn't qualify as a cave, it was really just a depression in the rock. As we'd gotten used to doing, we slept close to one another to get any warmth we could. At dawn we woke up to the sound of gunfire. We assumed it was coming from where the rest of our comrades were. It wasn't far off. We headed in that direction, but with the ice and snow, it was slow going.

"By the time we got to the area we thought the firing was coming from it was quiet. Then we came to the top of a rise and were stunned to see, below, the bodies of our comrades. I don't know how many, exactly, but it must have been almost all of them. Some Greek soldiers—they had on a strange combination of uniforms, so maybe they were guerrillas, I don't know— were going through the bodies, kicking them, prodding them with their guns, and so forth. Some of the Greeks were searching through pockets for whatever they could take, the bastards.

"We weren't concealed at this point, and let me tell you, between the shock of what we were seeing and the pitiful state we were in, we weren't moving very fast. Before we knew it some of the Greeks spotted us and began to shoot. We hit the ground and began to shoot back, but they were crawling out of the woods now and there was no way they weren't going to overwhelm us.

"The three of us looked at each other. We all had the same thought. We'd surrender. That was the only chance we had. From our prone position, Tisara, one of the guys I was with, the other was called Panzo, starts yelling—in Greek, no less—for them to stop, we surrender, and so on. But they didn't stop, and the three of us threw our rifles out in front of us to make sure they understood. It was then that they stopped shooting. The closest ones were still maybe thirty yards away, and we began to stand with our hands in the air.

"All of a sudden I see first Panzo, then Tisara blown away. I leapt backwards, down the hill we came up. I rolled and ran between the trees like

I was possessed. For once, the ice probably worked in my favor, because I was sliding and falling downhill faster than the Greeks could get up to the ridge and follow me down. They took a few shots at me but none came close. By now their hearts probably weren't in the chase. What was one more dead Italian? It wasn't worth the effort."

"Then what happened?"

"Everything I just told you happened without thinking. I just reacted. But then reality hit me. I was lost in enemy territory. I was alone. I'd abandoned the small amount of gear I had, including the few bits of food, and my rifle of course. All I knew was that I wanted to get home. I wanted to live. I wanted to get warm. I wanted to eat something. I would have surrendered for these things, but after what had just happened when the three of us tried to give ourselves up even that seemed impossible.

"I did have a compass, and I did have a general idea of where our lines were—or had been, at any rate. But I couldn't move during the day, only at night. The only thing I was able to accomplish during the day was occasionally to find a place that was sunny enough to melt some snow for drinking water and get some sleep.

"I wandered like this for three days. My feet were already in bad shape, but then I took a step onto what looked like solid ice. The ice gave way and my right foot got drenched. The next day it got even colder. I could barely walk. I couldn't even think about taking off the boots to inspect my feet. I didn't have to anyway—I knew I was really in trouble. I fashioned a crutch out of a fallen branch. Still, I pushed myself forward, one step at a time.

"On the third day, I made it to a main road that I prayed was still under our control. That was when one of our lorries came by. I should have been jubilant, but that would have taken more energy than I had. They stuffed me inside and got me back to a medical tent. That's where my toes came off, but to tell the truth I was too out of it to know what was happening, or to care."

Daniel looked at Alfredo and cocked his head. "I still don't understand what you're ashamed of. It sounds as if you acquitted yourself admirably."

Alfredo said softly, "I had to tell you all of this so you would understand what happened next."

"Go on."

"I was out of my head for some time. An orderly told me it was a week before I started to come back. It took about another week for things really to

169

come into focus. I started hobbling around on crutches. The pain was tough to take. I was still incredibly depressed. On top of the hell I'd been through I got to see how chewed up other soldiers were. I had expected to be evacuated to a real hospital, but that didn't happen. This was probably before the Germans stepped in to help us, because people were talking about how we were short of everything, including lorries and what not, so I assumed I would just have to stay put for a while. In any case, my war was over.

"At least that's what I thought. All of a sudden I start hearing guys in the tent talk about people being patched up and sent back into the line. I'm not talking about guys with little wounds. I'm talking about guys like me who had parts missing. Then one day a doctor comes in to take a look at me. He says my foot is healing well and that it won't be long before they'll be able to fit me with a special shoe and send me back out there. He says this like it's good news, like I'm supposed to be happy.

"At first, I didn't think he was serious. But I kept hearing more and more talk in the tent about how bad things were and how guys were being sent back out." Alfredo's voice had changed to a hoarse whisper. "I couldn't do it, Daniel. I just couldn't. Whatever I had to do, I just couldn't go out there again."

"So you went missing," Daniel said.

Alfredo nodded. "There were some civilians working in the camp. They had a dressing area. I stole some clothes and took off."

"How long did it take to get back here?"

"A long time. Weeks. I lost track. I had to be careful. They're looking for deserters." Alfredo stopped suddenly, as if he had shocked himself to hear the word out loud. "For all I've given, I suppose that's what I am now," he said softly with pain in his eyes. "After all I've given," he repeated hollowly, "and even knowing now how fucked up this country is, I'm still ashamed. I feel like a disgrace. Isn't that something?"

At this, tears came to his eyes.

* * *

THREE DAYS LATER, Paola was shopping for that night's supper when she ran into Renata Buca. The coldness of their greeting left no doubt that the incident that had occurred when she and her father visited had taken a toll. They made small talk for a minute, and that might have been the end of it but for a parting remark.

"Oh, I almost forgot," Renata said after they had made their goodbyes. "Father told me he received an interesting phone call yesterday. It was from a friend of his, a Captain Greve. It seems that, among other things, the captain called to say he was sorry that he had not been able to locate Alfredo, as my father had asked some time earlier. The captain said he wanted to let him know this before he contacted your family to tell you that he had no choice but to list Alfredo as missing. Of course, my father was happy to share the news that Alfredo is home, safe and sound!"

The import of this message only became clear to Paola when she related it casually to Daniel and Alfredo that evening, along with her observation that everything Renata had said was infused with her usual malice.

The next morning, Alfredo was gone.

~ ~ ~ ~ ~

~ ~ ~

Chapter 22

OA   14 May 1943

I STILL DON'T KNOW how it happened, but I received a letter from Nora in America. It must have followed a circuitous route, indeed! It's dated 26 November 1942 and was opened at least twice by censors.

Nora and Victoria are well. There's not much news about Nora, herself, which isn't surprising, as she has become less communicative over the years. I suppose I have been less communicative as well. Strange to say, most of a decade has somehow slipped away. The distance and my work are partly to blame, and there is my life with Paola and the children, and, of course, the war. In the meantime, we tend to think time has stood still for the people we knew back when.

Nora does allude to a new man in her life, which surprised me even though I know it should not. Being logical about it, the real surprise is that a woman possessing as many charms as Nora should not have found someone long ago. Nora also says in her letter that, thankfully, she and her family have been spared any tragedy. So far, no one close has been lost in the fighting.

Victoria is almost thirteen now. Nora included a photo of her taken at school. She's dressed in her school uniform—gray pleated skirt, white blouse, blue blazer with the school's shield over her heart—more handsome than pretty (I'm afraid she looks more like me than Nora), with a keen intelligence in her eyes. She's a good student, Nora says. Somehow she's become quite grown up. It pains me deeply to say it, but if I met her on the street, I wouldn't know my own daughter. Who could have predicted such a thing? When Victoria was born, I assumed without question that I would be simply a normal, fatherly part of her growing up. Now, amid this infernal war, it seems too much to hope for the simple pleasure of seeing her before she is completely grown.

The impetus for Nora's writing me is amusing. It seems she received a letter from the draft board directing me to report for an induction physical! Surely, at my age, they have the wrong person in mind. Maybe the standards for physicians are different. Either way, if they can get to me, I'll report!

Actually, Americans arriving here may not be so far-fetched. Talk is everywhere about an Allied invasion of Italy. Fascist propaganda notwithstanding, for several months it's been clear to almost everyone that the Allies have gained the upper hand. The Nazis are in retreat in the east, having suffered a debacle at Stalingrad. It's an open secret that many Italians were lost—killed, wounded or captured—on the Russian front. The Allies are in control in North Africa and threatening Italy itself. Amazingly, if I'm reading the tea leaves right, that prospect seems to be welcome to many people here. After twenty years of Fascist misrule, people are fed up. It's not just the usual deprivations of wartime, either—the shortages, the rationing, and so forth. The fundamental emptiness of the Fascist program, not to mention its brutality, is apparent to many. It's finally dawned on Italians that they've bet on the wrong horse and are about to lose big.

Of course, the Fascists aren't necessarily rolling over. While some of them are hedging their bets by cozying up to the anti-Fascists who are themselves just now venturing forth in greater numbers, others are digging in. That could make them even more dangerous, at least in the short run. Among our neighbors, the dividing line is clear. The Bucas, with whom we've had very little to do since Alfredo ran off, seem to have opted for the diehard position—or in any event I've seen no outward sign of their wavering. They travel conspicuously with both the Blackshirts and the Germans. It will be interesting to see whether they waver if the Duce's declining fortunes don't turn around.

On the other hand, the Rosettis have become increasingly outspoken in their opposition to the party. As one might expect, that goes doubly for Paola, whom I must constantly caution not to be premature in her anti-Fascist campaigning. The Rosettis' sacrifice of Luca provides the family with a measure of political cover, but that has been diminishing steadily in the face of Italy's worsening military position, the ever-increasing commonness of such loss, the business of Alfredo's desertion and flight (which the Bucas seem to take pleasure in keeping as current news around town), and of course, the frequently intemperate remarks of my darling wife.

My own status, strangely ambiguous at best, seems to be improving. Perhaps how one treats an American in these times is a barometer of public sentiment toward the Fascists and the war. Lord knows there have been anxious moments. Within days of the U.S. entry into the war I was visited by a member of the carabinieri*, who informed me that my status as an American citizen (even one married to an Italian) was something they would be required "to monitor." I am supposed to report to the local police, the* vigile*, once a week, and I need special permission to travel more than fifty kilometers from home.*

For the first few weeks I complied with these demands. But this is Italy, after all, and often as not such things are honored in the breach. The local police to whom I reported already knew me (one of the men is a patient), so they treated my calls as a social event. No one got too upset if I was too busy to report for a week, and then for a few weeks, and so on. An amusing moment occurred when a new officer who apparently hadn't gotten the word came to my office, presumably for the purpose of reading me the riot act for being overdue. My patients leaped to my defense and practically ran him out of the office! It may be my imagination, but now, as things deteriorate for Italy and the Fascists are in ever worse odor, the people around here seem to be cozying up to me. I suppose they figure an American might come in handy one of these days. Never let it be said of an Italian that he doesn't watch which way the wind is blowing!

In a strange way we are insulated from the swirl of events around us. There are hardships, of course. Many things are rationed or unavailable, as one would expect in wartime. The same would be true if I were at home. Traveling is difficult, especially given my political status. I miss the political activities I engaged in before the war, such as the work I did for the League, even though that work seems to have been for naught.

But these are trivial things in such times as these. There is much for which we must be grateful. Paola and the children are in good health. Francesco is five and showing signs of becoming an actual person! He's bright, active but not especially athletic. Isabella is a delightful, amazingly sweet-tempered baby. We have sufficient money so that we are not deprived of necessities. There is no shortage of useful work for me to do. If I become complacent, I need do no more than treat one of my patients who has returned (one of the few who has returned, it would seem) from Russia to be reminded of just how horrific this war is for so many people. Beyond the loss of Luca, which sometimes seems very long ago, and the uncertain whereabouts of Alfredo, our family has been spared much of that. Paola sometimes says she feels guilty that she's the reason I'm stuck here. But she may have been right to insist on coming. This may be the safest place for our family to ride out the war, after all.

Victoria put down the journal and looked off into space. There it was—the natural tension of historical discovery: elation at the ability of the historian to inhabit, however briefly and superficially, another human being's skin; poignancy over the things known by the historian but not by the subject of the inquiry—the godlike knowing of how things turned out and the yearning to be a puppeteer. Things would get much worse for Daniel, Paola, and their children. The historian knew that; the actors didn't.

Also, he mentioned her, Victoria. Across all this time there he was, her natural father with whom she had almost no connection, this oddly familiar stranger mentioned her. Did it really pain him, as he said, that he wouldn't have recognized her, or is that just what one says in the circumstances?

Was it really possible that even now she was a little hurt at being called more handsome than pretty? He expended so few words on her, could he have not chosen others? Yet she had to admit, the words were on the mark. She was more handsome than pretty. The keen intelligence in her eyes was manifested in her being a good student. But these things aren't necessarily assets in a thirteen-year-old girl, and indeed they were not for Victoria, who remembered herself at that time as being lonely and unpopular. She had friends, but they were girls much like herself, whereas the popular girls, while they didn't exactly spurn her, didn't welcome her either. It was not until she was older that handsomeness balanced prettiness and keen intelligence began to count for something socially.

But then, Daniel didn't know any of this. He confined his thoughts of her to a few sentences prompted by her mother's letter. And, wonder of wonders, after all this time, she was miffed! Miffed over being called more handsome than pretty! The small, but potent Calvinist streak in her, which she ascribed to her mother's side of the family and which she had spent a lifetime battling, would permit her only a moment of self-pity before she reminded herself how fortunate she had been to escape the horrors of the war. Here she was in Italy, surrounded by people, not least Francesco and Chiara, who were not so fortunate. Would she even be alive today if Daniel had stayed married to her mother? Then again, move one piece on the chessboard and everything changes. If they had stayed together there would be no Francesco, and she herself might have siblings conceived sometime in the 1930s, perhaps after Daniel and Nora were forced to give up on Europe and return to America. Instead, the man Nora only alluded to in her letter soon after became Victoria's stepfather, while Daniel and his new family entered the regions of suffering and death.

By now she had read enough of Daniel's journals to not be surprised by the contradictory accounts of the Bucas' place in these events. One could be forgiven for concluding that Daniel then, and Chiara now, were referring to different people. Victoria had to allow for the possibility that things had changed subsequently. There was still much to read. In the meantime, the subtle openings she created for Chiara to alter her version were met with steadfastly guileless recounting of the Bucas' honor, bravery and tragedy. On the other hand, what else could be expected? After all, the impetus for Chiara's work, and the reason for Victoria's presence, was to pay tribute to the righteous, and above all that meant the Buca family.

OA   5 June 1943

An extraordinary thing happened today. As it was a lovely Saturday, Paola and I decided to go hiking in the woods around Borgo a Mozzano. We intended to take the children, but Isabella has the sniffles and Paola's mother overruled the doctor's judgment that it wouldn't hurt to take her out. So only Francesco came with us (I'm sure he enjoyed having us to himself).

We decided to take a little-used trail above Borgo that Paola knew. It was a steep climb—hard on Francesco's short legs—and well designed to ensure we would appreciate a rewarding lunch.

As we neared the top of our ascent, where we had agreed we would turn around and take a connecting path back down the mountain, a man with a rifle stepped out from behind a tree and blocked our way. The man had a thick beard and was dressed in mismatched military clothing. He pointed the rifle at us and ordered us to stop, but said nothing else. Francesco began to whimper. I tried to reassure him and brought him around behind me to shield him, while Paola, using what I have learned to recognize as her gutter Italian, demanded to know what the hell the man was doing.

He remained silent and motioned to us to sit in a small clearing a few yards away. We did so, and before long we were joined by three other men, all of whom were dressed like the one who stopped us and also were armed. Two of them had pistols strapped to their waists in addition to their rifles.

One of the men—I call him a man but he looked no older than seventeen— motioned to the others to lower their weapons. "What are you doing here?" he asked in a no-nonsense voice.

I was determined to keep the situation calm. "We're out for a hike, that's all."

"Why here?"

"Why not here?" Paola retorted.

The man ignored her, turned to me. "Just out for a hike you say?"

"Yes." In the distance I could see two other men approaching.

"Or maybe you intend to tell the Fascists what you see."

"If you hadn't stopped us, there would have been nothing to tell even if we wanted to," Paola said, without compromise.

The two new men came closer, and suddenly I knew everything would turn out all right. One of them was Alfredo.

When Paola realized who he was, she leaped to her feet and ran to him, causing the others to raise their guns.

Of course, the mood lightened considerably once Alfredo identified us. There was a brief moment of tension as one of the men, whom we later learned was a not entirely rational Croat named Niko, asked, "What about the boy? There's no telling what a child might say."

I started to give him our assurances that Francesco would do nothing to jeopardize the group—and of course, the very idea was absurd, how could he jeopardize anyone?—but Alfredo stepped in and finished the declaration for me. The expression on Niko's face said that he wasn't convinced, but he didn't raise the matter again.

Alfredo still walked with a limp, as he always would, but otherwise appeared fit. We were not completely surprised to find him well, as he had sent us cryptic notes from time to time since he ran away. But we had no idea where he was.

We accompanied the men to a small farmhouse nearby, which was hidden by the dense sylvan growth of summer. The exterior of the house was full of mold, but inside it was dry with just a hint of mustiness. Makeshift mattresses were scattered around the periphery of the main room. A large distressed wooden table and chairs occupied the center.

Over a misto of sausages, cheese, olives and bread we talked about the situation in the country. Alfredo said it was clear the Fascists' days were numbered. It wouldn't be long before he and the others would come out of hiding and pay the squadristi back in kind. And their friends, too, he added in what we took as a not very veiled allusion to the Bucas.

One of the partisans, whom we later heard referred to as deputy commander Lazio and who had been silent until then, said to me, "You look fit. Why don't you join us and end up on the winning side?"

"We already are on the winning side," Paola declared. "As my brother can attest."

Lazio shrugged. "There are those who support us, and there are those who support us. The distinctions will become clear with time."

I smiled at him. "I'm a little old for your band, don't you think? I fought in the last war," I added, not bothering to mention the oath I had sworn to myself as a result never again to fire a gun in anger. To my surprise—Alfredo obviously had talked about me before—Lazio seemed ready for my answer.

"Doctors are different. We can always use a doctor."

"So can our town," Paola interjected.

"It will help to have an American with us when the Americans come through here," Niko said, ignoring her.

Alfredo looked on in silence, presumably content to let others do the recruiting while he avoided the wrath of his sister.

"Anyway," Lazio said, issuing his first smile of the day, "you're not so old. Believe me, we've seen older."

OA   10 July 1943

The Allies have landed in Sicily. Now we shall see.

OA   26 July 1943

We are euphoric! Yesterday, the king showed the kind of courage none of us thought he had and arrested Mussolini. Field Marshal Badoglio has been named head of government, though who knows what that means. We all assume that peace is imminent. Italy will pull out of the war.

When we heard the announcement we could barely contain our excitement. It was stunning. As sick of the war and the government as we were, no one imagined change could come so quickly. After putting up with Mussolini for twenty years, the king himself finally staged what can only be called, wryly, a palace coup.

For perhaps understandable reasons, the jubilation in the streets is already being marred by vengeance. The victims of the Fascists are emboldened. In town this morning the shops of some ardent Fascists (and of some not so clearly ardent) had their windows smashed. A few were looted. It's all well and good to have a new government, but will the government be able to control things in the face of pent up anger? This morning I saw one official surrounded by a group of young men who proceeded to shove and spit on him. It might be good for these men to bear in mind that the Fascists aren't dead, and many of them still retain the brutal impulses that brought them to, and kept them in, power.

The Bucas and other prominent pro-Fascist families are keeping their heads down. They've been nowhere in evidence as I've walked around. Some of their homes are shuttered tight.

One of the many unanswered questions is, what are the Germans going to do? Not that there are that many of them in this area. Still, I wonder what our friendly liaison officer, Major Eberhard, would have to say. Did the Germans expect this turn of events? I don't know what they'll do, but they'll do something. The Nazis may be a lot of things, but they're not indecisive.

OA   27 August 1943

There is much anxiety in the air as many of the events we have anticipated for the past month have failed to occur. For reasons unclear to me, the government in Rome has yet to sign an armistice. There is much speculation in the streets as to why, but no one has a good answer. Perhaps it was too much to expect that the arrest of Mussolini would be sufficient to satisfy the Allies. As far as I know, the Allied demand for unconditional surrender applies to Italy as well as Germany and Japan. This must be complicating any steps toward an armistice.

Of course, there are many Italians who want not merely to stop fighting, but to declare war on Germany. Without doubt to do so would place Italy in a better position vis-à-vis the Allies. It's a fascinating problem: how does an army stop fighting its enemy and turn overnight to fighting its friend? It must be particularly difficult for professional soldiers in whom loyalties to Germany have been inculcated over many years.

Many Italian soldiers apparently began solving the problem the day Mussolini was arrested when they simply left their units to return home. We were hopeful that Alfredo might return home to stay, but that has not happened. We did see him last week. Clearly he feels comfortable enough with the current situation to come and go. He surprised me by saying that he expected his little band of anti-Fascists to grow. When I asked him why this should be if the Fascists were out and the war over, he said he expected Italy to change sides and fight the Germans. In that case, I asked, why would the partisan groups not join (or rejoin, as the case might be) the regular army?

He explained that the various partisan groups are organizing around two basic, and often irreconcilable, political philosophies. There are the Communists, many of whom want to follow the example of Tito and Mihailovic in Yugoslavia. And there are the Republicans, like himself, who want no part of the monarchy. The king could go to hell, as far as he was concerned. The king tolerated Mussolini for twenty years and got Italy into the mess it was in. Alfredo would have nothing to do with a monarchist army, he said. He is determined to fight Germans and recalcitrant Italian Fascists on his own terms.

In the meantime, we've heard that the Germans have been hedging their bets by sending large numbers of troops through the Brenner pass into northern and central Italy. There is evidence of this close by. I've seen more Germans in Lucca than I can remember. What's more, the anti-Fascist bands that last month had become so emboldened now seem to be more discreet.

Still, the anti-Fascist sentiment remains high. The other day, Bruno Buca was roughed up in town. He wasn't seriously hurt, just shoved around and subjected to verbal insults—which I'm sure he felt keenly.

~ ~ ~ ~ ~

~ ~ ~

Chapter 23

CHIARA SEEMED TO BE lost in thought when Victoria passed the open door of her study. Nevertheless, not wishing to appear rude, Victoria gave a slight wave and said "ciao" as she went by.

"Please come in, Victoria," Chiara called.

Victoria, who had already gone a few steps down the hallway, stopped and went back. Chiara was sitting behind the large desk that faced the door. The room was filled floor to ceiling with books, one of the few places in the house where artwork did not predominate, though many of the books were art books. A large vase of yellow tulips on the desk added a welcoming cheer.

"You appeared to be busy," Victoria said from the doorway. "I hope I didn't disturb you."

"Not at all. I was only working on the program for the ceremony." The room was illuminated by sunlight streaming through the window behind Chiara, throwing her face into shadow and making it difficult to read her features. "Please come in and sit with me," Chiara added.

Victoria smiled and stepped inside. Chiara motioned to an armchair on the other side of the desk. "This is a lovely room," Victoria said, taking a seat.

"It's one of my favorite places. I believe your father may have used it sometimes when he lived here to see patients. Forgive me if I haven't been sufficiently attentive to you," Chiara went on. "I've been busier than I thought I would be preparing for the ceremony. I thought everything would be done by now."

"Please don't concern yourself with me," Victoria said with a dismissive wave. "I know how such things are. Besides, I've had lots of time to enjoy myself, and the reading I'm doing is turning out to be fascinating. Francesco said I might learn some interesting things about my father, and indeed I have."

Victoria considered whether this might be an opportune time to ask Chiara about her recollections of her family, and in particular about the tensions she had been reading about between her family and Francesco's. She settled on a more innocent question, though one she hoped might veer off down revealing paths. "One thing I've wondered about, Chiara, is how you and Francesco met and married."

Chiara smiled broadly, softening a face that might otherwise have been overly defined by the coolness of elegance. As usual, even in her daily routine she was simply but finely dressed, a single strand of pearls setting off a brightly colored print cotton dress. Her hair was meticulously done, with carefully placed streaks of silver. Her hands were perfectly manicured, her nails glossed in a dark geranium red. "Meeting Francesco was a gift from God," she said, and Victoria detected in the remark none of the shallow hyperbole or fashionable irony she was accustomed to from her New York friends when God was invoked. She was certain that, in Chiara's mouth, God was a word that required no nuance. "After my husband died and Francesco's wife died," Chiara continued, "it was as if we were both given wonderful second chances."

"That's delightful to hear. I wish I could say I was equally fortunate. There has been no one important in my life since my husband died. I'm a little confused, though, when you say you met Francesco. Didn't you always know him? You grew up practically next door to one another."

Chiara sat back in her chair. For a moment, as the sun passed behind a cloud, her face was more completely in shadow. "You might think so," she said, leaning forward again to reveal an expression of pleasure at the opportunity to talk about Francesco. "But we were, as one says, like ships passing in the night. We were both children during the war, and after the war we were rarely in the same place at the same time. As you know, for several years he traveled with his—that is, your—father."

"When you say traveled, what do you mean exactly?"

"Oh, well, you know, your father did take up his international work again. He traveled often to meetings and conferences. And he lived for a while—

Francesco too, of course—in Geneva and New York. I don't know exactly when. You should ask Francesco about it."

"Lived in New York?" Victoria repeated to make sure she had not misheard.

"Yes." Chiara's expression suggested surprise that any of this should be news to Victoria. "In the late forties or early fifties, I think. He worked at the UN, if I'm not mistaken."

Victoria had to force herself to concentrate on what Chiara was saying, so distracted was she by the thought of Daniel living in the same city and still not contacting her. When she was young it had been difficult enough to come to terms with the thought that he occasionally visited the city and did not do so. But he lived there! It seemed a slap in the face. And yet, considering how much time had passed, she was surprised at the intensity of her feelings. Perhaps all the reading she had been doing had restored a sense of connection to the time. And yes, it was true, Daniel did eventually contact her. But by then it was she who had no desire to see him.

"What about you, though? Where were you during this time?" Victoria managed to ask.

"Oh, dear," Chiara replied with a small laugh. "It would be easier to say where we were not. Milan mostly, I suppose. After the war ended, we stayed in Ponte di Maddalena for a short time. Things were awful here. My father hadn't come home yet. My mother was dead, of course, as you know, murdered the same day as my grandparents. Somehow, my older sister took charge of things. She was hardly more than a child herself. It just goes to show what one is capable of if there is no alternative. My most powerful memory is of the two of us crying for weeks without stopping."

"What about your father? Where was he when your mother died?"

"In a prisoner of war camp. Of course, I understood none of this at the time. Not long after he returned home, we moved to Milan." Chiara gave a dismissive wave. "Anyway, many years later I moved back to my family home, the one we visited. At about the same time, Francesco came back here to his home. For all practical purposes we were complete strangers. It was only after we got to know each other better that we realized just how much history our families share. And, of course, like me he had suffered terribly in the war. Do you know, for many years he refused to accept that his mother and sister were not coming home?"

"Really? Refused to talk about it?"

"Not only talk about it. He refused to admit it even to himself. For a time the doctors were concerned for his sanity."

"Amazing. When did he finally return here?"

"That's a good question. As I said, it was near the time I returned, but I don't know exactly. This house was occupied, though. There was one surviving son of the Rosettis. His name was Alfredo. He stayed here and actually raised a family of his own."

"There are references to Alfredo in the journals," Victoria offered. "Whatever happened to him?"

"Oh, Alfredo died many years ago. In the early nineteen-eighties, I think. His wife was from Lombardy. She returned there after he died. We've lost track of her, though. His children must be grown up." Chiara absently fingered the papers in front of her. "Sometimes I wonder if we might not be happier if we had less complicated histories," she said with a wistful smile.

Victoria laughed lightly. "I suppose so, but then fewer of us would be inspired to be historians." She nodded toward the papers in Chiara's hands. "How is the planning coming along? The ceremony is coming up fast."

"A little too fast. Just a week from tomorrow. I'll tell you, Victoria, I'm not sure I would have started this project if I had known how much work it would be."

"What can I do to help?" Victoria asked, feeling remiss for not volunteering sooner.

"Oh, thank you so much for offering, but really, I don't know what you could do."

Victoria nodded, reminded that one reason she'd not offered to help was the feeling she had from the beginning that this was Chiara's project alone. The proprietary air she exuded extended even to Francesco, who had followed the project's progress not with disinterest, but rather from a certain remove that suggested a desire not to interfere. "I understand," Victoria said. "There are times when it takes longer to explain something than to do it oneself."

"Exactly."

"Still, if you find yourself in need of help, I'd be only too happy to have the diversion. As much as I've enjoyed my little family history project, I sometimes feel odd about not getting out more. It's a curse of my profession,

I suppose, this shutting oneself off with the documentary remains of a previous world."

"I understand. Francesco sometimes says he spends so much time looking at paintings of landscapes and gardens, he fails to notice the real thing. Come to think of it, perhaps you can help with one thing."

Victoria smiled. *"Volentieri,"* as I think I've heard you say."

"Very good." Chiara smiled broadly. "I was thinking maybe I could tell you what the program will be and maybe read one or two of the things I plan to say—just to get a different point of view and let me know if I'm overlooking something."

"Of course, I'd be glad to read it."

"Ah, well, it's not so simple. It's all in Italian."

Victoria laughed heartily. "I would expect so," she said, bringing a self-mocking palm to her forehead.

"I'll read it to you in English."

"That would be excellent. It hadn't even occurred to me that I came all this way for the ceremony and won't be able to understand it."

"Oh, well of course I planned to have you sit next to someone who could translate. Anyway, here is what the program calls for." Chiara shuffled the papers and went through them. "The ceremony is on 25 April, Liberation Day."

Victoria nodded.

"As of course you know," Chiara affirmed quickly and went on. "We'll assemble in the town piazza at nine-thirty in the morning—that's Italian time, not German . . ."

"For this occasion in particular I should hope so," Victoria said with a laugh.

Chiara shared the joke and continued. "Yes, so sometime around nine-thirty, maybe closer to ten. The monument will have been delivered to the piazza the day before and kept covered. At ten-thirty—again, Italian time—we'll begin. Organizers and honored guests will stand on a covered stage set up for the occasion. There will be many Italian flags in evidence, of course."

"Of course."

"And flags draped from the windows around the piazza. How do you call them in English?"

"Bunting I think is what you mean."

"Ah. Then the procession will start. Everyone in the procession will be held ready in the southeast corner of the piazza. The military guard of honor comes first. There are representatives of all the military services, in dress uniform of course. We have two people each from the army, navy, and air force, and a larger contingent of local carabinieri."

Victoria was taken aback at this in light of the almost uniformly negative things she had been reading about the wartime carabinieri, but she said nothing.

"The honor guard will be followed by a marching band and a number of surviving soldiers and partisans from the war. Then local associations will come in. These are various organizations from Ponte di Maddalena and nearby towns.

"When everyone is assembled, we will begin the speeches. I will briefly welcome everyone. I hope there is a good crowd, though I'm nervous about speaking. I'm much better behind the scenes."

"I understand all too well," Victoria said sympathetically.

"But I won't say much. I'll introduce the mayor, who will do most of the speaking."

"What do you plan to say?"

"I want to give some of the reasons for the ceremony. I want to explain that it's been too long for the people of our town and the towns in the area to have gone without their sacrifices being properly observed. I want to say a few things about my parents." Chiara smiled self-consciously. "This is the main benefit of being the organizer. I can single out my family."

"What will you say about them?"

"Well, I . . ." Chiara stopped abruptly. "There's no reason to describe it. Let me read some of what I've written." She shuffled through the papers in front of her and pulled one out. She began to read, then stopped. "Ah, no, here is where it begins. Excuse me if I stumble; I'll have to translate as I go along."

"Certainly."

"Here's the main part." Chiara mouthed the words quickly, barely audibly, in Italian, then translated. "The people of this town should take satisfaction and pride in what they have overcome. Not everyone who lived here during this terrible period looks back with pride. This was a difficult time for us all, and not everyone was able to rise to the challenge."

186

As Victoria listened she thought that perhaps this would be Chiara's way of offering a rationalization of the things she had been reading about the Bucas. She wondered how much of Chiara's version was a reflection of simple denial, or even a willful desire not to know—a suspicion reinforced a few days earlier by Francesco's surprising revelation that, for all her championing of this historical commemoration, Chiara had not bothered to read through Daniel's papers.

But the notion that this might be an opportune time to broach some of these questions was quickly dashed as Chiara went on, leaving Victoria grateful she had not done so.

"My mother's dear brother, my uncle, was lost in the Balkan campaign," she said. "Then, with the end of the war in sight, my mother herself and her parents, who had distinguished themselves by their antifascist labors and sacrifices, were murdered. To this day we don't know the name of the assassin.

"But this is not a day for recrimination. This is a day for healing. Whether or not people fought nobly as my family did, everyone suffered. And the fact that we as a community survived and healed is reason enough to hold this ceremony."

When she was finished reading Chiara sat back. "What do you think?"

Despite Victoria's misgivings that what she had heard might be resented by some of those in attendance—in particular the inference some would make that their families did not behave honorably, no matter how much charity Chiara was willing to bestow in her remarks on the need to let the past rest in peace, or some who perhaps remembered the Bucas in a different light—the look of satisfaction she read on Chiara's face convinced her that the only possible critique was a positive one. "It's very moving," she said, and Chiara returned a proud smile.

~ ~ ~ ~ ~

~ ~ ~

Chapter 24

INCREASINGLY, TALK AROUND THE Rosetti family table as around so many others turned to what they had come to refer to simply, incontrovertibly, as the lost summer. This was the summer of waiting for the armistice. This was the summer of waiting for the Badoglio government to assert control.

What could be the reason for the delay? Mussolini was gone. Many of the soldiers had laid down their weapons. Indeed, they seemed everywhere to be returning to their homes. Was the king holding out for better terms from the Allies? Would Italy henceforth be neutral, or would it have to change sides? Could one do that so easily—could one change from German ally to enemy? Perhaps that was the reason for the delay. Perhaps some kind of interregnum was required. A period in which fair warning was given. A period in which Italy could, in essence, proclaim the marriage to be in trouble, on the verge of dissolution if not actually dissolved. People might be sick of the war, but even war required a certain etiquette.

Some likened Italy to a man in a duel who waits for his opponent to fire the first shot. That shot wipes the slate clean. There can be no perfidy in the riposte. Let the Germans decide whether Italy would be neutral or hostile!

Others said, but what if the first shot is a kill?

And still others said, the point is not to fight a new enemy; the point is to stop fighting.

That is impossible, their interlocutors would respond. The Allies demand unconditional surrender. Only a demonstrated willingness to join them will persuade them to treat us well. Italy must act, not merely declare itself neutral and supine.

And on it went, day after sultry day, during which time two things were becoming apparent. First, there were more German soldiers in evidence, and the prospect of their being abandoned by Italy made them resentful. There was no armistice, so there was no resolution of the Germans' status on Italian soil. Toward their former allies the Germans increasingly showed a sneering contempt and acted as occupiers.

Second, the Italian Fascists—the officials and their sympathizers—who in July were on the defensive, had as a result of the increased German presence, regained some of their swagger. At the very least they could count on the Italian genius for wind-watching to prevent all but the most extreme elements—outlaw Monarchists, Communists, and Liberal Republicans—from harassing them.

At last, the anxiety of August gave way to the depressing certainty of September. For all the anticipation, when the armistice was announced it seemed to catch everyone by surprise.

Yet, if the armistice was a surprise, the succeeding events were a shock. First, the king and his government abandoned Rome for the safety—and, no one doubted, the irrelevancy—of Brindisi.

Then, the most preposterous event of all: the German rescue of Mussolini. Surely the government could have prevented this—could have taken him with them to the south? The failure to do so could not conceivably have been an oversight. No government could be that feckless. Within days the Duce was in the embrace of the Führer and proclaiming the intention of reconstituting a government.

In Lucca, people watched in depressed silence as the proclamation went up on every wall in sight, addressed to the citizens of the city and province from Randolf, the new commander of what was referred to as the military zone of Lucca, a position assumed "in the name of the Führer." A state of emergency was declared. German soldiers harbored no hostile sentiments toward the Italian people, it said, but any attack on the Germans would be treated with utmost severity.

In case the threat wasn't clear enough, the following day new proclamations were posted warning that attempts at sabotage would be punished immediately according to the rules of war. Other proclamations followed: making German currency legal tender; reconstituting the authority of the Fascist Party under the leadership of the Duce and his Republic of the

North in Salo`, on Lake Garda; restricting travel; and setting forth requirements for new identity documents and permits.

Even more alarming, rumors began to circulate about Nazi treachery and brutality toward the Italian military. Units that had surrendered to the Germans in good faith were being sent north in boxcars to German labor camps where the conditions were appalling. Often the soldiers didn't survive the journey. Some soldiers were presented with the option of reconsecrating themselves to the Duce. Any who resisted were being treated not as prisoners of war, but as traitors. Many were summarily shot.

And still, attacks by partisans increased. Their numbers swelled as Italian soldiers, left with the choice between execution, forced labor, or renewed allegiance to Mussolini, created another alternative: guerrilla warfare. In this the partisans could often count on the covert support of their neighbors. But it did not take long before they made it clear that when they could not—when they were betrayed to the Germans—they could be as brutal as any in retribution.

*   *   *

ONE NIGHT, FOR a fleeting moment through the gauze of sleep, Daniel became aware of a sound—something dropped, perhaps, or a door closed too hard during a late-night trip to the bathroom—and tried to determine whether it required leaving the seductive warmth of the bed to investigate. Paola slept on next to him. With effort he concluded it was actually something he had heard and not dreamt, but he willed the sound into insignificance and returned to an unconcerned slumber.

In the morning he awoke as usual without the aid of an alarm clock. Paola stirred. She would give him a brief head start and then tap on the bathroom door just as he was wiping the last of the shaving soap from his face.

Downstairs, Mama had made what these days passed for coffee. Daniel drained one cup, filled another, took a thick slice of bread and honey, and went to his office.

He turned on the two table lamps in the waiting room. He had about half an hour until his first patient was due to arrive and was looking forward to the quiet time.

The light from the waiting room filtered in from behind as he opened the door to his office. Even before his hand touched the wall switch he could see that something was amiss. His routine was to carefully clean and organize

190

the office before he left for the day. He liked arriving to a well-prepared space, hated having to begin the day cleaning.

His hand stopped at the switch. As he scanned the room, light from the waiting room behind him glinted off the glass door of the cabinet that held surgical supplies. The cabinet was open. There was the shadow of something large on the examination table.

He stepped back into the waiting room and put down the cup and bread. As a precaution he stood on the waiting room side of the door and reached around, feeling for the light switch on the wall.

He found the switch, took a breath in anticipation of whatever might happen when he turned it on, and flicked it upward.

Nothing. He peered into the room, now brightly illuminated. Cotton wool and surgical dressings were scattered on the floor below the open cabinet. He could see now that what he thought was a shadow on the examination table was in fact the body of a man. He hadn't moved.

Daniel approached slowly. The man was heavily bearded. His skin had an unnatural pallor, the color of blanched ivory. He wore muddy army pants, boots also caked with mud, and a dark green sweater. Daniel prodded the man tentatively. A folded piece of paper was tucked under his belt. Daniel took the paper on which was written in a hurried, childlike scrawl, "Please do what you can for our comrade."

But it was plain to see that there was nothing he could do for the man.

There were no obvious wounds, but under the man's sweater he seemed to be unnaturally padded around the abdomen. Daniel lifted the sweater. One layer after another of cloth and bandages was soaked through with blood, most of which had already dried stiff. Even before getting down to the man's skin it was clear that he had been shot.

With a start, Daniel could hear his first patient arriving at the front door. It was a woman, Signora Fiorella. She was chatting with Mama. He couldn't make out what the woman was saying, only that the tone was full of the resignation of the chronically ill.

He composed himself and left the office, closing the door behind him. In the kitchen Signora Fiorella sat at the table with Mama. Paola was preparing breakfast for Francesco before taking him to school. Mama held Isabella in her lap; the child squirmed away from a biscuit proffered by Signora Fiorella.

The women looked up in surprise to see Daniel, who usually didn't return from his office until lunchtime.

"Have I kept you waiting for Signora Fiorella?" Mama asked. "I thought she was early, but it's my fault if we lost track of the time," she added. "I asked her to join me for coffee."

Francesco called out, "Good morning, Papa! Come see what I can read."

Paola said in English, "Good morning, darling."

He turned to Mama and his patient, reminding himself to keep the mood calm. "You're not late at all. In fact, I'm the one who is running late this morning. Please, signora, finish your coffee."

Signora Fiorella, a homely, heavyset woman with thick lips and a pronounced gap between her teeth gave a brief smile, which she allowed to dissolve into a slight grimace, as if to suggest that she hadn't forgotten that this wasn't a social call and neither should he.

Paola gave him a quizzical look.

"Something has come up," he said to her calmly, in English. "It's not an emergency, but I'd like to cancel as many of my patients today as possible. I wonder, could Mama take Francesco to school while perhaps you try to get in touch with some of them?"

"All right." She turned to her mother and asked in Italian if she would take Francesco, though Mama would have understood Daniel's English.

Mama looked only slightly curious as she said of course she would. Francesco said, "Papa, I want to read this to you."

"A little later, Francesco," Daniel said, and then praised the boy automatically as, undeterred, he read from a school workbook. To the others Daniel announced, "I'm afraid my office is a bit of a mess this morning. What I want to do is use the waiting room to examine patients. Mama, perhaps you would be kind enough to receive any others in here?"

"Certainly. And I'll help straighten up your office."

"Thank you, but it's really something I have to do myself."

Before leading Signora Fiorella to the waiting room where he would examine her, Daniel blew a kiss to Isabella who ignored it as she continued to squirm. He kissed Francesco and admonished him to be good in school. "Is your father awake?" he asked Paola matter-of-factly.

"I'm not sure. Why?"

"I'll tell you in a few minutes. Could you see if he can come down and then cancel as many of the appointments as you can? I'll examine Signora Fiorella in the meantime."

"All right. Will she see you alone?" Paola asked in English.

"She'll have to today."

Thirty minutes later, Daniel showed the signora out and went to find Paola. "You only had three others scheduled for this morning," Paola said. "I managed to postpone two of them, but there's still one at eleven o'clock."

"All right, that should be enough time."

"Not to mention the ones who always show up without an appointment," she added with a small smile.

"Mama can receive them here. Unless they're urgent she can send them away. Get your father and come to the office and I'll explain."

After a few minutes Paola appeared in the waiting room with Antonio, who was grumbling about not having had time for his breakfast.

"We have a problem," Daniel began and recounted what had occurred, trying to prepare them for the sight.

"Do you know who the man is?" Antonio asked.

"No. There's no identification on him. I was hoping you might know him."

Daniel led them into the office. Neither was squeamish or easily rattled, but he had taken the precaution of pulling down the man's sweater to lessen the impact of the gore.

"What happened to him?" Paola asked, her voice somber, anxious.

"Shot in the abdomen. Do you know him?"

She shook her head.

Antonio came closer, touched the man's face. "I don't know him either. How did he get in here?"

Daniel produced the note. "During the night I thought I might have heard something from down here. Obviously, I shouldn't have dismissed it. But no force was used to get in. Whoever it was brought the man in through the garden door."

Paola looked at him. "How do you know?"

"It was closed but unlocked when I checked it this morning. I'm certain I locked it last night. And there are no signs of force—no broken windows or anything."

"Alfredo," she said.

"Must have been, though there must have been others as well. Alfredo couldn't have managed this man on his own."

Antonio nodded agreement. He returned to the waiting room. The others followed. He sat down and lit a cigarette.

"What do we do with the body?" Daniel asked.

"I need to think for a minute," Antonio said through a cloud of smoke.

Daniel sat in a chair opposite Antonio, then leaned forward. "Do you know anyone who can make this right? If we were to go to the carabinieri and basically tell the truth? We could say he was left by the partisans who were hoping the doctor could help him. That wouldn't necessarily incriminate us."

Shaking his head, Antonio turned to Daniel. "In these times," he said through pursed lips, "there's no one we can trust. We must get rid of this man's body in secret. There's no choice. It doesn't even matter whether we can find a sympathetic ear among the carabinieri. There are too many others who would use the incident against us, if only to curry favor with the Nazis and the Fascists."

"That idiot brother of mine," Paola fumed. "To place us in danger like this! It's one thing if he insists on getting himself killed. Or even to involve me or you. But we have children here. He has no right!"

Daniel nodded, his face a grim mask. During the heady month of July, with the Fascists in retreat, Alfredo had ventured to make brief visits home. He showed caution in these visits, either out of lessons imbued in the partisan life or out of a newly mature comprehension that the game was still in the balance—things might yet go wrong for his side.

On one occasion, shortly after the armistice was announced, Alfredo took a greater risk. He appeared in the house late at night and asked to see Daniel alone. At first Daniel thought Alfredo might need him to examine his foot.

"No, it's something else," Alfredo said, taking a seat on the corner of Daniel's desk. Daniel pulled up one of the visitor's chairs for himself. "I think I know what your answer will be, but I've been instructed to ask, so I'm here."

"Who instructed you to ask what?"

"The who is not important at the moment. The what is for you to reconsider the question of helping us."

"In what way?"

"Medical help."

"What kind of medical help do you need?"

"It's not so much for right now. All the signs are that we're in for a rough time with the Fascists and the Nazis. We expect to need the services of a doctor."

Daniel exhaled loudly as he ran his fingers through his hair. "Surely you know you're asking the impossible." When Alfredo didn't respond, he continued: "How could I abandon your family—abandon my wife and children—to help you? If you're right and things get worse, it would leave all of them completely vulnerable. Suspicions are already high because of you. If I were to leave . . . "

"I told them that's what you'd say," Alfredo interrupted bluntly.

It occurred to Daniel that, aside from Alfredo's obvious irritation, he also might be relieved. Daniel's concerns surely must be shared by him. Yet now Alfredo could report that he had undertaken his assignment in good faith. But Alfredo surprised him by not letting the subject drop, and his next proposal was more difficult to reject out of hand.

"What if, sometimes—if we could ensure security—we were to bring people to you?"

"There's no way you can ensure security," Daniel responded after collecting his thoughts.

"Well, not perfectly of course."

"So, we come back to endangering our family."

Now Alfredo seemed to speak more from the heart, and not so much as directed. "Do you think this is easy for me? Do you think I want to endanger my family? In these times, who can entirely escape risk!"

"I understand, Alfredo. It would be one thing to risk my own safety, but that of my wife and children? It's impossible."

Daniel was preparing to go another round, but Alfredo merely nodded. He stood, took a fraction of a second to secure his balance on the bad foot. As he reached the door he turned, and in the low, sad voice of one much older—one much battered by experience—he said: "These people we're fighting . . . I wonder if you're able to comprehend just how evil they are."

There had been little word from him since September—just enough contact, usually in the form of an anonymous letter or surreptitiously passed note, to let the family know he was well. And now this.

Daniel nodded toward the body. "We'll have to get rid of him somehow."

"I think I know how," Antonio said after a moment. "There is a place near the garden, off in the far corner, where I dump dried clippings, weeds and such. The pile is shielded from view by trees and fencing, since it's an eyesore. I could dig a grave in the soft earth below the pile. No one would think twice about me working there. Everyone knows the garden is my pride and joy."

"That's too much of a strain on your heart," Paola objected, and Daniel agreed.

"A shallow grave, then," Antonio said with a small shrug. "As a practical matter it will become deeper as we put more dead leaves and such on the pile."

"No, Babbo. It's too dangerous for you alone. I'll help you dig."

Antonio shook his head. "You know I do the gardening myself. Your going out there with me will call attention. Don't worry. I'll take my time. We should be able to bury the man as soon as it gets dark tonight."

While Antonio went off to begin his digging, Paola found an old blanket in which to wrap the man's body. It was hard work in the small office. Rigor mortis was taking hold of the man, who because of his size would have been difficult to cope with in the best of circumstances.

They were almost finished when Daniel heard Mama call his name from the front door. "Damn," he said, slightly breathless from raising the corpse high enough for Paola to wind it a final time in the blanket. "It must be a patient."

A moment later, they heard steps coming toward the office, along with Mama's voice and a man's, in officious tones. When Mama referred to the man as sir, they looked at each other in rising panic.

"Daniel," Mama called through the closed door. "I'm sorry to bother you, but there's an officer from the carabinieri out here who would like a word with you.

"I'll be out in a moment, Mama." To Paola he whispered instructions, which he thanked God for once she didn't question. Then, with all his strength, he moved the dead partisan into a corner of the room, out of view from the doorway.

"Wait!" Paola whispered as Daniel got ready to open the door. She smoothed his hair and straightened his shirt. "Wipe your brow," she whispered.

Daniel took a towel to the perspiration on his forehead. He collected himself and opened the door just wide enough to step out while shielding the interior from view. "Yes?" he asked, hoping his voice conveyed more irritation than anxiety.

Daniel thought he saw a flicker of confusion and fear pass across Mama's face, and he remembered that she was unaware of what was going on. She did know something was amiss, though. Fortunately her voice was steady when she said, "This is Corporal Stesso. He was asking about a partisan fighter who might have come this way. I told him no, but he wanted to see you."

Daniel nodded, maintaining an expression of severity and annoyance. He knew most of the local carabinieri on sight, but didn't recognize this one and concluded that he must be new. He was young, his face scarred by acne. "You want to know if I've seen a partisan fighter here?"

"Yes, doctor."

Mama excused herself, saying she wanted to be available in case other patients arrived.

"No. Why would a partisan come here?" Daniel asked in a tone still determinedly annoyed by the interruption and hoping he might intimidate the young officer.

"I was ordered to check here because we heard the man was wounded. This would be a logical place for him to come."

"The answer is no. I haven't seen anyone."

"I'm sorry, doctor, but this man we're looking for is important. I've been instructed to search your office to ensure he's not here."

"I just told you he's not," Daniel said, allowing his voice to rise. "Do you think I'm lying to you?"

"Oh, no, doctor, I know you would not want to. But these men are ruthless. They could make you say things you would not want to say."

Daniel was surprised at the young officer's poise. He was about to respond when Mama called to say that two patients had arrived unexpectedly. She asked if he could see them.

Relieved at the prospect of having more normal activity for the officer's benefit, he called back that Mama should send them to the waiting room. A moment later, two older women whom Daniel knew came into the room. Their faces registered surprise at the presence of the officer. Daniel greeted the women, asked them to take a seat and said he would get to them as soon as he could. "I have a patient inside my office and Corporal Stesso was about to leave."

Daniel could see that, again, the officer was nonplused by his brisk demeanor. "As I said, doctor, I don't mean to disturb you. I'll be glad to leave as soon as I check your office."

"That's not possible at the moment. I have a patient in there."

"Sorry, doctor, but this is more important than your patient." The officer stepped around Daniel, knocked quickly and began to open the door."

In a shocked instant he saw the naked woman sitting on the examination table trying to cover up and yelling, "Who are you . . . what do you think you're doing?" and other things that probably didn't register on him. He slammed the door shut.

"Are you satisfied?" Daniel demanded to the officer's bright red face. He had been prepared to have to explain that, yes, even his own wife needed his services, but the officer obviously had not recognized Paola. In the meantime, the women in the waiting room adopted indignant, condemning looks toward the officer, who now couldn't leave soon enough. His face still brightly colored, he apologized repeatedly and said he could now satisfy his superiors that the man they were looking for was not there.

That night they buried the still unidentified partisan behind Antonio's garden.

~ ~ ~ ~ ~

~ ~ ~

Chapter 25

PAOLA SLIPPED UNDER THE covers, shivered ostentatiously against the January cold and put her lips to Daniel's. Candles flickered on the nightstand, their glow caught in the mirror over Paola's dressing table.

"They're asleep?" he asked as he entwined his leg with hers like the first strands of a rope.

"Yes, thank God," she said with feigned exhaustion and not so feigned exasperation. While Francesco slept soundly through the night as usual, Isabella, a bit colicky—and, Daniel and Paola were almost convinced after several sleepless nights, a bit malicious—had finally begun to emit the signature soft breathing that let Paola sneak away.

They kissed deeply and held each other close. She reached and stroked him in the way he loved. He undid the buttons in the front of her nightgown. His hand glided over her breasts, barely, tantalizingly touching, and down to the place where his fingers parted her gently and swirled around her slipperiness.

He felt her tense. "What?" he whispered.

"Isabella."

"I didn't hear anything." But then he did; heard the familiar start of her cries, which he knew even as he hoped otherwise would become insistent, incessant. "God damn. You'd think she'd let us have one night."

"Shush," Paola whispered. "Maybe she'll go back to sleep." She kissed him and stroked what was left of him.

"She won't." His voice conveyed defeat, frustration. Isabella's cries began to spike, to his ears more a demanding bleat than an expression of need that, this night at least, made him more angry than sympathetic. "Christ!" he sighed. "For one lousy night can't she just disappear?"

Paola pulled her nightgown tight and got out of bed. "She's just a baby, Daniel. What's going on with you tonight? Where's your patience?"

He puffed out his cheeks. "Sorry, you're right. I was enjoying being just us, alone."

"Let me see if I can get her down."

"Not bloody likely," he said, knowing how churlish he sounded but not feeling up to the labor of self-control.

Paola ignored the remark, padded next door to Isabella's room. After a moment the crying stopped. Daniel assumed Paola had picked her up. For the next several minutes he could make out the low notes of the melody she improvised, usually off key.

After awhile she returned to bed. But no sooner had she touched him softly, saying "Why don't we try again?" than Isabella's cries resumed. As if choreographed, they rolled onto their backs, stared at the ceiling and exhaled.

"I'll go to her," Daniel said, his voice full of resignation.

She put a hand on his arm. "No, let me. The mood you're in, you'll probably smother her."

"Very funny."

She gave him a quick kiss on the lips and got out of bed. "There will be other nights," she said, and Daniel both resented the mature stoicism of the remark and wondered if indeed there might ever come a time when Isabella would stop crying.

The next day, a Monday, was a holiday and a break from school for Francesco. Paola had awakened with the first signs of a cold, and Daniel offered to take Francesco with him into Lucca, where he was helping out at the hospital. Mama said she would look after Isabella, and Francesco always enjoyed his excursions with Daniel. On previous occasions Daniel had been pleased to see that Francesco was good at entertaining himself.

Daniel hoped to complete his work by lunchtime, then treat Francesco to a restaurant meal before returning home. Affecting a stern professional demeanor, he instructed Paola to stay in bed and drink plenty of tea. He bent to kiss her goodbye, but she turned her head away, saying she didn't want to pass her cold to him and eliciting a laughing response to the effect that, if he hadn't already caught it the previous night, he should be safe. Still, she insisted there was no reason to incur further risk, which all the more made him want to feel the lovely fullness of her lips as he settled for a kiss blown in his direction.

It was cold but the sun was out as they walked to the station. He held Francesco's mittened hand and listened to him talk animatedly about the things he would draw and color with crayons that day. As he often did, Daniel encouraged him to speak in English, and the small Italian-inflected lilt that issued forth made him smile. Francesco had brought three crayons, one each black, yellow and red, the red worn to half the length of the others. They were wrapped in paper to prevent them smearing the inside of his coat pocket. In his free hand he carried a pad of drawing paper, the first few sheets of which had been crayoned in. "I'll draw things for Mama and Nonna," he said.

"What things will you draw?" Daniel asked.

Francesco spied a stone and kicked it skittering ahead of him. "Don't know. Maybe animals."

"Will you make a picture for Nonno too? He likes when you draw cows. And how about one for your sister?"

Francesco pondered this for a moment, as if judging her worthiness. "Maybe." He kicked another stone. "I'm cold," he said with little conviction.

"Already?" The sun had gone behind a bank of clouds, but there was only a short distance left to the station. "Here, hit yourself like this. It will get your blood moving and warm you up." Daniel struck his chest with both hands in a crossing motion. The blows made a thudding sound against his coat.

"Like this?" Francesco asked, laughing, as he mimicked Daniel.

"Faster!"

"Like this?"

"Exactly! But be careful not to knock yourself out!"

* * *

FROM THE HARD wooden seat on the weakly heated train, Daniel looked out the window at a dull winter landscape.

"When will we be there?" Francesco asked.

"In about ten minutes. Three more stops. You can count them."

"And then more walking," Francesco said in voice filled with prospective exhaustion. He slumped exaggeratedly in his seat, then laughed when Daniel smiled at him. "Can we take a bus?" Francesco asked, with sudden enthusiasm.

"We could, but it's not such a long walk to the hospital. We'll have fun."

Francesco looked at him incredulously, in response to which Daniel gave him a tickling poke in the ribs, eliciting a squirming laugh.

At the hospital, Daniel took longer than he had anticipated. It was nearly one before he finished. Only in the last hour, though, did Francesco's impatience begin to show. Until then he had been content to sit at a vacant desk and draw. He drew pictures for all of his family members, Isabella included. Nurses rushed by but still found the time to praise his work and, less welcome, hug and fuss over him. When he tired of drawing he played with wooden models of a knee and an elbow, making the joints flex in ways intended and unintended.

"You've been a good boy," Daniel said at last, tousling Francesco's hair. They walked to Neni, a new trattoria near Piazza San Michele. Along the way, Daniel stopped to read a newly posted announcement reporting the execution of partisans "and their supporters" who had been caught sabotaging government property. The specific property was not mentioned. The previous day a priest had been executed near the Elisa Gate to the old city. Daniel made certain to avoid the gate with Francesco, lest there be some remnant of the incident.

*   *   *

IT WAS AFTER three o'clock when they caught the train home. A north wind had brought thick clouds and a blustery cold. Daniel was bareheaded, having forgotten his hat at the hospital. The coach offered a welcome haven, and barely after the train left the station Francesco fell asleep, his head against Daniel, who relieved Francesco of the drawings that were slipping from his hand and placed an arm around him.

They stayed like this until the train approached the stop before theirs. Daniel prodded Francesco gently. "We're nearly home, sleepy boy. Time to get up."

Francesco stirred, stared vacantly for a moment. "We're home?"

"Almost." Daniel buttoned Francesco's coat and placed the mittens back on his hands.

The train made its normal, brief stop and began to pull out. It picked up speed, and within a minute was passing an area of brush and overgrown weeds.

Then, without warning, the train screeched to a halt as if someone had pulled the emergency brake. Daniel and Francesco were thrown forward. There was loud confusion as the passengers struggled to understand what was happening.

Within seconds, two men appeared at the end of the car. They were dressed unexceptionally in laborer's clothing and woolen caps, but as they came up the aisle both produced pistols and swept them through the air in case anyone was considering challenging them. Some of the passengers cried out and pressed themselves as well as they could into their hard seats.

In the instant he had to look behind him, Daniel saw another man coming down the aisle from the opposite end of the car. He was dressed like the other two, roughly and for warmth. He, too, brandished a gun. Daniel put his arm around Francesco and drew him close. "Don't worry," he said, keeping his voice even.

At once the three strangers converged on Daniel and Francesco. "Right now! Come with us!" one commanded while the others covered him.

Daniel held Francesco closer to him. "Why? Who are you?" he managed to ask.

"Stand up! Now!" the man said again, at the same time grabbing Daniel's arm.

"All right, I'll come. Leave my son alone!"

"He comes too!"

One of the other men reached in to help the first. In an instant they jerked Daniel and Francesco to their feet, eliciting a cry from Francesco, and pushed them down the aisle toward the exit, followed by the third man. The cold air hit them as they opened the door. Without a platform, the drop to the ground was high. One man jumped and waved his gun to clear the area. The engineer was peering from his cabin. From the rear a conductor was walking along the side of the track to investigate what had happened. The first man fired a shot into the air and the conductor dropped to the ground, while the engineer pulled back into the cabin. From behind, Daniel was pushed off the train. He was barely able to keep his feet when they hit the ground. Another of the strangers followed and reached back to pull Francesco off. Finally, the third man jumped down.

"Follow me!" the first man commanded. One of the others fired another shot into the air, but no one was following from the train.

In an instant Daniel and the others were hustling away from the tracks, through brush that, though denuded of green, was thick and full of stickers. One of the men was carrying Francesco, who wore a silent terror on his face.

"Why do you have to take my son?" Daniel demanded as he was pushed along.

"Orders. Now shut up and keep moving. We're not here to hurt you."

"Whose orders?" Daniel managed to say, breathing hard. He was trying to get his bearings, but everything had happened so quickly.

They reached a clearing next to a road. There a large black sedan was waiting. "Get in! Quickly!" one of the men commanded. Two of the men bracketed Daniel and Francesco in the back seat, while the third got in front and the waiting driver took off.

The men put their guns away. The man in the front passenger seat turned around. He was younger than the others but seemed to be in charge. "Don't be afraid. We won't hurt you. But if we're stopped, don't try to escape. That will be bad for everyone."

"Who told you to do this?" Daniel tried again.

Again, the question was met with silence.

"Well, if you're not going to hurt us, at least tell us why you've taken us and where we're going."

The two men in the rear remained silent. The driver, a man large enough to take up more than his share of the seat and whose face Daniel could see in the rear view mirror but did not recognize, had not said a word since they'd got in. The one in the front answered without turning around. "We're not going far. I can't tell you why you're coming with us. All I know is that something happened today and we were told to take you off the train but not to harm you."

Daniel hugged Francesco close to him. "Everything will be all right," he whispered in the boy's ear.

The car drove higher into the hills. It was getting dark, but the driver hadn't turned on the headlights. As they drove through a small town they were forced to slow as they approached an intersection. Two cars were in front of them.

"What's up?" the front seat passenger asked the driver.

"Possibly a carabinieri checkpoint. There's sometimes one here."

"Then why did we take this route?"

The driver gave a quick, impatient look. "You know this area as well as I do. If you can think of any other roads to take, I'd like to hear about them."

The leader turned to Daniel. "Remember what I said. We're not going to hurt you. But if we're stopped, don't do anything stupid or many of us will get hurt, including the two of you."

A moment later the car in front of them came to a stop. Two carabinieri approached it, one on either side. There was only one person, the driver, in the car.

Francesco sat rigidly against Daniel. "Make believe you're sleepy," Daniel whispered. "Just lean against me with your eyes closed." The men sitting on either side of them drew away and leaned against the doors in what Daniel assumed was an effort to appear relaxed.

Ahead of them one of the officers was holding a flashlight to the driver's papers. He said something to the driver, then to the other officer.

"These cretins," the driver of Daniel's car said under his breath.

"You have papers, right?" the leader asked.

"Yeah, but no permit to be on the road after dark. I thought we'd be there by now."

"Shit. All right. Let's stay calm. You all know what to do if they ask us to get out of the car."

At last the car in front of them was waved on. The officers motioned for their car to come ahead. Before the officer could ask for their papers, the driver, with window already rolled down and in an urgent, scatterbrained manner said, "Madonna! We're ten minutes from home. We're not supposed to be on the road after dark, and you're keeping us from making it on time!"

For a moment the officer on the driver's side was taken aback by the earnest assignment of blame. The driver pressed his advantage, going on in an uninterruptible stream about how he needed to get to his sister's house and how he couldn't afford to be in trouble, strongly implying that he could not have done anything wrong and that if he was in trouble it must be the fault of the officers who stopped him.

Daniel noticed that, in the gesticulating hand he had out the window, the driver held a discretely folded banknote. As the driver kept up his patter, the second officer motioned for the front passenger to open his window and peered in with a flashlight.

"Everything okay?" the officer by the driver asked his comrade, who had just finished scanning the passengers. Daniel could see that the bill was no longer in the driver's hand.

"I suppose so," the one with the flashlight said.

"You'd better go," the first officer said to the driver. "Your sister is waiting," he added with a thin smile as he waved the car on.

They only drove for a short time before the driver pulled off the road into a small clearing. "We get out here," the leader announced. "Don't leave anything behind."

Outside the car and the close-packed bodies the air was bitterly cold. Daniel knelt down to Francesco and made sure he was buttoned up. "Don't be afraid. Everything will be okay."

"I'll bring up the rear. Stay in single file behind Tito," the leader said.

So, at least the driver has a name, Daniel thought. Tito had a flashlight in his hand, but he obviously knew the way and didn't switch it on. It was difficult to tell if they were on an actual path. If so, it must have been very narrow, as they constantly had to push away branches. Brush and sticks grabbed at his pant legs. Francesco kept up as well as he could, but within a few minutes Daniel had to carry him.

"Not much farther," Tito said. Still, it was not long before Daniel, breathing hard, had to stop.

"Here," the man behind him said. "Give the boy to me."

Daniel's impulse was to refuse, but he quickly concluded there wasn't much point to not trusting these men. If they meant to do harm, there was nothing standing in their way. He did his best to reassure Francesco and handed him to the man, who carried him for the next ten minutes of climbing and then passed him down the line. They walked on in silence and in the pitch dark, which it seemed Tito must be able somehow to see through, so sure were his movements. When finally they stopped it took Daniel a moment to realize that they were standing in front of a small stone house.

They entered and were startled by the lantern light and the fireplace that had been blocked from view from the outside by the closed shutters. As

Daniel's eyes adjusted he could see three men in the room. One of them was Alfredo.

"You did it!" Alfredo said loudly in the direction of the man Daniel had considered the leader. "Fantastic, Lido!" he said, providing another name.

"It wasn't easy," Lido said, unbuttoning his coat. "By the time we found out where they were, they were on the train, nearly at their stop. We barely had time to halt the train and pull them off."

"Thank you," Alfredo said, surprising Daniel—surely this was a strange comment on the events of the last couple of hours.

Francesco smiled at the sight of Alfredo, who said, "Come here and give your uncle a hug!"

Daniel began to form the first of his many questions, but he was cut off by one of Alfredo's comrades who, sitting in a crude chair with his feet propped on the raw table in the center of the room, said to Alfredo, "If it wasn't for you, we shouldn't have bothered. It's not as if the doctor has earned our help."

Alfredo ignored the remark but the ebullience of a moment before was gone as he said to Daniel, "Get comfortable. Have something to eat and I'll explain."

"A little explanation might be helpful right now."

Alfredo frowned, pulled him aside. "This is a small place, as you see," he said in a low voice. "I suggest you let Francesco go to sleep before we talk. Something happened today and you were in grave danger. There are things Francesco shouldn't hear. I suggest you let it go at that for now."

Daniel started to protest, but then only nodded.

They ate a simple meal. Francesco sat by the warmth of the fire. Soon he began to nod off. Alfredo handed some blankets to Daniel, who wrapped Francesco tightly. Some of the men had taken bedrolls into an adjacent room, apparently the only other one in the house. "We draw straws to see who has to sleep in there," Alfredo explained. "Short straw wins the honor. There's hardly any heat. They get a couple of extra blankets, though." In one corner of the main room the men Daniel knew as Tito and Lido began a game of chess with a well-worn set and a makeshift board.

Alfredo motioned Daniel toward an opposite corner, as far away as possible from Francesco. "Over here," he said just above a whisper as Daniel braced himself. The ebullience of the rescue over, Alfredo seemed haggard and barely in control of his emotions. "The family was arrested today," he said.

"What!" The exclamation made Francesco stir. Tito looked up from the board. "What are you talking about?" Daniel demanded in a lower voice.

"Last night we got word that there was to be a mass arrest of people considered opponents of the Duce's new government and the Germans."

"What does that mean?" Daniel interrupted. "That would probably include two thirds of the people around here."

"That may be," Alfredo said with a resigned shrug.

"And Paola was arrested?" Daniel asked without trying to conceal his alarm.

"Yes. We didn't know last night who they were taking, only that the arrests were to occur today. At noon we found out that our family . . ."

"Everyone?"

"Yes. Paola, Mama, Babbo," Alfredo answered with growing alarm in his voice, as if prompted by Daniel's panicky questions.

"Where's the baby?"

"As far as I know, with Paola."

"What the . . . "

"Listen, Daniel, we don't know much more at this point. Some of our contacts are trying to find out. Right after we learned about the arrests we tried to discover why they had been taken. The only thing we learned for certain was that you were supposed to be taken with them, and I assume that would have meant Francesco, too."

"But none of us has done anything, as you know very well." Even as the words came out he wondered whether the dead partisan might have been discovered.

Alfredo nodded.

"Are they still in custody? Perhaps they were taken and released."

"Anything is possible."

"Christ!" Daniel sat down and leaned forward in the chair, holding his head in his hands. "I should be with them, Alfredo," he exclaimed suddenly. "At least I could try to protect them, especially if it was me they really wanted for God knows what reason. Maybe being an American citizen is enough."

"Don't be absurd, Daniel!" Alfredo's voice was a whispered shout. "In the best case, if this is some kind of mistake or maybe a warning of some kind to intimidate suspected opponents, they'll be released and that will be the end of it. But I shouldn't have to tell you how these things work. It was bad enough before, when the squadristi were in control. They were mean bastards but at least we knew the rules. Now the Germans are calling the shots. Don't flatter yourself to think you could reason with them."

Daniel's voice was taut with anguish as he said, "This is my wife and child you're talking about. I should be with them, no matter what."

"Fuck you, Daniel!" Alfredo almost shouted. Francesco didn't stir, but Daniel was taken aback. "You think I don't care about my sister and my mother and father? Fuck you, then!" Alfredo added in a more controlled, but strained, voice.

"I didn't mean that."

"No? How did you expect me to take it? Do you think we won't try to help them if we can? When we found out about the arrests we did all we were able to do, which was to track you down and keep you—and your son, I should add, or haven't you considered him?—from being snatched up too. And if you think that was so easy to do, think again."

"I'm sorry," Daniel whispered. "Thank you."

But Alfredo was not finished. More quietly he said, "And do you think these guys who saved you"—he nodded in the general direction of the others in the house—"give a damn about you? As far as they're concerned, you're just the snooty doctor who couldn't be bothered to help us."

"You know that's not fair."

"Fair or not, that's what they think. And you know what?" Alfredo added before Daniel could respond, "Maybe you should try and see things from their point of view. Or maybe you think they're out here sleeping in this shithole for the fun of it—that they don't have their own families to worry about. You're not the only one trying to protect a family, you know."

Daniel stared at Alfredo. He had a flash memory of the callow, naive soldier he had met less than six years ago. The rough, bearded man with the limp who now lectured him couldn't be more transformed. "What do we do now?" he asked, softly.

"Tomorrow we'll see what more we can find out about the arrests. Then we'll have a better idea of where we stand. Get some sleep if you can. We'll have to move on from here tomorrow in any case. We've already been here for two days. That's one day too long if you want to be safe. As you'll see, there's nothing glamorous about this life."

~ ~ ~ ~ ~

~ ~ ~

Chapter 26

FRANCESCO WAS STILL ASLEEP when Daniel stirred next to him the following morning. It had been a fitful night. After a period when his mind raced with the events of the day, exhaustion overtook him and he fell into a deep sleep. But he awoke an hour later and spent the rest of the night alternately dozing and anxiously anticipating what lay ahead. The room was cold, the fire having gone out. Traces of light from cracks in the shutters provided the only indication that day had arrived.

Tito was moving toward the door. "Toilet's out here," he said.

A moment later, Francesco opened his eyes. Brief confusion gave way to a small smile as he recognized Daniel next to him. Rattling snores were coming from the other room.

"I have to go to the bathroom," Francesco announced.

"It's outside," Daniel responded. "I'll take you in a minute. You'll have to dress warmly."

Alfredo approached and stood over them. He was already fully dressed.

"I'm cold," Francesco said as he burrowed into his blankets. "What happened to the fire?"

"It went out while we were sleeping," Alfredo explained.

"Can we have another one?" Francesco asked from his burrow.

"Sorry, we can't. No smoke during the daytime."

"There are some people we don't want to know we're here," Daniel tried to clarify. "There's no reason for you to worry," he added, weakly. Indeed, he had spent much of the night wondering how to explain events to Francesco. How could any of this be explained to a child? And yet, it occurred to him that, precisely because Francesco's entire cognizant life had

211

been spent in the circumstances of the war—because normal to him meant the mysterious comings and goings of people, the bandages and stumps, the absence of certainty in the answers to simple questions—he wanted to avoid glib responses to his concerns. Most children were more perceptive than the adults around them believed, and that certainly was true of Francesco. Daniel and Paola had tried hard to find balance in what they told him. Amid the clear evidence of the horrific things that could be done to people—all the more so given the condition of many of Daniel's patients—they had tried to make him feel safe. The dark or bloody subjects that would surface in his play and his drawings suggested he continued to fear otherwise.

"When will we see Mama?"

"Soon. As soon as we can."

The front door opened. Tito entered and slammed it hard against a cold wind. "Well I don't think we're going anywhere today," he announced. The others in the room were stirring.

"What do you mean?" Alfredo asked.

"There's nothing but ice out there. You can't walk two steps without falling on your ass."

"Well we can't stay here all day doing nothing," Daniel protested, his voice rising.

Tito shrugged. "See for yourself. If you can cover a hundred meters in an hour, I'll give you a prize."

In the light of day he appeared older than Daniel first thought. Mid-forties, Daniel concluded. About my age. But there the similarities ended. Tito had the rough look of a mountain man. Daniel could understand why he had been able to lead the way in the dark. He probably knew every bit of the surrounding woods. His warning about the ice was not to be dismissed lightly.

"Maybe conditions will improve," Alfredo said.

Tito shrugged again, as if to say, "Believe that if you like."

"In any case," Alfredo went on, "the good news is that, if we can't move, our enemies won't be able to either."

"That won't help Paola and the others," Daniel said.

"Is something wrong with Mama?" Francesco asked.

Daniel knelt down and looked into his face. "I'm sure Mama's fine. There was a problem yesterday. The police needed to ask Mama and Nonna and Nonno some questions."

"What kind of questions?"

"That's what we have to find out. But you shouldn't worry. You're here with me and your uncle."

"But I want to see Mama."

Daniel touched his face. "Me too. And we will. I'm sure it won't take long."

They spent the morning trying to stay busy and warm. In the afternoon, the sun came out strongly and the ice began to melt. One of the men who had taken Daniel and Francesco off the train and the one who questioned why it was worth doing so—neither of whom ever were introduced to Daniel— announced that they were leaving. All Daniel heard was that they were headed east. That left, in addition to Daniel and Francesco, Alfredo, Tito and Lido. Late in the afternoon as darkness was falling, those three caucused in the corner of the main room, while Daniel and Francesco lit a fire.

The room began to warm. Daniel took wood from a pile next to the fireplace, rejecting some pieces in favor of others, and handed them to Francesco to feed the flames. "We want to use these hard woods," he explained. "They last longer and don't smoke so much."

Dinner consisted of the last of the bread, olives, and cheese the group had laid by, as well as some watered down red wine. Afterward, Lido and Tito withdrew to the corner to resume their chess game. Lido encouraged Francesco to come and watch. "Go on," Daniel said to him. "You know how to play chess. Maybe they'll let you play." To Tito's look of skeptical annoyance at the thought, Daniel added, "I'll put my money on my son."

"You remember Lazio?" Alfredo asked Daniel as they sat across from one another at the table.

Daniel thought for a minute, picked a dry breadcrumb off the table with a saliva-moistened finger, then shook his head no.

"You met him that day you, Paola and Francesco went hiking."

Daniel smiled. "Ah, yes, the one who tried to convince me I wasn't too old for this life."

Alfredo returned the smile. "He's the one. He's the second in command in this sector. Assuming we're not frozen in again overnight, we'll meet up with him tomorrow morning. He shouldn't be too far from here and we'll leave first thing. Anyway, we might as well get going early. We have no food left, and we've been here too long."

"But what about Paola and the family? How will we find out what happened to them?"

"If anyone will know, it will be Lazio. Look, for all we know, they've already been released and are at home worrying about us."

Daniel looked at his hands.

"Really, Daniel, there's no point in assuming the worst."

"I thought assuming the worst was one of the basic rules of survival on the run."

"You know what I mean. You can drive yourself crazy . . . "

"I already am. Here's a question for you. What if everyone is really back at home safe? Can I go back to them after I've been taken away by the partisans?"

"Well, that's the point, isn't it? In such a case you could always say you were taken against your will. I mean, it's time for the doctor to take some advice. You should only dwell on things you have a chance of affecting. It's one thing to plan how you might explain being taken off the train to the authorities. It's another to indulge—and I do mean indulge—in fantasies about things you have no way of knowing or affecting. We all miss our families, but what would be the point to sitting around and imagining the worst things that could happen to them? If you're going to stress your heart, doctor, at least do so about things over which you have some control."

The group set out at first light. Daniel still wore the clothes he had on in Lucca, and which, in addition to making him feel dirty and malodorous, were ill-suited—especially his shoes—to the rural paths on which they had to rely. It was slow going. In many places the ice had melted the previous day and refrozen overnight. Daniel was surprised at how well Alfredo was able to move with his bad foot.

Before they'd left, Alfredo pulled Daniel aside. "You'd better take this," he said, as he handed him a pistol.

Daniel shook his head no.

"We'll try to avoid fighting," Alfredo said, "especially with Francesco with us. But you never know . . . "

"I won't use it," Daniel said, and Alfredo seemed taken aback by the vehemence of the remark.

"Even to save your own life?"

Daniel's face remained set.

"What about the life of your child?" Alfredo's voice was harsh, condemnatory. He held out the gun again.

Daniel stared for a long moment, as if to decide whether Alfredo personally was responsible for the dilemma in which he found himself. He took the gun and put it in the pocket of his coat, then turned to go.

Although for the most part they were able to remain on the back paths, at one point they had to use the paved road and only barely avoided a German patrol. They traversed several olive groves and then, after about two hours of walking, arrived at a small stone house similar to the one they had left.

Tito slowly pushed open the door, which was heavily planked and had rusted iron fittings. He had to duck to enter. The house was deserted, but there were signs that it had been recently occupied. The fireplace retained some residual warmth. On the table near the fireplace were breadcrumbs and bits of food, and a still-wet ring from a bottle or glass.

"Is this the right place?" Daniel asked.

Lido spoke up. "Yes, we've been here before. It's owned by a family farther up the hill who are friendly to us. We should be safe."

In spite of its rustic and cramped appearance, the house was more commodious than the first one. There was a well-outfitted kitchen, a bedroom off the main room, an indoor toilet, and a staircase leading up to two additional bedrooms. Francesco asked if he could go up there. Daniel was about to suggest he not do so when Lido said he would take him.

Looking out the window, Alfredo said, "Here they come."

Four men had come into view. Daniel recognized one of them as Lazio. None of the others looked familiar. All of them had rifles slung over their shoulders.

Alfredo went outside to meet them. Brief expressions of pleasure at seeing one another gave way to looks of concern and worry. Even through the window, Daniel could see that Lazio was considerably more haggard than the last time they had met. Lazio said something to Alfredo, which caused him to slump and cover his face.

Daniel started to go outside, but stopped as the men moved toward the house. Alfredo said to Lazio as they came through the door, "You remember my sister's husband, Daniel Gideon?"

Lazio gave a thin-lipped smile, said he did, and extended his hand.

The three other men were unloading packs of food as Lazio introduced them. "The one who looks like a bankrupt banker is Marco. He's carrying the lightest pack, of course."

"Except for you, Lazio, who carries no pack at all," Marco called back.

"The only benefit of leadership," Lazio responded. "Then there's Michele over there. Michele ran a bar in a village across the valley until the Fascists drove him out of business. And Nicola, the rugged one over there, is the only one among us who actually has some experience growing food and butchering animals."

All in turn nodded toward Daniel. Francesco and Lido returned from upstairs. Lido greeted the others. Daniel was becoming increasingly worried as he stole glances at Alfredo, who seemed distracted and had a kind of panic behind his eyes.

"Do you remember me?" Lazio asked Francesco. "I remember you."

Francesco nodded uncertainly as he came closer to Daniel.

"What's happening, Alfredo?" Daniel asked. The question seemed to startle him.

"Come outside for a minute," he said. Lazio followed them both.

"There's bad news, Daniel," Alfredo said as soon as the door was closed behind them. He seemed to be struggling to maintain control.

Lazio touched Daniel's arm. "We found out this morning. The people who were rounded up . . . including your family," he added before Daniel could utter the question, "were sent away . . . "

"What do you mean, sent away?" Daniel exclaimed. "Sent away where?"

"They were sent north, by train. We don't know exactly where, but we know the train goes at least as far as Bolzano, not far from Austria. They may move on from there."

Daniel felt his insides drain out. His legs felt rubbery and he had to fight to control them. "Oh Jesus," he said, quietly. "How can this be?" he added. "What could they have done?"

Alfredo kept his eyes on the ground.

"Who knows?" Lazio said, his voice sympathetic. "It's not as if one must actually do something wrong to get in trouble with these people. We'll try to find out more, of course. In the meantime . . . "

"Well I'll make my own goddamn inquiries! I know people in that town!"

Lazio and Alfredo appeared startled by the outburst.

"Don't be ridiculous, Daniel!" Alfredo said. "Do you really think you can go back there as if nothing's happened? There's room for you and Francesco on the next train to Bolzano, I guarantee it."

"Alfredo is right," Lazio said in a calm voice that suggested he had the experience of too many conversations such as this.

Daniel looked at him, the anguish plain. "These trains . . . what do we know about them?" The anger in his voice was replaced by a tentativeness in this question, a halting step toward a fearful answer.

The tenor of Lazio's reply suggested his desire to be mindful of a fragile object. "We don't know for certain." He touched Daniel's shoulder. "There are labor camps . . . "

"And perhaps worse," Daniel managed to get out.

Lazio regarded him for a moment, taking his measure. "And perhaps worse," he nodded. "But," he added before Daniel could respond, "probably not. I would be lying if I said anything was beyond our enemies, but from what we know it's more likely your family will actually be sent to labor camps than . . . something worse."

It crossed Daniel's mind that, of those taken, only Paola would be considered fit for any kind of labor. It was a thought he could not bring himself to utter aloud. "What do we do now?" he asked, his voice barely a whisper.

"You'll stay with us," Lazio said, matter of factly. "We can use your help. In the meantime, we'll find out what we can about your wife and family. We can make some arrangements for your son."

"What kind of arrangements?" The alarm returned to Daniel's voice and expression. "I'm not letting him out of my sight."

Alfredo looked to Lazio to answer, which he did, his voice sympathetic but leaving no room for compromise. "That's impossible, doctor. Our whole purpose is to attack our enemies. We cannot have a child with us."

"Well, then you won't have me with you, either."

Lazio shrugged, as if to say, "Suit yourself."

217

Now it was Alfredo who responded. "You must see reason about this. You can't protect Francesco by keeping him with us. We know a convent not far from here. The sisters will take him and keep him safe. That's all we can do."

~ ~ ~ ~ ~

~ ~ ~

Chapter 27

OA   11 March 1944

DEAR GOD, WHERE ARE they? I spend every waking moment trying to imagine what Paola is doing, precisely, at that instant. Is she sitting there, bored or afraid, trying to entertain Isabella? Are Mama and Antonio all right, or is Paola forced to care for them as well? Are they able to keep warm? Do they have enough to eat? I am crazed. Yesterday, I was suddenly taken by a vision of Paola, freezing and hungry, holding Isabella to her breast. Before I realized it, I came within a hair's breadth of giving a man a lethal dose of morphine. I was so shaken by the near disaster that I ran outside and vomited. Is it the nature of this diabolical chain that, rather than being the alleviator of death and suffering, I will now be their source?

The fact is, we still know nothing more about Paola and the others than we did the day they were sent away. Lazio assures us everything possible is being done to discover what happened to them. The more time passes the more I must rely on hope alone, no matter how groundless. I must hold on to something.

At every turn I am overwhelmed by guilt over having escaped the dragnet. Alfredo reminds me constantly that this isn't rational—that it's not as if I deliberately tried to save my own skin at the expense of the others—and that Francesco is safe. Certainly he's right about Francesco. But rational or not, I can't stop thinking that I should be with my family. I am their protector, and if I cannot protect them, I have an obligation to die trying. Instead my efforts are devoted to staying alive. Again, Alfredo says, this is my real obligation. I'm of no use to anyone dead. And again, he makes sense in a realm of senselessness.

OA 26 March 1944

There is a growing feeling of desperation in the air, and I don't think I'm merely projecting my own desperate state of mind. A climax is coming—some resolution, some falling to earth of all the pieces that have been thrown skyward. I'm not sure when it will happen, though I think I can see the broad outlines. And I'm certain that, between now and then, there will be much suffering.

North of the so-called Gothic Line, where the Germans and Mussolini's "republic" are in control, the situation is becoming ever more brutal. With the support of the Germans, Mussolini has organized new Italian divisions, which newspapers and newsreels tout; and the Duce himself is shown at his strutting best even though everyone knows he survives solely at the whim of his German patron. It is said that Hitler has a soft spot for his old fascist mentor. More likely, Hitler is making the best of a bad situation.

In our area there continue to be many arrests (not to mention general harassment) of those deemed insufficiently loyal. Many are being sent north, which gives me hope on some days, despair on others. The things we hear range from the logical to the lunatic. The lunatic things turn out to be true often enough to make one fear the worst. It's clear, for example, that the Italian soldiers who after the armistice did not immediately swear fealty to Mussolini and the Germans were—if they didn't manage to escape—killed or sent to work in German labor camps. At first, these things were rumors, and hard to believe at that. For instance, we heard that surrendering Italians were piled into boxcars and shipped to Germany. We heard that many didn't survive the journey and that those that did were put to work in slave-like conditions. In the beginning, we chalked up many of these stories to the wild rumors that usually go hand in hand with a chaotic situation. But the substance of the stories has been so consistent over time that they have gained credence, especially as they've come from trusted sources. And, of course, I cannot hear any of this without feeling sick with worry for Paola and the baby. On days that pass for good ones, I have confidence in Paola. I know how smart and strong she is. But then, there are the other days . . . and more of them.

Almost every day it seems there are Fascist army call-ups of young men, who become eligible at ever younger age. Those who refuse to serve have little choice but to flee. I heard that in one village the Germans got tired of the parents of these men lying and making excuses about their whereabouts and so arrested the parents, saying they would be held until the sons surrendered. At the urging of the village mayor and the local priest, the Germans let the parents go. Still, the incident gives some indication of how bad things have become and suggests how much worse they may yet be if the Germans become desperate.

OA   29 March 1944

Overnight I have gone from being a town doctor, respected if not always trusted, to being a fugitive. Our group—Green Flames we are called, or call ourselves, I'm not sure which came first—is constantly on the move, and in ever-changing combinations. I have stayed close to Alfredo, and often it seems we end up with Lazio, though I'm not sure whether that's by design. At the end of the day, we might end up in a place with anywhere from two to ten of us.

Sometimes we're joined by escaped POWs. When Italy pulled out of the war many of the camps holding Allied prisoners, especially Brits, threw open their gates. As I understand it, in the confusion that followed, some prisoners opted to remain in the camps, fearing they would be hunted down. As the Germans have taken control of the camps, many of these more timid souls have come to regret the decision. Still, there are many POWs on the run. Their usual objective is to reach Allied lines in the south or to get to safety in Switzerland. The Swiss are willing to take in soldiers who reach their border, but these soldiers cannot be repatriated until after the war. They are out of the game, which probably suits some of them just fine. For those who remain on the run, the partisans help as many as they can, and some simply join the partisans in the hope they can continue the fight and survive until the Allies, who are creeping up the peninsula, reach them.

The trick for any of us on the run—but especially for the POWs, who often understand neither the language nor local customs—is to know whom we can trust. When we stop at a farm for the night we are at the mercy of the farmer. Of course, over time the partisans have learned of many places where they will be safe. In this regard, many of the villagers have displayed remarkable bravery. Sheltering a partisan brings the same penalty as being one, and the Germans become more ruthless by the day. And yet, partisans and POWs often can find shelter and food, for which no compensation is asked. To be sure, not all the helpers do so willingly. In talking about German brutality it's easy to forget that the partisans can be equally brutal. A farmer who betrays a partisan fighter is likely to have his throat cut, or worse. The local people are caught in a vise. Both sides demand their support, and either side is willing to kill those who withhold it or, even more dangerous, support the enemy.

OA 2 April 1944

The fact that Francesco is at a convent nearby both gives me relief and drives me mad. I want so much to see him, and to reassure him, even as I have so many days of needing reassurance myself. The understanding with the nuns is that children left in their care will be treated as orphans. All of the sides seem to have honored this, as so far the nuns and the children have been left alone. But there is no way for me to see Francesco without endangering him and many others as well.

The weather has taken a turn for the better, after a very rough winter. While the group talked about the attacks they wanted to carry out, it was all we could do to stay warm and fed. Now attacks by both sides have picked up. The partisans have hit bridges and roads used by the enemy. But their favorite target is German supply convoys; a successful strike on one of them can mean additional supplies for their own use. The convoys are becoming harder to hit, though, because the Germans are paying more attention to protecting them. Two nights ago, I was brought to a house nearby to attend to two of our fighters who had been wounded in an attempt on a convoy. The attack went badly. Three partisans were killed outright. Of the two I treated, only one is likely to survive.

When I say I've treated someone, this often means little more than providing the services that anyone who has taken a basic first-aid course could provide. I can set bones and suture wounds (though even these simple things sometimes must be done with makeshift supplies). I have performed more serious operations on rough-hewn farm tables. The result is almost never good, but everyone understands that these are instances in which there is nothing to lose by trying.

My presence among the partisans is viewed with considerable ambivalence. Most of them like having a doctor at hand, finding the thought comforting despite the reality that often there isn't much I can do for them. Some, however, can't tolerate that I won't fight. I tell them doctors are in shorter supply than fighters. They say fighting is a matter of principle, a visible demonstration of my commitment and a sign that I will live and die with them. At the end of the day, I am left trying to explain that it's a matter of principle to me, too. I will put myself at risk, but I will not take a life. They make little effort to comprehend this. One of the men was cruel enough to suggest that, if I had been willing to kill, I might have been able to protect my family. It's not true, of course, but it seared me just the same.

One good thing that happened over the winter was that a party returned to our house in Ponte di Maddalena and retrieved some of my instruments and supplies. The house itself has suffered considerable damage. Ransacked is probably the right word. Which made it all the more surprising that any of my things were left intact. It didn't take long for me to use up the few medicines and bandages, though the more durable things—instruments and the like—remain useful.

I've been able to get some additional supplies from the Allies, delivered in air drops I'm told, but the manner of their getting here is of little concern to me. This is partly a question of prudence. It's wiser not to ask about operational things I have no real need to know, even when my comrades—I do consider them as such, though some would be skeptical to hear it—would be willing to tell me. I haven't received much, but there's a promise of more to come.

OA   5 April 1944

The other night I awoke to find Lazio getting dressed. Without thinking, I asked where he was going, and he surprised me by telling me he was going— alone, another surprise—to meet another partisan and an American OSS officer. When I heard this, I told him I wanted to go along to ask the American's help in getting to Paola.

Lazio refused, saying I had no need to be there, and in any case he would talk to the American for me. I got angry. "We haven't been able to find out a damn thing," I said. I had gotten out of bed and stood over him. "He's my countryman. He might do something for me that he won't do for you." I knew even as I said it that the argument was weak.

It appeared that Lazio would refuse again. But I was becoming angrier. It didn't seem like too much to ask of him, and I began to think that, if he refused again, I would tell him point blank that I was leaving the group. When I threatened to do so my first night with them, he merely shrugged, as if I had no choice but to stay. Since then, I know that he has come to value my presence, not only for my medical work, but for other reasons as well.

He cocked his head, then nodded. "Why not? It can't hurt to have our own American there. I have one condition. You won't say anything until I tell you to."

I had no problem agreeing to that, but before I could respond, he said, "I don't mean to offend you, but the fact is, you don't know these people."

"I'm not offended. All I want to do is ask his help in finding my family."

"Agreed. I'm going to talk to him about getting more weapons, so you might as well tell him what medical supplies you need, too."

Lazio led me to a ruined stone church—more of a chapel, really, perhaps part of a former estate. It wasn't far away, but because it was necessary to avoid the main roads it took a couple of hours to reach it. Only one room of the church was intact, and even then there were places where the roof had collapsed and been covered over by wooden boards.

The place must have been used for meetings before, as there was an oil lamp sitting on the floor in the corner. Lazio lit it and asked me to go outside and tell him how much light was visible. I reported that only a very little could be seen leaking through cracks in the mortar, which seemed to satisfy him.

It felt colder inside the church than outside. I stood with my hands in my pockets. Lazio sat back on his haunches, using the wall for support. He fished in his coat pocket and drew out a pack of cigarettes, saw it was empty, crumpled it into a ball and (cautious man that he is—that he has to be) put it back in his pocket to dispose of later. He asked if I had a cigarette to spare, then said immediately, "Right, you don't smoke," before I had a chance to remind him.

Lazio cocked his ear toward the door and placed his hand on the pistol in his belt. There was a soft knock followed by the quick entry of two men. Lazio relaxed as soon as he recognized the first man, who for an instant seemed startled to see me before he set eyes on Lazio. The second man—to my eyes obviously an American, and I wondered if he would take me for the same—closed the door.

Lazio introduced me simply as Daniele, and I nodded without saying anything. The Italian's name was Mario. The American, a solidly built man of medium height in his early thirties, was introduced as Tom. Tom quickly demonstrated that he spoke Italian surprisingly well, though it was clearly Italian of a standard classroom variety. He wore a bulky jacket and simple gray pants. He explained that he had come through Bologna and was trying to meet with as many resistance cells as possible to provide them with supplies (the bait) and to get them to work in concert with one another under Allied direction (the hook). I still had not said anything, and I didn't get the impression it would make any difference if he knew I was an American. Even in textbook Italian he spoke with the assurance and conviction of his own logic typical of my countrymen and which I found somehow—some kind of nationalistic atavism no doubt at work—refreshing and comforting. There was a common enemy to face, he said, and the only sensible way to face that enemy was cohesively, cooperatively. His tone of voice left no room for acknowledgement of the reality that, among scores of groups and factions covering the entire spectrum of ideologies and motivations, facing a common enemy often takes a back seat to facing one nearer at hand.

Lazio allowed Tom to go on without interruption, but I knew him well enough to know that his silence did not signal anything like consent. In spite of his wiry energy, Lazio can be patient when he believes it's in his interest to be, which is why he makes a better leader than the more impulsive types—like Alfredo, the more I see of him—who believe leadership is defined only as action. Tom continued, his remarks seeming ever more a scripted sermon. The script included a long passage on the Allies' desire to support the resistance and an equal need for the resistance to demonstrate its reliability.

While Lazio remained impassive, his counterpart, Mario, visibly seethed, then erupted as Tom went on. "Who are you to lecture us about reliability?" he all but shouted. "Where's the invasion force that was supposed to come ashore at Livorno? While you take your time moving up the boot my people are dying."

Tom held his ground, though. He apologized for his poor choice of words, then added, "Surely you can see that, with limited resources, we're more eager to supply the groups that are most willing to work with us and not waste the supplies fighting among themselves."

When he was finished, Lazio simply nodded and said, *"And what is it you'd like us to do?"*

"The most important thing you can do is disrupt the German and Fascist Republican supply and communication lines. Hit railways, bridges, roads . . . ."

"We already do all those things," Mario interrupted.

Tom looked to me, as if he expected me to say something, but I remained quiet. *"That's true,"* he said, returning his attention to Mario. *"But the resistance groups—not only yours,"* he added—*"are spending too much time assassinating individual soldiers."*

"If you'd give us the weapons we need, we could do more than kill individuals," Mario said.

"You're missing the point. Killing Germans may be emotionally satisfying to your people, but it doesn't do as much good as disrupting their movements and supplies. In the meantime, as you know all too well, increasingly the Nazis are taking their revenge on the local population. In our opinion, all that does is create resentment against the resistance. I'm sure you'll agree that can't be in your interest."

"Why don't you leave that decision to the people who know the Italians best," Mario said.

Lazio let the two go on. When they seemed spent, he said, simply, *"This is what we need from you,"* and proceeded to tick off a list of supplies: Sten guns, ammunition, dynamite, grenades, mortars, radios, boots, medical supplies. With this he turned to me and said, in English, *"Doctor, tell Tom what you need."*

Tom looked at me in surprise as I began my list. *"You're an American!"* he exclaimed, ignoring the things I'd mentioned. *"I thought you looked like one. An escaped POW?"* he asked. *"Or . . ."* and here his eyes narrowed as he perhaps considered less agreeable alternatives. Possibly he thought I was a member of his organization working at cross purposes. In any event, he relaxed visibly when I explained I was married to an Italian and had been caught here when the war broke out. I explained what had happened to Paola, and asked if there was anything he could do to help.

He puffed out his cheeks. *"I'd like to tell you that I will . . ."*

I assume my frustration was immediately visible to him, because he added, quickly, "I hope you'll believe me when I say it's not that I don't care."

"Don't tell me you care, tell me you'll help."

He looked at me and must have seen the pain that was coming to my eyes even as I fought it. He said softly, "Look, I'll be glad to take your information, but I'm simply not in a position to learn what you need to know. To be honest with you, this war is so fucked up, I don't know anyone who is. You really are a doctor?" he asked after a pause, as if he had to realign all of the pieces.

"Yes."

"That's good. Always helps to have one on the ground. You understand the point I was making about the need for the partisan groups to work together under our direction," he added, apparently happy to have found a kinsman to whom the logic of his argument must appeal.

I assume therefore that he was disappointed to hear me reply that I was only concerned with medical issues. "I'm not a tactician," I added. "Lazio makes those decisions."

"It's getting late," Lazio interjected. "Tell Tom what you need and let's get going."

"I'm running out of almost everything," I began, and proceeded to write down the things I needed and hand the paper to Tom.

"I'll do what I can," he said, looking at the list. He turned to Lazio and Mario. "As for the other things you need, we'll have to see. I'll have to report to my superiors."

"When you do," Mario said, "make sure to remind them that we're still expecting an invasion near Livorno, and also that we'll be able to do more to help if we're properly armed."

With that the meeting broke up. Lazio and I made it back to our base just as dawn was breaking. We didn't speak along the way, and when we returned I went off to be by myself.

OA   7 May 1944

The partisans have stepped up attacks on all types of targets, especially (coincidentally or not) railways, roads and bridges. There is a better sense of organization among the groups, which have allocated themselves into zones. Our group is in Zone 9. We have been receiving more supplies from the Allies lately. Perhaps this is a sign of confidence in us.

As a consequence of the increased attacks we have been on the move constantly. With the attacks have come German and Fascist patrols everywhere, and reprisals. In this area it would seem the warnings issued by the OSS man, Tom, were on the mark. As the Germans' frustration has grown over the partisans' attacks, they have taken it out on the local populace without regard to guilt. This is particularly true in response to the frequent assassinations of German soldiers. The Germans have been executing suspected partisans and partisan supporters at will. In one village four men were chosen at random, stood up against the church wall, and shot.

With some success, the Germans have renewed the tactic of arresting the families of young men who have fled. I have heard two versions of this tactic. In one, the Germans announce that, if the wanted man doesn't appear within such and such a time, they will take the family members in his place and ship them to labor camps. They actually did this a few times to demonstrate that they weren't bluffing. In a second version, the Germans threaten to execute the family members, and I know for sure of at least one instance in which they followed through. Of course, this creates enormous pressure on the young men, some of whom surrender—no doubt to their parents' anguish.

The Germans have used similar tactics in their attempts to capture partisan leaders. About two weeks ago, searching for our zone commander, called Pippo, who has gained fame for his exploits, the Germans rounded up the entire population of Montefegatesi, a beautiful mountaintop town in which Dante once took refuge. All the town's men were herded into the main piazza—conveniently located across from the German headquarters for that area—and accused of harboring Pippo. A machine gun was set on a tripod opposite the men. Meanwhile, the town's women and children were assembled to watch. The commanding officer announced that, unless Pippo was produced, the town would be destroyed, beginning with the execution of the men.

As the townspeople huddled together in terror, a man, who apparently had been ill, fainted. He was removed from the crowd and taken into the German headquarters—my comrades, engaging in the kind of humor that gives momentary release, say the Germans wanted to revive him so he could feel the full effect of his execution. As the story goes, the man spoke German, which he learned during his service in an Italian army unit on the Russian front. The man had been wounded and discharged (or so he said) and had returned to the town only the week before.

As the people continued to wait in the piazza, the man inside was able to convince the Germans that the town was not guilty of harboring Pippo. He knew them all, he said, and it simply was not true.

After another hour the commander marched outside and announced that, this time, there would be no execution. As horrible as it is to contemplate, no one doubts that next time there will be no reprieve.

OA   16 May 1944

We go from place to place, never sleeping in the same bed for more than a night. Our numbers swell and shrink, depending on the time and activity. I continue to be pretty much attached to Lazio, who has taken on an ever larger role. He is the clear number two to Pippo, whom I have seen only once. I continue to have a great deal of respect for Lazio as a man of both bravery and sound judgment. Alfredo is with us a fair amount of the time, but increasingly he is leading his own squads. I am constantly busy. If I'm not treating wounds of war, I'm treating the routine maladies of the group or whatever household we happen to be in. Last week, I delivered a baby boy, and the contrast between the mother's joy and the dismal situation into which the baby has come couldn't have been more striking.

I am glad to be busy, though. It keeps me from obsessing over the thoughts of Paola and Isabella. Every place we go, we seek information on the fate of our family. Nothing.

Tensions within the group often run high. Not long ago, we were joined for one night by a man, called Radio for reasons unclear to me, whom I remembered criticizing my reluctance to become involved with the resistance. Over the past few months I have become so used to traveling with the partisans—indeed, I am as hunted as any of them—that I was taken aback when Radio made it clear that he had not changed his opinion of me. "Still afraid to shoot anyone?" he taunted. There were five or six of us, including Lazio, and he looked at Radio as if to warn him off starting something.

"Not afraid," I said in a measured voice. "Determined. I got my fill of shooting in the last war, while you were a child. My job now is different." I was hoping Radio would let it go at that, but of course, he wouldn't.

"So, what you're saying is you're some kind of universalist. You proclaim you have a higher purpose than the rest of us."

"Not true," I began to protest, but he cut me off. I don't know what sparked his ire, but something was driving him on.

"Well, I've had my fill of people who proclaim high principles. If you can't choose between good and evil, you end up as a whore for evil."

"That's enough," Lazio interjected. "Daniel risks his life as much as you do. Now just keep quiet."

For a moment Radio retreated into silence, but then, like a river that couldn't be contained within its banks, he said, "Let me ask you a question, doctor. If tomorrow morning I walked through the door with two wounded people, one a comrade and the other a bit of Nazi scum, what would you do?"

"Unlike you, I would treat them both."

"Well, you're right that I wouldn't save them both. I'm speaking purely hypothetically, of course. The fact is, I never would have brought the Nazi back here in the first place. If he was alive when I found him, he'd be dead when I left." Radio snorted and a couple of the others laughed. "But you would treat them both," he continued. "All right, which one first?"

Lazio stood. "I said that's enough."

"No, that's all right, Lazio," I said. "I'm not ashamed of my stand. Perhaps it's Radio who should be ashamed of his, since he apparently thinks it's all right to adopt the most barbaric actions of his enemy." I turned back toward Radio, who was leaning back in his chair with a look on his face that suggested he'd never in his life been ashamed of anything. "The answer," I continued, "is that I would treat the man first who was in the most grave condition."

Radio rocked his chair forward onto all of its legs and leaned in. "Which means, as far as I'm concerned, that you can't tell the difference between good and evil. Or maybe you just refuse to admit to a difference.

"And let me tell you something else, dottore" (he gave the word as much derision as he could put into it). "If you're willing to treat each patient equally, you might as well travel with your German friends. That way they

230

can feed you and take care of you, and we all get treated anyway, right? But, of course, you know how ridiculous that suggestion is for the simple reason that these people you would treat equally wouldn't for one second let you minister to us, would they? They'd shoot us and you, too, before they allowed that. In the meantime, you eat our food and are willing to help the very scum who killed your wife and daughter."

"Arrested, not killed," I started in a voice that I'm sure suggested something more desperate than the need to make a mere correction.

"Arrested and sent north in the trains, right?" he responded without giving way.

I nodded.

He shrugged. "Same difference."

Without thought or hesitation, I was on him, pinning him still in his chair against the wall. And before he could recover and just as I regained control, Lazio pulled me away.

For a moment after we were separated I thought Radio might come at me. But he remained seated. He clucked his tongue and smiled dismissively. "So, it seems, dottore, you are capable of violence in the right circumstances. I wonder. If I were brought in together with a wounded Nazi, would you treat me at all?"

It took everything in me not to say no.

~ ~ ~ ~ ~

~ ~ ~

Chapter 28

O N A LATE JUNE evening so sweet it was almost possible for him to forget the war—almost possible to lighten the stone in his chest that held a place for Paola and Isabella—Daniel stood in a small clearing above the town of Castelnuovo di Garfagnana. From there he could see the town with its medieval fortress and the Serchio River flowing past slowly, for there had not been much rain. Farther on, the river would pass Lucca and empty into the sea near Pisa.

Perhaps an hour of twilight remained, and Daniel was determined to take full advantage of this first day in weeks his services had not been called upon, nor had it been necessary to move to another place. No doubt the next day would be different, but he considered one of the only good things about war to be the heightened imperative to live each moment fully. He breathed in the smells of wildflowers and warm grass and herbs, all of which grew in profusion. He reached down and pinched the soft spines of wild rosemary, and held his fingers to his nose to take in the scent.

In recent weeks Daniel and various members of the group had covered a great deal of ground. They had ranged as far south as Massaciuccoli in the hills and caves above the sea, and as far north as their present location in the Garfagnana. The tide of war was turning. The Allies had landed in France. Rome had been liberated at last. The outcome, if not imminent, was clearer every day.

Along with this optimism came an almost frantic craving to reunite with Paola and his children. It was a craving borne of nearness, a long distance runner's scent of the finish line. He still had no word about their fate, but he was confident in their ability to survive. No one knew better than he the amazing fortitude and determination Paola possessed. Perhaps it would be only months before the war would end. Then they would find each other. They would make love with the passion of the saved. They would promise, earnestly, that it would always be so. This is what he could tell himself with the heightened conviction of a perfect summer eve.

The next morning, Daniel and two others—Tito and a young *contadino* named Pietro—were again on the move, this time headed south toward Lucca. Over the months Daniel and Tito had spent much time together. Daniel had come to respect Tito for his seriousness of purpose and an overall dignity of bearing unexpected in such a burly, rough man. In turn, Tito had come to demonstrate respect for Daniel's quiet professionalism and, unlike many of the others who saw heroism only in terms of a willingness to fight, for his bravery, because in spite of his refusal to harm others, Daniel did not shy away from danger.

Two days later they arrived at a stone farmhouse in the hills, which Daniel recognized at once as the place where he and Francesco had been brought after they were saved—for he had come to appreciate this word as the definition of what had happened to them—the previous January. They had been there for only a few hours when they were joined by Alfredo, two strangers, and a man the group had taken prisoner.

It was late in the afternoon. Daniel happened to be outside the house as the group approached. The prisoner's head was covered by a makeshift hood. His hands were bound behind him; a rope around his neck joined another around his waist and a second rope by which his captors led him. The rope between neck and waist was too short for the man to stand upright, and so, trussed like an animal bound for market, he was pulled forward, blind, bent, and stumbling. The man wore a carabinieri uniform, and judging by the insignia and the amount of soiled braid, he was of high rank.

Standing in sharp contrast with this dismal picture were the man's captors. Alfredo in particular was exultant. He smiled and greeted Daniel with a hug and a kiss on both cheeks. "Hail Caesar!" he proclaimed with a laugh and a Roman salute that had more Fascist than Roman resonance. "We arrive bearing a great prize!—that is, if you believe shit in a uniform is a great prize!" he added as he embraced Tito. "Take the shit prize into the back room and tie him to a chair," Alfredo told Pietro. He put his arm around Daniel's shoulder. "Come inside and I'll tell you all about it."

"Today we scored a great victory," Alfredo continued as he put down his pack and rifle. "And we were lucky," he added with a smile.

"Who is he?" Daniel asked, cocking his head toward the back room. As he said this, Pietro opened the door long enough for Daniel to see that the prisoner had been bound to a chair in the center of the room. He was still hooded and his head still forced forward by a shortened rope.

"He is Major Silvio Petresco—whom we affectionately call *Putanesca*," Alfredo added with undiminished high spirits, playing on the word for a spicy sauce that meant, literally, whore-style—"and he is also the reason we're lucky. Last night several of us carried out a raid on the small carabinieri barracks in Ponte di Maddalena. Of course, I was happy to be attacking the barracks in my very home town. We took them completely by surprise. We shot four officers plus one German soldier who was there for who knows what reason—bad luck for him—and captured Major Putanesca here, which was incredibly good luck for us. We still don't know why he happened to be there, but I guarantee we'll find out that and a lot of other things before we kill him."

Daniel stared at Alfredo, not bothering to hide his revulsion at the blithely jubilant proclamation. For his part, Alfredo gave no sign that he noticed. "Is it our policy now to kill our prisoners?" Daniel asked, coldly.

"Oh, well, maybe not," Alfredo replied with a dismissive wave, as if he couldn't be bothered with such details. "Maybe we'll kill him, maybe we won't. Depends on how cooperative he is, I suppose. He has a lot of important information in his head. We'll do whatever we have to in order to get it out. And I almost forgot to mention—we were able to take boxes of files from the barracks. We don't know what's in them yet, but they'll probably be useful. Lazio has the boxes. He's supposed to meet us here with them."

Daniel nodded, relieved to hear that Lazio's sound judgment might prevail in the treatment of the prisoner but, even more so, hopeful that something might be learned about his family.

Lazio joined them the following morning, accompanied by Lido and two pimply faces whom Daniel presumed had only recently become eligible for conscription and chose the partisan alternative. Over the next few days, fighters came and went, taking what they could of the prisoner's information. Lazio and some of the others pored over the cache of files. Occasionally, one of them would take a piece of paper into the back room in the hope of getting the prisoner to provide clarification.

But the prisoner was proving a tough nut to crack. Deprived of sleep, food and water, and beaten but so far more to intimidate than to damage, he remained defiant. The result was usually the sound of slaps and threats, but not much information.

One night, Lazio, obviously tired and frustrated at the lack of progress, said to Daniel, "Well, doctor, perhaps you can offer something from your bag of tricks? What's that stuff called? Sodium-something, maybe?"

Daniel smiled wanly. "Sodium pentothal. Sorry, I have nothing like that. Such drugs are more mythical than effective anyway."

"I was afraid you'd say that." Lazio sighed audibly. "We're going to turn up the heat, you know," he said as if he were seeking permission.

Daniel remained silent, and Lazio continued. "This man knows too much for us to let him keep the knowledge to himself. If he continues to resist our less severe methods . . ." Lazio let the thought hang in the air. "Oh, I know what you're going to say, doctor," he added, holding up his hand in a preemptive gesture before he went on. "You think we've not been so humane. But I guarantee, if the tables were turned—if I were the prisoner, for instance—you would understand just how forbearing we've been."

"You may be surprised to hear it, Lazio, but I believe you." Daniel let out a short, ironic laugh. "I don't know whether to be pleased or put upon that I seem somehow to have taken on the role of conscience for the group. But since I have, I'll just say that the enemy should not be allowed to set the standard for our behavior."

"So you've made clear to Radio."

"Ah, yes. And how is our heartless friend Radio? All is lost if he's our standard. It's clear enough that you, Alfredo, and the others will do what you think you have to with this prisoner and that there's nothing I can do to stop you. All I can say is, I hope you won't sink to the depths of our enemies. Our first duty as humans may be to survive. Our second should be to not have to regret every minute that we do. And I won't be a torture room doctor. I won't revive him only so he can be beaten again."

"That's all well and good, but you should bear in mind that this man may be your best hope for discovering the fate of your family."

235

The same night word reached the group that the Germans had taken revenge for the attack on the carabinieri barracks in Ponte di Maddalena—and in particular for the death of one of their soldiers there—by rounding up a dozen men—all of them beyond conscription age and none members of the resistance—and executing them in the town's piazza. Before they opened fire the Germans apparently thought it necessary to justify their actions by reminding the condemned and anyone within hearing that they had been warned that such would be the consequence of attacks on their forces.

Daniel recognized the names of some of the men as his patients and struggled to quell the murderous bile that arose by reminding himself of his words to Lazio only a short time before. The next day, the test would be infinitely greater.

* * *

SHORTLY AFTER SUNRISE, Daniel was awakened by a tug on his shirtsleeve from Alfredo, who said that a farmer from up the road had come to see if Daniel could take a look at his sick wife. The woman had been vomiting all night, and the man was afraid for her. Daniel rubbed his eyes and sat up slowly. He noted to himself that, for the first time in days, he had been able to sleep through the night. He felt no less tired for it.

Alfredo, who had been taking turns with the others interrogating the prisoner and combing through the captured documents, looked haggard. Daniel could hear nothing from the back room. "What's going on back there?" he asked, fearful of the answer.

"Nothing," Alfredo responded, clearly irritated. "The bastard's tough. I'll give him that. We're letting him get a few hours sleep before we start in on him again. He was getting so confused, he probably couldn't have told us much if he wanted to. I'm running out of patience with the guy, though."

Daniel didn't respond, but stared at Alfredo, who brought his face close. His eyes were bloodshot and his breath reeked of make-do tobacco. "Listen to me." He kept his voice low, but it had the force of steam being pushed through a pinhole. "This man can tell us about our family. I know it." Daniel remained silent and Alfredo continued. "He's high up. He has to know what's going on. There's no way people are being sent north on trains and this guy doesn't know it."

"But does he know anything that can really help us? We know they were sent north. The question is, what happened to them? I hope you're right, but

I'm not optimistic. His job is probably done when the doors to the train close."

Daniel stood. He had slept fully dressed except for his boots, which he pulled on. Outside, the farmer, a middle-aged man with few teeth and leathery skin whom Daniel had seen before, extended his callous-encrusted hand. Daniel took it and listened patiently as the man described his wife's symptoms, then asked him to wait while he got his kit.

Inside, the others were stirring. In the far corner of the room, Lazio and Lido were discussing something in a low voice. Daniel approached to let them know where he was going. He expected to return within a couple of hours.

"Right," Lazio said, looking up from his seated position. "Lido and I were just talking about some things we need to get done today. We may not be here when you return, but we shouldn't be back too late. Anyway, we've been here too long for safety. No doubt the enemy is searching madly for Petresco. We'll need to move on."

"What about the prisoner?" Daniel asked.

"I'll leave a couple of people behind—probably Alfredo and one of the young guys—to stay with him."

Daniel's visit to the farmer's house took longer than expected. He was able to treat the wife, who was suffering from a routine intestinal ailment, but was delayed when he was asked to examine one of the couple's daughters, who was displaying similar symptoms. Afterward, he took his time returning to the group's base, enjoying the moment of freedom and the warm summer's day.

As he approached the stone house, the door opened and Lazio stepped out. He appeared agitated. Sweat soaked through his shirt and dripped from his brow.

"What's happened?" Daniel asked, stopping in front of Lazio, who blocked the door.

"Come with me," Lazio commanded, putting his hand on Daniel's shoulder and steering him toward a woodpile about twenty yards beyond the house. "Did you run into Alfredo on your way back here?" Lazio asked.

They stopped next to a tree stump near the woodpile. "No, why? Is something wrong?"

Lazio took a deep breath. "I'm afraid so."

"Something's happened to Alfredo?"

Lazio shook his head no. The usual dark intensity of his eyes was heightened by circles of sleeplessness and a profound sadness. "About an hour ago," he began, "we returned here and went into the back room to check on the prisoner. When I opened the door, I saw Alfredo standing there, his fists clenched, blood and sweat everywhere. The kid I left with him was sitting on the floor, dazed and bleeding from his mouth. The prisoner was still tied to the chair, but he was covered in blood too. His head was slumped forward."

"What . . . "

Lazio put his hand on Daniel's arm. "Let me finish. Alfredo looked up at me and I could see he'd been crying. His face was contorted. Tito came to the door behind me. Alfredo only stared at us for a second, almost as if he didn't recognize us, before he turned back to the prisoner and started hitting him with his fists as hard as he could.

"I screamed at him to stop. But he kept hitting the man and crying until Tito pushed past me and tackled him." Lazio stopped to collect his thoughts.

"Go on," Daniel said, his heart racing.

"The prisoner was dead. And he looked like he must have been dead for some time."

Daniel felt himself sink, but his dejection quickly changed to anxiety when the look on Lazio's face indicated he had not yet told him the worst part of the story. "Why?" he asked, hoarsely. "I don't understand what happened."

"At first, I had no idea," Lazio said, holding his arms wide like a supplicant. "I was astonished. I yelled at him. Are you crazy! What have you done! And so forth. He seemed to be calming down, so Tito got off him and helped him up. It looked like Alfredo was going to explain but he said a few incoherent words and bolted—headed for the woods. In the meantime, the kid just sat there on the floor, dumbstruck. What the hell happened? I asked him. I helped him up, and he said he didn't know. He said one minute he was standing next to Alfredo watching him ask the prisoner questions—slapping him around a little but not beating him."

"Did the kid know what Alfredo was questioning him about?" Daniel interrupted.

"He said it had something to do with people the carabinieri had arrested. Alfredo had a sheaf of papers from the captured files and was reading from them. Did you know so and so? Why was he arrested? What happened to him? And so on. According to the kid, the prisoner kept insisting that he didn't know the people on the list. Then, suddenly, Alfredo stopped and stared at one of the papers. The kid said Alfredo turned white and held the paper in front of the prisoner and forced him to read it. He asked the prisoner whether it was his signature on the bottom. The prisoner nodded yes. Alfredo asked what more he knew about the list and the prisoner said nothing, that was all he knew; he'd signed a thousand pieces of paper.

"Alfredo kept reading from the papers in his hand. Then, all of a sudden he went crazy and started beating the man. The kid said he tried to stop him, but Alfredo hit him in the face and threw him to the floor."

Lazio stopped, now looking truly ashen.

In a whisper, all that remained after a wrenching act of volition, Daniel said, "Tell me."

Lazio reached into his pants pocket and pulled out several sheets of paper that had been folded and creased repeatedly. They were smeared with blood and dirt. He unfolded them and, wordlessly, handed the first several pages to Daniel.

Daniel scanned the first page. On it was a typewritten heading, "Train #070144LULIPI January 1944," followed by pages of names, which were organized under locations in Lucca and adjoining provinces. Lazio stood silently while Daniel went through the list. Not until the fourth page, under Ponte di Maddalena, did the names appear that he dreaded to see. The Rosettis were listed. And there, under Gideon: Paola Rosetti and child, unnamed.

Daniel's hands shook as he continued to read. He tried to calm himself with the thought that this was nothing more than a confirmation of what he already knew—that following their arrest they had been sent north by train.

Lazio remained silent as Daniel stared at the list and then at the next pages. The last sheet contained an asterisk and a handwritten note in the margin, which it took him a moment to decipher: "Colonel, this was the train that was the subject of the letter to the Duce, a copy of which is attached." The note was signed, "Petresco."

Lazio nodded toward the paper. "I assume that was the signature Alfredo was asking about."

Daniel looked up. Before he could ask, Lazio handed him the remaining pages he held in his hand. It was a carbon copy of a letter, dated 12 February, from the administrative chief of Lucca Province to Mussolini in Salo`. "This is what was attached."

Duce,

I am writing to call your attention to a growing problem and to beg your intercession with our German allies in the matter of the transport of Italian citizens for labor in the north. Allow me to preface my remarks by stating that, as you have said, in these times of grave labor shortage we must be willing to take extraordinary steps. Since last autumn, the Republican government and its provinces have taken such steps, among other things assisting the Germans by assigning certain of these citizens of dubious loyalty to support the war effort in factories within German territory; in particular, in Bavaria.

The problem to which I refer and which I hope you will take up with our allies at the highest level is that of the occasionally harsh and abusive treatment of our citizens. You are no doubt aware of the almost inhuman conditions in which many of our soldiers found themselves last September when, after the Germans instructed them to lay down their arms, they were shipped north in conditions worse than those typically endured even by British or American prisoners of war.

It is my sad duty, Duce, to ensure that you are equally aware of the deleterious effect on morale that has occurred over the state's mistreatment of private citizens in a similar fashion. Here I would point out that, even if the stories that have reached us were fabrications, they would be nonetheless of considerable propaganda value to our enemies. If I may be frank, as such tales gain currency, they make governance of the provinces ever more difficult. People are ever more willing to take drastic steps—including joining partisan ranks—to avoid being sent north.

In our province, one case in particular has caused great popular fear and consternation. On 7 January, we dispatched a train full of workers (Train #070144LULIPI, for your information should you wish to make further inquiries) to Bolzano for onward travel. Several days later, we were informed that, in Bolzano, for reasons which are not yet clear, the wagons from Lucca and Pisa Provinces were decoupled and sent to a siding where they were allowed to sit in the freezing cold without water, food, or any method of producing warmth.

Duce, I know it will touch your heart and that you will appreciate the grave effect it had on popular morale in our province when word reached us that everyone aboard that train died of exposure. I also know this is a matter you will bring to the attention . . .

The rest was a blur through Daniel's tears. He brought his hand to his eyes, but the tears would not be contained. They trailed down his cheeks and fell to the papers in his hand, striking with the crisp staccato of the first raindrops on a tin roof.

~ ~ ~ ~ ~

~ ~ ~

Chapter 29

OA   28 August 1944

IN QUIET MOMENTS WHEN the fury is spent, it is the hopelessness of eternal loss that sneaks up on me like a bank of fog. I am beset by images, or fragments of images, from my former life. Paola and the artist Jospin on the Seine. Fits of jealousy over Paola and Alessandro (how foolish it makes me feel)! Francesco being born, and the fear that Isabella might be born on a crowded, desperate train ride. I try to remember the last time we made love, and can only remember the last time we tried and were interrupted by Isabella's cries—and of course I feel guilty when I remember the puerile, hateful thoughts that came to me. It's foolish, I know. I was—am—a good father. But rational or not, it is a terrible thing for the last thoughts of one's child to be thoughts such as these. And then, that last morning. Such a simple thing—a kiss blown at me rather than risk passing on her cold. Oh, God, how I wish she would have risked it! How I think about the soft fullness of her lips and how I want to feel them again against mine. It's such a small thing, and such an enormous, overwhelming thing too.

There are times when I will begin to cry and only become aware of it when others avert their eyes or a kind hand rests briefly on my shoulder. And then there are the days when it is nothing but rage within me. Churning, roiling, seething rage, cataclysmic in its scale, fulminating and unquenchable except, perhaps, or so I think, by the unalloyed poison of revenge. These are the days when, if I'm lucky, I remember to pray for deliverance from the poison, the days when I may have the wit to recognize the thug Radio when I look in the mirror, or the days when the better part of good fortune may be as simple as not having a convenient target on which to vent the fury.

And then I am amazed to find that the world moves on. My suffering is unique only to me.

Meanwhile, the Allies are closing in on Lucca, and the partisans are emboldened. They have stepped up attacks everywhere, and casualties are high. The Germans respond to each attack with more punitive killings. It is the people in the towns and villages who suffer most. There is nowhere for them to go. A German retreat is inevitable at this point, but this doesn't prevent the killings and destruction on both sides. The outcome may no longer be in doubt, but there will be much new misery before it is realized.

We continue to move frequently from place to place but, increasingly, our moves are more for offensive rather than defensive purposes. The decision is never mine, of course. To me, it is all but meaningless. I am a sort of glorified medical corpsman. I go where I'm needed, though to the extent I have what would be called a home unit, it is with Lazio's group.

I have no complaints about this. Of all the partisans I've dealt with, I continue to rank Lazio at the top. He possesses the qualities of toughness, bravery and good judgment that make for a good leader. He's managed to hold onto a sense of compassion, too—not an easy feat and one that, unfortunately, many otherwise good men have not been able to pull off. Sometimes I fear I must add even myself to the ranks of the soul-hardened, though if I'm being charitable I tell myself that my compassion, like most of my senses, is anesthetized, not dead. I sincerely hope so.

Francesco is still safe, and I've decided there is no point to telling him now about Paola and Isabella. Even if I could see him to tell him, I wouldn't be able to stay long enough to help him through the grief. If the war continues on its present course, we will have to cross that bridge soon enough. I often wonder exactly how I will break the news to him. Then I remember that he is a child of this war and will have readier comprehension than is healthy for any human being to have.

I continue to avoid Alfredo as much as I can. The seeds of bitterness, rage and vengeance that have long been present in him are now in full flower, having been perfectly nurtured by the events of June. He will not be reasoned with—though I shouldn't imply that I'm the one to reason with him. He interprets all events, no matter how banal, through a screen of his wounds and his cynicism. Nothing that passes through this screen can have happened for reasons less than malign. The only alternative explanation he allows is incompetence and stupidity. In his world there is no room for randomness. In his world the only relief comes from vengeance. He is never happy, but after he has killed someone or blown up something he embodies the temporary relief that can be experienced when an abscess is lanced but not cured.

Yet even as I write these things I am aware of my disingenuousness. Everything I say about Alfredo is true, except that the main reason I avoid him is not his caustic demeanor, however unpleasant it may be. No, the truth is that I'm afraid of my own emotions—afraid of becoming what Alfredo has become, afraid that it is the rage that will win out. When I see Alfredo, everything gets stirred up. And if I manage to control the demons, he looks at me with a strange contempt, as if such control represents nothing more than an inability to feel.

Of course, he just might be right. If he is filled with hot pus, what am I filled with? What afflicts me? When it is not fury, is it the chronic inflammation of sadness or grief? Is sadness enough? Does mere grief dishonor my loved ones? What about grief mixed with a desire for revenge— whatever Alfredo thinks, that desire in me is the major reason I don't want to be near him. He is contagious.

Sometimes I think perhaps the very ability to suppress feelings of violence and rage is a sign, not of humanity or civility or progress as I want to believe, but of a fundamental weakness—a vulnerability—that exists as part of the Darwinian order of things. What if the impulse to decency on the part of some people is really nothing more than a fatally flawed evolutionary branch—a defective line to be winnowed out, leaving only the carnivores behind? Some are content to throw up their hands and assign such questions to the will of God, but hard as I've looked I can find no evidence of a God, or at least not of one who wishes to or can deliver more than Darwin can.

It has occurred to me that my desire to fight the urges of revenge—deny them perhaps is a more accurate description—might be nothing more than a perverse form of selfishness or self-preservation, not the noble ideal I typically ascribe to it. It is the equivalent of curling into a fetal ball and willing away the unpleasantness of the outside world. After all, one can't simply go on lancing the abscess forever (and, witness Alfredo, the lancing has no lasting benefit anyway). Like so many others, I am already a victim of this war. If I am unable to cure my abscess—unable to control the poison in me—when it is over, I will surely drown in my own pus as Alfredo seems destined to drown in his.

OA   30 September 1944

It is hard to believe that over a year has passed since Italy switched sides. Hope then that the armistice would lead to better days has long since been proven not merely false, but profoundly so. And yet hope, that defrocked shaman, persists.

The Gothic Line is pushed back beyond Barga. Lucca is in Allied hands. Yesterday, for the first time in ages, we entered Ponte di Maddalena without fear or furtiveness. While many arrived on foot, many others, myself included, arrived in (and atop!) cars and trucks with victory horns blaring. Such displays may be premature but even the normally circumspect Lazio was photographed posing triumphantly on the hood of a dusty old sedan.

The Rosetti home is in the derelict state in which we last saw it when we snuck into town. I always assumed that such a lovely place would be requisitioned for officers or party functionaries. Instead, parts of it obviously have been used by squatters. Of course, I know firsthand how the desperation to find shelter can trump property rights. God only knows how many houses we've appropriated for our own use during this past year.

One of the amazing things is the chameleon quality of many of the local inhabitants. Citizens who survived by currying favor with the Fascists act, with surprising success, the part of liberated slaves. They cheer the partisan fighters and praise our leaders as conquering heroes.

Most of these chameleons—or I should say would-be chameleons, for they are not all successful in changing colors—can be placed into categories defined by the partisans. The partisans, who know well the local environment from which they've sprung, are quite decisive about this placement—that is, they know the terrain well enough to see through the transmutation of the creatures.

One category consists of those whose basic color was never in doubt. These are the people who secretly, actively cooperated with the partisans. They are the ones who, by day, gave the appearance of supporting the Fascists (or Nazifascisti, as we've taken to calling the blended form), while by night gave active help to the resistance. These people are now celebrated. Ordinarily, I would say the townspeople's public acceptance of this praise and celebration might be premature—we could suffer new reverses, after all. But there is a defensive aspect to it as well in that open acceptance of the partisans' praise and public identification with them inoculates this group against hotheaded retribution by those who might not have gotten the word that they should be considered friends, not enemies.

Which brings me to the second category, the failed chameleons. This group includes those who have been identified as collaborators of the Nazifascisti and who now try to portray themselves otherwise. Many of the worst of these collaborators long ago met their fate at the hands of the partisans, while others who have been unable to change their hue effectively are, even as I write this, being subjected to unspeakable retribution by (it pains me to say it) the likes of Alfredo or, even worse, the cretinous Radio. Even this morning, a collaborationist merchant was shot and hanged upside down near the piazza. I understand all too well the rage that motivates such actions, but I am sickened by them nonetheless.

The third, and largest, category consists of those poor souls who have simply had to live day by day doing their best to appease both sides just to survive. They have had to walk the tightrope. Stumbling or leaning too far in any direction would prove disastrous. What they had going for them was experience in performing this balancing act over millennia in the face of countless invaders.

But perhaps the most surprising group of chameleons is the one containing prominent people who somehow have managed to change from one side to the other and remain prominent. These people, for reasons I can only guess at, have been adjudged untouchable despite clear association with the old regime.

To find an example of this phenomenon one need look no further than the welcoming crowds that lined the streets when we returned to town. There, wearing the armband of our Green Flames, smiling and waving, were the Bucas! There they were! Bruno and Hilde, Renata (but not her husband, whose whereabouts are not known) and her children, whom she was encouraging to cheer. Bruno looked relatively well, as appropriate to one who no doubt has been deprived of little. He'd obviously learned some kind of lesson since he was roughed up last year. To look at them one would think they never had a pro-Fascist thought. Alfredo told me they even waved at him, which he regarded as a theatrical performance worthy of a blue ribbon.

Here's the interesting thing. Alfredo of course hasn't forgotten the role the Bucas played in bringing his desertion to the attention of the authorities. For that matter, neither have I. It was nothing more than a mean-spirited riposte to Alfredo's (undeniably intemperate) remarks. Ever since, he's been talking about getting even. But he's been told by Lazio that the Bucas are off limits. Neither Alfredo nor anyone else is to touch them. Lazio wouldn't explain, so it's left to us to imagine what bribes were paid, debts called in, and so on, to keep the Bucas safe.

In the meantime, there's no shortage of targets for Alfredo's retribution. And the question he will pursue—with my assistance and encouragement, at that—is, what were the events that led up to our family's arrest? For all of our nosing around since last January we have been unable to discover any reason for it. Now we may get our chance.

~ ~ ~ ~ ~

~ ~ ~

Chapter 30

O N THE DAY BEFORE Christmas 1944, Daniel awoke to a brittle morning. It had sleeted the previous day and now a shimmer of ice covered the landscape in the faint light. He dressed quickly, putting on a heavy blue wool sweater Paola had bought him three Christmases and worlds ago. It had begun to pill and he stopped for a moment to pinch off the most egregious of the tiny balls from the left shoulder.

He was back in the house in Ponte di Maddalena. His return, at the end of November, followed several long talks with Lazio, who wanted him to remain with the group as it pushed the offensive. The subject of Daniel's leaving, which he began to broach shortly after the town was liberated at the end of September, was one of a very few points of contention between the two men, who had developed respect and liking for one another. Lazio maintained that Daniel's services would continue to be most valuable in the field. "If I get shot, I want you right beside me," he'd said with a smile that only barely masked an undercurrent Daniel interpreted as a charge of disloyalty or ingratitude.

"I don't think it's a good idea to be that close to anyone who gets shot," Daniel responded with an equally superficial lightness. "Listen," he went on, deciding to venture beneath the surface, "you know that I will forever be a part of this group. I'll never forget what you did for me and Francesco."

"But you'll remember from afar, is that it?" The smile was still there, thinner now.

"Not exactly. The fact is, I can do much more good for many more people if I can reestablish myself in one place. Making house calls over mountain roads is not a very efficient use of my time. I can treat many more patients if they come to me."

Left unsaid was his growing desire to infuse a sense of order into the jumble his life had become. Immediately after the world-altering discoveries of June, he had welcomed the distractions of life on the run, when keeping his mind occupied was less a matter of self-discipline than imposed need. Now he wanted to establish a new center of gravity, and to draw Francesco into it. Of course, none of these things could be discussed with Lazio, who would immediately rebuke him for selfishness and remind him that he was hardly the only one who had suffered during the war.

Lazio shot Daniel a skeptical look. "If you were talking about treating common colds and diarrhea, I might agree with you. But those who suffer battlefield wounds won't be reassured by the efficiency of your central location."

With a promise that he would come in an emergency, Daniel held his ground.

The decision was not without regret. The Rosetti house often overwhelmed him with what he perceived as its vast emptiness. Memories of happier times found him and battered him, filling him at turns with grief or a desire for vengeance. He cleaned up the bedroom he shared with Paola as best he could, then found he couldn't occupy it. Especially he couldn't sleep in their bed, and slept instead in one of the small guest rooms that were better suited to his penitential state of mind. He made a halfhearted effort to restore some kind of order to Isabella's room, knowing even as he did that, once finished, he would close the door and not open it again.

Francesco's room was a different matter. Daniel's emotional state was less important than the obligation he felt to ease the devastating homecoming that awaited Francesco. So he cleaned and polished the room, keeping himself warm with the cathartic effort of the scrubbing during which, on his knees, he was sometimes surprised to find tears mixed in with the sweat that dripped from his forehead onto the soapy swirls on the terra cotta floor.

Daniel had contacted the nuns in October and expressed a wish for Francesco to come home as soon as possible. They responded that Francesco was now adjusted to his surroundings, was doing well in his studies, and had made friends. They suggested it would be better for him to finish out the term.

Daniel had agreed, reluctantly, because he missed his son. At the same time, he was relieved—though not without guilt—at the prospect of putting off the difficult time to come. Now he was determined, amid an overload of patients, to find time to make the homecoming as cheerful as possible. The sisters had told Francesco to expect Daniel on Christmas Day.

On this day before Christmas Daniel was preoccupied with the many small tasks that remained before Francesco returned. He had done the big things. He had gotten the house in order, found gifts he thought Francesco would like—a clever wooden train set and an artist's kit he assembled from several sources and packaged neatly in a red enamel metal box that had previously held automotive tools—even as he knew how much these things inevitably must pale in the face of the emptiness and sorrow that would be Francesco's true find. Now he set about last-minute chores.

He made his way to the kitchen and put on a pot of coffee that consisted only in the tiniest fraction of coffee and mostly of chicory and herbs and which, Daniel often thought wryly as he recalled his love of Parisian cafés, was one of the best daily proofs that one could get used to anything. The actual coffee, which he rationed as if it were diamond dust, was received from a Brazilian soldier whose hand he had bandaged, the Brazilian contingent being one of the components of the Allied forces in his area. Many of the town's inhabitants had reacted with surprise at the sight of, not the British or American forces they expected, but a stew of Moroccans, Brazilians, and most surprising, American Negroes who constituted the bulk of the US Army's 92nd Division.

As usual, Daniel had entered Christmas week determined to limit the number of patients he would see. As usual, he was nearly supine in the face of callers asking for his help. Thus, he still expected patients that day, considered it a victory that he was able to schedule them later than first light, and pleasantly surprised that, so far, none had decided to come early.

Twenty minutes later, as he finished a piece of bread and unconsciously grimaced following a sip of now tepid coffee, a knock on the door announced the arrival of Giancarlo Ferretti and his severely arthritic septuagenarian mother. Their entrance was accompanied by a blast of bitterly raw air. Daniel quickly pushed the door closed.

"*Buon Natale*," the woman declared, straining to look up from her stooped position. The effort had the painful aspect of trying to bend back a warped board.

"And to you," Daniel responded, leading them to his office. "Who is my patient today?" he asked with a smile as he helped the woman out of her coat. Giancarlo, in his mid-forties, was missing his left eye, the result of an accident at the forge he operated. The injury was not recent but, as a consequence of improper treatment at the time, continued to trouble him. His mother suffered mostly from the predictable ills of her age.

"Mama's arthritis is making her miserable," Giancarlo said.

The woman nodded gravely in agreement. "It's terrible," she added, "or you know we wouldn't have troubled you on a holiday."

"Don't give it a thought," Daniel responded. "Let's examine you and see what we can do." Even as he said this he knew that any relief he was able to offer would be mostly in the form of professional solace and, perhaps, a new supply of aspirin. Ironically, the supplies available to him had diminished since the Allies arrived. Although he had talked to an American doctor, a Captain Sullivan, about securing the supplies he needed, he had received nothing. In the meantime, the things he had been receiving in air drops to the partisans had ceased to arrive, either because the front had moved past them or because the partisans were keeping the supplies for themselves.

"I hear your boy is coming home," Giancarlo said as he helped Daniel move his mother into a more comfortable position.

"Tomorrow."

"Sad about his mother and the others," the old woman said, shaking her head.

"How is he taking it?" Giancarlo asked.

"He doesn't know yet." Daniel briefly explained why he had delayed giving Francesco the news. "What have you been doing for the arthritis?"

Giancarlo answered for his mother. "Warm compresses, mostly, and she tries to keep moving as much as she can, as you suggested. The cold weather makes it worse."

"How's her diet? She's getting enough to eat?"

"On and off. You know how it is."

"She's taking the aspirin?"

"No. She said it made her feel sick to her stomach."

"Did she take it with food, as I suggested?"

"It ruins the taste of the food," the woman offered.

"Signora," Daniel began in a voice of professional reproach, "we have very few tools at our disposal in these times. Try taking the aspirin a half hour after you've eaten."

"It still gives a bad taste."

"Nevertheless," he said sternly, "it is the most powerful thing we have." He cocked his ear at the sound of a door opening and closing; presumably his next patient had let himself in. Giancarlo began the deliberate process of helping his mother into her coat. "You must see to it she takes the aspirin— but with food to make it easier on her stomach," Daniel said to him.

A moment later, there was a knock on the office door. "One moment," Daniel called out. "I'm with a patient."

"It's Alfredo," a voice said. "Hurry up. You're needed."

Daniel and the others looked up in surprise. "What do we owe you, doctor?" Giancarlo asked as they made for the door. "Money is a little difficult, but we have some very nice potatoes and herbs."

"You owe me nothing," Daniel said, his hand on the doorknob. "We're neighbors. All we did was talk, after all. Have a happy Christmas," he added before Giancarlo could protest.

When they opened the office door Alfredo was standing there with an expression that suggested he would not have waited much longer before he barged in. He was bundled against the cold, including a woolen watch cap pulled down below his ears. After a brief exchange of greetings, Giancarlo said he and his mother would show themselves out.

"What's wrong?" Daniel asked Alfredo.

"You've got to come with me. Lazio has been wounded."

* * *

ALFREDO TOOK DANIEL north by car to a villa situated between the small city of Barga and the village of Sommocolonia. Lazio had been shot in the abdomen, Alfredo explained during the drive. "He was in a lot of pain when I left."

"When did it happen?"

"Early this morning. Lazio and three of the other guys—I think Tito's the only one you know—stumbled on a German patrol. Two of the guys were killed outright. Lazio was hit in the gut. I don't know how they missed Tito, big as he is, but he ran and has a twisted ankle to show for it."

"He's not the fastest guy around, either. I'm surprised he got away."

"He said he scurried over a ridge and that they only pursued him for a minute or two. And they must have been in a hurry, because they didn't do anything with the ones they shot. Lucky for Lazio. If they'd gotten their hands on him, he wouldn't have bothered struggling to stay alive, that's for sure. After they left, Tito went back to check. Bad ankle and all he was able to carry Lazio to the place we're going to now."

"Of course I'll do what I can for him," Daniel said, "but sometime tomorrow I'll need you to drive me to the convent to pick up Francesco."

Alfredo blew out his cheeks. "Tomorrow, right. Tomorrow's Christmas. I will if I can, but don't count on it."

"Listen, Alfredo," Daniel began, his voice rising, "Francesco's waited long enough. He's expecting me tomorrow. Actually, he's probably expecting me and Paola. I intend to get to him."

"I understand," Alfredo replied with new softness, his eyes on the road. "But listen to me. There's something funny going on."

"What . . ."

"The place where Lazio ran into the patrol . . . "

"It's not like Lazio to be so careless," Daniel interrupted.

"No. Or Tito, either. Tito said they were surprised because as far as they knew the German lines were farther north. He thinks the fact they didn't mop things up after the fight is suspicious. As I said, not only did they not go after Tito, they didn't bother to check on the ones they'd shot. After all, it's not every day that they have a chance to grab up a fighter of Lazio's importance."

"Meaning?"

"We're not sure. Tito thinks it was a reconnaissance patrol. Maybe the Germans and Fascists are planning an attack."

Daniel gave Alfredo a skeptical look. "Doesn't sound very likely. They've been in retreat for months. If they counterattack anywhere, my bet would be toward Florence, from around Bologna where they're still in control. The Gothic Line's not very strong here, is it?"

"We didn't think so. A few German units and a bunch of reconstituted Fascists. We've seen evidence that the Duce is trying to build up the Monte

Rosa Division, but we've assumed it was for defensive purposes—to do his bit in anchoring the line."

"So?"

Alfredo shrugged, then grimaced as the car's suspension bottomed into a deep pothole. "I don't know what to say. That patrol bothers me. I contacted a few of the other groups in the area to let them know about Lazio and ask if they'd seen anything suspicious. Only one of them said they'd seen anything out of the ordinary—a small column of SS about twenty kilometers from here. I suggested a few reconnaissance patrols of our own might be in order, but they all thought it could wait until after Christmas."

"Because we all know how reverential the Nazis are," Daniel said.

Alfredo laughed. "No, the real problem the Nazis would face would be getting any of their Italian Fascist brethren to work on a holiday."

They arrived at the villa, the home of a sympathizer, early in the afternoon. Daniel couldn't help but notice, wryly, that it was far nicer than any of the places he had stayed in when he was traveling with the group. The villa had come through the war remarkably unscathed. Nevertheless, the final stretch of road to the main house, washed out and iced up, was too much for Alfredo's expropriated rattletrap Fiat sedan, and they had to get out and walk.

A limping Tito greeted them and immediately led Daniel to the bedroom where Lazio lay, unconscious. Alfredo followed. "How long has he been out?" Daniel asked.

"He woke up when I picked him up to carry him here," Tito responded, "then he passed out again. He's stirred a few times since then, I think mostly from the pain."

"We've given him morphine," Alfredo added. "But we're running low."

Daniel pulled back the covers to inspect the wound. "His pulse and color aren't too bad."

"He doesn't seem to be bleeding so much," Tito observed as Daniel removed the bandages.

"Not externally, anyway." He probed the wound lightly. Lazio stirred. "The entry looks fairly clean. The problem is, we don't know how much internal damage was done. Why didn't you take him to the hospital at Barga?" he asked Alfredo.

"Barga's still too close to the front line," Tito said.

"There are still too many spies—too many people who would be willing to make a few pieces of silver by turning him in," Alfredo added.

Daniel began to clean the wound. Lazio's eyes fluttered open as Daniel touched him, then closed again. Between grimaces a faint smile crossed his lips as he murmured, "I told you I needed you by my side."

"Can you remove the bullet?" Tito asked.

"I'm not sure." Daniel packed the wound and rebandaged it. "Let's talk downstairs. Stoke the fire first. We need to keep him warm."

They went into the kitchen, where three partisans whom Daniel recognized were gathered around the table eating cheese and olives. All had sullen, worried expressions on their faces.

"Welcome back, doctor," one of them said, somberly, and the others added their welcomes.

"How's the commander?" one of the men asked, motioning for Daniel to take a seat at the table.

Tito also sat down, grimacing as he shifted his weight.

"You've done the right things for him," Daniel said, focusing on Alfredo, who remained standing. "In truth, I can't do much more."

"Doesn't the bullet have to come out?" Alfredo asked.

"That depends. He seems to be stable, which suggests the bullet may have missed vital organs. His temperature is slightly elevated, as is to be expected. There's been some internal bleeding, but I can't tell how much. Septicemia is always a danger. How is your supply of sulfa drugs? Mine ran out a long time ago," he added.

"We have some left," Tito said, "and we're expecting more soon."

"I know you're concerned about the safety of the hospital in Barga," Daniel continued. "Nevertheless, that's where Lazio should be, so the wound can be explored properly. Anyway," he waved his hand to erase the slate, "it's water under the bridge. At this point he probably shouldn't be moved until we know more by observing him."

"I don't understand, Daniel," Alfredo said. "Why can't you do the surgery? You've pulled bullets out of guys' guts plenty of times, and in worse places than this."

Daniel nodded. "That's true, but what you're forgetting is how many of those men died. I operated because there was no alternative. It seems to me, there is an alternative here."

Alfredo's response was cut short by the sound of explosions in the distance. The men looked up, then ran outside.

They stood in a small clearing behind the house. New explosions could be heard coming from several points along the line to the north.

"Artillery," one of the men volunteered.

"No, smaller," Alfredo suggested. "Mortars, maybe."

"A Christmas present, you think?" Tito asked.

Just then the dying afternoon light was augmented by flashes along a wide horizon.

"Bigger than mortars," Alfredo revised.

"Most of it's coming from over there," Daniel said, pointing beyond Barga. "It appears they found someone willing to work on Christmas after all," he added, turning to Alfredo.

A moment later another of the men raced from the house. "We've got to get moving!" he yelled. "I've been on the radio," he said as he approached the others. "They're counterattacking all along the line. I talked to Stefano in Barga. He said from the duomo he can see tanks leading the way for Nazi and Fascist Republican infantry."

"All right," Alfredo said in a voice that assumed command. "Start packing up." He turned to Daniel, who answered before the question could be formed.

"It's dangerous to move him."

"What if we take him in a car to Lucca?"

"You never know for sure, but I don't think he'd make it. Too much bouncing and jostling on the road."

"What choice do we have?"

Daniel looked away, scanning the mountains, then turned again to Alfredo. "I might as well stay here with him. It's probably as safe here as anyplace else that would be close enough to get him to. I should have a clearer idea of his condition within the next twenty-four hours. Then we'll see."

Tito had rejoined them and looked on in silence.

"No way," Alfredo said to both of them. "I'm speaking for Lazio. There's no way he'd allow that. You know as well as I do what will happen if he's captured. You'd have it easy by comparison," he added, looking at Daniel. "They'd only shoot you."

"I'm willing to risk it," Daniel said firmly, "and Lazio has no say."

256

"But I do. It's not just your lives at stake. If he's captured and interrogated, we're all dead."

"For Christ sake, Alfredo! How much more can we be at risk than we already are? Besides, I'm betting the offensive fails. It's a stunt—a Christmas surprise courtesy of the resurrected Duce with his master's support. I'm willing to bet they're desperate," Daniel added with more bravado than real conviction.

Tito, who had stood by quietly, said, "Maybe, but it wouldn't be the first time we've been too optimistic. And, if you're right that this is just a sign of desperation, it's all the more reason to get the hell out of here until the Allies can beat them back. The fucking SS are bad enough to deal with when they're not desperate."

"This is a big house," Daniel said. "There must be someplace where the two of us can hide."

Tito shook his head. "I've checked the place out thoroughly. There's nothing they wouldn't discover in five minutes. They've become pretty good at the discovery game."

"What if we get Lazio out of here but not as far as Lucca?" Alfredo asked Daniel. "To Borgo a Mozzano, for instance."

"I suppose we could try. But listen, there are houses and villas all over these mountains. There's no reason to assume the enemy will stop at this one. We're probably as safe here as anywhere. And if this is the real thing, there's no reason to suppose they also won't make it as far as Borgo."

Alfredo considered this for a moment, then said, "That's not true. We're close to the main road. I'm telling you, we can't chance Lazio being captured. He'd be the first to agree. He'd kill himself first. We have to try and get him to Borgo at least."

Alfredo directed Tito to take charge of the others and arranged to meet up with them as soon as he and Daniel got Lazio to safety. He told Daniel to do whatever he could to get Lazio ready to travel.

But when Alfredo reached the bedroom, it was immediately obvious that the plan they'd settled on would have to be changed. "It's not going to work," Daniel said, looking up from Lazio. "He's definitely bleeding internally. I'm going to have to open him up by myself. There's no other choice, though I don't think much of his chances. And I'll need someone to give me a hand.

Is there someone you can spare? Tito maybe. He can't move too fast on his bad foot anyway."

Alfredo's face set. He pushed his hand through his hair. "No, I'll stay with you. No one knows the terrain like Tito. Even on a bad foot he'll be more useful than me." He smiled thinly and added, "As you'll remember, I'm not running sprints these days either. But I'm telling you one thing: you'd better pray you're right about not being overrun. None of us will be captured alive." He touched the pistol in his belt. "It'll be my job to guarantee that."

Daniel and Alfredo struggled to bring the kitchen table upstairs. It was a heavy, trestle-legged piece of furniture, but Daniel determined it to be the best surface to work on and the right height. He would have preferred to do the surgery in the kitchen, close to water and the stove, but he didn't want to move Lazio more than necessary.

They placed the table next to Lazio's bed and transferred him as gently as possible. While Daniel prepared, Alfredo worked in the kitchen to sterilize the instruments. Electricity in the villa, never reliable, was behaving especially erratically, and Alfredo gathered as many oil lamps as possible, as well as mirrors to enhance the light.

As darkness fell, they closed all of the shutters. Gunfire reverberated all around the area, especially from Barga and Sommocolonia. Alfredo was concerned about smoke from the chimney, but Daniel insisted it would have to be risked.

For once, Daniel had basic anesthetics available, but he was concerned about Lazio's weakened state and especially the loss of blood, which he had no way of replacing. Morphine was controlling his pain, but there was confusion about how much he had been given before Daniel arrived, and he had to be careful not to overdose him. Underlying everything, though, was the perverse sense of reassurance that accompanies the lack of an alternative.

* * *

DANIEL BEGAN HIS work amid the distracting sound of firing in the hills all around them. They could feel the rumble of heavy vehicles on the road below the villa and could only hold their breath as they silently urged them to keep going, a grim form of body English.

He forced himself to focus and was rewarded with a relatively uncomplicated surgery. He was able to locate the bullet, which thankfully had not penetrated too deeply or fragmented. He was therefore able to keep his probing to a minimum and to repair the internal wound with a minimum of further blood loss. He showed Alfredo where the bullet had just missed an artery. "Lucky man, our Lazio is," Daniel said. Lazio's basic weakness and the risk of infection meant he was still in grave danger, but Daniel could take some satisfaction in the thought that he had done everything possible to save his friend. Now they could only wait, keep him as comfortable as they could, and hope for the best.

Daniel slumped into a chair and watched Lazio while Alfredo went downstairs to find something to eat.

"Bread, cheese and olive oil," Daniel said with a smile when Alfredo returned. "How unusual. We haven't had anything like it for at least several hours."

"And these," Alfredo responded, holding up a tin of onions. "And I wouldn't make fun if I were you," he added, putting the food within Daniel's reach on the corner of the table on which Lazio lay. "When this is used up, all we have is hardtack, for which you can thank your countrymen."

"Right." Daniel gave a small laugh.

"How's he doing?" Alfredo asked with a nod toward Lazio and taking a seat. His bad foot was obviously bothering him as over the last few hours his limp had become more pronounced. "Sorry about Francesco," he added without waiting for a response. "I guess the homecoming will have to be delayed."

Daniel's mouth set. He nodded.

"Don't worry, it won't be for too long. As you said, this attack is probably just a desperation move. It will be repulsed."

"Let's hope so."

"Until then, maybe it's for the best that Francesco is with the sisters."

Daniel nodded again. After a pause he said, "Thanks for staying behind. I couldn't have done it alone."

"It's okay. Someone has to be here to shoot if the Nazis arrive."

"Our last stand, perhaps." Daniel shook his head and smiled thinly. "It's like a bad western movie: A soldier, a doctor, and their wounded leader. Can their ammo hold out?"

"Well I'll tell you this," Alfredo responded, not sharing in the jest, "the last three bullets are for us."

They were quiet again. The only sounds in the room were the reassuring breathing of Lazio and the less reassuring, but at least now sporadic, echoes of gunfire.

"Have you had any luck learning anything about the traitors?" Alfredo asked suddenly. It was unnecessary to clarify that the allusion was to whoever was behind the family's arrest and fatal deportation.

"I've asked around town, especially my patients," Daniel responded. "No one knows anything."

"Ah, well. Not exactly a surprise, is it?"

"I'm not sure what you mean." Daniel looked over at Lazio, who had moaned briefly before settling down again.

"They're Italians, after all. Even if they knew the answer they might not tell you. They know in their bones what we're seeing evidence of tonight—that there's no such thing as certainty. In a blink, everything can change. And when you get down to it, no matter how much your patients might like you, respect you, or pity you, you're still a foreigner."

"I suppose that's true." Daniel's voice contained a note of fatalism. "What about you? Have you been able to find out anything?"

"Nothing solid. My money's on those bastards, the Bucas, though. And if it turns out to be true, I'm personally going to kill every last one of them."

"Why the Bucas?" Daniel considered, then rejected the impulse to add that they might know more and have to speculate less if Alfredo hadn't murdered their best source, Major Petresco. "You're not exactly unbiased where they're concerned," he added, reasonably, though he could feel the bile rising within him anyway at the thought of having someone to blame. Over the past several months the desire for vengeance had remained strong no matter how hard he fought against it. Indeed, he was often surprised by the intensity of the desire he felt to wreak havoc upon whoever had been responsible for the deaths of those he loved and the uprooting of his world. "I can understand why there's no love lost between you and the Bucas," Daniel added, "but why would they have attacked the rest of the family? What was to gain?"

"When I find out, I'll let you know."

They ate in silence. Daniel hadn't realized how hungry he was. After he finished, he got up to check on Lazio. "No change," he said in answer to Alfredo's unasked question.

Using blankets, Alfredo made a place for himself on the floor. "I'll let you have the bed," he said to Daniel. "One of us might as well be comfortable."

"Thanks, but I'll join you on the floor. We may want to put Lazio in the bed. I'll give him a little more time without moving him, though. I want to make sure the bleeding has stopped."

Alfredo found more blankets in a nearby bedroom and arranged them for Daniel on the floor. They lay there quietly, the lights now dimmed except for two lamps near Lazio, one electric and another, smelly but reliable, oil.

"Have you thought about what you and Francesco will do after the war?" Alfredo asked, breaking the silence. "Will you stay in Italy?"

Daniel didn't answer immediately, and Alfredo looked over to see if he had fallen asleep. "It's hard to say," he said at last. "Francesco is the main thing. I have to do what's best for him. That probably means staying here. It's hard to say," he repeated. "I find it difficult to think about the future. I keep telling myself the only way to survive the war is by putting on blinders and focusing only on getting through each day. Like a horse pulling a wagon—head down, one weary step in front of another."

"I know what you mean. Every time I think about the future, I think about the people who won't be in it. Then I become enraged and all I want to do is get even. So I try not to think about the future."

Daniel wondered at this tale of self-control, of which he had not seen much evidence.

"Anyway," Alfredo continued, "you're lucky. At least you have a profession you can practice almost anywhere. You're needed. Me? I'll be lucky to get a job as a contadino."

"Don't sell yourself short," Daniel replied, though he hoped Alfredo wouldn't press him for specific suggestions.

"Then again," Alfredo said, "assuming I survive the war, which I never assume, it will be a different world. Who's to say what any of us will have to do? Doctors, though, they'll always need doctors."

"I suppose so. Sometimes," Daniel added after a pause, "I think about working for peace again. I was so successful after the first war, after all."

Alfredo laughed.

"It is funny, isn't it?" Daniel said. "Ludicrous, really. But I believed in the League of Nations. I still do. I think the world needs international rules, international order. I mean, this war is evidence of that, not of the contrary.

Once, Paola was giving me a hard time over my idealism. She never missed an opportunity to tell me how naive I was. It made me mad as hell. Why shouldn't I work for peace? I asked her. What's the alternative?" Daniel laughed at the memory. "Why does there have to be an alternative?" she said. "Just because you want there to be one?"

Alfredo shared the laugh. "Yes, that sounds like something Paola would say."

Daniel sat up, looked at Alfredo earnestly. "But she was wrong, you know. The alternative to peace is this." He waved to embrace their surroundings. "The alternative is this miserable existence we've created for ourselves. I sometimes think preserving my idealism is all I have left to do."

"I understand," Alfredo said.

Daniel was certain he did not.

* * *

THROUGH THE NIGHT they would doze off and on in tag-team fashion, exhausted by the events of the previous day and the vigil over Lazio, who would awake in pain as the morphine wore off. At times he began to thrash, and they would have to restrain him.

Just before six, Alfredo nudged Daniel awake. Lazio was moving and calling out. "You'd better take a look at him," Alfredo said.

Lazio's sheets and pillow were wet with perspiration. His eyelids fluttered when Daniel approached. "How do you feel?" Daniel asked. He was pleased to see that Lazio's pulse was strong. Apparently he had succeeded in stanching the internal bleeding. Now, if infection could be staved off, things might turn out well.

Lazio's eyes closed, but then he surprised Daniel by saying, "My gut hurts like hell."

"I know. But we need to limit the amount of morphine in your system."

"How about a little bit?" Lazio asked. His eyes were still closed but there was a slight smile on his lips.

"Right, I . . . . "

"Daniel! Quiet!" Alfredo said. "There's someone outside. Turn out those lights!"

Alfredo grabbed his rifle and slid along the floor to the window, which overlooked the front yard. He cracked open the shutters and peered out. "Shit."

"What . . ." Daniel started.

"There are one, no two guys looking around," Alfredo whispered. "Fascists, I think."

"Not Germans?"

"It's dark. Hard to tell for sure. They look like Fascist regulars. Probably Monte Rosa Division. Scum," he added.

On the main road a column of heavy vehicles rumbled by.

"Andiamo," one of the soldiers in the yard was heard to say.

"In a minute," the other responded. "I want to check this place out. It's a nice place. There's probably something good inside." A moment later, from the front door, the man yelled, "Open up!" and without waiting for a response kicked at the door and then, when it wouldn't give, shot out the locks.

From the bedroom, the soldiers could be heard throwing things about, opening and slamming doors in their search for loot.

"Move over there," Alfredo hissed, motioning Daniel away from the door. "Wait. First help me move Lazio."

They went to either end of the table on which Lazio lay. He was quiet, but Daniel wasn't sure whether he had drifted off again or was aware of the need for silence.

"Let's get him close to that wall," Alfredo, whispered. "Out of the line of fire. We'll want a clear shot at the door."

The table was heavy even without Lazio on it. They had struggled to bring it upstairs. "I don't know if we can do this without making noise," Daniel whispered.

"We've got to try," Alfredo responded. The men downstairs began again to throw things around.

"Now," Daniel said, hoping to mask their movement with the men's crashing and clattering.

They strained to lift the table, and they had succeeded in moving it with mincing steps just near the far wall when Alfredo's bad foot caught on an irregular floorboard. The trestle leg thumped as it hit the floor.

"Whoever's up there, come down now!" one of the soldiers barked from the bottom of the stairs.

They held their breath, but Lazio began to moan, at first softly, then louder. Daniel grabbed a pillow. He placed it lightly over Lazio's face just long enough to muffle the sound, then raised it and held it poised to muffle further cries.

"I said come down," the soldier repeated. To Daniel, the man sounded drunk. There was no sound of his climbing the stairs.

"Behind the bed, quickly!" Alfredo whispered. Leaving Lazio on the table next to the wall, they knelt behind the empty bed, Alfredo using it to prop up the rifle which he aimed at the door.

Daniel and Alfredo tensed as they heard the soldier take a step, then another. He stopped. "Come with me," they could hear him say to the second man.

Alfredo pulled his pistol from his belt. "Here," he whispered, holding it out to Daniel.

Instinctively, he began to reach for the gun, his heart hammering inside his chest. Then he stopped and shook his head, no.

"Stupid bastard!" Alfredo hissed. He left it on the floor within Daniel's reach.

The steps outside resumed. Alfredo sighted down the barrel of his rifle. A klaxon blared suddenly from the road. Daniel flinched and Alfredo nearly pulled the trigger. They listened, frozen, as the steps came right outside the door.

Lazio moaned.

The door was opened for only an instant before Alfredo fired, a hellacious sound followed an instant later by the Fascist's riposte, a wild shot caused by the automatic squeezing of the trigger as his chest was holed.

Alfredo fired again and the second soldier, framed in the doorway behind his now fallen comrade, screamed, dropping his rifle and clutching his shoulder. The man tried to pick up the rifle, saw he could never do so before Alfredo would shoot again. "Wait! Don't shoot!" the man shouted. He began to raise his good arm slowly in surrender.

The next thing Daniel saw was the man crashing backwards, his hand never making it to the top of the surrender arc before Alfredo shot him in the chest.

Daniel raced over to him, stepping over the first man, who was clearly dead.

"What the hell!" Alfredo said, his voice full of disgust. "You're going to try to save him? That piece of dog shit?"

Daniel knelt over the man. But he could see immediately that he had been shot in the heart. He stood and looked at Alfredo. "He was trying to surrender."

Alfredo stood, and pointed his finger at Daniel. He was shaking with anger. "Don't you tell me what he was trying to do!" His voice quavered. "If it were up to you we'd all be dead! If it were up to you your son would be an orphan! So don't give me any of your damned pacifist sermons. Guys like you survive because you let guys like me do your killing for you." He pushed past Daniel and limped out of the room.

"He was trying to surrender," Daniel insisted, evenly, to Alfredo's back.

"So he was," Alfredo said, not bothering to turn around. "Too bad for him."

~ ~ ~ ~ ~

~ ~ ~

Chapter 31

OA   18 February 1945

I'M WORRIED THAT I may have overestimated Francesco's resiliency. It's been a month since I brought him home and broke the news to him. I did my best to anticipate the problems that would ensue. I was ready for tears, anger, explosions of irrationality, periods of melancholy. In the months leading up to his return, and especially during the unexpected delay while the Allies beat back the Christmas Eve offensive, I was diligent about trying to prepare for these reactions. I thought about the things that might sooth him, the ways in which I might try to comfort him. I had images of forcing him into my arms to control a tantrum, then both of us crying tears of deep, cathartic grief.

None of these things has happened. Instead, there has been a prolonged period, which continues as I write this, during which Francesco has steadfastly refused to believe that anything bad actually happened. He has yet to deviate for one second from the disbelieving face he presented to me the moment I told him about Paola, Isabella, and his grandparents. He has acted as if I were suffering a delusion, a temporary dementia for which I was to be humored.

On several occasions I've tried to force the issue. I sit him down and explain again what happened. Sometimes I think I'm getting through. Do you understand about your mama? I'll ask gravely, and he'll say yes, he does. Do you understand that Mama and Isabella and Nonno and Nonna aren't coming back? I'll ask, risking what in my own ears sounds like heartless interrogation—as if I'm bound and determined to weasel out of him the cruel truth and, perhaps, a few tears of recognition and normalcy. Yes, he says, he understands. And then, when he is convinced my strange game is over, he goes on as if we never had the conversation. He talks about Paola and the others in the present tense (Isabella likes this, Mama doesn't want me to do that) and will go on without a hint of reservation or self-consciousness to discuss what he and Paola will do for Easter. It's not even a question of his talking about when Paola comes home; his denial of reality is so strong, it's as if he refuses to acknowledge that she's not already home.

I tell myself, on some level he must comprehend. How could he not? The evidence of our loss is everywhere. We can't go out without receiving the solicitous looks and hearing the condoling tones of our neighbors (and often must return them in kind for the losses they've suffered). This house we share is so completely transformed—so lacking in the vitality that suffused it when we were all together. I've thought about moving somewhere else, and we probably will.

There have been changes in him, even if they're not the ones I anticipated. He refuses to speak to me in English, even though he couldn't have forgotten everything since he's been away (in fact, I seem to recall one of the nuns remarking on his ability to speak it, though I didn't make anything of it at the time). He's somehow maintained his sweet nature. He has a lovely smile. He's grown, too, in this past year, though he's still small for his age. What's missing—the thing that breaks my heart as much as anything—is the easy, natural delight he used to take in the smallest things—in the smallest discoveries.

Given the circumstances, perhaps I should be grateful he is not somehow worse. What keeps me from this meager gratitude is the fact that his denial is so extreme, so strangely compartmented. I've seen plenty of cases of shellshock, from mild to severe, and though I've read about cases like Francesco's, I can't remember actually seeing one where behavior was so selective. It seems certain there must be another shoe still to drop.

In the meantime, I just have to be patient and assume Francesco will turn around. And then I dread the moment he does.

OA   22 February 1945

Alfredo came to see me today. He said he's more convinced than ever that the Bucas are somehow involved in the family's arrest.

267

Alfredo has good reason to hate the Bucas, and that is reason enough to worry about a rush to judgment. So I keep pressing him on what he knows. He tells me about whispered conversations here or there. He raises the strange untouchable status the Bucas have managed to achieve on both sides.

However suspicious this may be—as much as I want an answer to this mystery—I'm not sure why this points to guilt as far as our personal tragedy is concerned. Yet Alfredo is convinced the link, whatever it is, is strong, which leaves me in the uncomfortable position of feeling obligated to be his voice of reason. It is perhaps the salutary side of an impulse I've developed to challenge him automatically about almost everything. In so many ways he has, by his righteous anger and matching vengeful temperament, come to embody the worst, most dehumanizing aspect of this war. He is (or has become) the kind of person who is so impulsively cynical—and so certain in his cynicism—that he creates in me a Newtonian opposite impulse. Even as he says something I know is probably correct, I am so eager to prove that his world view is a myopic one, I automatically take the other side. No doubt there is a good deal of self-justification embedded in this—a deep-seated desire to rationalize what now appears to be the great irrelevancy of the pacifistic philosophy to which I've devoted most of my life.

As we've ended similar conversations in the past, we ended this one with my encouraging Alfredo not to do something he'll regret. He promises he won't, then immediately follows by saying as soon as he's sure, he'll kill every last one of them.

Shortly after we had this conversation, Francesco came into my office. He smiled that sweet, sad, smile of his, and all I could think of was how much I yearned for the simplicity of Alfredo's solution.

OA   27 February 1945

As if there has been a shortage of cruel jokes, here's another. I received word today that Lazio has died—of a ruptured appendix. He had recovered quite well, and amazingly quickly, from the surgery I performed on him. He spent a week or so in the hospital in Lucca and then, though weakened, insisted on returning to the field. Not long after, he fell ill and (predictably, I suppose), refused to seek help.

His loss saddens me greatly. It saddens me, too, to think that there is so much I don't know about him. This is a contradiction as profoundly odd as the one that marks Francesco's behavior. In some ways, I feel as if I got to know Lazio deeply–got to know his nature and his character. And yet, I am startled—almost embarrassed—by the realization that I don't know his real name.

~ ~ ~ ~ ~
~ ~ ~

Chapter 32

VICTORIA WAS LOOKING AT the paintings in the living room while she waited for Francesco to conclude a phone call. She was accompanying him to see the gallery in Forte dei Marmi, then they would have lunch at one of the seaside restaurants nearby.

In the brief time she had been in Italy much of the artwork in the house had been changed as pieces were sent to or received from the gallery. Currently, the majority of the paintings in the room were oils, most on canvas but quite a few on wood panel. Some were mixed media. All were beautifully framed for their subject and style. About half the themes were traditional—still lifes, portraits, religious themes, historical depictions. Some were clearly quite valuable. The other half comprised a wide range of expressionist styles, from pastel impressionist pieces to paintings that all but overwhelmed the senses in their strength of color or line.

Amid this eclectic coexistence some works suggested to Victoria an air of permanence and entitlement in the room, others suggested the transience of migrant workers. Some appeared not to have been moved in anyone's memory. Others, suspended on adjustable wires or other clever devices, could be moved at a whim.

"Do you like our home gallery?" Francesco asked with a smile as he returned. As usual, he was dressed casually in clothes of obviously fine quality. His slacks and shirt were beautifully tailored, every line falling precisely on his thin frame. He was relaxed and that day appeared to Victoria years younger than his true age.

"Very much. I have to admit, I sneak in to look at every opportunity— that is, when I'm not eyeing the many other lovely things you have just hanging here and there around the house."

"I'm glad you enjoy them," he smiled, appearing genuinely appreciative. "No sneaking is necessary," he added.

She gave him a coy smile. "I think I've figured out which are your favorites."

"Wonderful! I can't wait to hear your selections. I assume you've done more than merely count the ones that haven't been moved in awhile," he said, cocking his head and returning the smile.

Victoria laughed. "Oh, Francesco, surely you can give me a little credit!"

"Yes, of course. Not to mention that such a process would be very misleading. Many of the paintings that have been in their places longest are there either for sentimental reasons or because others like them."

"You know, Francesco, it's interesting to me that if I had taken you up on your challenge immediately after I arrived, I would have chosen different paintings to define you."

"But we still don't know whether the ones you have selected are right," he pointed out.

"Fair enough. So, come along and I'll go out on a limb and explain my choices."

"Fair enough, indeed," Francesco said, his smile still in place.

"First of all," Victoria began, "I'll eliminate the things that are definitely of only sentimental value." She led him to the opposite side of the room and stopped next to a buffet table against the wall. There were several photographs on the table: Daniel at several stages in his life—she had already spent a considerable amount of time looking at these, wondering, trying to inhabit them; Paola, in perhaps her early thirties, reflecting a natural insouciance at odds with the formal, dignified pose in which the photographer had placed her; Paola's parents in the late twenties or early thirties, smiling and prosperous; a sepia photo of Chiara in her mother Renata's arms with the rest of the Buca family looking on. On the wall above the table, an oil portrait of Paola at about fifteen, which Victoria now pointed to. "Photographs and paintings such as these I'll simply assume are important to you, Francesco, but more because they're part of your heritage than because you have any deep aesthetic attachment to them."

271

He nodded.

"But while I'm at it I'll risk saying that the portrait of your mother over the buffet is not among your favorites. From what I know about her—and from what I can see in her photos—the portrait fails to capture her essence. It makes her more classically beautiful than she was while failing to capture the spirit that was the true source of her beauty and which clearly captivated Daniel."

Francesco turned to Victoria and clapped his hands. "Brava! That is exactly how I feel about it. It has pride of place in the room because there is so little else of her to choose from. It amuses me to think, however, that my grandparents probably liked that portrait very much for precisely the reasons it misses the mark for me. As you said, the painter makes her classically beautiful. Ironically, by showing little of her spirit, the portrait was probably reassuring to her parents. It gives the illusion that my mother's spirit might, after all, be reined in." Francesco laughed with a mischievous mirth at this thought.

"So, having got the disclaimer settled," Victoria continued, "let me show you a few paintings I believe are very important to you."

She turned to her right. "I believe you are very attached to this one," she said, pointing to an intensely colored abstract landscape. "I've noticed that, beneath your elegant, well mannered exterior, which might suggest a liking for softer work, you have a taste for things that break out—things that are determinedly bright, exuberant, striving to be happy. No dead saints for you," she added with a laugh. "Right so far?"

"Indeed," Francesco nodded. "I'm impressed."

"Therefore, I think you are also very partial to the abstract painting over there, on the far wall next to the pointillist number, which you probably don't care for."

"Also true."

"So, going on: Although you favor exuberance, I sense you don't care very much for things that are bold in random or completely abstract ways, like that geometric painting over there, which is well executed but I suspect not the kind of thing that moves you. The same goes for that Pollock-like drip painting, which I suspect is too anarchic for your tastes."

"Also correct, though I may like that one better than you think I do."

"All right, I'll interpret that as being on a roll. So, that said, I believe there is a sweet, sentimental side of you that would be partial to Cézanne-like still lifes. There are two that caught my eye, hanging side by side in the dining room, and I think you probably like the one on the left better for its balance."

Francesco gave Victoria's arm a gentle squeeze and smiled sweetly. "You are remarkably perceptive in your selections. It is a pleasure for one to feel he is understood."

She returned his smile. "It is more gratifying than I can say to gain understanding of such an agreeable subject. You've always loved art, I think," she added, seriously.

"Yes, always. As a child, I drew and painted all the time."

"And yet I don't see any works of yours in the house. No evidence at all of your passion."

"Not quite none," Francesco said with a smile. "You've missed my materials."

Victoria looked at him, not comprehending.

"Come." He led her to a small table on which rested a red enamel metal box, which he opened to reveal drawing pencils and crayons. "My supply box. Father bought it for me—assembled the kit from its various parts would be a better way to say it—when I was a child. For a particularly difficult Christmas," he added.

"Difficult?"

"Yes. It was the year I found out about my mother and the others."

"Oh, I'm sorry." She touched his arm, feeling awkward about the way the remark came out—as if she had really just found out about the tragedy rather than it being the subtext of her visit. "But why didn't you continue drawing or painting?"

"I did for a while. As I grew older, though, I'm afraid I had to acknowledge that I had no talent."

"Oh, I can't believe that."

"It's true—and I'm old enough to say so without looking for sympathy. It's not really so sad anyway. I never would have made anything of myself as an artist. Well, I would have made myself frustrated!"

Victoria laughed. "It's like that old joke where the farmer is asked what he grows and he responds, 'Tired.'"

"Ha! Yes! But I'm a very happy student of art, and I never could have appreciated art as much as I do if I hadn't tried my hand at it."

"I understand what you mean." As she said this she felt a rush of affection for Francesco and wondered that she had never made time for him. "Now," she added after a pause, "let's get on with our outing so I can quit while I'm ahead."

They had just closed the front door behind them when Chiara's car pulled into the drive. She got out quickly, not bothering to smooth her dress and not acknowledging Francesco and Victoria's hellos from the top step. Victoria looked to Francesco, but he appeared, first, mildly confused, and then, as Chiara reached into the trunk, withdrew something and slammed it shut, concerned. They descended the steps.

"Is everything all right, cara?" he asked as she approached. Her face was set, pinched, angry. Victoria could see now that she had taken from the car rolled up posters of some kind.

"Again?" Francesco asked with a fretful expression.

'Again. And worse. Look!" Chiara unrolled the posters, holding them top and bottom to keep the glossy papers from springing back to their closed form. "These are just the ones I saw near the piazza. I just ripped them down. This one and this one," she said, peeling them like the layers of an onion. The poster she held up, a graphically bold announcement of the forthcoming Liberation Day activities, including the dedication of the memorial, had been defaced with spray paint. "All of the posters in the piazza have been ruined," Chiara said in disgust.

What caught Victoria's eye as Chiara paged through the posters, dropping each one at her feet, was that several were not merely defaced but contained a pointed message, which even she with her limited Italian could get the gist of. "Don't Glorify the Fascists," one said. "Remember the Real Heroes," said another. A third, requiring no language facility at all, covered the words "Memorial Dedication" with a line of swastikas.

It surprised Victoria even more when Chiara didn't comment on the messages and focused instead on the "childish vandalism," as she called it, and complained about the additional work it would create to replace the posters.

"Some little barbarian also spray-painted on the pavement where the monument will go," Chiara added as, with Francesco's help, she picked up the posters she had shed and proceeded to roll them tight as a window shade. "That will take some work to clean," she said as she marched up the stairs to the house.

"There's time," Francesco called after her in a reassuring tone. "I'm sure everything will work out fine."

"I gather from what you said that this has happened before?" Victoria asked.

"Yes. It's very upsetting. Ah, well," he went on, his natural optimism returning to his face, "these are just the nonsensical things one has to expect."

Victoria was silent, once again unsure how far to press some of the questions that troubled her. This time, however, she resolved not to let the opportunity pass. "I must confess, Francesco," she began tentatively and interrupting what she could see was to be an imminent change of subject, "I'm surprised that Chiara is so upset by the vandalism as such, and not so much by the political message."

"I understand your confusion," Francesco responded, nodding. "You must keep in mind that just about every conceivable point of view gets expressed in spray paint around here."

"But, Francesco, you've read Daniel's papers, and I've read enough of them to know that Chiara's family was, how shall I say it . . . "

"Controversial?" Francesco volunteered.

"Well, yes. And I must say, quite different from Chiara's portrayal."

Francesco nodded again and shifted his weight in a way that Victoria took for discomfort. "There are differences in the accounts, that's true. But you must remember that those were very complicated times. It's very hard to know what exactly was the truth, and as always there is the problem of selective memory."

"From what I've been reading about the events surrounding your uncle Alfredo, I can understand why some people might not think so highly of the Buca family."

"Exactly my point," Francesco said quickly, still seeming to Victoria anxious to cap the subject. "Where Alfredo is concerned I'm sure you can see how people might regard him as a"—he searched for the word—"a hothead, I think. And don't forget, the main reason Chiara has been pushing hard for the memorial is precisely to end the bitterness of the past. Honoring her family is important to her, but it's secondary."

Victoria was tempted to press him. The more she had read, the clearer it had become that, if what he had just said about Chiara was true, the main goal of reconciliation was being undermined by the secondary one, as Francesco put it, of singling out her family. That Chiara did not acknowledge the opposition her project aroused made her seem not just obtuse but, Victoria suspected, willfully so. But in the time it took her to form a question in a way that would not offend Francesco, Chiara appeared again at the front door to tell him he had a phone call, and the opportunity slipped away.

~ ~ ~ ~ ~

~ ~ ~

Chapter 33

ARLY ON THE DAY before the ceremony Victoria accompanied Francesco, Chiara and Roberto to witness the final preparations in the piazza. The monument itself was to be installed. Chiara had checked and corrected it several times during its casting and construction; only its delivery and installation remained to be done. The offending spray paint had been cleaned from the pavement. Still, she had a long list of last-minute inspections and tasks which, Francesco commented, was just as well, since there would be less time for her to fret over the more improbable things that could go awry.

"*Calma, calma,*" Francesco said to her as they prepared to leave the house.

Chiara took a deep breath and smoothed her dress. "All right. I'm ready."

A few minutes later they arrived at the piazza. Chiara immediately excused herself as she spotted friends who had worked with her. Roberto announced that he needed to go to the corner bar for coffee and invited Francesco and Victoria to join him. Francesco declined, saying he was happy to simply take in the glorious morning, and Victoria said she would keep Francesco company.

"I'm looking forward to seeing the monument," Francesco said.

"I've been impressed by the photos I've seen," Victoria responded. "It's a lovely, dignified design."

The monument featured a simple bronze sculpture depicting a scene of phoenix-like resurrection. From a base of ashes and molten houses, tanks and guns, flames of intertwined hands met in an apex of unity and hope. The sculpture sat on a cylindrical base of rose marble onto which were fitted curved bronze plates bearing the names of the local victims of Nazifascism.

Chiara was proud of the design, which she had participated in creating, and equally proud of the success of raising the not inconsiderable funds to pay for the project.

At the center of the piazza workmen stood on a flatbed truck preparing to lower the monument, still in its crate, into place with a hydraulic arm. Once it was put in position and inspected for a final time it would be draped in fabric until it was unveiled at the ceremony.

Victoria looked on, shielding her eyes against the morning sun. Francesco stood next to her. "I'm very happy for Chiara," he said, breaking the brief silence. "She has worked very hard to make the ceremony a reality."

"Yes, it's a great accomplishment," Victoria responded before retreating again into silence. She had spent a restless night during which she had been troubled by her continuing inability to reconcile the contradictory accounts, current and historical, of the period they were about to commemorate. She was still cautious about pressing the matter, not wishing to offend either Chiara or Francesco, yet she was upset by her increasing certainty that crucial information was missing. Not merely nonexistent, but missing. She didn't want to hurt Francesco by suggesting he had been in any way dishonest, but nor did she like the feeling that she was being misled. Resentment over this possibility grew palpably during the night.

"I'm so glad you were able to be here with us at this time," Francesco said, and Victoria thought he seemed uncomfortable with the silence that had descended again. "Tell me," he went on, "aside from the things that I'm sure have interested you as a historian, have you learned things that surprised you about Father—I mean surprised you about him as your father?"

Victoria thought for a moment, then said, "Yes, I suppose I have. Not so much in the sense of the part he played in my life. There really isn't much to be added on that score. He was absent from my life. Period. And absent from my mother's, which probably hurt both of us even more. The fact that he may have felt bad about this—that's one of the things that comes across from his papers—doesn't change very much, though I must admit it was a humanizing discovery. It made him less cold, less a malicious perpetrator and more the victim of his and my mother's mistake."

"Mistake?"

"Yes. Even though you could say it should have been obvious, I was struck by just how young and mismatched he and my mother were. What I see from this vantage point in my life is not that he was such a bastard—which is what I suppose I expected to find. It's clear to me now that he and mother never should have gotten together in the first place. That was the real mistake. I was merely an unfortunate byproduct, as it were, of their youthful error."

Francesco smiled at the characterization. "Surely that is too strong."

"Perhaps. But I'm sure you can see what I mean. Once I accepted that, it was easier to look at Daniel more objectively, and I found him much more sympathetic. He was a decent person. His friend Bemis called him a striver and someone worth knowing, and I believe those things to be true. Daniel's idealism seems quixotic now, but that may be because no idealism could have survived that horrible time. Besides, idealism generally seems quixotic now, don't you think? And quaint. We're all cynics now, aren't we?"

"I'm afraid you may be right," Francesco nodded.

"In any case, there's a question that wasn't answered, and I was wondering if you might be able to shed some light."

"Certainly, if I can."

"The other day, Chiara told me you and Daniel lived in New York for a time, in the late forties I think."

"Yes, that's right. Father was doing some work for the UN. But it was an off and on thing. We'd spend a few months in New York, then a few in Geneva. Father did his best to time the moves to coincide with my schooling, but sometimes it was quite disruptive. I suppose one thing the war years taught me was the value of flexibility."

"You were still quite young then, so you may not know the answer to this, but did Daniel ever talk about why he made no effort to contact me or my mother during that time? Maybe it sounds silly to be bothered by such things at this stage in our lives . . . "

"Not at all . . . "

"But it does bother me all the same. I think I can understand the loss of contact as the war approached, and certainly during the war, but here he was, minutes from us, and not a word."

"Are you sure?"

"That I didn't see him?" she asked, incredulously.

"That he didn't try."

She was conscious of an effort to keep a tone of derision from her voice. "If he did it's hard to imagine him being defeated by the challenge. Finding us wasn't exactly the equivalent of climbing Mt. Everest."

"I think there must have been a reason."

"The subject never came up then?"

Francesco sighed. "I realize I'm not being very helpful, but it wasn't until after that time—I was about fourteen or fifteen and we had left New York—that I even knew that Father had been married before."

Victoria looked at him in surprise and gave a sudden, sharp laugh. "You know, for all my absorption in this question—maybe because of my absorption in it—it didn't occur to me that you wouldn't have known. But as I think about it, why would you have? In fact, given your own wartime trauma, I can more readily understand why Daniel wouldn't raise such a complicating subject."

"I do remember, years later, when Father did tell me about you, I think it was because he had decided to contact you. You would have been grown up by then, of course."

"Yes, that's right. By that time I'd decided I didn't want to see him. It was my way of paying him back, I guess. It all seems so stupidly childish and pointless now," she added, shaking her head. "I suppose I was using the only weapon I had."

They sat quietly for a moment. Francesco broke the silence. "Anyway, I'm happy you were able to learn the things you did."

Victoria's response, "I am, too," which was somewhat atonal, or its austerity, as she didn't follow with enthusiastic elaboration, may have disturbed him, because he turned to her with a concerned expression.

"Something is wrong?" he asked.

"No, no," she said, automatically. "You have all been lovely." But before he could respond, a determined curiosity gained the upper hand and she added, "Francesco, I don't wish to offend you . . ."

His eyebrows arched in surprise, but she placed a hand on his arm and continued. This time, she tried to lighten her words with a smile. "I'm a historian, you know, so I hope you'll forgive my natural inclination always to think there is a piece of critical information that has eluded me."

"Of course," Francesco said, recovering with a smile—but a thin one—of his own.

"You've read Daniel's journals, so you won't be surprised to hear that I am disturbed, to put it mildly, about the discrepancy between his account of events regarding Chiara's family and her own version. It's not, after all, merely a case of differing details, but of completely different versions. What's more," she went on, deciding to go for broke before he could respond, "I'm as certain as I can be that there are journal entries that I haven't seen. And I have to confess, I am very curious—mystified, really—as to why these things don't seem to trouble you."

Now it was Francesco's turn to be quiet, as what appeared to Victoria the beginning of an anodyne response stopped in mid-formation. He looked across the piazza, where Chiara was still engaged in animated discussion. Farther on, at the bar, Roberto was having his coffee and chatting with another man.

Francesco turned to Victoria. "I had no intention to deceive you."

"Then there is more."

"Yes, but I would like to explain."

Victoria nodded, and he continued. "When I discovered Father's papers, I thought of you immediately. I thought how lovely it would be to have you turn your historian's eye upon them and at the same time join us for the ceremony. I became caught up in my enthusiasm. When I called to invite you, I had only just begun to read the papers. I hadn't even figured out the OA entries. I was so pleased when you said you would come . . . "

"Your enthusiasm was infectious," Victoria interrupted, moved by the sweet earnestness of Francesco's explanation and wanting to encourage his continued telling.

"Of course, then I continued to read—though I'm sure not nearly as carefully as you have done—and, like you, I was struck by the different versions. It wasn't that I didn't suspect what Chiara has told me over the years to be at odds with things I knew or thought I knew. But I hope you'll understand when I say that, in my love for Chiara, I was predisposed to give her version at least equal weight. But . . . "

"But then you had doubts."

Francesco nodded and remained silent for a moment. "It isn't merely the different accounts," he said. "I could live with such differences—whereas perhaps you cannot. But I fear the things revealed by Father would deeply affect Chiara. I have no doubt they would."

"Of course."

"They would hurt her," he went on, "and possibly even change the way she sees me. You're right, Victoria, the entries you've read are not the last ones. Certainly, it was hoping for too much to think you might be content without seeing them, but I do hope you'll understand that by the time I had read them you were practically on your way here, and as I said, my first thoughts were to protect Chiara."

Victoria looked off into the distance, quietly surveying the piazza. A workman was installing Italian flag bunting in the upper story windows. "I won't press you for them," she said, suddenly. "But I do thank you for telling me about them."

"No, Victoria, you must see them," Francesco responded emphatically. "I could not live with myself now if you did not. I would only ask one thing. I would be very sad if you brought these matters to Chiara's attention, especially right now."

~ ~ ~ ~ ~

~ ~ ~

Chapter 34

THAT AFTERNOON, VICTORIA RETURNED to her room to read the missing entries Francesco had given her in solitude. She removed her dress and with a small gesture of revenge kicked off the shoes that had begun to pinch, then propped herself up in bed with the door closed so that she would not be disturbed by the activity that had begun to overtake the house. Chiara had invited a large group of friends and family to lunch after the ceremony the next day, and now the house was in the grip of last-minute preparation. There was cooking to be done, of course, as well as cleaning and straightening for which two women had come in the afternoon.

Ever since Francesco had confirmed the existence of the missing entries she had been filled with dread. It was bad enough that he had confirmed her reading of events; it would be bad enough if she found nothing worse than she already had. Even now it was difficult for Victoria to be in Chiara's presence, both because she felt a visceral disdain for her and because she was afraid it would show. However much she tried to rationalize Chiara's behavior, reminding herself that there were cultural differences she could not understand and so many other things about Chiara's life that she could not know, she could not think of her without being washed over by resentment.

She recognized that her resentment was at least in part a reflection of anger at herself for waiting so long to press the things she suspected to be true almost from the beginning of her visit. But her disdain stemmed at least equally from what she saw as Chiara's weakness in preferring delusion. As far as Victoria was concerned, truth was something to be sought after and confronted. Wasn't that why she was here, after all? She was proud of this trait; it was a strength. One of the hardest things she ever had to do was keep from her mother almost to the end of her life the diagnosis of her illness as terminal. She hated every minute of the deception, and did it only because Nora had signaled so strongly that she didn't want to know the truth.

For all the love Victoria felt for her mother, for all the understanding she wanted to have for this weakness, she did in fact see it as a weakness, just as she saw Chiara's failure to confront her past.

She was more understanding—it occurred to her that because she liked him so much she was determined to be understanding—of Francesco, who at least, in desiring to protect Chiara and perhaps, as he said, her feelings for him, had a reason to want to shunt the truth to the side. She was more forgiving of him even as she dismissed his explanation that the invitation had been issued before he knew the truth. Even without Daniel's papers surely he had reason to suspect over the years that Chiara's version of events was wrong. There might be nothing concrete to link the Bucas to his mother's death, but surely he suspected what they stood for? Surely there was an indirect connection? Surely they did not deserve to be honored? And was she now to swallow hard and sit there in silence?

She placed the papers in her lap and smoothed them carefully.

OA   23 May 1945

It may be foolish to record the events I'm about to describe, but I need somehow to see them in detail, hard in front of me, even if subsequently I destroy these pages.

Late one morning only days before the war officially came to an end, I had seen my last patient and decided to get out and run some errands. Francesco was still in school and was to go to the home of a friend after he was released at one o'clock. It was a lovely day and I was more relaxed than I'd been in a long time, looking forward to the mindless wandering for which my errands provided an excuse. For whatever reason, it was a day in which I was being spared the usual tugs on my heart, and I was willing to take this gift at face value.

I stopped for a quick coffee, then went on to buy a newspaper, some sundries and a few vegetables. The people I met greeted me cheerfully, as if, like me, they had chosen to ignore their abundant sorrows and their ample reasons to view the future in terms of stunted possibilities and new hardships, and to concentrate instead on the loveliness of the moment. After all, the end of the war was in sight, a mere formality—Mussolini was already dead and the outcome certain—though a formality that mattered, a reminder of the importance of ritual in people's lives.

It was not until after lunch that I returned to the house, feeling mellow and hoping to enjoy the luxury of a brief nap. Yet as I approached the front door, my contentment was suddenly rattled by the vague sense that something was out of place.

I entered the house cautiously and looked around. Nothing seemed to be wrong. I walked from room to room and became easier as each one showed no sign of disturbance. A quick scan of the kitchen revealed everything to be in order. The breakfast dishes sat next to the sink where I had left them to drain. The sun threw indirect light into the room and cast the parts of the room farthest from the windows into shadow.

Perhaps it was this uneven lighting that caused me at first not to notice the piece of paper in the center of the dining table. Or perhaps it was that the paper occupied the place where I usually keep a bowl of fruit or flowers and thus served as a kind of visual substitute.

In any event, the deception was short-lived. As I approached the table I saw that the paper, held in place by a small, smooth stone, was a note hastily written in large, emphatic cursive. It said, simply, "Daniel: There is no longer any doubt. They are the ones."

The note was unsigned, but of course I knew who wrote it, knew who "they" alluded to, and all but shuddered at the implications.

It couldn't have taken me long to traverse the back path to the Bucas' home, but every step seemed an eternity that afforded a cataclysmic opportunity for my mind to race from one extreme to another.

My first impulse was to stop Alfredo from acting on his threats. I had no doubt he planned to do so.

But somewhere along that path, in syncopation with the fear I felt and the anger I had at Alfredo's recklessness, came the beat of vengeance that I had worked so hard to suppress. What if, I asked myself, Alfredo was right? What if he did have proof that the Bucas were responsible for the arrests? What if they were in fact the cause of the misery our family had experienced and in which we who survived continued to exist every day? Why should we not ensure that the Bucas suffered in proportion to the suffering they caused?

With each step I took, the image in my brain altered with the rapidity and unpredictability of a rubber ball flung against the walls of an enclosed room. At the same time, underlying the staccato of my thoughts was the hope, which occasionally surfaced, that I wouldn't find Alfredo. Perhaps his note was meant only to alert me to his discovery for later action. I didn't believe it, but the comfort of illusion is often found in the smallest parcels.

I was out of breath as I came over the rise at the rear of the Bucas' villa. I stopped to scan the area. The house and property had suffered some neglect during the war but otherwise had come through in good shape. Even the neglect was cloaked by spring growth, which gave everything a deceptively prosperous, luxuriant aspect. There was no sign of Alfredo or anyone else. Nothing appeared to be out of order.

I was about to conclude that my worst fears were unfounded when something caught my eye in a small, secluded part of the garden near the outer wall of the villa. I eased closer to the rear gate and stopped to listen.

From the direction of a small stand of olive trees I heard the sound of low voices. Though I couldn't make out what was being said, there was an unmistakable agitation in the atmosphere—a hum of fear and anger.

I called out hello. At that moment my thoughts had nothing to do with anger or revenge. I simply hoped my ears were mistaken and that I could turn around and take the path home.

It was a futile hope.

"Over here, Daniel," came Alfredo's clear voice.

I pushed open the gate and threaded through the garden. As I approached the small patio that had been carved out of a clearing in the olive trees, I saw Alfredo training a gun on Hilde and Bruno Buca, who were seated next to one another at a rough garden table. Bruno's cheek was swollen and raw, and there was a smear of blood on the left side of his lip.

"Oh, thank God, Daniel!" Hilde exclaimed when I came into view. "Alfredo has gone mad!"

Yet if there was a madness in Alfredo, it was unlike any I'd seen in him before. He was not outraged and flailing; he didn't appear irrational or emotional. If his blood had been up when he hit Bruno, as I assumed, there was little sign of it now as he stood with the gun trained on them, more calm and resolute than enraged.

"Daniel, thank God," Hilde said again. "Tell this crazy man to put the gun down. We haven't done anything wrong."

"I know differently," Alfredo said. His voice was cool and unemotional.

To my surprise, I heard myself defend him. "Really?" I asked Hilde. "How would you describe what you did when you gave Alfredo up to the army as a deserter, even though it was plain to see how bad his condition was when he returned home? What would you call that?"

"We did no such thing!" Hilde asserted.

Bruno, however, remained silent. He glared at Alfredo and then at me.

Alfredo gave a short, sharp laugh. "You're either incredibly stupid, Hilde, or an incredible liar. Tell her, Bruno." He waved the gun in Bruno's direction.

"It wasn't on purpose," Hilde protested before Bruno could respond. "Someone from the army was going around looking for you. Bruno was gone and they asked me about you. It's true, I told them you were home, but what did you expect me to tell them? It was easy enough to check. How could I lie about it? Tell him, Bruno. I said I had seen you, that's all. We were upset, you know. Stefano had just . . . "

"You're a liar, Hilde!" Alfredo interrupted. He turned to Bruno. "Tell your wife," he commanded. "Tell her how it really was, you Fascist whore. No one was looking for me. You took it upon yourself to make sure someone came looking."

To my surprise, no denial was forthcoming from Bruno.

"But it turned out that wasn't nearly enough for you, was it?" Alfredo continued.

"What are you talking about?" Hilde interjected in a high, panicked voice. "How can you say such things? You have no proof we did anything wrong . . . anything to hurt you."

As I stood watching, the color drained out of Alfredo's face. "She wants proof, Daniel," he said, turning to me. Without another word he walked around the table toward Hilde. He reached down and grabbed a fistful of hair down to the roots and jerked her upright. She issued a brief scream. Bruno started to rise to her defense, but before he could reach his feet, Alfredo whipped him across the face with his gun. He didn't connect hard, but the sharp edge of the hammer left a red welt across his cheek. Bruno fell back, stunned, small beads of blood rising in places along the welt where the skin had broken. "Yes, Bruno, that would be very nice. Give me an excuse to shoot you. One move, that's all it would take."

Alfredo returned to my side of the table and addressed his remarks to me again. "She wants proof, Daniel," he repeated. "The final stand of the guilty. Listen to her. Does she say they didn't do it? No, she says, what proof do you have?"

I was struggling to keep my voice even, "What's happened?" I asked him. "What have you discovered?"

"As I said, Daniel, I know for sure now. What I don't know for sure is why." He turned again to the Bucas. "You want proof? I have a counterproposal for you. You tell me why you gave up my parents, who you used to call your friends, and my sister, my baby niece, and—let's not forget—Daniel and Francesco, who would have met the same end if you'd had your way. You tell me why, and I may let you live. On the other hand, you make me prove you did it, and I will prove it. And then I'll splatter your brains all over the garden. Which, I'll add, is an easier end than you gave my family."

I could feel myself growing cold. "What proof, Alfredo? What are you talking about? Don't turn this into a game. Don't do that. It dishonors the memory of our family."

Hilde looked up at me hopefully as I said this, as if I'd thrown her a lifeline. Bruno, however, showed little reaction, though that may have been because he was still stunned by Alfredo's blow.

"They're the ones playing a game, Daniel." Wordlessly, Alfredo pulled a piece of paper from his pocket. It was folded into quarters and I immediately thought of the last time I had seen such a paper on that horrific day in June. He held it out to me and I took it with unsteady hands.

I stared at it for a long minute. When I looked up, I could feel the kind of rage surging within me that I thought I'd managed to conquer. My hands shook more noticeably now as I tossed the paper to Bruno. "Let him read it," I said to Alfredo.

Hilde was crying openly now as Bruno picked it up.

"Tell us all what it is," Alfredo commanded.

For a moment Bruno remained silent. "It's a denuncia*—a complaint," he said at last, looking first at Alfredo and then at me. The truculence that had* been in his eyes a few minutes earlier was gone. But he didn't look frightened, either. He appeared more sad or resigned than scared or defiant.

"A complaint against whom?" Alfredo asked.

"It is a complaint issued against the members of your family," Bruno responded, evenly, almost vacuously.

"Who issued the complaint?" Alfredo pressed.

"The local police headquarters—the Questura."

"On whose authority?"

"The party's."

"And who is listed as initiating the complaint?"

Bruno looked Alfredo in the eye, then said, "I am."

"Come on, Bruno, don't be coy. And who else?"

"My wife. But only if necessary for corroboration," he added, as Hilde began to weep harder.

"Corroborate what?"

Now it was I who demanded to know. "Corroborate what?" I echoed, and now it was my turn to begin to lose the little control I had. "What crime could Hilde have possibly corroborated? What could my family possibly have done to warrant their deaths?" I yelled, hoarsely. Hilde's weeping became louder and more frightened as she seemed to conclude that, in my rage, she had lost the only ally she could have had in settling Alfredo down. "I want to know, Bruno! I want to know the crime my infant daughter was accused of!"

As Hilde sobbed, Bruno remained stonefaced. I heard a metallic click as Alfredo drew back the hammer of his gun.

"It wasn't supposed to happen that way," Bruno said, and for the first time something approximating sorrow seemed to seep into his expression.

"Tell me," I said, and he must have heard me even though my voice was barely audible in my own ears. Hilde's weeping was quieter now, but in a way more intense, as if it welled from a place deeper inside. She had no handkerchief and seemed oblivious to the tears dripping down her face and onto her dress.

"It happened in about November of forty-three, or perhaps early December," Bruno said as, with his right hand, he reached over to stroke Hilde's arm. "The Duce was attempting to establish the republic up in Salo` and the party people were trying to reassert control. You may recall that those of us who were faithful to Italy"—he said this without a hint of doubt, remorse, or self-consciousness—*"had been treated badly when the king signed the armistice.*

"I don't deny I was angry at your family. They had been patriotic and loyal once, even to the point of sacrificing a son. Now you"—he looked at Alfredo without apology—"had besmirched your brother's sacrifice. At first, I tried to be understanding. Of course your parents would stand by you. That was natural. But then there was your sister, whose sympathies she never tried to hide, and the slow conversion against Italy to which your mother and father were succumbing."

The numbness I felt listening to this clinical recitation of self-justification was briefly jarred by Alfredo's plaintive, almost shrieking cry. "And you took it upon yourself to condemn them to death!"

"No!" Hilde cried with a start. "It wasn't like that!"

"Some men from the party came to the house," Bruno continued. "They asked us what we knew about certain people who might or might not be loyal to the Duce. You must remember this time. No one knew who was on whose side." Bruno looked hard at Alfredo. "Just as you chose your side, the men who visited us made it clear that we must choose ours. We looked at their list of names and confirmed that certain people on the list had chosen the other side."

"This was the least we had to do to save ourselves," Hilde interrupted.

"Save yourselves or save your exalted positions?" Alfredo demanded.

"The names were already on the list," Bruno said, matter of factly. "Do you really think we were about to change anyone's mind?" Now he looked at me. "Besides, I swear to you we had no thought that the people on the list would be treated as they were. Yes, it's true we had to assume they might be harassed in some way, but I swear we had no idea what would actually happen."

"You're lying!" Alfredo screamed and again cocked the gun.

"It's true, I swear!" Hilde blurted through her tears.

Bruno, however, maintained the strange, serene countenance of the condemned. "It's the truth," he said evenly to Alfredo. "No matter how much you wave that gun and threaten us, it will still be the truth."

We stood locked in this impasse for what seemed like hours. And yet, in that time, which in reality must have been measured in seconds, my emotions raced out of control. All of the vengeful thoughts I had been harboring and allowing to fester came to the surface. These two old people sitting before us, beaten down, fearful, and stoic were the faces of evil I had sought. I imagined them shot—raw and bleeding.

And then, just as suddenly, I found that the images gave me no satisfaction or comfort. I understood that to kill these people for their crimes would be at one and the same time just and inadequate. It could never be satisfying and, in its finality, it would deprive the future of any hope that the future might contain.

"Put the gun down," I said at last to Alfredo. "Just put it down and let's leave."

But he kept the gun trained on Bruno and said, "I haven't heard the truth from them yet. I want to hear the truth from their lips, and then I may or may not let them live."

"But you have heard the truth!" Hilde cried. "You have. I swear it."

"What about that, Bruno?" Alfredo asked, bringing the muzzle closer to his head. "You've told us everything?"

"Yes, everything."

"Put it down, Alfredo," I said again. "Killing them won't help anything now."

"It will help me."

"No, it won't," I said, softly, and with my hand shaking I touched his arm. He lowered the gun slowly to his side.

"Come on," I said. "Let's go."

He had tears in his eyes when he looked at me, but I wasn't certain whether I was witnessing tears of grief or frustration. His look also struck me as accusatory, as if I had turned against him, as if I were standing between him and the peace he believed would flow from the retribution I was denying him.

Still, he turned his back on the Bucas.

"Let's go," I said again, though the utterance struck me as gratuitous, since Alfredo had already begun to walk away. What happened next, therefore, caught me completely by surprise.

More to himself than to me, Alfredo said, "The least he could have done was tell the truth."

Before I could react Alfredo said it again, louder, and whirled and rushed back to the table. He leaned across it and put the gun to Hilde's head. And pulled the trigger.

The sharp report was repeated an instant later when Bruno, too stunned to move, was knocked backward by the bullet Alfredo put through the center of his forehead.

I began to scream at Alfredo, but he shook his head and pursed his lips, as if to say, "Don't bother, it's done."

"Why?" I screamed again.

He shoved me and I stumbled backward. "God damn it, Daniel! Don't you understand? They lied. They sat here and lied and then lied more. Our family is dead and they caused it. And then they sat here and lied."

"No, I don't understand," I managed to get out. "How did they lie? They said they confirmed the names on the list."

Before he could answer I saw Renata running toward us from the house. She must have heard the shots and now as she came closer I could see the terror growing in her eyes. She screamed when she saw her parents—a wild keening sound—and I thought she was going to throw herself on Alfredo.

But she pulled up suddenly, and when I looked over at him, he had raised the gun again and was aiming it at her.

Automatically, I yelled, "No, Alfredo! You can't!" and took a step toward him. Renata's shrieking hadn't diminished, and if anything, she seemed oblivious to her own danger.

With his free hand Alfredo pushed me back, and in a voice as icy as any I have ever heard or hope to hear, he said, "For right now, Daniel, you are just going to have to believe me." And with that, he raised the gun again and aimed at Renata.

I will spend the rest of my life anguishing over that moment. Could I have stopped him? I think perhaps I could have. But that's not even the question that will haunt me. The question, for which I have no answer, is, Why didn't I try? Was it something in that calm assurance of his voice that somehow convinced me not to interfere? Was my desire for revenge so deep, so completely wormed into me, that I didn't care on whom it was meted out? He aimed with all deliberation. I stood there almost as if I had given consent. And he killed her.

How could I not have tried?

And then, standing there spattered with the Bucas' blood, he said simply, quietly, "Now we can go."

How could I not have tried?

All I can say as I write this is that I was so stunned by the turn of events— so stunned by their finality—that I hardly remember our walk home. We had left three people dead in their garden and were walking home on the rustic path as if we were day hikers.

When we reached the house Alfredo went to wash the gore from himself while I sat on the terrace silently overlooking our own garden. My senses were so saturated that any emotion, from grief to violence, might have felt normal. And in fact, what I was feeling was probably a muddle of all these things. When Alfredo returned and sat down next to me, all I could do was ask, "Why?"

He was completely composed when he looked at me. Whether or not revenge could ever help me, it must have helped him, because I could not recall seeing him so much at peace.

"You almost convinced me to let them live," he said, evenly. "But I couldn't do it—not without their at least admitting the truth. In the end, full confession was the least I could accept."

"But how are you so sure they were lying?"

At this he reached into his pocket and pulled out another document, this one a few pages long. Like the one he had shown the Bucas, he had folded it in quarters. Perhaps he had planned to present it to them as he had the first one, as part of his indictment. He unfolded the document and handed it to me. "This is how I know."

I stared at the pages, but it wasn't necessary to read them as Alfredo went on immediately to explain what he had given me. "This," he said, "is the final gift from that pig Petresco. It's what I finally found after looking for every scrap of paper of his I could get my hands on.

"As you can see, it's a memorandum—a report by Petresco on his activities to identify opponents of the Fascist government. He describes how he went about his task, including his meetings with loyalists like the Bucas. About this the Bucas weren't lying."

Alfredo looked at me unflinchingly, with the certainty of righteous conviction. "But, Daniel," he went on, "if ever there was a half truth, that was it. If you look at the second page of the report you'll see a list of people who were considered unreliable and subject to arrest. Petresco goes on to explain that his interviews confirmed that these people deserved a place on the list. Now, Daniel, look at the names."

I read through the list once, then looked up at Alfredo. My expression must have reflected the confusion I felt, because he said, "Read it again."

I read it, more carefully this time.

"Where is our family?" he asked as I got to the end. "Their names aren't there, are they?"

I shook my head.

"Now," he said, with more triumphant condescension in his voice than I was prepared for, "read the next section, beginning on page three."

I turned the page. It took only a minute to comprehend. This section of the report explained that other names had been added based on information that had been volunteered during the interviews with the loyalists. I looked at Alfredo.

"Keep going," he said, and I turned to the next page. There I came to the following, which Alfredo had underlined, and which hit me so hard I felt my chest constrict:

"It should not be overlooked that, among the volunteers, Bruno Buca and his wife were especially helpful in bringing to my attention persons of concern. These included their long-time neighbors, the Rosetti family (including the daughter's husband, an American citizen), whom we subsequently added to the list of those who should be arrested for interrogation."

As I read, Alfredo stood and began to wander the terrace. I looked up and asked, "Why didn't you show this to them?"

"Why didn't I show it to them?" he echoed as if the thought had just occurred to him. "I intended to," he went on, looking at me again. "But then I said to myself, no, I'm not a public prosecutor. There was no judge sitting there who had to be convinced. The least we had a right to expect under the circumstances was a full confession and a plea for mercy."

I sat quietly for a moment, trying to take it all in, then said, "Tell me, Alfredo, if you had heard the confession and the plea for mercy, would you have spared them?"

At least he was honest. "I don't know. Probably not."

And then there was Renata. Revenge for Alfredo, pure and simple. How will I ever come to live with the image of Renata?

~ ~ ~ ~ ~

~ ~ ~

Chapter 35

V ICTORIA HAD PLANNED ONLY a short absence from the preparations going on downstairs. Yet she was so disturbed by what she had just read, she needed time simply to digest it. Earlier she had quickly and without hesitation promised Francesco that she would keep these particular writings of Daniel's between them. Now she reproached herself for not qualifying the promise in some way. She was at a loss for what to do. She could not confront Chiara now, with the ceremony less than a day away. But she also could not imagine how she could attend.

As troubled as she was by what she had read, she was not really surprised, and this in itself confirmed the harsh judgment she rendered against herself for failing to confront Francesco, and perhaps Chiara, earlier. Though she might not have predicted the specific course of events—especially the killing of Renata—the roles of the actors, including the Bucas, Alfredo, and Daniel, had been clearly demarcated. There was a certain trajectory to the play, even if the final act could have taken other forms.

All of which still left her to grapple with a desire—a need—to do something. The prospect of sitting through a ceremony that was so false in all of its particulars made her sick at heart. It would be one thing if she were simply a casual, ignorant observer. She could take in the speeches and tributes with little regard for the truth of what she heard. She could listen to Chiara talk about her family's gallant defense of freedom in the face of fascist oppression, while her father was lauded in the same breath for his actions.

But she was not ignorant. Knowing what she did, she now faced the prospect of being not merely a casual observer, but a participant in deceit.

The truth was that, far from being noble, the Buca family played hard for all they could get and ended up in a direct line of responsibility for the horrific deaths of her father's wife, his child, and his wife's parents—crimes made all the worse by the special treachery of betraying old friends and neighbors.

And in return? Francesco's uncle murdered Chiara's mother and grandparents. And Victoria's own father—who had long championed, and even after the fact continued to champion—a noble ideal, by his own admission had not even tried to intervene to save Chiara's mother and presumably paid a price in anguish to the end of his days.

To know these things and pretend not to know them; to sit mute while a new version of history was being planted, solidified, made the lasting version, was abhorrent to her.

And yet, what was the alternative? Would it really change anything to stay away? To do something as tepid as plead illness was as inconceivable as challenging Chiara at this late date. To have advance knowledge of a wrong and not act on the knowledge when it is possible to do so is itself morally wrong; to avert one's gaze as the wrong is being committed also is wrong. Weren't these the very things that had so consumed Daniel? But was it really possible for her to act without creating a greater harm?

There was a knock on the door followed by Chiara's inquiry, "Victoria? Are you there?"

The very sound of Chiara's voice not only startled her, but caused a flinch of indignation. "Yes, come in," she said, shuffling Daniel's papers among some others she had in her lap.

But she didn't open the door. "I just wanted to tell you we'll have tea downstairs in a few minutes."

"Thank you. I'll be down."

* * *

FRANCESCO WAS WALKING through the garden, idly picking up fallen branches and other detritus, when Victoria stepped out onto the terrace. He caught sight of her, waved and began to return along the path leading to the terrace steps, but she motioned that she would join him where he was. She made her way down the steps and onto the path. New gravel crunched under her feet.

"Let's sit over there," he said, nodding toward a small clearing as she reached him. He dropped the leafy debris onto a pile that had been raked together but not yet picked up, and brushed his hands against one another, each pass catching slightly as if snagged by a residue of sap. "You've read it, then?" he said, looking at her.

"Is it so obvious?"

"It is. Your face is sad. Troubled."

"I suppose I'll never make a spy," she said with a small smile.

"America's loss," he smiled back.

They began to walk slowly toward the clearing.

"I'd be lying if I told you I wasn't troubled, Francesco. As you know, I was troubled even before I read the last entries. But at least then I could force myself to rationalize the contradictory accounts." She looked at him frankly. "Let me ask you something. I can understand Chiara's not knowing the truth about the final, bloody day, but has she never questioned all of the other things she believes about her family?"

He shook his head slightly, pursed his lips. "I think she got a certain version of events, first from her father, and then from her older brother, and these accounts satisfied her. She had no reason to question them. And, of course, it's human nature, isn't it, to become less and less willing as we get older to challenge the things we know to be true?"

"But what about you? I can't believe this doesn't hurt you." She was aware of her voice rising to strike an unwanted note of incredulity. "This is your mother and sister we're talking about. The Buca family is responsible for their horrible deaths. And Daniel's account aside, you must remember things from that time, surely?"

When they reached the clearing Francesco invited Victoria to sit with him on the stone bench. The stone was porous and cool to the touch. For a moment they both glanced back toward the house.

"Do you remember," Francesco began, "not long after you arrived I told you that Chiara's efforts to put together the ceremony over the years had met with resistance?"

Victoria nodded. "You said it was a time most people would just as soon forget."

"Yes, that's right. Having read our father's papers, you can see why, I'm sure."

"I can, yes." She put a hand on his arm and added, "And I don't want you to think I'm not grateful for the opportunity to discover some of the things I did about Father." She paused for a moment at the odd sound of the word where Daniel's name normally had been. "The thing is, I feel fortunate to have found out so many things about him that are praiseworthy."

"Did you really not think you would?" Francesco interrupted, his face openly surprised.

"Oh, yes, of course, on some level I did. Daniel's friend Bemis was very emphatic about that. He said I would. But I was hardly unbiased where Daniel was concerned. Chiara's are not the only versions that may have become fixed over time," she added with a self-deprecating smile. "I decided—with the impetus of your kind invitation—that, at my age, it was now or never as far as learning about him. I was happy to discover some of the things I did, but I would have accepted—some might say I was looking for—a worse picture.

"But tell me, Francesco," she rushed on before he could respond, "Don't you think it diminishes—actually dishonors, in a way—the memory of our father, and even more so your mother, to have Chiara's version of events get proclaimed to one and all as the truth?"

Francesco considered this for a long moment. "I love Chiara very much."

Victoria looked at him in surprise. "I never doubted it."

"I suspect, Victoria, that the ways in which we have come, respectively, to know the truth are very different and therefore the truth carries different weight and value to each of us. For you, the truth—these discoveries you've made—has a feeling of epiphany. Yes, I understand that, on some level, you've dealt with Father's legacy all your life. But so much about him was revealed to you in such a short time and, I might add, discovered at an age when we tend to be more philosophical about things."

"But it seems to me that you are the one who is being . . . I won't say philosophical as much as stoical."

"Perhaps you're right. But consider: the things I've read recently did more to confirm what I may have suspected or known in some way for many years, as opposed to revealing new things. It's true, I had no reason to think Father might have played a part in the death of Chiara's mother—at least to the extent he might have been able to prevent it.

"But the things I've learned about my history I've learned slowly, over many years, in pieces of memory. Especially after we moved away from here I had not much reason to think about Chiara's family one way or the other, and Father never gave me any reason to do so either. To the extent I have thought about them and those terrible times since, I suppose it has been through the special prism we Italians have devised for ourselves. It's a wondrous device that somehow allows light to be focused clearly everywhere except on those things on which we have an aversion to clarity. On those things, happily, the prism is flawed. It sheds only an amorphous light that permits the viewer a glimpse at color and vague shape and then to move on."

Victoria considered this and began to say something, but Francesco continued. "One of the things that intrigues me most in art is the power of myth. Myth has the power to bind people together and let them live with themselves and one another. You have discovered your father, Victoria, and I have discovered some new things about him as well. We have also discovered many other things about that time."

"Yes, we have. But from my point of view myth is not something we should deliberately nurture in the way that will happen tomorrow. What's more, defective prisms or not, such truths as will not be faced tomorrow have a way of bubbling up. There are people out there who defaced those posters, after all. They cannot be dismissed as mere vandals. Their target was not random. If these people bother to attend the ceremony at all, they will certainly resent what they hear."

"If there is a difference between us, Victoria, it is that I am willing to take such revelations as we've had in a pragmatic way. Tomorrow, Chiara will stand up in front of our citizens, many of whose families have lived here for more years than we can imagine. She will tell these people some things that you and I know are not true.

"And then she will tell them, implicitly, what they know in their bones—that we cannot move forward on a foundation of recrimination. We must foreswear making judgments on others so long ago, and allow that time to be softened by the light of our defective prisms. That may not be historical truth, but it is wisdom."

"And those who do know the truth—about the Bucas, for example—will they sit still rather than spit out the tainted soup they're being fed?"

"I don't know. We'll see."

"Even if they do sit still for it, it's really more of a deal with the devil, I think. You will sacrifice enlightenment in the service of a more hopeful future based on a carefully constructed myth. There's an opiate in that solution, isn't there?"

"Yes, I suppose there is. But for me it's also an expression of will. It's a way of saying I will not allow us to be mired in the past. It's a way of saying to Chiara that the past is less important than my love for her today.

"You know, Victoria, one thing you may not realize about our father is that in the more than twenty years he lived after the war, he never allowed himself to be defeated by what he suffered. My guess is that after he sealed his papers behind the wall in the cantina he never considered opening the wall again."

Victoria stared off into the garden. "Would he have opened it tomorrow?"

"I hope not."

She smiled and gently touched Francesco's face, looked into the kind eyes that seemed to reflect more happiness than they had taken in. "You are a very dear person, but I cannot find it in me to do what you ask. I promised not to reveal any of this to Chiara, and I will not. But I also cannot attend the ceremony."

Francesco's face tightened. "I do hope you'll reconsider. Keep in mind that we are honoring those who deserve to be honored—including our father—even if we also include a few who don't deserve it."

"And you're willing to allow the perpetrators of murder to be lauded and placed in the same tomb as their victims?"

"If it allows us to move on, yes. Our father worked for peace. Would he have accepted a deal in which peace could be had for the price of a lie? I think he would have."

She looked down at the fingers she had unconsciously woven tightly together in her lap. When she looked up it was with fresh resolve. "But I cannot, Francesco. Father's principles and dreams aren't the only ones at stake here. I, too, have spent a life in a certain way. As the American author James Baldwin put it, the past is all that can make the present coherent. I believe this. I have devoted myself to the idea that if you can show people what they've done and why, eventually they may live their lives in a better way."

"Oh, Victoria, there must be some way around this. What could I say to Chiara—to all of the people who are expecting to see you there?"

They looked up at Chiara's sudden call of Francesco's name.

301

"Let's talk about it later," he said earnestly, placing his hand over Victoria's, before calling back to Chiara to say he was coming. "For now just tell me I haven't had your final word."

She took a breath, then seemed to cut her response short and only nodded. When he had taken a few steps away he turned around as if to make certain she hadn't already changed her mind. "I'll be there in a few minutes," she said.

After he had gone, she stood slowly and unconsciously rubbed the back of her thighs, which had gone cold from the stone seat. She looked into the distance, into the fading daylight, wondered how she could possibly make things right.

She walked slowly back to the house, hoping to avoid Chiara. The more she thought about it, the more she resented being placed in this position. She resented Chiara, of course, but was also angry at Francesco for not being fully honest with her sooner. If he had been, she might have been able to do something. She might have been more forceful the day Chiara read her speech. Even now she wondered if it wasn't too late to tone down her remarks. Perhaps she could be prevailed upon to say fewer things that specifically praised her family's actions and focus more on the general difficulty of the times and need for healing. Victoria smiled ruefully at the thought, as the label that sprang to mind for this solution was the general amnesty.

But how could the subject even be broached at this point? Had it been possible to raise it earlier perhaps Chiara would have made some changes. Or, failing that, Victoria would have had the opportunity to take the stand that she now felt compelled to take even as she also felt it both reckless and inadequate. Rather than an act of principle, it had the feel of petulance. For this reason her pique at Francesco flared again. Even if she accepted his well-meaning explanation at face value—accepted that he wanted to protect Chiara and allow a healing myth to be perpetrated—it was at the very least grossly condescending to Chiara, who was, after all, no child. Was Chiara really so incapable of facing the truth?

And a worse thought, still: that even now Francesco wasn't being completely honest—that Chiara in fact knew the truth and was deliberately ignoring it. But Victoria quickly deflected this notion, not because it was impossible but because it was so distasteful. She certainly didn't want to confront the actions that must flow from such a conclusion, assuming it could be proved. Bad enough to feel deceived for reasons that, if she accepted Francesco's explanation, could be rationalized. The alternative was to be a dupe and a fool and to cast a pall over all of the good things that had occurred during her visit.

Yet one way or another she still had to decide what to do, whether that meant sticking to the stand she took with Francesco or finding some alternative. It also meant she had to get through the coming evening. She was never a good liar—never good at concealing her feelings—and she had to be in Chiara and Francesco's company and not give away anything until her decision was firm.

As she approached the house she saw Chiara bustling from place to place on the terrace, moving chairs a certain way, then changing their direction by a degree or two, then picking up extraneous leaves or stones that might have been trailed in from the garden. It was a nervous—and to Victoria's eye, a dismayingly happy—energy. Victoria girded for performance. "May I help you?" she asked with as much generic brightness as she could produce.

"Victoria! I didn't see you coming. I'm only doing some last-minute straightening. If it's all right with you, I think we'll go out for dinner so we don't have to fuss here. Just something casual and easy, close by."

"That's a brilliant idea," Victoria responded with some relief at the thought of not spending the evening at home alone with Chiara and Francesco. Her acting skills were not up to a one-woman performance in an intimate theater. Such a setting might have offered the best opportunity to worm into the subject that so troubled her. But as she intended to honor her promise to Francesco not to confront Chiara, she could more readily envision the evening as one of awkward evasion and false bonhomie. Dinner out could at least provide distraction and cover, even if it would not bring her closer to a resolution.

They went to a trattoria in sight of the piazza where the ceremony was to be held. Chiara kept up her excited chatter, but also took frequent, nervous looks toward the piazza. Victoria thought she was worried that there might be a repeat of the recent vandalism. The memorial sculpture was draped and all seemed in order.

Throughout the meal friends and neighbors stopped to chat. It was at these moments that Victoria tended to let her guard down. When she caught

Francesco looking at her anxiously, she realized her mind had returned to the subject of its real interest. She excused herself to go to the bathroom, but instead of regaining her composure, she regained more fully, more resentfully, the feeling of entrapment. As, upon her return to the table, she observed Chiara engaging happily with her friends and neighbors, did she also observe some who maintained a cool detachment? Did they know, or was Victoria just imagining that they did?

"It's been a long day," Chiara said at last, looking around the table for confirmation that Francesco and Victoria were ready to leave.

"And a longer one in prospect for tomorrow," Francesco said, making to rise.

Victoria smiled wanly and said, "I'm ready."

* * *

WHEN DAWN ARRIVED following a sleepless night, Victoria was no closer to a way out of her dilemma. She grew increasingly anxious at the thought that, if she didn't take a stand one way or another, time would take one for her. She concluded it would be the worst of all of the bad alternatives before her to simply drift into either being at the ceremony or not being there, perhaps delivering some weak excuse; the plea of illness that she rejected out of hand the previous day now seemed not so much out of the question.

The minimum that was required, she concluded, was a conscious, deliberate decision. If she wasn't going to attend—no matter the excuse she settled on—she needed to tell Francesco. She still leaned strongly in this direction.

But if she changed her mind, she also felt a need to tell Francesco directly. The one thing she could not allow herself to do was to be passive, to be swept by time into a wraithlike attendance.

She was sitting on the terrace, bundled against the morning chill, coffee cup in hand, lost in thought when Francesco appeared and took a seat next to her. Victoria's impulse was to look around for Chiara.

"Chiara's upstairs getting dressed," he said, reading her thoughts. "You've come to a decision," he added in a matter of fact voice.

"Oh, Francesco . . ."

"You're not going to come, are you?"

"Francesco, I can't. It's not only what Father stood for, it's what I must stand for."

304

Yet hardly had the words escaped than she understood they would be honored in the breach. It took only one look at the new sadness in Francesco's countenance. It took only the piety she heard and hated in her voice. It was a pronouncement she had to make. In the circumstances, it was the least she could do, and it would never be enough. But she understood it would have to be enough for now.

Would Daniel make the bargain Francesco suggested? Peace for a lie? The greater good for a high price? Would he make this bargain? Perhaps he would answer yes to both questions. In the course of a journey she had begun halfheartedly she had learned many things about Daniel, and perhaps a few about herself. She had discovered that Daniel was principled, and that he was flawed—an observation that, had anyone offered it to her, she would have dismissed as absurdly obvious but which, at this moment, felt like revealed truth. In the end, what could be said about Daniel Gideon—her father—was what Bemis said about him: He was a striver. He pursued the things he believed in and, often, he fell short. If there was nobility in him, it was in the striving, not the attaining.

And, she discovered, looking back on her own life, perhaps there was something of the striver in her, too. Both in her professional and private lives she could take pride in honest purpose—pride in striving to leave things better than she found them. Not a bad legacy, if that's what it was. There was an epitaph she had read once. "Saved by grace, if saved at all." Do we ever really know? We can only try.

She looked over at Francesco, took in again the sadness in his face over her pronouncement, and knew that, whatever came afterward, she would be at the ceremony. She would sit still for Francesco's bargain, allow herself to hope for the magic of his defective prism.

She reached out and touched his hand, and when she smiled she could see in his face he understood these things too.

The End

Richard Samuel Sheres

Acknowledgments

The story of the Italian people's suffering and bravery has often been relegated to second place in the histories of the Second World War, but is no less profound for it. Their sacrifice is depicted in the monuments and memorials that are at once ubiquitous and surprising in their seeming ability to materialize out of nowhere all around Italy—and perhaps that is as it should be: not so much places visited by those who already remember as cautionary snares for those who might fail to do so.

Many people and organizations helped in the research, writing and general encouragement of this book. Friends and strangers in our adopted home of Lucca, Italy, and beyond provided vital historical knowledge and context for the Mussolini years and those awful years when the country managed the difficult trick of being at war with both the Allied and Axis powers, while at the same time being torn apart by myriad internal factions. In Lucca, I was helped greatly by the Museo Storico Della Liberazione and the archives of the Istituto Storico della Resistenza, both of which have struggled to keep the memories alive as the War generation recedes.

Jessie Thorpe, a brilliant writer, editor, and reviewer, helped me through several drafts. The manuscript was read at various stages by Jack and Donna Salem, Alex and Maureen Bory, Jill and Jeremy Bishop, Vivien Arcoleo and Laura Flaherty (aka LaLaFlaFla), all of whom offered valuable, if sometimes painful, comments and insights. Thanks also to the marvelous people in the Creative Writing Program at Princeton University.

My family, especially my parents and children, gave the priceless combination of honest criticism and encouragement. Above all, love and thanks to my wife Jo—Giovanna—who has somehow found the enthusiasm to read more iterations of the manuscript than should be asked of any sane person and who at crucial times of doubt urged me on nonetheless.

This is a work of fiction. While taking the usual novelistic liberties with people, events and places, I have endeavored to create a true sense of the times depicted in the story. I apologize in advance for any errors or misrepresentations; they are inadvertent but in any case my responsibility alone.

Richard Samuel Sheres
Lucca, Italy, 2006

Afterword to the Second Edition

For the author, a good thing about releasing a second edition is having an opportunity to experience the frisson that may come with seeing through new eyes something produced many years earlier. Does the story stand the test of time? This is particularly relevant for a historical or political novel, not only in terms of accounting for subsequent events, but for the author's possible reinterpretation of history or changed perspectives.

It cannot be said without appearing to be self-serving, but upon rereading, I was pleased to find that the story and the "lessons"—the takeaways, as they say now—continue to come across as intended.

Daniel Gideon is portrayed as a man with noble ideals and his share of faults. He is, as his estranged daughter, Victoria, concludes, a striver. He has spent a life—which is to say, most of the twentieth century—in a cauldron. He has made significant errors and misjudgments. But he has strived to do right, however much he may have fallen short.

A persistent debate among readers over the years involves the book's ending. Without giving too much away to new readers, the conclusion poses the moral dilemma faced by Victoria and the way she resolves it. Or doesn't, depending on one's point of view. In a word, some readers were content with the ending, others felt dissatisfied with what they saw as its ambiguity.

I'm comfortable with this schism. But then, I may be unusually comfortable with ambiguity . . . with the notion that few things in life beyond such verities as the Golden Rule are certain—that those who hold tightly, rigidly to their beliefs with little room for emendation will (if they are honest) only rarely have the satisfaction of being proven right. In a confessional spirit, I'll also allow for the possibility that I'm simply reluctant to make choices.

It is understandable that people hold on to certainty, often using it as a defensive tool against the challenges of daily existence among a species that is always in danger of meeting the same fate as the extinct beings that came before. Not for sissies this thing we call life. As he often did, in his novel *Villages*, John Updike may have said it best:

> *The human animal, evolved in trees and then dropped down to run in the grasslands of Kenya, arrived at a highly conscious position awkward beyond any easements of philosophy. At three in the morning, our brains churn within the self, trying to get out of what we know to be a sinking ship. But jumping out of the self is not a Western skill. The walls of the skull stay solid, sealing us in with our fears."*

Although it was not planned this way, since the original publication of *Keeping Gideon* in 2006, there has been a consistent theme about the pitfalls of certainty running through my work, including in the novels *Ingersoll* and the recent, aptly titled, *An Imperfect Certainty*. Each in its way is a caution against the dangers of rigid belief. Or, as Voltaire had it, "Doubt is not a pleasant condition, but certainty is an absurd one."

The characters in *Keeping Gideon* could count on nothing with certainty. *Ingersoll* deals with a struggle by true believers to fundamentally change the way of life and Constitution of a not-so-farfetched United States. *An Imperfect Certainty* looks at how we learn from history and the challenges of passing useful knowledge from one generation to the next. In *Keeping Gideon*, Victoria quotes James Baldwin to observe that the past is all that can make the present coherent.

I maintain that the solution to the over-certainty dilemma is to strive to be open to new ways of seeing and thinking. Daniel Gideon might say, more simply, it is always to strive.

R.S. Sheres
Alexandria, Virginia, 2020

About the Author

Richard Samuel Sheres is a novelist and former U.S. Government foreign affairs and intelligence senior executive. Born and raised in New York City, he has visited or resided in over sixty countries. He researched and wrote *Keeping Gideon* while living in Lucca, Italy, with his wife, Jo. In addition to *Keeping Gideon*, he is the author of the acclaimed novels *Ingersoll* and *An Imperfect Certainty*. He and Jo currently live in Alexandria, Virginia.

Made in the USA
Coppell, TX
21 October 2020